"*A Lesson in Vengeance* is at once dark and mesmerizing, with spine-tingling suspense and mind-bending twists. I loved it."

Kara Thomas, author of *The Cheerleaders* and *That Weekend*

"A smart, layered, thought-provoking thriller about female desire and the intimacy of violence."

Ava Reid, author of *The Wolf and the Woodsman*

"Darkly radiant and brilliantly wicked, *A Lesson in Vengeance* is a sharp dissection of queerness, ambition, and the forbidden luster of the occult. This book will possess you from first pages to its haunting, final words."

Ryan La Sala, author of *Be Dazzled* and *Reverie*

"*A Lesson in Vengeance* is the witchy boarding school story I always knew I wanted, a gorgeous take on the complicated bonds of female love and friendship, told in lyrical, creeping prose as haunting as the tale itself. The ghosts of Felicity, Ellis, and Alex—and of Dalloway School and its historical witches—will linger with you long after the final page."

Lana Popović, author of *Wicked Like a Wildfire*

"With queer primary characters, an irresistible gothic atmosphere, and unrelenting creeping dread, this propulsive work of dark academia is both thrilling and thought-provoking."

Publishers Weekly, starred review

"A layered, stylized, brooding mystery that will draw readers in."

Kirkus

"[A] twisty, immersive thriller."

Booklist, starred review

A LESSON IN VENGEANCE

VICTORIA LEE

TITAN BOOKS

A Lesson in Vengeance
Print edition ISBN: 9781789099768
E-book edition ISBN: 9781789099775

Published by Titan Books
A division of Titan Publishing Group Ltd
144 Southwark Street, London SE1 0UP
www.titanbooks.com

First Titan edition: February 2022
10 9 8 7 6 5 4 3 2 1

This is a work of fiction. All of the characters, organizations, and events portrayed in this novel are either products of the author's imagination or are used fictitiously. Any resemblance to actual persons, living or dead (except for satirical purposes), is entirely coincidental.

A CIP catalogue record for this title is available from the British Library.

Printed and bound in Great Britain by CPI Group Ltd.

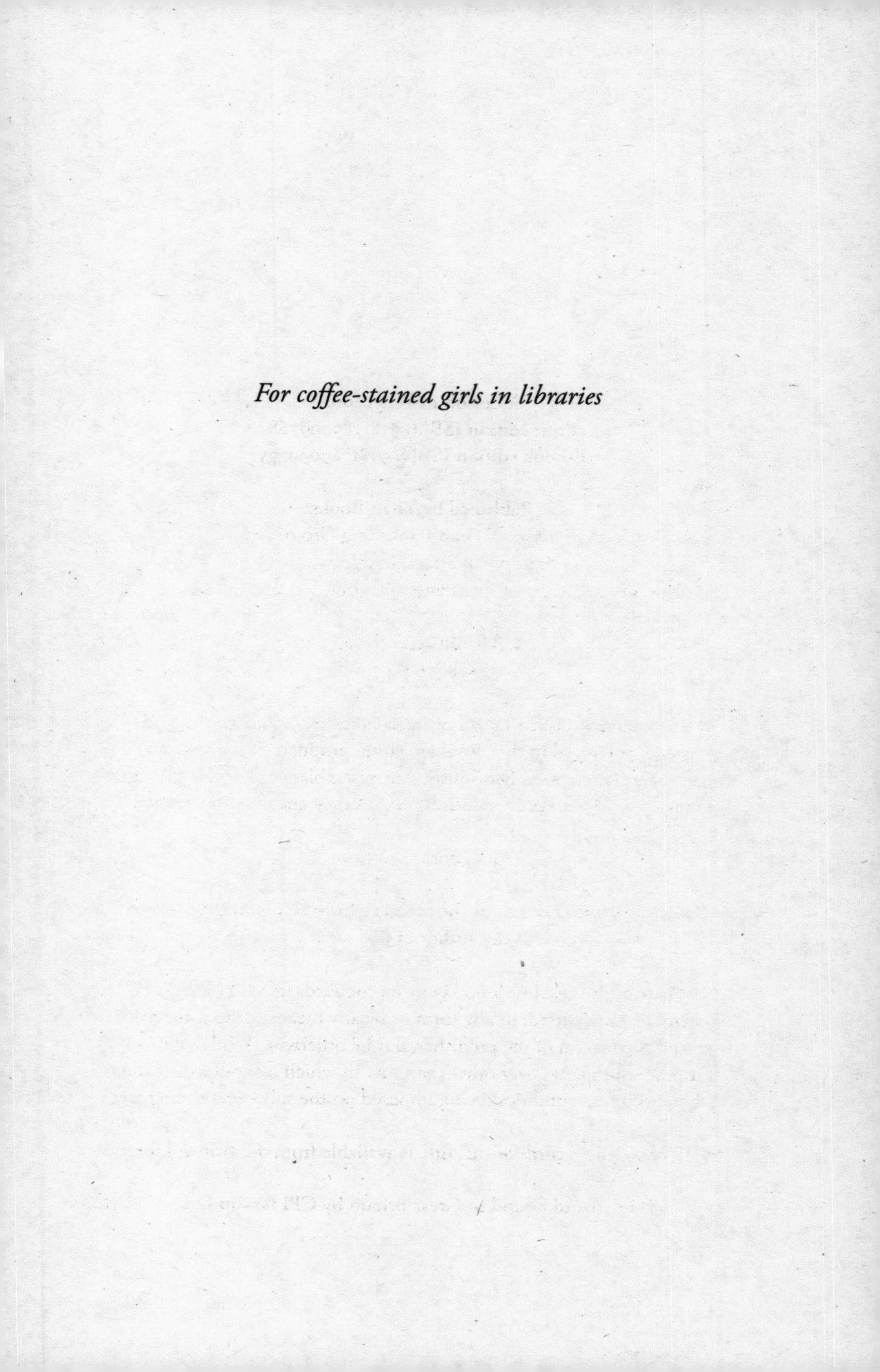

For coffee-stained girls in libraries

DALLOWAY SCHOOL
1
2
3
4
5
6
7
8
9
10
11
12
13
14
15
16
17
18
DALLOWAY SCHOOL
KEY
1. Godwin House
2. Yancey House
3. Chopin House
4. Maud Hall
5. Wharton Hall
6. Walker Hall
7. Eliot House
8. Boleyn House
9. Butler Hall
10. Atwood House
11. Sybil Hall
12. Befana House
13. Library
14. Lemont House
15. Dining Hall
16. Claremont House
17. Farquhar House
18. The Quad

Thirteen thousand feet above sea level, you can drown in air like water.

I read that drowning is a good way to go. By all accounts the pain fades and euphoria blooms in its place like hothouse flowers, red orchid roots tethered to the stones in your pocket.

Falling would be worse.

Falling is barbed-wire terror ripping down your spine, a sharp drop and a sudden stop, scrabbling for a rope that isn't there.

My cheek is pressed against the snow. I don't feel cold anymore. I am part of the mountain, its frigid stone heart beating alongside mine. The storm batters against my back, tries to peel me off this rock like lichen. But I am not lichen. I am limestone and schist, veined with quartz. I am immovable.

And up this high, pinned against the eastern face with thin air crystallizing in my lungs, I am the only thing left alive.

No live organism can continue for long to exist sanely under conditions of absolute reality.

—Shirley Jackson, *The Haunting of Hill House*

The legacy of Dalloway School is not its alumnae, although those include a variety of luminaries such as award-winning playwrights and future senators. The legacy of Dalloway is the bones it was built on.

—Gertrude Milliner, "The Feminization of Witchcraft in Post-Revolutionary America," *Journal of Cultural History*

1

Dalloway School rises from the Catskill foothills like a crown upon an auburn head. Accessible only by gravel road and flanked by a mirror-glass lake to the east, its brick-faced buildings stand with their backs turned to the gate and their windows shuttered. My mother is silent in the front seat; we haven't spoken since New Paltz, when she remarked on how flat the land could be so close to the mountains.

That was an hour ago. I should be glad, I suppose, that she came at all. But, to be honest, I prefer the mutual indifference that endured between me and the hired driver who met me at the airport every year before this one. The driver had her own problems, ones that didn't involve me.

The same cannot be said for my mother.

We park in front of Sybil Hall and hand the keys to a valet, who will take care of the luggage. This is the downside to arriving at school four days early: we have to meet the dean of students in her office and then tramp across campus together, my mother and the dean chatting six steps ahead and me trailing behind. The lake glitters like a silver coin, visible in the gap between hills. I keep my gaze fixed on the dean's wrist, on the bronze key that dangles from a string around that wrist: the key to Godwin House.

Godwin House is isolated from the rest of campus by a copse of balsam firs, up a sharply pitched road and perched atop a small ridge—unevenly, as the house was built three hundred years ago on the remains of an ancient avalanche. And as the ground settled, the house did too: crookedly. Inside, the floors slope noticeably along an east-west axis, cracks gaping beneath doors and the kitchen table wobbling under weight. Since I arrived at Dalloway five years ago, there have been two attempts to have the building condemned, or at the very least renovated down to the bones—but we, the inhabitants, protested vociferously enough that the school abandoned its plans both times. And why shouldn't we protest? Godwin House belongs to us, to the literary effete of Dalloway, self-presumed natural heirs to Emily Dickinson—who had stayed here once while visiting a friend in Woodstock—and we like our house as is. Including its gnarled skeleton.

"You can take your meals at the faculty dining hall for now," Dean Marriott informs me once she has deposited me in my room. It's the same room I always stayed in, before. The same water stain on the ceiling, the same yellowing curtains drifting in the breeze from the open window.

I wonder if they kept it empty for me, or if my mother browbeat the school into kicking some other girl out when I rematriculated.

"Miss MacDonald should be back by now," the dean goes on. "She's the housemistress for Godwin again this year. You can go by her office sometime this afternoon, let her know you've arrived."

The dean gives me her personal number, too. A liability thing, most likely: After all, what if I have a breakdown on campus? What if, beneath the tailored skirt and tennis sweater, I'm one lonely night away from stripping off my clothes and hurtling naked through the woods like some delirious maenad?

Better to play it safe.

I take the number and slip it into my skirt pocket. I clench it in my fist until the paper's an inky nugget against my palm.

Once the dean is gone, my mother turns to look at the room properly, her cool gaze taking in the shabby rug and the mahogany dresser with its chipped corners. I imagine she wonders what becomes of the sixty thousand she pays in tuition each year.

"Perhaps," she says after a long moment, "I should stay the night in town, let you settle in. . . ."

It's not a real offer, and when I shake my head she looks relieved. She can fly back to Aspen this afternoon and be drinking cabernet in her study by nightfall.

"All right, then. All right. Well." She considers me, her shell-pink fingernails pressing in against opposite arms. "You have the dean's number."

"Yes."

"Right. Yes. Hopefully you won't need it."

She embraces me, my face buried against the crook of her neck, where everything smells like Acqua di Parma and airplane sweat.

I watch her retreat down the path until she vanishes around

the curve, past the balsams—just to make sure she's really gone. Then I drag my suitcases up onto the bed and start unpacking.

I hang my dresses in the closet, arranged by color and fabric—gauzy white cotton, cool-water cream silk—and pretend not to remember the spot where I'd pried the baseboard loose from the wall last year and concealed my version of contraband: tarot cards, long taper candles, herbs hidden in empty mint tins. I used to arrange them atop my dresser in a neat row the way another girl might arrange her makeup.

This time I stack my dresser with jewelry instead. When I look up I catch my own gaze in the mirror: blond hair tied back with a ribbon, politely neutral lipstick smudging my lips.

I scrub it off against my wrist. After all, there's no one around to impress.

Even with nothing to distract me from the task, unpacking still takes the better part of three hours. And when I've kicked the empty suitcases under my bed and turned to survey the final product, I realize I hadn't thought past this point. It's still early afternoon, the distant lake now glittering golden outside my window, and I don't know what to do next.

By the middle of my first attempt at a senior year, I'd accrued such a collection of books in my Godwin room that they were spilling off my shelves, the overflow stacked up on my floor and the corner of my dresser, littering the foot of my bed to get shoved out of the way in my sleep. They all had to be moved out when I didn't come back for spring semester last year. The few books I was able to fit in my suitcases this year are a poor replacement: a single shelf not even completely filled, the last two books tipped forlornly against the wood siding.

I decide to go down to the common room. It's a better reading atmosphere anyway; me and Alex used to sprawl out on the Persian carpet amid a fortress of books—teacups at our elbows and jazz playing off Alex's Bluetooth speaker.

Alex.

The memory lances through me like a thrown dart. It's unexpected enough to steal my breath away, and for a moment I'm standing there dizzy in my own doorway as the house tilts and spins.

I'd known it would be worse, coming back here. Dr. Ortega had explained it to me before I left, her voice placid and reassuring: how grief would tie itself to the small things, that I'd be living my life as normal and then a bit of music or the cut of a girl's smile would remind me of her and it would all flood back in.

I understand the concept of sense memory. But understanding isn't preparation.

All at once I want nothing more than to dart out of Godwin House and run down the hill, onto the quad, where the white sunshine will blot out any ghosts.

Except that's weakness, and I refuse to be weak.

This is why I'm here, I tell myself. I came early so I'd have time to adjust. *Well, then. Let's adjust.*

I suck in a lungful of air and make myself go into the hall, down two flights of stairs to the ground floor. I find some tea in the house kitchen cabinet—probably left over from last year—boil some water, and carry the mug with me into the common room while it brews.

The common room is the largest space in the house. It

claims the entire western wall, its massive windows gazing out toward the woods, and is therefore dark even at midafternoon. Shadows hang like drapes from the ceiling, until I flick on a few of the lamps and amber light brightens the deep corners.

No ghosts here.

Godwin House was built in the early eighteenth century, the first construction of Dalloway School. Within ten years of its founding, it saw five violent deaths. Sometimes I still smell blood on the air, as if Godwin's macabre history is buried in its uneven foundations alongside Margery Lemont's bones.

I take the armchair by the window: my favorite, soft and burgundy with a seat cushion that sinks when I sit, as if the chair wants to devour its occupant. I settle in with a Harriet Vane mystery and lock myself in Oxford of the 1930s, in a tangled mess of murderous notes and scholarly dinners and threats exchanged over cakes and cigarettes.

The house feels so different like this. A year ago, midsemester, the halls were raucous with girls' shouting voices and the clatter of shoes on hardwood, empty teacups scattered across flat surfaces and long hairs clinging to velvet upholstery. All that has been swallowed up by the passage of time. My friends graduated last year. When classes start, Godwin will be home to a brand-new crop of students: third- and fourth-years with bright eyes and souls they sold to literature. Girls who might prefer Oates to Shelley, Alcott to Allende. Girls who know nothing of blood and smoke, the darker kinds of magic.

And I will slide into their group, the last relic of a bygone era, old machinery everyone is anxiously waiting to replace.

My mother wanted me to transfer to Exeter for my final

year. Exeter—as if I could survive that any better than being back here. Not that I expected her to understand. *But all your friends are gone,* she'd said.

I didn't know how to explain to her that being friendless at Dalloway was better than being friendless anywhere else. At least here the walls know me, the floors, the soil. I am rooted at Dalloway. Dalloway is mine.

Thump.

The sound startles me enough that I drop my book, gaze flicking toward the ceiling. I taste iron in my mouth.

It's nothing. It's an old house, settling deeper into unsteady land.

I retrieve my book and flip through the pages to find my lost place. I've never been afraid of being alone, and I'm not about to start now.

Thump.

This time I'm half expecting it, tension having drawn my spine straight and my free hand into a fist. I put the book aside and slip out of my chair with an unsteady drum beating in my chest. Surely Dean Marriott wouldn't have let anyone else in the house, right? Unless . . . It's probably maintenance. They must have someone coming by to clean out the mothballs and change the air filters.

In fact, that makes a lot of sense. The semester will commence at the end of the weekend; now should be peak cleaning time. No doubt I can expect a significant amount of traffic in and out of Godwin, staff scrubbing the floors and throwing open windows.

Only the house was already clean when I arrived.

As I creep up the stairs, I realize the air has gone frigid, a cold that curls in the marrow of my bones. A slow dread rises in my blood. And I know without having to guess where that sound came from.

Alex's bedroom was the third door down on the right, second floor—directly below my room. I used to stomp on the floor when she played her music too loud. She'd rap back with the handle of a broom.

Four raps: *Shut. The. Hell. Up.*

This is stupid. This is . . . ridiculous, and irrational, but knowing that does little to quell the seasick feeling beneath my ribs.

I stand in front of the closed door, one hand braced against the wood.

Open it. I should open it.

The wood is cold, cold, cold. A white noise buzzes between my ears, and suddenly I can't stop envisioning Alex on the other side: decayed and gray, with filmy eyes staring out from a desiccated skull.

Open it.

I can't open it.

I spin on my heel and dart back down the hall and all the way to the common room. I drag the armchair closer to the tall window and huddle there on its cushion, with Sayers clutched in both hands, staring at the doorway I came through and waiting for a slim figure to drift in from the stairs, dragging dusk like a cloak in her wake.

Nothing comes. Of course it doesn't. I'm just—

It's paranoia. It's the same strain of fear that used to send me lurching awake in the middle of the night with my throat torn raw. It's guilt reaching long fingers into the soft underbelly of my mind and letting the guts spill out.

I don't know how long it is before I can open my book again and turn my gaze away from the door and to the words instead. No doubt reading murder books alone in an old house is half my problem. Impossible not to startle at every creak and bump when you're half buried in a story that heavily features *library crimes.*

The afternoon slips toward evening; I have to turn on more lights and refill my tea in the kitchen, but I finish the book.

I've just turned the final page when it happens again:

Thump.

And then, almost immediately after, the slow drag of something heavy across the floor above my head.

This time I don't hesitate.

I take the stairs up to the second floor two at a time, and I'm halfway down the hall when I realize Alex's bedroom door is open. Bile surges up my throat, and no . . . *no—*

But when I come to a stop in front of Alex's room, there's no ghost.

A girl sits at Alex's desk, slim and black-haired with fountain pen in hand. She's wearing an oversized glen check blazer and silver cuff links. I've never seen her before in my life.

She glances up from her writing, and our eyes meet. Hers are gray, the color of the sky at midwinter.

"Who are you?" The words tumble out of me all at once, sharp and aggressive. "What are you doing here?"

The room isn't empty. The bed has sheets on it. There are houseplants on the windowsill. Books pile atop the dresser.

This girl isn't Alex, but she's in Alex's room. She's in *Alex's* room, and looking at me like I just walked in off the street dripping with garbage.

She sets down her pen and says, "I live here." Her voice is low, accent like molasses.

For a moment we stare at each other, static humming in my chest. The girl is as calm and motionless as lake water. It's unnerving. I keep expecting her to ask *Why are you here?*—to turn the question back around on me, the intruder—but she never does.

She's waiting for me to speak. All the niceties are close at hand: introductions, small talk, polite questions about origin and interests. But my jaw is wired shut, and I say nothing.

At last she rises from her seat, chair legs scraping against the hardwood, and shuts the door in my face.

2

The girl in Alex's room isn't a ghost, but she might as well be.

A day passes without us speaking again; the door to Alex's room remains shut, the only sign of the new occupant's presence the occasional creak of a floorboard or a dirty coffee cup left out on the kitchen counter. At noon I spot her out on the porch, sitting in a rocking chair with a cigarette in one hand and *Oryx and Crake* in the other, dressed in a seersucker suit.

I split my time between my bedroom and the common room, venturing once to the faculty dining hall to load up a box of food and abscond with it back to Godwin House; nothing seems worse to me than the prospect of trying to eat while all the English faculty wander up to me to remind me how sorry they are, how difficult it must be, how brave I am to come back here after everything.

If I keep moving—bedroom, common room; common room, bedroom—then maybe the cold won't catch up to me.

That's what I tell myself, at least. But in the end I can't outrun it.

I'm in the reading nook when it happens. I've curled up lodged on the window seat at the end of the ground-floor hallway, shoes kicked off and sock feet tucked between the cushions, the books from Dr. Wyatt's summer reading list stacked on the floor by my hip. My eyelids are heavy, sinking low no matter how hard I fight to keep my gaze fixed on the page. I've lit candles even though it's still late afternoon; the flames flicker and spit, reflecting off the window glass.

A moment, I think. *I'll just close my eyes for a moment.*

Sleep swells around me like groundwater. The dark pulls me under.

And then I'm back on the mountain, hands numb in my gloves as I cling to that meager ledge. The storm is unrelenting, sleet battering the nape of my neck. I keep thinking about dark water rising in my lungs. About Alex's body broken on the rocks.

The snow beneath me isn't shifting anymore. I perch light on its back, light like an insect, motionless. If I move, the mountain will shiver and swat me away.

If I don't move, I will die here.

"Then die," Alex says, and I snap awake.

The hall has gone dark. The tall windows gaze out into the black woods, and the candles have blown out. My breath is the only thing I can hear, heavy and arrhythmic. It bursts out of me in gasps—painful, like I'm at altitude, like I'm still so far above the earth.

I feel her fingers at the back of my neck, nails like shards of ice. I jerk around, but there's no one there. Shadows stretch out through the empty halls of Godwin House, unseen eyes gazing down from the tall corners. Once upon a time I found it so easy to forget the stories about Godwin House and the five Dalloway witches who lived here three hundred years ago, their blood in our dirt, their bones hanging from our trees. If this place is haunted, it's haunted by the legacy of murder and magic—not by Alex Haywood.

Alex was the brightest thing in these halls. Alex kept the night at bay.

I need to turn on the lights. But I can't move from this spot against the window, can't stop gripping my own knees with both hands.

She isn't here. She's gone. She's gone.

I lurch up and stagger to the nearest floor lamp, yank the chain to switch on the light. The bulb glares white; and I turn to face the hall again, to prove to myself it's empty. And of course it is. God, what time is it? *3:03 a.m.* says my overly bright phone screen. It's too late for the girl in Alex's room to still be awake.

I turn on every light between there and my bedroom, pulse stammering as I keep climbing the stairs past the second floor—*Don't look, don't look*—and up to the third.

In my room I shut the door and crouch down on the rug. If this were last year I might have cast a spell, a circle of light my protection against the dark. Tonight my hands shake so badly I break three matches before I manage to strike a flame. I don't make a circle. *Magic doesn't exist.* I don't cast a spell. I just light three candles and hunch forward over their heat.

Practice mindfulness, Dr. Ortega would say. *Focus on the flame. Focus on something* real.

If anything supernatural wanders these halls, it doesn't answer; the candle flames flicker in the dim light and cast shifting shadows against the wall.

"No one's there," I whisper, and no sooner have the words left my lips than someone knocks.

I startle violently enough that I knock over a candle. The silk rug catches almost instantly, yellow fire eating a quick path across the antique pattern. I'm still stamping out sparks when someone says, "What are you doing?"

I look up. Alex's replacement stands in my doorway. And although it's past three in the morning, she's dressed as if she's about to walk into a law school interview. She's even wearing collar studs.

"Summoning the devil. What does it look like?" I answer, but the heat burning in my cheeks betrays me; I'm humiliated. I want to kick the rest of the candles over and burn the whole house down so no one knows I got caught like this.

One of the girl's brows lifts.

I've never been able to do that. Even after ages staring at myself in the mirror, I've only ever been able to muster a constipated sort of grimace.

I expect a witty comeback, something sharp and bladed and befitting this strange girl with all her unexpected edges. But she just says, "You left all the lights on."

"I'll turn them off."

"Thank you." She turns to go, presumably to vanish back downstairs and from my life for another few days.

"Wait," I say, and she glances back, the candlelight flickering across her face and casting odd shadows beneath her cheekbones.

I step gingerly over the remaining flames, but I still feel the heat as my legs cross over. I hold out my hand. "I'm Felicity. Felicity Morrow."

She eyes my hand for a moment before she finally reaches out and shakes it. Her palm is cool, her grasp strong. "Ellis."

"Is that a first or a last name?"

She laughs and drops my hand and doesn't answer. I stand there in the doorway, watching her head back down the hall. Her hips don't sway when she walks. She just goes, hands in her trouser pockets and the motion of her body straight and sure.

I don't know why she's here early. I don't know why she won't tell me her name. I don't know why she never speaks to me, or who she is.

But I want to find a loose thread on the collar of her shirt and tug.

I want to unravel her.

3

Everyone returns two days later, the Saturday before classes commence. Not in a trickle, but in hordes: the front lot is a hive of cars, the quad flooded with new and returning students and their families—often dragging younger siblings to gaze through the looking glass at their own potential future. Four hundred girls: a small school by most standards, all of us students divvied up into even smaller living communities. Even so, I can't quite bring myself to go downstairs while the new residents of Godwin House are moving in. But I do leave my door open. From my position on my bed, curled up with a book, I watch the figures crossing back and forth in the third-floor hall.

Godwin House is the smallest on campus—only large enough to fit five students in addition to Housemistress MacDonald, who sleeps on the first floor, and reserved exclusively for upperclassmen. Expanding Godwin to fit more students was another cause we fought against. Just imagine this place with its rickety stairs and slanted floors appended to a modernized glass-and-concrete parasite of an extension, wood and marble giving way to carpet and formica, Godwin no longer the home of Dickinson and witches but a monstrous chimera designed to maximize residential density.

No. We've been able to keep Godwin the way it is, the way it *was* three hundred years ago, when this school was founded. You can still feel history in these halls. At any moment you might turn the corner and find yourself face to face with a ghost from the past.

There are two others assigned to this floor with me: a brown-skinned girl with long black hair, wearing an expression of perpetual boredom, and a pallid, pinch-faced redhead, whom I glimpse from time to time half-hidden behind a worn paperback of *The Enchanted April*. If they notice me in my room, perched on my bed with my laptop on my knees, they don't say anything. I watch them direct hired help to carry boxes and suitcases up the stairs, sipping iced coffees while other people sweat for them.

The first time I spot the redhead, a flash of hair vanishing around a corner like sudden flame, I almost think she's Alex.

She isn't Alex.

If my mother were here, she would urge me up off this bed and force me into a common space. I'd be shepherded from girl to girl until I'd introduced myself to them all. I'd offer to make tea, a gesture calculated to endear myself to them. I wouldn't be late for supper, a chance to congregate with the rest of the Godwin girls in the house dining room, to trade summer anecdotes and pass the salt.

I accomplish none of those things, and I do not go to supper at all.

I feel as if the next year has just opened up in front of me, a great and yawning void that consumes all light. What will emerge from that darkness? What ghosts will reach from the shadows to close their fingers around my neck?

A year ago, Alex and I let something evil into this house. What if it never left?

I shut myself in my room and pace from the window to the door and back again, twisting my hands in front of my stomach. *Magic isn't real,* I tell myself once again. *Ghosts aren't real.*

And if ghosts and magic aren't real, curses aren't real, either.

But the *tap-tap* of the oak tree branches against my window reminds me of bony fingertips on glass, and I can't get Alex's voice out of my head.

Tarot isn't magic, I decide. It's fortune-telling. It's a historical practice. It's . . . it's essentially a card game. Therefore, there's no risk courting old habits when I crouch in the closet and peel the baseboard away from the wall, reaching past herbs and candles and old stones to find the familiar metal tin that holds my Smith-Waite deck.

I shove the rest of those dark materials back in place and scuttle out of the closet on my hands, breath coming sharp and shallow.

Magic isn't real. There's nothing to be afraid of.

I carry the box to my bed, shuffle the cards, and ask my questions: Will I fit in with these girls? Will I make friends here?

Will Godwin House be anything like what I remember?

I lay out three cards: past, present, future.

Past: the Six of Cups, which represents freedom, happiness.

It's the card of childhood and innocence. Which, I suppose, is why it falls in my past.

Present: the Nine of Wands, reversed. Hesitation. Paranoia. That sounds about right.

And my future: the Devil.

I frown down at my cards, then sweep them back into the deck. I never know what to make of the major arcana. Besides, tarot doesn't predict the future, or so said Dr. Ortega, anyway. Tarot only means as much as your interpretation tells you about yourself.

There's no point in agonizing over the cards right now. Instead I check my reflection in the mirror, tying my hair back and applying a fresh coat of lipstick, then go downstairs to meet the rest of them.

I find the new students in the common room. They're all gathered around the coffee table, seemingly fixated on a chess game being played between Ellis and the redhead. A rose-scented candle burns, classical music playing on vinyl.

Even though I know nothing about chess, I can tell Ellis is winning. The center of the board is controlled by her pawns, the other girl's pieces pushed off to the flanks and battling to regain lost ground.

"Hi," I say.

All eyes swing round to fix on me. It's so abrupt—a single movement, as if synchronized—that I'm left feeling suddenly off balance. My smile is tentative on my mouth.

I'm never tentative. I'm Felicity Morrow.

But these girls don't know that.

All their gazes turn to Ellis next, as if asking *her* for permission to speak to me. Ellis sweeps a white pawn off the board and sits back. Drapes a wrist over her knee, says: "That's Felicity."

As if I can't introduce myself. And of course it's too late now; what am I supposed to say? I can't just say hi again. I'm certainly not going to agree with her: *Yes indeed, my name* is *Felicity, you are quite correct.*

Ellis met these girls a few hours ago, and already she's established herself as their center of gravity.

One of them—a Black girl with a halo of tight coils, wearing a cardigan I recognize as this season's Vivienne Westwood—takes pity on me. "Leonie Schuyler."

It's enough to prompt the others to speak, at least.

"Kajal Mehta," says the thin, bored-looking girl from my floor.

"Clara Kennedy." The red-haired girl, her attention already turned back to the chess game.

And it appears that concludes the conversation. Not that they return to whatever they'd been talking about before; now that I am here, the room has fallen silent, except for the click of Clara's knight against the board and the sound of a match striking as Ellis lights a cigarette.

Indoors. And not only does no one tell her to put it out, MacDonald fails to preternaturally manifest the way she would had it been me and Alex smoking in the common room: *Books are flammable, girls!*

Well. I'm hardly going to leave just because they so clearly want me to. In fact . . . I belong here as much as they do. *More* than they do. I was a resident of Godwin House when they were still first-years begging for directions to the dining hall.

I sit down in an empty armchair and pull out my phone, scrolling through my email while Clara and Kajal exchange incredulous looks—like they've never seen someone text before. And maybe they haven't. They're all dressed as if they've just emerged from the 1960s: tweed skirts and Peter Pan collars and scarlet lipstick.

Ellis finishes the chess game in eight moves—a quick and brutal destruction of Clara's army—and conversation resumes, albeit stiltedly, as if they're all trying to forget I'm here. I learn that Leonie spent the summer at her family's cottage in Nantucket, and Kajal has a pet cat named Birdie.

I don't learn anything I want to know—and frankly, nothing I didn't know already. Leonie's family, the Schuylers, are old money; and I'd seen Leonie around school before, I realize, although she had straight hair then, and she certainly hadn't been wearing that massive antique signet ring. The surnames Mehta and Kennedy are equally storied, their wielders frequent guests at my mother's holiday home in Venice.

I *want* to know why they chose Godwin . . . or Dalloway altogether. I want to know if they were drawn here, as I was, by the allure of its literary past. Or if perhaps their interest goes back further, paging through the years to the eighteenth century, to dead girls and dark magic.

"What do you think of Dalloway so far?" Leonie asks. Asks *Ellis,* that is.

Ellis taps the ash from her cigarette into an empty teacup. "It's fine. Much smaller than I expected."

"You get used to it," Clara says with a silly little giggle. More and more I dislike her; perhaps because she reminds me too much of Alex, and yet not enough of her, either. Clara and Alex look alike, but that's where the similarities end. "You're lucky to be in Godwin. It's the best house."

"Yes, I know about Dickinson," says Ellis.

"Not just that," Leonie says. "Godwin might be the smallest house on campus, but it's also the oldest. It was here before the rest of the school was even built. Deliverance Lemont—the founder—lived here with her daughter."

"Margery Lemont," Ellis says, and I am frozen in the armchair, ice water in my veins. "I read about what happened," she adds.

I should have gone upstairs when I had the chance.

"Creepy, right?" Clara says. She's smiling. I can't help but stare at her. *Creepy:* the word fails to encapsulate what Margery Lemont had been. I can think of better terms: *Wealthy. Daring. Killer. Witch.*

"Oh, please," Kajal says, waving a dismissive hand. "No one really believes in that nonsense."

"The deaths were real. That much is a historical fact." Leonie's tone is almost pedagogic; I wonder if her thesis involves archival work.

"Yes, but witchcraft? Ritual murder?" Kajal shakes her head. "More likely the Dalloway Five were just girls who were too bold for their time, and they were killed for it. Like what happened in Salem."

The Dalloway Five.

Flora Grayfriar, who was murdered first, by the girls she'd thought were friends.

Tamsyn Penhaligon, hanged from a tree.

Beatrix Walker, her body broken on a stone floor.

Cordelia Darling, drowned.

And . . . Margery Lemont, buried alive.

Before last year, I had planned to write my thesis on the intersection of witchcraft and misogyny in literature. Dalloway seemed like the perfect place for it, the very walls steeped in dark history. I had studied the Dalloway witches like an academic, paging through the stories of their lives and deaths with scholarly detachment—until the past reached out from parchment and ink to close its fingers around my throat.

"You're lucky you got accepted to Godwin your first year at Dalloway," Leonie says to Ellis, deftly guiding the conversation out of choppy waters. "It's so competitive; most people don't get accepted until they're seniors."

"*I'm* a junior," Clara points out, to general disregard.

I resist the urge to retort: *I was, too.*

"Didn't they say all the witches died here at Godwin House?" Ellis says, lighting a fresh cigarette. The smell of her smoke curls through the air, acrid as burning flesh.

I can't be here.

I shove back my chair and stand. "I think I'll head to bed now. It was lovely meeting all of you."

They're staring at me, so I force a smile: *polite, good girl, from a good family.* Ellis exhales her smoke toward the ceiling.

By the time I make it upstairs to my dark room and its old familiar shapes, I've identified the feeling in my chest: defeat.

The tarot cards are still on my bed. I grab the deck and shove it back into the hole it came from, push the baseboard into place.

Ridiculous. I'm ridiculous. I should never have used them again. Tarot isn't magic, but it's close enough; I can practically hear Dr. Ortega's voice in my head, murmuring about fixed delusions and grief. But magic isn't real, I'm not crazy, and I'm not grieving.

Not anymore.

4

I debated attending the party at all. The inhabitants of Boleyn House throw the same soiree at the start and finish of every semester—Moulin Rouge themed, girls with long cigarette holders sipping absinthe and checking glued-on lashes in the bathroom mirror—and I'd always attended before. But that was when I had all of Godwin House with me. Alex and I used to dress monochrome: me in red, her in midnight blue. She'd have a hip flask tucked into her beaded clutch. I'd lean out the fourth-story window and chain-smoke cigarettes—the only time I ever smoked.

This time it's just me. No dark mirror-self. And the red dress I wore last year hangs off me now, my collarbone jutting like blades from shoulder to shoulder and my hip bones visible through the thin silk.

I recognize some of the faces, students who had been first-years and sophomores during my first attempt at a senior year; they wave at me as they drift past, on to more promising prospects.

"Felicity Morrow?"

I glance around. A short, bob-haired girl stands at my elbow, all big eyes and wearing a dress that has clearly never seen an iron in its life. It takes a second for the realization to sink in.

"Oh—hi. It's Hannah, right?"

"Hannah Stratford," she says, beaming still wider. "I wasn't sure you'd remember me!"

I do, although only as a vague recollection of the little first-year who'd tagged along after Alex like Alex was the very embodiment of sophistication and not a messy girl who always slept too late and cheated a passing grade out of French class. No, outside of Godwin House, Alex was seamless, refined, the model of effortless perfection, who managed to wear her parvenu surname like a goddamn halo.

My stomach cramps. I press a hand against my ribs and suck in a shallow breath. "Of course I remember," I say, drawing a smile onto my lips. "It's good to see you again."

"I'm so glad you decided to come back this year," Hannah says, solemn as a priest. "I hope you're feeling better."

All at once, that smile takes effort. "I'm feeling fine."

It comes out sharply enough that Hannah flinches. "Right. Of course," she says hurriedly. "Sorry. I just mean . . . sorry."

She doesn't know about my time at Silver Lake. She can't possibly know.

Another breath, my hand rising and falling with my diaphragm. "We all miss her."

I wonder if it sounds disingenuous coming from my mouth. I wonder if Hannah hates me for it, a little.

Hannah chews her lower lip for a moment, but whatever she'd thought of saying she abandons in favor of another bright grin. "Well, at least you're still in Godwin House! I applied this year, but no go, unfortunately. But then again, *everyone* applied. I mean, obviously."

Obviously?

I don't even have to ask the question. Hannah rises up on the balls of her feet, leans in, and whispers it like a secret: *"Ellis Haley."*

Oh. *Oh.* Mismatched puzzle pieces slide, at last, into place. Ellis is Ellis Haley. Ellis is Ellis Haley, novelist: bestselling author of *Night Bird,* which won the Pulitzer last year. I'd heard about it on NPR; Ellis Haley, only seventeen and "the voice of our generation."

Ellis Haley, a prodigy.

I manage to say, "Isn't she homeschooled?"

"That's right. You wouldn't know, I guess. She transferred here this semester, for her senior year. I suppose she wanted to get out of Georgia."

Hannah is still talking, but I don't really hear her. I'm too busy combing through my memories of the past week, trying to remember if I did anything humiliating.

Everything I'd done was humiliating.

"I'm going to get a drink," I tell Hannah, and escape before she can announce she'll join me. The only thing worse than listening to Hannah tell me how *sorry* she is about what happened would be listening to her wax rhapsodic about Ellis Haley.

The Boleyn girls have set up a makeshift bar in their kitchen, their faculty adviser conveniently absent—as all our faculty go conveniently absent whenever we throw parties; our parents don't pay this school to discipline us after all—and there are more varieties of expensive gin than I know how to parse. I pour myself a glass of what's closest, then a second glass when that one's gone.

I don't even like gin. I doubt that any of the twenty girls who live in Boleyn House like gin; they just like how much this particular gin costs.

No one talks to me. For once, I'm glad. Instead I get to watch them talk to each other, their sidelong glances skirting past me like they're trying not to be caught looking, conversation dropping low when they realize I'm there.

Everyone knows, then.

I don't know how they figured it out—or, well, maybe I do. Gossip travels fast in our circles. Even with Ellis Haley at Dalloway School, I am the most interesting person here.

I tip back the rest of my drink. They'll get over it. Once classes start, someone will invent a worse story to tell around the fireplace than *Felicity Morrow, the girl who . . .*

Even in my mind, I can't say it.

I pour myself another glass.

Every house at Dalloway has its secrets, a relic of the school's history. As Leonie had so astutely pointed out, Dalloway was founded by Deliverance Lemont, the daughter of a Salem witch and allegedly a practitioner herself. Some secrets are easier: a secret passageway from the kitchen to the common room, a collection of old exam papers. Boleyn's, like Godwin's, is darker.

Boleyn's secret is an old ritual, a nod from the present day to a time when bad women were witches and passed their magic down to their daughters, generation to generation. And if the magic has died by now, diluted by technology and cynicism and too many years, students of certain Dalloway houses still honor our bloody inheritance.

Boleyn House. Befana House. Godwin.

When I was initiated into the Margery coven, I pledged my blood and loyalty to the bones of Deliverance's daughter, the dead witch Margery Lemont. I might not be part of Boleyn House, but the initiation ritual bound me to five girls each year from these three houses, chosen to carry Margery's legacy.

More or less, anyway; last year I saw one of the Boleyn initiates drinking tequila out of the Margery Skull's eye socket like it was a particularly macabre sippy cup.

The Skull is supposed to be here, at the Boleyn House altar. I could drift down the hall with gin running hot in my veins, find the girl in red standing guard by the crypt door, and murmur the password:

Ex scientia ultio.

From knowledge comes vengeance.

I close my eyes, and for a moment I can see it: the single slim table draped in black cloth and bearing thirteen black candles. The thirteenth candle atop the Margery Skull, wax melting over its crown like a dark hand grasping bone.

But the Skull isn't there anymore, of course. It's been missing for almost a year.

None of the Boleyn girls seem concerned. Even the girls I recognize from previous visits to the Boleyn crypt are drunk and laughing, liquor sloshing over the rims of their cups. If they worry about a dead witch seeking revenge for her desecrated remains, it doesn't show.

We've all heard the ghost stories. They're told at Margery coven initiation rites, handed down from older sister to younger like a family heirloom: Tamsyn Penhaligon seen outside a window with her snapped neck, Cordelia Darling with her sodden clothes dripping water on the kitchen floor, Beatrix Walker murmuring arcane words in the darkness.

Tales meant to frighten and entertain—not meant to be believed. And I hadn't believed. Not at first.

But I still remember the dark figure blooming from the shadows, the guttering candlelight, and Alex's white, stricken face.

I turn and stalk down that hall toward the crypt. The girl in red is there, but she isn't the somber, stoic figure she ought to be. She's on her phone, tapping away at the screen, which lights her face in an eerie bluish glow, smirking at something she's just read.

"Remember me?" I say.

She looks up. The grin drops from her face between one heartbeat and the next, a new expression stealing its place: something flat and guarded and hard to read. "Felicity Morrow."

"That's right. I've been enjoying the party."

Her weight shifts to the other foot, and her arms rise to hug around her waist, fingertips pressing in against that red cardigan. "I heard you were back at school this year."

She's afraid of me.

I shouldn't blame her for it, but I do. I hate her, all at once. I hate that she is the one standing in scarlet to guard the crypt, I hate the invisible threads that tie her to the other girls in our coven, the knots between her and Bridget Crenshaw and

Fatima Alaoui and the rest of them, tethers I used to think were unbreakable.

I hate that I don't even remember her name.

"I haven't received a note yet," I say.

She shakes her head very slightly. "You won't be getting one. Not this year."

I knew it. I *guessed* it when none of them wrote to me while I was gone, despite all those flowers they sent to Alex's mother for the funeral, their figures like a murder of crows huddled at Alex's grave site even though none of them knew her. None of them *really* knew her, not like I did.

Suddenly I'm coldly, brutally sober. I set my empty glass aside on the nearest table and look at this girl with her scarlet Isabel Marant sweater and expensive manicure, her lipsticked mouth that would have whispered about Alex when she thought Alex couldn't hear: *scholarship, rustic, aspirant.*

"I see," I say. "And why is that?"

She might be afraid of me, but now it's for a different reason entirely. I know how to adopt my mother's crisp consonants and Boston vowels to effect. It's an introduction without ever having to repeat my name.

The girl's cheeks flush as red as her cardigan. "I'm sorry," she says. "It wasn't my decision. It's just . . . you took this all so seriously, you know."

It's a comment that demands a response, but I find myself voiceless. *So seriously.* As if the skull, the candles, the goat's blood . . . as if that was all a joke to them.

Or maybe it was. Alex would have said that witchcraft was about aesthetics. She would tell me that this coven was created for sisterhood—for the Margery girl with a knowing smile at that corporate gala introducing you to the right person at the right time. *Connections,* not conjure.

My smile feels tight and false on my lips, but I smile all the same. That's all we ever do at this school: insult each other, then smile.

"Thank you for the explanation," I say. "I understand your position completely."

Time for another drink.

I make my way back into the kitchen, where the gin has been replaced by an unfamiliar green drink that tastes bitter, like rotten herbs. I drink it anyway, because that's what you do at parties, because my mother's blood runs in my veins and, like Cecelia Morrow, it turns out I cannot face the real world without the taste of lies in my mouth and liquor in my blood.

I hate that it's true. I hate *them* more.

My thoughts have finally tilted hazy, all blue lights and blurred shapes, when I see her. Ellis Haley has arrived, and she's brought her new cult in tow: Clara and Kajal and Leonie. None of them dressed for the theme, but somehow they become the knot around which the rest of the party shifts and contorts. I'm no better. I'm staring, too.

Ellis is wearing lipstick for the occasion, a red so dark it's almost black. It will leave a mark on everything her mouth touches.

Our eyes meet across the room. And for once I'm not even tempted to turn away. I lift my chin and hold her gaze, sharp beneath straight brows, somehow clear despite the empty absinthe glass she holds in hand. I want to crack open her chest and peer inside, see how she ticks.

Then Ellis tilts her head to the side, bending down slightly as Clara rises up to murmur something in her ear. That rope tethered between us draws taut; she doesn't look away.

But I do, just in time to catch the twist to Clara's pink lips, the brief and brutal gesture with two fingers: scissors snapping shut.

Something cold plunges into my stomach; even chasing it with the rest of my drink doesn't thaw the ice. I abandon my empty glass on the table and push my way through the crowd, using elbows where words fail.

I make it all the way outside before lurching forward to spill my guts across the lawn. I'm still gasping, spitting out bile, as someone yells from the porch: "Go to rehab!"

Oh. Right. It's only nine p.m.

I wipe my mouth on the back of a shaky hand, straighten up, and dart down the walkway toward the quad. I don't look back. I don't let them see my face.

At Godwin House I brush my teeth, then pace the empty halls, a terrible restlessness crawling up and down my spine. I can't sleep yet. I can't climb into my chilly bed and stare at the wall, waiting for the rest of them to get home, craning my ears to hear the sound of my name on their lips.

I make a cup of tea instead, stand at the kitchen counter sipping it until some of that dizzy drunk feeling fades. That gets me to nine-thirty, and then I have to put the dishes away and figure out something else. I draw a three-card tarot reading: all swords. I glimpse a light on, through the crack beneath

Housemistress MacDonald's door, but I'm not quite so pathetic yet as to seek her company.

As usual I end up in the common room.

The problem is, I don't have anything I want to read. I peruse the shelves, but nothing jumps out at me. I feel as if I've read everything—every book in the world. Every title seems like a reiteration of something that came before it, the same story regurgitated over and over.

I make a fine literature student, don't I?

This house seems too quiet now. The silence bears down on me like a weight.

No, it *is* too quiet—it's unnaturally quiet—and when I glance back I see why.

The grandmother clock that sits between the fiction and poetry shelves has gone silent. Its hands are stuck at 3:03.

The same time I had the nightmare.

I draw closer, steps slow. The floorboards creak under my weight. I stare at the white face of that clock, at those black blades pointing nearly at a right angle to each other, mocking me. The silence thickens. I can't breathe; I'm suffocating in thin, depressurized air—

"I suppose we'll have to get it repaired," someone says, and I spin around.

Ellis Haley stands behind me, both hands tucked into her trouser pockets and her attention fixed past me at the grandmother clock. She's still wearing that red lipstick, the lines of it too crisp and perfect to have just come from a party. After a moment her gaze slips down to meet mine.

"You left early," she comments.

"I felt sick."

"They didn't sweeten the absinthe enough," she says, and shakes her head.

For a second we both stand there staring at each other. I remember Clara's pale hands in the darkness: snip, snip.

"Where's everyone else?" I ask.

"Still at Boleyn, as far as I know. I came back alone."

I struggle to imagine any of those girls letting Ellis Haley go anywhere by herself. *You must've had to peel them off like tiny well-dressed leeches.*

I realize I've said that out loud, a beat after my mouth falls shut again.

Ellis laughs. It's a sudden bright sound that breaks the silence like an egg, that fills the room. "I did tell them I was just going to freshen up," she admits. Her eyes crinkle at the corners when she smiles. "Clara tried to come with me."

"How fortunate you managed to escape."

"By a hair," Ellis says, pinching her fingers. "I made coffee, by the way. Would you like some?"

"It's late for coffee, isn't it?"

"It's never too late for coffee."

This whole night already feels bizarre, like the world viewed through a kaleidoscope. "Why not," I say, and Ellis goes to retrieve a tray from the kitchen: the coffee in a silver pot that appears vaguely Moroccan, our own chipped teacups a little forlorn when adjacent.

Ellis pours two cups, sitting on the floor with both legs tucked beneath her. She hasn't brought cream or sugar; apparently we're both meant to drink our coffee black.

"Why were you here so early?" I ask her after she's picked up her cup and taken her first sip. It's a brash question—not the kind of conversation starter my mother would approve of—but it seems all my restraint was expelled with my vomit. "Most people aren't so desperate to get back to school."

"Only two weeks early, really," Ellis says. "I needed a retreat. Time away from the world to work on my book. It's peaceful here when everyone else is gone."

I'm surprised the administration let her stay.

Or, actually, maybe I'm not. The publicity—*Ellis Haley's sophomore novel, written in seclusion on the campus of Dalloway School*—would be worth the extra cost of sustaining a single student for two weeks. Dalloway can align itself with the Villa Diodati, with Walden.

I'm not sure what my mother had to do to convince Dalloway to let me arrive four days early, but I imagine it required more than mere asking.

"What are you writing now?"

Ellis lowers her cup, gazing down at the black surface of her coffee for a moment as if she'll find inspiration there. "It's a character study," she says. "I want to explore the gradations of human morality: how indifference can slide into evil, what drives a person toward murder. And I want to interrogate the concept of the psychopath: whether villainy exists in that truest form or if it's simply a manifestation of some human drive that lurks in all of us."

It's chilly in this room; I hold my coffee between both hands, trying to borrow its warmth. "And what will you conclude?"

"I don't know yet. That's what I'm trying to figure out." Ellis traces her finger along the circumference of her cup. "Although I suppose in some ways I don't need to speculate. The deaths in the story are inspired by the Dalloway Five."

The Dalloway Five, again. No matter what I do, it seems like I can't escape them. I left for almost an entire year—I spent nearly a *year* away from this place, in my own brand of seclusion, but as soon as I come back, there are ghosts at my heels and stories of dead witches on everyone's tongue.

I don't recall people being nearly so interested in Dalloway's history last year. If anything, I felt self-conscious of my thesis subject; discussing it always earned me scrunched noses and twisted mouths.

"What do you mean?"

"I'm writing about them," Ellis says. "Well, about Margery Lemont specifically. The story is from multiple perspectives, but ultimately questions whether Margery was really a witch, as her accusers claimed, or whether accusations of witchcraft merely reflected a pathologization of female anger."

I don't know how to respond to that. My mouth is dry; my tongue sticks to my palate like old gum.

"So of course I had to transfer here, to Dalloway. There's nowhere else to write this kind of story, is there?"

I suppose there isn't. Even so, a part of me wants to warn her not to get too close. Margery Lemont has a way of sucking you in and refusing to let go. I wonder if Alex's ghost is watching us right now, her dead gaze drinking in this scene. Judging.

"Well, good luck," I offer.

Ellis smiles at me, right as her lips close around the rim

of her cup, is still smiling as she takes another sip. "And you? What's your senior thesis?"

For a moment, last year's answer perches on my lips. Ellis waits in patient silence while I struggle to swallow it down.

"I don't know yet."

I can barely stand to exist in this place anymore. Dalloway might be in my blood and bones, but as much as I was unable to stay away, Dalloway's history—and mine—hangs over the campus like a heavy fog. I wonder if Ellis feels it. If Ellis is scared of it, or if she hopes a shadow of that evil will seep up from the ground and infect her, the way it infected Margery Lemont.

At last, I bite the inside of my cheek and admit: "I thought I wanted to study the witches, as well. But I'm not sure that's such a good idea anymore."

Ellis's brow arches at a perfect angle. "Curiouser and curiouser," she says.

Her amusement hangs on the words like antique lace.

Does she know? Can she tell that, for me, the study was never academic?

Maybe she's been warned, Wyatt or MacDonald drawing Ellis into her office: *Be careful with such stories, Miss Haley. Take care you don't start to believe they're true.*

"How so?" It comes out a little more aggressively than I expect. "It's a good story. Clearly you agree, or you wouldn't be writing about it."

"A perfect story," Ellis corrects. "Dalloway School: founded to teach the arcane arts to young witches under the guise of an expensive finishing school. Dalloway's first headmistress:

daughter of a witch. And of course the Dalloway Five, who murdered one of their own in a satanic ritual. Reality only aspires to such perversity."

"It's not all untrue. We know the founder came from Salem, after all. And don't forget the occult collection in the main library." A collection donated by an alumna of Dalloway, a now-famous historian of seventeenth-century religious practices. A collection I had hoped to get my hands on, as soon as I was a third-year and had a faculty member willing to sign the permission slip. I wanted to breathe the dust off those scrolls, trace my gloved fingers along ancient spines. The administration—and Wyatt—had tried to talk me out of my thesis a hundred times. Maybe they'd known what would become of me if I flirted too well with old magic. "How many finishing schools do you know with rare book rooms crammed full of pentacles and pages made out of human skin?"

Ellis waves a hand as if to say *Fair enough.*

"But of course, you're right," I add. "They weren't really witches. They were just girls."

Just girls. Just clever, bright young women. Too clever and bright for their time.

And they were killed for it.

"One other fact was real," Ellis says after a long moment. Her gaze is as cool as silver lake water, and as steady. "The death of Flora Grayfriar."

She's right. I'd almost not come to Dalloway for that precise reason; I'd found the idea of attending a school where a girl was ritually murdered, even if three hundred years ago, to be horribly gauche. All I'd really cared about was Godwin House.

Yes, all five of the Dalloway witches had been found dead on Godwin's grounds—killed by each other, or by small-minded townsfolk, depending who you believe—but *Emily Dickinson.* How could I resist?

It wasn't until I came here and learned more about the history of the school, about the witches, that I fell in love with the dark.

The front door bangs open, and the murmur of voices in the foyer heralds the return of the other Godwin girls. Ellis sets her empty coffee cup aside and stands, offering me her hand. After a moment, I take it, and she pulls me to my feet.

"Ellis," Kajal says once she appears in the common room entryway. "You should have told us you were coming back here."

Ellis glances toward me, the corner of her mouth curling up; and for once, I smile back.

The spell is broken now. The other girls eat up all the oxygen in the room, circling around Ellis like asteroids around a black hole. I escape upstairs to wash off my makeup and scrub the scent of cigarette smoke out of my hair. I'm exhausted, but even once I've curled up under my duvet with my pillow slowly going damp against my cheek from the shower water, it takes me a long time to fall asleep.

Flora Grayfriar haunts the late-night silence of Godwin House. My skin holds the sense memory of the Margery Skull, cool bone and warm wax dripping over my fingers. And I can't forget what Ellis wondered: whether the drive to murder sleeps quiet in all of us, if we're all two steps away from the ledge, waiting for an excuse to throw out both hands and *push.*

I think about the moment the rope snapped and the world went quiet and still, my body weightless without Alex dragging it down, the snow in my eyes and the emptiness on the mountain. The hollow feeling that carved its way into my chest.

And the relief.

5

Dalloway semesters never begin slowly.

Unlike other prep schools, Dalloway allows its students remarkable leeway in terms of what we study. We have a general education requirement, taught with the Harkness method—all discussion-based. And after our second year, students are encouraged to adopt a concentration: a passion project to pursue that will eventually become our senior thesis. There are Dalloway students who spend most of their year enmeshed in internships at the nearby aerospace laboratory, students who sleep in the classics building and only speak in ancient Greek. And then there's us: the literati, the bookish intelligentsia with an affinity for horn-rimmed glasses and pages that smell like dust.

I had thought I might get away with an unannounced thesis for a few weeks at least, that the administration's sympathy over Alex, or at least their repulsion over my former subject, would translate into a long leash and emails saying things like *Take your time.* I should have known better. But as it turns out, I'm a slow learner.

Wyatt calls me into her office the first day of classes and

passes me a can of store-brand soda; she keeps it in a minifridge under her mahogany desk, and the aesthetic of the chilly aluminum can juxtaposed with that desk and Wyatt's antique rug makes me oddly uneasy.

"So," she says, perching her reading glasses on the bridge of her nose. "As I told you over email, I think it's best we find a new subject for your senior thesis. Yes?"

"Yes." I got used to responding as people wanted to hear while I was at Silver Lake. *Yes* is what Wyatt wants to hear. "I don't want to waste the research I did before, so I was thinking I'd stay in a similar genre. Horror."

Wyatt nods slowly. "Is that a good idea? Horror can be . . . very gruesome."

"I'm better now," I reassure her. "I can handle reading Helen Oyeyemi. I promise."

Wyatt's pen taps a quick rhythm against the edge of her desk. I crack open the drink she gave me and take a small sip; the tropical-flavored soda bursts on my tongue with an eruption of fizz and synthetic citrus. It tastes like formaldehyde.

"Very well," Wyatt says at last.

I didn't realize how tense I'd been until she says that—and now I feel my body sinking back into the chair, shoulders retreating from where they'd scrunched up toward my ears.

I was never small and frightened before. I didn't used to be afraid of anything.

"Your thesis will need to be more specific than that, of course. What question will you be trying to answer with this work?"

"The same question." It's easier now. My prepared speech falls from my lips cool as a lie. "Misogyny and characterizations of female emotionality in horror literature. It'll be written through an intellectual history lens: How were these works in conversation with the social norms and mores of their time? How were they influenced by catalytic historical events and literature? And how did they influence history and literature in turn?"

"How did perceptions of women's emotions change throughout history," Wyatt translates.

"As viewed through the gaze of contemporaneous horror writers."

This earns me one of Wyatt's rare smiles. She uncaps her pen and signs her name on my thesis application form, then passes it back over her desk and says, "I very much look forward to reading this, Miss Morrow."

By the time I leave Wyatt's building, though, I already wonder if I've made a mistake. If reading about witches was foolish, reading about ghosts is surely more so. Ever since I came back here, I've felt Alex's presence like an unfinished sentence—*waiting.* And no matter how many times I tell myself ghosts don't exist, that doesn't dilute my fear.

I feel dizzy in the sunlight, heat prickling over my skin and fermenting there, spreading like a quick fever. Before I can lose my balance, I catch myself on the handrail and stand at the foot of the stairs, students flowing around me like water around a rock, oblivious.

I'd known it would be hard coming back to Dalloway after Alex died. But I didn't expect the way I'd smell her perfume lingering on an armchair in Godwin House, or the chill that rolls up my spine when I pass near her old room.

I didn't expect to feel so . . . *unmoored.*

I can practically hear Dr. Ortega's voice in my head, insisting that I should never have stopped my medication. That I'm not ready, that I'm fundamentally and biologically *not well.* She'd tell me all this would go away if only I was good and obedient and swallowed what they gave me.

All those old ghosts would wither and die in the light of day—if only I did as I was told.

But I am tired of being a good girl. I'm tired of obeying.

I don't need a babysitter. I certainly don't need a woman whose medical degree bought her a cushy job at a pricey private clinic telling me *It must be difficult* and *It wasn't your fault.*

Not that anyone else agrees on that point. Wyatt handles me with kid gloves, as they all do.

Sometimes I wonder what would happen if I just stopped cooperating.

Leonie is in the Godwin House foyer when I return. She jumps a little when I kick the door shut; she was waiting for me. "Hi," she says.

"Hi."

"How was your first day of classes?"

"Fine." I don't know why she's talking to me. Not knowing makes me suspicious.

"We're making dinner in the kitchen. If you wanted to . . ." She doesn't seem to know what word she's looking for to finish the sentence, just stares at me with these big brown eyes.

I think about letting her hang there, awkward and off balance. It would be a nice kind of social vengeance—repayment for that horrible night in the common room, for the invisible walls the four of them constructed to keep me out.

But I can't let them make me that person, so I relent. "Sure, I'll help."

I know this isn't Leonie's idea, of course. Ellis sent her. It's the only explanation, the only reason any of them would tolerate my presence for longer than absolutely necessary. But when I get into the kitchen, they're all there—sharp elbows and broth-splattered cookbooks and wooden spoons rapping against countertops—and Kajal passes me a gingham apron, and somehow it's easy to slip in among them.

"We're making balsamic mushroom ravioli," Clara says, tipping her head toward the wooden basket of shiitakes at her side. She's sliced what looks like half a pound already, soil ground into the cutting board.

"I'm not a very good cook," I admit.

Ellis glances up from where she's set up shop at the end of the island, a steel pasta-maker affixed to the side of the counter. She has a bit of flour swiped across her cheek. "None of us are. But we need someone to fold the ravioli, if you think you can manage that."

I can manage it.

Their conversation resumes around me, effortless as placing the needle back on a vinyl record and continuing where the melody left off.

"I can't believe I'm with Lindquist this year," Clara moans from her spot in the corner. There are too many girls in the kitchen and too few tasks, so after she finished with the mushrooms, she set up with her books open in her lap and a fountain pen fiddling between her fingers. "She hates me."

"You were with Yang last year?" asks Kajal.

"Yes. And now I've been cruelly abandoned."

"Yang only advises first- and second-years," I comment, pinching the edge of a ravioli. "It's Lindquist, MacDonald, and Wyatt for juniors and seniors."

"I know," Clara sighs, "but I'd hoped she might make an exception."

It's so like the conversations we used to have in Godwin House before I left. Although perhaps ours were more vicious; we'd created the definitive ranking of Dalloway English faculty, an algorithm including points for toughness, intelligence, susceptibility to various late-work excuses, and probability of dying of old age before the semester ended. Lindquist was at the top of our list, MacDonald at the bottom (although the algorithm, to be fair, didn't favor an instructor who lived in Godwin House and could know for sure that our essays were late because we were up all night partying, not because our third grandmother died).

"Who are you with?" Leonie asks, meeting my gaze and offering a tentative smile. And although I still suspect she's sympathetic only on Ellis's orders, I smile back.

"Wyatt."

"Kajal's with Wyatt, too," Leonie says, gesturing toward Kajal herself, who crushes another garlic clove under the flat blade of her knife and doesn't look up.

I'm not used to feeling uncertain in social situations. My junior year at Dalloway—the year before everything fell apart with Alex, before that climbing trip and its aftermath, my subsequent withdrawal from classes—I was popular. Or if not popular, then at least *envied;* my mother sent large allowances every month and had little interest in how I spent it, so I wasted all that money on tailored dresses and hair appointments and weekend trips to the city for my Godwin friends. And although I was far from the richest girl at Dalloway, the way I chose to spend my money bought me a certain immunity from social faux pas. Everyone has awkward moments; I was forgiven mine.

At least I didn't have to buy *my friends,* Alex had said the night she died, cheeks blotchy with rage; and even then I'd known she was right.

But I don't have any interest in buying the friendship of Ellis Haley or her cabal. I find it hard to care about social hierarchies these days.

Alex would have been proud.

"What is your thesis on?" I ask Kajal, because I no longer think feigning indifference proves superiority, and she looks up—surprised, I suspect, that I'm still talking to her.

"Female thinkers and philosophers of the Enlightenment," Kajal says. "Work from the *salons.* Macaulay, d'Épinay, de Gouges, Wollstonecraft . . ."

"Mary Astell? *A Serious Proposal*?"

"Of course." Kajal's posture has eased; she chops up the garlic with quick, smooth motions of her hands. "She was a little too religious for my preference, but I suppose that was unavoidable at the time."

"Although that relatively Cartesian approach produced her concept of virtuous friendship," I say, "so one can't fault her too much."

Kajal shrugs, probably preparing the same old argument:

whether Astell's conceptualization of friendship was truly virtuous or, as Broad argues, merely reciprocal.

"Just so," Ellis interjects. "As Astell said herself: 'It were well if we could look into the very Soul of the beloved Person, to discover what resemblance it bears to our own.' "

When I look, a slight smile has taken up at the corners of Ellis's mouth—there only for a moment, her gaze flicking over to meet mine before she turns back to the dough.

"I like Lady Mary Chudleigh," Clara supplies from the corner, a smudge of ink on her cheek.

"Hmm," says Ellis. "I've always found Chudleigh rather derivative."

Clara's pale face goes scarlet, and she says, "Oh. Well, I mean . . . yes, she was clearly influenced by Astell, so . . ."

Ellis has nothing to say to that, which only makes Clara flush worse. I don't completely understand why she's so upset by the prospect of disagreeing with Ellis, but then again, I don't pretend to understand the cult of personality the new members of Godwin House have constructed around Ellis, either.

"I think Chudleigh even admitted as much," I say, folding another ravioli and tossing it into the bowl. "Clara, maybe you could look it up on your phone."

The derisive look Clara shoots my way could burn through steel. "I don't have a *phone.*"

"None of us do," Leonie adds. "Technology is so distracting. I heard people's attention spans are actually getting shorter because they read everything online these days."

I glance toward Ellis, but she's moved to the sink to start washing up. No doubt she started this fad.

I finish the last ravioli and dust my flour-covered hands against my apron. It's not that I'm so very attached to my phone, but . . . still, I can't imagine eschewing it entirely. I'm not incredibly active on social media, but I *do* like to listen to music when I run. Me and Alex used to text each other constantly, our phones hidden under desks and behind books: *This class is interminable* and *Climbing this weekend?* and *Brush your hair—you look like a hedgehog.*

Maybe life's easier without all that.

We eat in the dining room, a white cloth spread over the mahogany table and candles burning between the array of cracked ceramic dishes. I don't talk much this time, either, but unlike the first night in the common room, I don't feel excluded. I'm here at the table with the rest of them, my chair between Leonie's and Clara's, my water poured from the same glass bottle as theirs. Ellis's slate gaze catches mine when Kajal mentions how quickly Ellis left the Boleyn party, a sharp cut of a smile before she looks away.

MacDonald doesn't join us. She would have, last year. I wonder if that's more to do with Ellis or with me.

"Shall we?" Ellis says when the last of us puts down her fork.

She leads us into the common room, where Kajal draws a slim green leather-bound book of poetry off the shelf and Ellis unearths a crystal decanter of bourbon concealed in a low cabinet, setting it down on the coffee table with a clink of glass on wood.

Leonie's brows lift. "What is that?"

"Bourbon. Castle and Key," Ellis says, lining a row of five glasses along the table's edge. "The very first barrel. My sibling got it for me when they went to the distillery last winter; the work the new owners have done on the Old Taylor restoration is really fantastic."

I have no idea how to interpret any of the words that just came out of Ellis's mouth. But Ellis discusses bourbon like she *knows* things, her slow southern drawl as calm and confident as if she were as much an expert with whiskeys as she is with literature.

She glances up. "Do you like old-fashioneds, Felicity?" Ellis has a little brown bottle in hand, squeezing a dark liquid from an eyedropper into each glass.

"What's an old-fashioned? It sounds . . . old-fashioned."

Ellis laughs. "Oh, you'll love this. Sit down."

"Ellis is on a whiskey kick," Kajal informs me, arching her perfect brows. She says it as if she's spent enough time with Ellis now to know everything there is to know about Ellis and her *kicks.* "Apparently the character in her new book likes whiskey. So of course that means Ellis has to like whiskey."

"How can you understand a character's mind without sharing their experiences?" Ellis says archly. She has a knife in one hand and an orange in the other, a twist of peel curling from under the blade. "If your writing isn't authentic—if you're just making it up—the reader will know."

"So, method acting," I say.

It earns me a sharp grin. "Precisely. *Method writing.*" Ellis squeezes the peel over the nearest drink; a fine mist sprays the glass.

"Once, Ellis slept outside in the Canadian winter for two weeks and bought heroin off a truck driver in an arcade bathroom," Clara says.

I find that incredibly hard to believe. It's the kind of Ellis Haley trivia you'd read in a literary magazine—hyperbolic and dramatized for effect, nothing whatsoever like the kind of behavior any parent would let their high-school-aged child get away with.

But Ellis doesn't deny it, either.

Because it didn't happen?

Or because it *did*?

Ellis finishes the cocktails and passes one to each of us. The fine crystal is heavy in my palm. Ellis, perched on the arm of the sofa, opens the little book of poetry and starts to read from St. Vincent Millay: *"Death, I say, my heart is bowed / Unto thine, O mother! . . ."*

I lift the glass and take a sip. The old-fashioned is surprisingly bitter, the heat of whiskey cut with something low and smoky. The sweetness, when it comes, is an afterthought. I'm not sure I like it.

Judging by the grimaces on the other girls' faces, I'm not the only one.

"This red gown will make a shroud / Good as any other."

Ellis passes the book to Leonie, who pages through with her free hand and chooses a new poem. We go around the room, each of us reading something; when it's my turn I choose Dickinson. From the glance Ellis shoots my way, shadowed under the fringe of her dark lashes, I wonder if she finds me as uninventive as Mary Chudleigh.

We take six rounds of the book, and after we've tired of poetry, Ellis makes coffee and ropes us all into a lively debate about the recursive feminine nature of birth and death; Leonie and Clara share a cigarette by the open window, the night breeze playing in Clara's russet hair and Leonie's sock feet tucked under Clara's thigh. Kajal falls asleep on the sofa with *Dear Life* draped over her face. Ellis reads in an armchair, teeth catching her lower lip and chewing till the skin flushes red. I go back upstairs, to the silent gray of my bedroom. But for once the shadowed corners don't hold threats.

I draw a card: the Page of Cups. My room smells like Alex's perfume.

Closed inside the books on my shelf are all the letters she ever sent me: notes passed in class, postcards mailed from those unbearable camping trips she used to take with her mother. I pin one of the postcards to the wall next to the mirror. Her signature—the big looping *A,* the spiky consonants—gazes back at me.

Alex is dead. And maybe her spirit is still here, maybe she still haunts the crooked halls of Godwin House. But I turn to face the empty room and say it anyway:

"I'm not afraid of you."

6

When classes fall into full swing, it's easier to forget I'm haunted.

The Godwin House poetry-and-existentialism sessions retreat from nightly to weekend occurrences over the next two weeks as attention turns away from dead poets and lyricism and toward homework and deadlines. More than once I catch Leonie sitting on the kitchen floor reading an assignment while dinner boils over, forgotten, on the stove behind her. My own reading list has gotten longer and longer; there's no shortage of female horror to consume, and not nearly enough time in the semester to read it all.

I find a first edition of Shirley Jackson's *The Haunting of Hill House* at a used bookstore in town and quickly discover it's impossible to read that book inside Godwin. There's nowhere to sit that doesn't position my back to either a window or door; I can't make it half a page without lurching around to look over my shoulder, half expecting to find a grotesque faceless figure gazing back at me from the dark corners. So I do a lot of my reading outside, during the day, a crocheted blanket tossed onto the quad grass and a thermos of tea at my elbow, devouring the dark and the macabre with white sunlight burning the nape of my neck.

The quad serves as the perfect vantage point to observe the full life cycle of a day's activities at Dalloway School. I watch the engineering interns dart down the sidewalks with ducked heads and arms full of blueprints; the artists meander over grass, trailing the scent of patchouli; instructors glare at wristwatches they can't afford as they hurry to the next meeting. I even spot Clara once, crossing from the library back toward Dalloway with a book held aloft. She doesn't seem to notice the way other students have to weave around her, her mind floating in a world very far away.

Ellis emerges from Godwin House just once, even though it's a Friday afternoon. Maybe Ellis Haley isn't required to attend classes. I watch her go across the yard, chin level with the ground and wearing a pantsuit, into the administrative building. She stays there about twenty minutes before I spy her again. This time she's holding an armful of paperwork. I raise my voice and call her name; she looks over and our gazes meet. But then she turns away and keeps walking, as if I'm not there at all.

It doesn't matter. I'm not an Ellis groupie. I must have done something to offend her—still using a cell phone would probably be sufficient crime to find myself permanently exiled from the clique.

But when I return to Godwin at dusk Ellis is there, cross-legged on the floor with the grandmother clock facedown on the rug and its insides strewn around her like war shrapnel.

"This is harder than it looks," she says, gesturing to the clock with a screwdriver.

"I'm sure we could call a professional."

She shrugs. "I was bored. And I found this in the library, so . . ." She has a book open by her knee, all clockwork diagrams. "Maybe I can write this into a novel, if I figure it out."

This seems like a lot of work for a scene that may or may not ever materialize. Then again, I suppose procrastination is universal. Not even the great *Ellis Haley* is immune.

I leave her there and retreat upstairs. I have an essay for Wyatt due tomorrow; I'm so absorbed in it that I ignore MacDonald's call for dinner, flicking on my desk lamp when the sun finally slips the rest of the way below the horizon. I've just written page seven and shut my laptop to push against the wall with my toes, arching my back and stretching both arms over my head, when someone knocks.

I expect MacDonald with a plate of leftovers, but when I call for her to come in, the door swings open and it's Ellis instead, coffee mug in hand.

"I thought you might need sustenance," she says.

More black coffee is the last thing I need at eleven p.m. when I have an early class the next day. I'm about to tell her that when she slides the mug onto my desk and I glance down.

"This isn't coffee," I say.

"It's chamomile," Ellis says. "One squeeze of lemon and a half teaspoon of honey. That is how you take it, right?"

I had no idea she'd even noticed how I drink my tea—or that I drink tea to begin with. And yet here she stands, hands clasped behind her back and the tea itself steaming right next to my potted echeveria. I arch my brows, pick up the mug, and take a tiny sip.

God, she even got it to the perfect temperature.

"It's good."

"I know."

It's things like this that make me entirely unsure where I stand with Ellis Haley. I don't understand how she could seem so patently disinterested in me on the quad earlier today, but within the crooked walls of Godwin House we might have known each other for months. I decide it's the dichotomy of Ellis's twin identities: Ellis Haley the famous writer, the prodigy whose face graced the cover of *Time* magazine, and Ellis the prep school student, who completely ruins antique grandmother clocks and tests new whiskey cocktails on her roommates, who shows up sweaty and flush-cheeked in the Godwin foyer after fencing practice with her épée scabbard slung over one shoulder and hair plastered to her brow, a modern Athena in lamé.

It feels like a peace offering, so after a moment I say, "How is the book going?"

She grimaces. "Not well. I'm starting to think writing about murder wasn't the best of plans, considering—"

"Considering you can't kill someone to see what it's like."

"Precisely." Ellis sighs. "Of course, the story isn't about murder, per se, it's a character sketch, but I'm sure when the book's out I'll hear all sorts of complaints from murderers regarding my insufficiently accurate representation of their pastime."

Ellis's gaze is steady, and there's nothing about her eyes or the set of her mouth that implies any deeper meaning than what she's said. But all at once I feel as if she has knotted her fingers in the threads that hold me together, pulling them taut and close to breaking.

"I suppose you could read memoirs."

Ellis laughs, which isn't at all the reaction I expected from a girl who—according to Hannah Stratford—takes her writing habits so seriously that she intentionally got arrested in small-town Mississippi just to see what it's like. "Yes, I suppose I could. Do you have any recommendations?"

This can't be innocent. Ellis is a writer; she knows how to choose her words. She's implying something. She's implying guilt.

My next words come out stiff and synthetic: "I'm afraid I'm not as well versed in the murder memoir genre as I should be."

"But your thesis is on the Dalloway witches," she says. "Surely you know quite a lot about these murders in particular. You can't imagine all the research I'm going to have to do in order to re-create their lives and deaths faithfully on the page."

My stomach has turned into a stone. I'm frozen with the tea halfway to my lips, all the excuses dead in my mouth—

Not that she would accept my excuses. How could I explain the way my past feels as if it's intertwined with theirs? The dark magic that bites at my heels no matter how fast I run?

She knows.

She can't possibly know.

But Ellis's gaze has already slid away from mine, fixing instead on my bookshelves. "What are these?"

I twist round to look. For a moment I think she's pointing at Alex's postcard—but no, it's right below that. I've stopped putting them in their hiding place.

"Tarot cards."

"Tarot?"

"You use them to read the future. Allegedly."

One of Ellis's dark brows goes up. "Are you a psychic, Felicity Morrow?"

"No. But they're fun to play with anyway. I don't really believe in . . . all that."

The words taste false on my tongue in a way they didn't before. Maybe it's how the air in the room has felt heavier ever since Ellis came in, a prickle rolling along the back of my neck. I shift my weight, and my chair—balanced on three legs with this uneven floor—wobbles.

Ellis picks up the deck and flips through my cards, pausing on Death. Everyone does.

"Can you read mine?" she says abruptly.

"Right now?"

"Unless you'd rather wait for the witching hour."

The choice of words makes me flinch. Even so, a part of me wants to say yes, just for the aesthetics. Another part of me wants to refuse entirely—because this feels like a play, like a move on a chessboard, a game for which I don't know the rules.

But if I say no, that would answer Ellis's suspicions in a different fashion. It would show her I can be rattled.

I slip out of my chair and we move to settle on my bed instead, Ellis passing me the deck to shuffle. She reclines back against my pillows, elbow propped on the mattress and her hair pooling black atop the duvet.

"Do you mind if I smoke?"

I do mind. But for some reason I shake my head, and she withdraws a silver cigarette case from her jacket pocket. There's a pack of matches with the candles lining my windowsill; she steals one, lights her cigarette, and waves the matchstick to quench the flame. The scent of red phosphorus lingers in the air.

"You need to think of a question to ask the cards." I split the deck again, reshuffle.

"Do I have to tell you what it is?"

"It will help me interpret the cards if you do."

"All right. Ask them about us. You and me." Her lips quirk. "Are we going to become friends?"

I almost laugh, but she seems serious, so I bite my cheek and draw three cards. "Fine. 'Are we going to become friends?' The first card is you." I tap the back of that card. "The second is me. The third card is us together."

Ellis pushes herself upright, crossing her legs and placing her hands in her lap like a child in school. "I'm ready."

I turn over the first card. It depicts a woman riding a stallion, her sword held aloft and her hair streaming out behind her like a banner. "The Knight of Swords," I say. "You're—surprise, surprise—ambitious and driven. You know what you want, and you pursue it at any cost. That can be a good thing, of course, but it has downsides; you can be impulsive and reckless, too, more focused on your goal than on its risks."

She nods, and from the set of her lips, I take it she's rather pleased with herself.

The next card: "The Hermit. This one's me." Cloaked and bearing a staff, my free hand extended to hold a lamp. The light cuts through the dark landscape around me, a star held in my palm. "I should prepare for a journey of self-discovery and introspection. Not everything will be clear at once; I'll only ever be able to see a few steps ahead. I have to trust myself and my own intuition."

I glance up at Ellis again. She has leaned forward slightly, her elbows braced against her knees and her gaze fixed on the cards: the twin pale faces of the Hermit and the Knight, the botanical design etched into the back of the third card still facedown.

"And the last one? Us together?"

I turn it over. It's the card from before, the same one that had so fascinated Ellis when she first looked at the deck.

Death rides a pale horse, the light of the setting sun glinting off the blade of her scythe. Peasants and queens alike are slain by her passing. In her wake, a white rose blooms.

"That doesn't look good," Ellis says dryly.

"Death isn't as fatal as you might think," I tell her, trailing my fingertips over the card's linen face. "It can mean change or upheaval of any kind. Something vital will come to an end. But"—I touch the five-petaled rose—"something new grows in its place."

There's an odd look on Ellis's face when our eyes meet again. A crack in the mask, something once hidden shifting behind the lacquered facade.

Ellis sweeps the cards into her hand and leafs through them one after the other. She lingers on the last again, skimming her thumb over Death's face. "Did you draw cards for her, too?"

For a moment I consider pretending I don't know what she means. But I do, and Ellis knows it. It's somewhat of a relief that she's finally brought her up after dancing around the subject for so long.

"Yes. A few times."

"Did you ever draw Death?"

My tongue flicks out to wet my lower lip; suddenly everything inside me feels brittle as leached clay. "No. Never."

She hands the cards back to me, and I shuffle them into the deck, then shut all the cards away in their box, where I don't have to look at them again.

Ellis never said Alex's name, but Alex's presence hangs like perfume in the air between us.

Even after Ellis has gone, the stench lingers. I can't erase the suspicion that this is why Ellis is speaking to me in the first place. She's the only one of them who has; she followed me back after the Boleyn party. Then again, that was two weeks ago. She's ignored me ever since, at least until she tracked me upstairs today and had me read her future. What has changed?

It's too easy to imagine Clara whispering in Ellis's ear again, old and rotten tales about missing girls and desolate mountain cliffs, how Felicity Morrow claimed it was an accident, but no one else was there to say for sure.

Maybe it's not the old murders at Dalloway that intrigue Ellis after all. Maybe it's me. I'm the key, that *lived experience* she so badly wants to exploit for her book.

I trace the lines on my palms and wonder if Ellis sees my hands drenched in red.

Ellis's absence has snapped whatever fragile nets had been holding the shadows at bay. Night fell hours ago, but it seems to deepen now, darkness creeping out from the corners and threatening to consume the house from the inside.

For a long time I lie in bed with my eyes squeezed shut and my heart pounding. My mind won't stop—it tumbles from one image to the next, like I'm being forced to watch a gruesome film. I see bones rotting in unmarked graves, crawling with maggots; Cordelia Darling's bloated body floating in the lake, hair a bloody halo around her face; a shadow figure with starlit eyes and skeleton fingers. Ellis's face peers out from the darkness, a pale mask that fractures to reveal the sunken features of Margery Lemont's corpse. Margery's mouth opens wide, wider, a gaping chasm, her tongue like a black snake swollen between her teeth—

I turn on my bedside lamp. Its soft glow is barely enough to illuminate this corner of my bed. Anything could lurk in the hidden spaces outside its orbit.

I light candles on all the windowsills until the shadows vanish, then crawl back into bed with my tarot cards clutched to my chest. I don't read them—it just makes me feel better having them near. I wish I held my crystals instead, black obsidian and staurolite heavy over my heart, their power like a golden field around me that no spirit could breach.

I can't, of course. I know I can't. Magic is dangerous for me. Maybe some people can toy with it, but me . . .

God. Just last week the party line was how *magic isn't real.* And yet it is; I know it is. The question isn't whether magic is real. It's whether I can touch it without being consumed by it.

I tighten my grip on my tarot deck, shut my eyes, and think about light in the darkness, my feet steady on whatever path is laid for me, protected not by magic but by my own will. *Your mind is powerful, Felicity,* Dr. Ortega had said. *You can summon terrible things. You also have the ability to banish them.*

But as I lie under the covers with the duvet drawn over my head, the tree branch outside once again tap-tapping against my window like bone fingers scratching for entry, I'm more certain than ever that even the Hermit's light won't be enough to keep the ghosts in their graves.

This day there being Complaint issued by Anonymous sources, whereby these named daughters are suspected of moste heinous Murder of one Flora Grayfriar in profane fashion, this court demands Apprehension of Margery Lemont, Cordelia Darling, Beatrix Walker, & Tamsyn Penhaligon of Dalloway School to appeare before us and speak truth before God and Justice, to face the graete damage and havock which hath beene wrought at the Devil's hands.

—Province of New York, Quarto Annoq'e Domini 1712, *Hudson Court Files,* vol. 32, docket no. 987

Is there no way out of the mind?

—Sylvia Plath, "Apprehensions"

7

Alex and I fell in love via a series of accidents.

My first semester at Dalloway, I lived in Farquhar House, sharing a room with a skinny, anxious girl named Therese who had a bad habit of picking at her scalp and eating the scraps. Eager to distance myself from Therese's orbit, I spent most of my time either in the Farquhar common room or pretending to belong to other houses: lurking in their common rooms, befriending their housemistresses, drinking their tea.

I met Alex at ten past midnight in the Lemont House common room. Normally I would have reluctantly returned to Farquhar—and Therese's dandruff—by that hour, but there was a blizzard, and a severe weather warning was in effect, so we'd all been advised to shelter in place until the danger passed.

"I think you should go," she said, standing in the doorway wearing a fleece jacket and hiking pants, her feet stuffed into those cozy wool booties that were popular for a few years despite how hideous they were.

"It's still snowing."

"I'm sure you've seen snow before."

"Mmm," I said, but all I could think was *I'm done talking to this girl.*

But she, clearly, was not done talking to me. Alex moved deeper into the room and planted herself in front of my chair with her arms crossed. There was no pretending not to notice her. I looked.

Alex was pretty. Maybe not in the conventional way—her jaw was too square, her eyes too far apart, her red hair always tangled and roped back into a fraying plait. But she exuded a fierce energy that ate up all the oxygen in a room.

I wanted her from day one.

First, though, we had to spend the whole night huddled on that sofa together, lighting a fire in the hearth to keep warm—because right as she had launched into a tirade about the moral faults of trespassing, the power went out.

It's hard to maintain a consistent standard of animosity when you spend eight hours with someone in the dark. Alex could have gone up to bed. I would have, if it had been me. But she stayed downstairs, bundled up in one of the blankets off the sofa, and we discovered that we both loved Daphne du Maurier and Margaret Atwood, that we hated the snobby STEM students with equal fervency, and, most important, that we were both determined to be accepted into Godwin House.

Midnight secrets weren't enough to build a friendship, though. I didn't see much of her after that; at least not until I broke my wrist in December and encountered Alex in the same emergency department waiting room. She was curled up on a stretcher, sweaty and grimacing, from what would later turn out to be appendicitis, but she somehow spotted me and called me over. Mostly to make me hold her hair back while she vomited, but still.

I stayed with her after my wrist had been bandaged up. Her mother appeared right before Alex was about to be wheeled into surgery, a panicked woman whose frantic hands flit about like wild birds. I managed to get Ms. Haywood to take a seat and calm down, stroking her hair like she was a little child while Alex made faces at me from the cot.

I remember being so fascinated by Ms. Haywood: her tears and her soft words, the way Alex seemed to bloom in her presence, even sick. The maternal way Ms. Haywood pressed her lips to Alex's temples.

"I'm so glad she has you, dear," Ms. Haywood told me, blotting her wet cheeks with her wrist. "Alex told me how horrible all the Dalloway girls have been. But you're so . . . so sweet. What a lovely friend."

It turned out Alex was at Dalloway on full scholarship, one of only three girls in our year. Ms. Haywood had raised her as a single mother working two jobs. Alex had attended public school, not prep. These factors had resulted in Alex's summary dismissal from every social group on campus.

Well, not anymore. I already had a generally low opinion of half the school, having seen how contingent their interest in me was upon whether they knew or didn't know my mother's name. Alex, I was fairly certain, didn't have the first clue who Cecelia Morrow was—and that suited me just fine.

Alex and I became our own clique: inverse images of one another, the rebel and the heiress. Alex had her own charm; it was impossible not to love her.

Our first kiss was at a rooftop party in the city. It was just an hour's drive away, so we'd gone out for Friday night, my mother's credit card covering bottle service at a bar I hoped my mother had never actually visited. I didn't want to hear the embarrassing stories if she had.

The roof was draped in greenery and market lights, which glimmered off the low reflecting pool that ran parallel to the bar. Alex and I were merely sixteen, but it didn't matter—no one had even glanced at our fake IDs. We were wearing enough makeup to pass for twenty-three, smoky-eyed and red-lipped, in designer heels. Alex was luminous in lavender, her hair drawn up into a chignon and exposing her bared back, a fine lariat chain falling along her spine and punctuated by a single glittering garnet. I knew Alex, so I knew the gem was fake. But in this strange, warm light, anything could have been real.

I'd never wanted to touch someone so much in my life.

"I still can't believe you failed the geography test," Alex said, both of us leaning against the iron railing with sparkling wines in hand. It was the fourth time she had brought it up that weekend, ever since I made the mistake of telling her about my dismal score on our drive down from Dalloway.

She was gazing out across the city, her hair shining scarlet. She looked like a Pre-Raphaelite painting.

I sipped my wine so I wouldn't speak. That was my third glass already; the alcohol had started to make me feel unpleasantly weightless, light-headed. Half the girls I knew at Dalloway drank, but all I could think about was my mother. I knew this feeling could be dangerous. I wondered what Alex would say if I poured the rest of my drink off the edge of the roof.

At last, I managed a response. "An off day, I suppose."

Alex looked over. "We studied," she said, half an accusation.

My glass was cold and sweaty in my hand; I twisted the stem between my fingers. "I know."

"What happened? You knew that material. You were quizzing *me* on it."

I chewed my lower lip until it hurt. I didn't know how to lie to Alex, even then. At last I sighed and tipped my head back, staring up at the stars. Or where the stars would have been if the sky weren't obscured by all that light pollution.

"I failed the test on purpose."

"You *what*?"

Alex grabbed my arm and tugged until I looked at her. I couldn't tell if the expression on her face was more repulsed or amused.

"I know," I said. "But . . . Well, you know Marie, from our class?"

Alex nodded.

"She loves geography. I was actually talking to her at a dinner thing the other day, and she said she's going to major in it in college. She wants to go to grad school and get her PhD. And I suppose I thought . . ."

Alex was staring at me like she'd never quite seen me before.

I shrugged. "I have the top score in that class right now. And I figured maybe I should let that be hers. Only I guess I overcorrected, and I . . . ended up failing the test."

It took a moment, but finally a small smile pulled at the corners of Alex's lips. "You're a good person, Felicity Morrow."

I didn't know what to say to that then. Now I know exactly what I would say.

I'm not good. I'm the furthest thing from good.

There on that rooftop, with the city alive around us, Alex slid her fingers along my cheek and stepped closer and kissed me. A breeze was picking up and my wineglass was shaking in my hand, but Alex was kissing me. Her lips tasted like chocolate.

But I can't think about her anymore. I can't remember that kiss now.

I don't want to.

I'd decided that for my elective this year, I would take Art History.

It was a choice I made on impulse that I came to regret after the final two weeks of summer, watching my mother entertain a dozen art curators in our living room, giving them tours of our gallery—the walls repainted and hung with fresh art, no evidence of violence, even though it hadn't yet been a month since my mother took a knife to her collection of priceless paintings and pushed over sculptures, shattering them on the marble floor.

I'd hidden in my room while she shouted and raged and broke things, and when I had finally ventured downstairs again I'd found her crouched in the middle of the wreckage, sweeping porcelain shards into a dustpan like they were nothing but spilled sugar.

"Come help me, darling," she'd said, her words still angled

and blurry from all the wine she'd had after dinner, and I didn't have a choice.

I'm not interested in art anymore, but it's too late to change my schedule. The first two classes, we went over the syllabus, and the prospect of all those looming projects and essays made me want to put my head in my arms and go to sleep.

Before last summer, I had vaguely anticipated all of us traipsing down the halls of an art museum in Kingston talking about patterns of brushstrokes and pigments mixed from arsenic. Now all I envision is endless hours of slides and falling asleep in a dim room to the *click-click* of an overhead projector.

I dread this class more than the rest, primarily because the syllabus says we will discuss our project assignments today. The word *group* isn't explicitly appended before the word *project,* but it's there nonetheless.

I slip into the room minutes before the bell, past our instructor, an emaciated woman with bird's-nest hair and a fringed shawl, standing at the head. I remember thinking on the first day that the instructor looked like she might have emerged from between time, a relic of Dalloway's witchiest years: the reincarnation of Beatrix Walker or Cordelia Darling.

Even now I wonder if I'd be able to tell. If she'd been possessed by the spirit of one of those dead girls, if she'd performed her own rituals in the dark, calling up spirits she didn't understand, spirits that would never leave her alone, would I scent it in the air like fine perfume?

I claim a seat near the windows, sufficiently far from the center of the room that I hope to go unnoticed if this is one of those group projects that lets students pick their own partners.

I'll happily accept the dregs of who's left after all the rich coven girls have been claimed.

I've just settled in and opened my laptop when I glance over and spot Ellis Haley sitting at one of the other desks, a plain black notebook in front of her and a fountain pen in hand. She must sense me watching, because she meets my gaze and one corner of her mouth quirks up before the instructor raps her knuckles on the chalkboard.

We begin inauspiciously, with a question—*What is the history of art?*—and a series of definitions. The project summary, when it's distributed, isn't as bad as I'd feared. There *will* be museum visits, even if most of them look as if they're meant to be done independently. And the project isn't due until the end of the semester.

"With your partner," the instructor says, "you will choose two works of art, and collaboratively you will write a research paper comparing these two works, situating them in their respective historical contexts. This is not the kind of project you can put off until finals week. To get a good grade, you will have to do extensive reading and research both into the construction of the works as well as their artists' biographies, the sociocultural issues of their time, and how the works entered into dialogue with their contemporary societies. My standards will be high."

I wonder how broadly she has construed the term *art*—if I might be allowed to use architecture, or a book of George Eliot essays.

Or I could write about art and the destruction thereof. About my mother's hand holding that knife, the sound canvas makes when it rips.

"I've randomly paired you up, with one group of three since we have an odd number. . . ."

The instructor reads off her list. Ellis is teamed up with Ursula Prince, who has an expression on her face like she's won an award; I'm assigned Bridget Crenshaw. The moment the instructor says my name, Bridget's hand snaps into the air.

"I can't work with Felicity," Bridget says without even waiting to be called upon. "She makes me uncomfortable."

That's code for *I won't work with a girl who killed her best friend.*

Under the desk, my hands clench into fists as every face in the room turns to stare at me. Bridget's pink-lipsticked mouth is set in a mean smile, and no—I immediately know exactly what this is. It has nothing to do with Alex. It has everything to do with the fact that Bridget applied to Godwin House every year and never got in, and since Alex and I were the queens of Godwin House, that became our fault. As if we'd hoarded our popularity just to make sure Bridget never got any. Never mind that Bridget is part of the Margery coven; never mind that Bridget had doubtless been part of the decision to excise me from that club.

I'm not queen anymore. This is a coup.

"I'll be Felicity's partner," a familiar voice says.

I look.

Ellis has one hand half raised, her pen thrust behind her ear. Ursula Prince, to her left, looks deeply disappointed.

The Art History teacher makes a mark on her clipboard. "Very well. Bridget, you can work with Ursula. Unless you have a problem with Miss Prince, too?"

A titter runs through the class, and Bridget's cheeks darken; she says nothing.

It shouldn't feel like a victory, but it does. If Bridget thinks less of me because of what happened, because I had to leave school, then I want her humiliated. If she's afraid of me because she thinks I killed Alex, well, then my wishes for her become even more uncharitable.

After class I catch up to Ellis halfway across the quad, the September wind cutting through my thin linen shirt and making me shiver; I should have worn a sweater. Ellis, in a turtleneck that looks at least as flimsy as what I'm wearing, hardly seems to notice the cold.

"You didn't have to do that," I tell her.

"Do what?" She spares me a sidelong glance. "I don't want to work with Ursula Prince. It's as simple as that."

As simple as that.

Somehow, I don't think it is.

Fall deepens, that chill breeze turning to cold as the leaves go yellow and then scarlet. Only three weeks have passed since school started, but by October, knit tights and cashmere sweaters have made their appearance and I discover all my winter clothes are too large now. I head into town, accompanied by Kajal, of all people, to buy more. We try on tartan skirts and blazers, Kajal examining herself in the full-length mirror with one hand pressed to her flat stomach and her lips curving downward.

"It looks good," I offer from two steps behind her, still doing up the buttons on my shirt.

She twists to the other side and looks at her reflection in profile. "It's not very slimming."

Kajal is already one of the slimmest people I've ever seen.

"You look fine," I tell her. "I like it with the belt—very vintage." It looks like something every single Ellis cliquer would wear. That's the part I don't say.

Not that I have any moral high ground; I've piled my dressing room with tweeds and cardigans and jackets that have elbow patches. The difference is that I've always dressed like this for fall. Alex used to say I cared more about the aesthetic of autumn than about comfort.

Kajal sighs. "I suppose."

Even so, she spends another minute staring at herself in that mirror, mouth knotting like she wishes she could take off her own body when she takes off that dress. For a moment I'm reminded of Florence Downpatrick, who'd been my roommate at Silver Lake. Florence had looked at herself the same way—always watching her reflection with narrowed eyes, like she hoped to find something wrong with it, or curling her fingers round her wrist as we sat reading in the common room, seeing how far she could slide those circled fingers up her forearm before they stopped touching.

"It looks good," I say again, but Kajal vanishes back into the dressing room without responding. I'm left standing in front of the mirror alone.

I avoid my own gaze and look at the clothes instead. The skirt hits past my knees, its dark-blue color drawing out the blue threads in my herringbone tweed blazer. I look like a university professor. I'm thinner than Kajal, but that has nothing to do with dieting and everything to do with the fact I couldn't keep food down for weeks toward the end of summer. It was as if something in my gut had rebelled against the idea of coming back here, rejecting everything I fed it like it hoped to wither away and die before I had the chance to face Dalloway again.

The way Kajal's always looked at me takes on new meaning now. Does she think I'm like her? Does she think we're in silent competition with one another, that my reassurances carry with them the smug satisfaction of victory?

Clara's in the common room when we return, bags slung over elbows. I try to hide my flinch—before she turned around to look at us, I'd only seen the glint of red hair in late afternoon sunlight and the book perched on her knee. My heart was still trapped between my teeth, Alex's name pressing against the backs of my lips. I could have sworn it was her.

"Have a good time?" Clara asks, ice frosting her words. I frown on reflex.

"Yes," Kajal says. "The weather was nice."

"You might have thought to invite me. I need new winter clothes, too, you know."

Kajal shrugs. "Sorry."

She sweeps away toward the stairs without another word. My bags are heavy, and I can't think of anything worse than staying down here with Clara when she's in this mood, so I follow.

"What's her problem?" I murmur to Kajal as we round the steps to the next landing.

"Clara's new," Kajal says, and waves a dismissive hand. "Ellis says she's insecure. She doesn't think she belongs with the rest of us because we already knew each other from before, and she just . . ."

Kajal trails off as she reaches her room, tilting her head in a voiceless farewell as she vanishes within.

Clara's new. But so was Ellis, and these rules didn't seem to apply to her.

But maybe that's precisely the problem: maybe Ellis is the one who ensures that you never really fit in.

Not that I fit here, either. My first attempt at a senior year, I'd been living in Godwin for a year already—had stitched myself into the fabric of Godwin with knotted threads. I remember I'd wanted so badly to be accepted to the house. I had applied to Boleyn and Eliot as well, but Godwin was the ground on which the Dalloway Five had stood, the land on which they'd lived—and died. I had read in the library about Tamsyn Penhaligon's death, her body found swinging from the oak tree behind Godwin eleven months after Flora Grayfriar's murder. Although Tamsyn had been ruled a suicide, one of the records in the occult library said her face had been painted with blood: unfamiliar sigils traced over her cheeks and brow.

That same tree stands right outside my bedroom. The first night I spent in Godwin, I'd pushed open the window and leaned out to press my palm against its bark. I'd imagined I could feel Tamsyn's heart beating inside it, an echo to my own. The oak didn't frighten me until later.

The moment I open my bedroom door, a curse escapes my lips. It looks like an autumn storm has swept through, the trash bin tipped over and its contents spilled across the rug, Alex's postcard torn from the wall and lying on the floor as if someone had read it and then, indifferent, discarded it.

Her ghost.

Only that can't be true, I tell myself, sucking in a series of shallow breaths and willing my pulse to slow. There's a more rational explanation: my window's cracked open, the gauzy drapes shivering and the air cold as night. The oak stands silent and watchful, branches like black fingers against the sky.

Ghosts don't exist. I have to keep my head on my shoulders; I have to stay sane. I have to prove I deserve to be back here. I need to prove returning wasn't a mistake.

I curse again and cross the room to shut the window, twisting the latch shut. I could have sworn I'd closed the window before I left.

I collect the detritus and put it all back in place. Some of Alex's old letters have fallen from their homes, tucked between books on my shelves. *That's more than a coincidence,* I think. *It has to be. It has to be.*

I retrieve her letters, carefully separating them from the wastebasket contents and putting them in my desk drawer this time. I find all except one, the card Alex sent me from her family's winter trip to Vermont. And no matter where I search—under the bed, behind my desk, even out on the lawn of Godwin House—I can't find it anywhere.

8

Here is the truth.

What happened to Alex was no accident. Not just because she fell, because we'd fought, or because I cut the rope—but because of what happened last October.

I'd recently decided on my thesis project: "I caution you against this," Wyatt had said when I told her I wanted to study representations of witchcraft in literature. "You will struggle to get a thesis on witchcraft approved by the administration, no matter how good your scholarship. Dalloway is a respectable school—this isn't the Scholomance."

"I don't see the problem," I'd said. "I'm not claiming the Dalloway witches were *real.* Just that conceptualizations of witchcraft existed in the eighteenth century, and that those were influenced by perceptions of female agency and mental illness at the time. I want to connect the reality of their lives to the fantasy of how women were presented on the page."

Wyatt had fixed me with a lancet gaze and said: "So long as you focus on the *literature,* Miss Morrow—not on flights of fancy." And she'd signed the papers.

But when I'd told my mother about my plans, she'd been appalled.

"That school is a bad influence on you," my mother had told me while I was home for Thanksgiving break a few weeks later. "I thought you knew better than to believe all that nonsense about witches."

Perhaps she was right to be afraid. Of course, at the time I'd scoffed. *I* don't *believe in witches,* I'd insisted, and it was true. Before Dalloway, I had fancied myself a rationalist—too rational, in fact, to entertain the possibility that reality might contain more mysteries than my feeble mortal mind could understand. But there was something about the Dalloway Five that drew me in, embraced me in their cold dead arms. They were real: there was historical evidence for their lives, for their deaths. And I imagined their magic stitched like a thread across time, passed from mother to daughter, a glittering link from the founder to Margery Lemont to me.

That had felt like a comfort once. After Halloween, it felt more like a curse.

By that night, I'd had plenty of opportunities to embroil myself in lore and legend. My room at Godwin House was littered with scanned grimoire pages and notes on the uncanny. Alex watched all this with a sort of academic fascination; she'd never been able to understand why I was so drawn to darkness. She had always belonged in the light of the sun.

"Don't you think you're taking this a little too seriously?" Alex asked the night everything went wrong, waving a match through the air to extinguish the flame. "You've been kind of over the top about this thesis business. Like, do you think you're starting to get a little confused about reality here? Magic doesn't exist, Felicity."

"Are you sure about that?"

"I mean . . . yes?"

She held my gaze for a long moment; I looked away first, back to the Ouija board set up between us. "This is important to me," I confessed to the planchette. I dipped a cloth into salt water and wiped it over the board itself, cleansing it for the summoning. "Not because I believe in it, necessarily, but because *they* did."

"And you're obsessed with them. The Dalloway Five."

"I'm not obsessed. This is our history—Godwin's history. They killed a girl. That really happened, whether we believe in witchcraft or not. And we know they held a séance—that was documented in the trial. Whether they thought it was real or just make-believe, they performed a ritual to raise a ghost. And Flora died a few days later."

The primary sources I'd read in Dalloway's library were inconsistent as to the nature of Flora Grayfriar's death. The account I'd read in the library described an almost ritualistic killing, Flora's throat slit and her stomach cut open, stuffed full of animal bones and herbs. But other contemporaneous writings said she was found with a musket ball in her gut, dead in the forest, shot like a beast. It should have been a simple thing, to determine how a girl died: Was she shot, or was her throat slit? Do I trust the trial documents, or the letters written by Flora's mother? Who had more motive to lie?

Either the Dalloway girls were witches, and they'd murdered Flora in some arcane deal with the devil, or Flora's death had a far more mundane explanation. A hunting accident, maybe. A lovers' quarrel. Or even a bigoted townsperson who heard about the séance and wanted to see the girls punished for meddling with powers they couldn't contain.

After all, Flora was the first death, but she wasn't the last. Following her, every one of the Dalloway witches died in ways that were impossible to explain. All of their bodies were found on the Godwin House grounds, like the house itself was determined to keep them. It was almost as if they were cursed, as if they'd raised a spirit that was determined to see them all dead.

The more likely explanation—that they'd been killed by religious mountain folk who feared women, feared the magic they'd assigned to women—didn't hold the same appeal.

Regardless, Alex was right. I hadn't been able to get the Dalloway Five out of my head for weeks. I'd even dreamed about them the previous night, Beatrix Walker's hair like spun corn silk and Tamsyn Penhaligon's bony fingers trailing along my cheek. They had found their way inside me, like fungal spores inhaled and taken root. Sometimes I felt like they'd always been there. I'd read about reincarnation, about girls born again and again, and imagined Margery Lemont whispering soft words in the back of my mind. Every time I touched her skull at Boleyn House, I felt her in my blood.

Maybe I was losing my mind. Or maybe this was what it was to appreciate history, to truly *understand* it. When I read books, the boundary between my world and others shifted. I could imagine other realities. I envisioned the tales so clearly that it was as if I lived them.

The story of the Dalloway Five was a story born in Godwin House. Why shouldn't their legend be real?

And if this ritual worked—if we spoke to them—we could put the mythos to rest once and for all.

The scent of sandalwood rose in the air. We'd already turned off the lamp; I could only see Alex by the flickering candles, her skin glowing warm silver in their light.

"All right, then," Alex said. "Let's summon old dead witches."

I'd written the summoning spell in my moleskin notebook: an incantation copied from an ancient tome in the library's occult section. The process had been painstaking; no one in the eighteenth century, it seemed, had been possessed of legible handwriting. Of course, they didn't have Ouija boards in the eighteenth century either, and this Hasbro-branded contraption I had bought at the independent bookstore in town hardly qualified as an accoutrement of real witchcraft. But it was better than nothing. I propped the notebook on my knees, and me and Alex both placed our fingers on the Ouija planchette, barely touching it.

And even though I hadn't spoken yet, all at once the room seemed darker—the corners deepening, the air heavy against my skin. I took in a shallow breath and read the spell aloud.

"Nothing happened," Alex said after several seconds. "It's not moving."

"You have to wait for it."

"You know that when the pointer moves, it's because *we're* moving it, right? Like, they've done studies on this."

I ignored her and closed my eyes. I'd stolen the Margery Skull; it sat at the head of our altar, close enough that I could have touched it. A part of me wanted to. The urge was almost overpowering. Maybe if I did . . . Maybe that's what this ritual *needed.*

I shifted forward, eyes still shut, fingers reaching. My touch grazed cold bone, and in the same moment, the planchette moved.

My eyes flew open. The pointer had darted across the board to cover the number 5.

"What does that mean?" Alex said, and I shook my head.

The Dalloway Five.

The candles guttered as if from an unseen wind. The room had gone chilly, and a strange sensation crept up my spine. My fingers quivered with the effort of keeping my touch on the planchette light; I refused to lend any credence to Alex's theory. If the board spoke, it wouldn't be because I forced matters into my own hands.

I'd never tried this kind of thing before. I didn't know what to expect.

Be real. I need you to be real.

"Are you really here?" I whispered. "Is this . . . Margery Lemont? Or—"

I stopped myself midsentence and stared at the lettering on the board indicating the word *yes.* But the planchette had gone still, the numeral 5 still visible through its aperture.

This wasn't enough. The incense, the candles—even Margery's skull smooth against my palm. It wasn't enough.

I'd read about this. I'd read dozens of books, hundreds, researching for my thesis. I *knew* how magic worked. I knew what these kinds of spirits required.

"We have to make a sacrifice," I told Alex abruptly. "Like the original Dalloway Five did in their séance, with the frog. If the Dalloway Five really were witches, they were powerful. Why should they speak to us if we don't give them something in return?"

Alex's mouth twisted, skeptical. "Well, I forgot to bring along my handy-dandy sacrificial goat, so . . ."

But I already knew what Margery wanted.

I released the planchette and grabbed the letter opener—the one I'd used to open the Ouija board box.

"Felicity, don't you *dare*—"

I sliced the blade into my palm. White fire cut along my veins, dark blood welling up in its wake. Alex lurched back as I held out my arm, but she didn't leave the circle, didn't retreat—just watched wide-eyed as my blood spattered the crown of Margery Lemont's skull.

The candles blew out.

Even Alex yelped. My heart pounded in my chest—too fast, too wild. Was that a figure stepping out from the shadows, eyes gleaming in the darkness like polished coins?

Alex struck a match, and the specter vanished. The place where it had stood was pitch black, and yet I could still feel its presence. Maybe it hadn't disappeared. Maybe instead it had *expanded,* consuming us.

Alex and I stared at each other across the board. Alex's shoulders shifted in quick, shallow little movements, her tongue flicking out to wet her lower lip. It felt colder now than before, like the temperature had dropped several degrees when the candles went out.

It's all right, I wanted to tell her, but my tongue was a dead thing in my mouth, heavy and ill tasting. As if I'd swallowed grave dirt.

Margery Lemont had been buried alive.

My blood was sticky against my palm, the scent of it high and coppery in the air, overwhelming the musk of incense. Alex lit the candles again—just the three nearest her. Their light cast unnatural shapes along the board, most of the letters fallen into darkness.

Neither of us were touching the planchette anymore, but its aperture was fixed over the word *yes.*

"Did you move the pointer?"

Alex shook her head.

My teeth dug into my lower lip. Together, we both tilted forward once more, our trembling fingers meeting atop the wooden planchette.

"Are the stories true?" I asked. "Were you really witches?"

If the ritual account of Flora's death was true, it had been clearly Druidic in inspiration: some bastardization of Greco-Roman reports that the ancient Celts performed human sacrifice at the autumnal equinox—that the future could be read in the way the victim's limbs convulsed as they died. Even the way in which the sacrifice bled had prognostic value.

The town midwife's diary told a version of the story in which Flora Grayfriar's body was found with her skin half-burned and her clothes in ashes atop a wicker altar. Silver mullein leaves were strewn about the ground, a wormwood crown laced through her hair, her throat wet with blood.

I knew the answer to my query, but I wanted Margery to say it nonetheless.

The planchette shifted under our hands, my breath catching in my chest—the planchette moved aside, then returned immediately to *yes*.

So many new questions swelled inside me. Too many. It was impossible to ask all of them. Impossible to ask with a board and a pointer the question I *really* wanted to know:

What can you teach me about magic?

I was about to ask the Dalloway Five the purpose of Flora's death, what ritual they were trying to perform that night at the autumn equinox—if they were even responsible for her death at all—when the planchette moved again.

"Get the notebook," Alex gasped, and I snatched my moleskin back into my lap and uncapped my pen with one shaking hand.

The planchette shifted across the board in jagged jerks under our touch.

"I . . . A . . ."

The air was frigid now, a bone-deep ice that crystallized in my blood. I didn't dare look away from the board, which meant that when the planchette finally went still—when I finally turned my gaze to the notebook—I could barely read my own handwriting.

"What does it say?" Alex urged after I'd been silent for several seconds.

"It says . . ." I shook my head, swallowed; my throat had gone dry. "It says, *'I am going to kill you.'*"

I looked up. Alex stared at me from the other side of the

board, both her hands clenched in white fists against her knees. Her face glowed greenish in the candlelight, eerie, and—

Something grazed the back of my neck, a cold finger tracing down my spine.

"Alex," I choked out.

"Are you okay?"

The touch vanished; I felt a breeze ripple through my hair as it passed. I was too afraid to look over my shoulder. "I swear, something just—"

The shadows deepened, coalescing like smoke. A figure rose behind Alex like a ghastly silhouette, long hair undulating like waves about its head, its hands like sharp claws reaching.

Reaching for her throat.

"Alex, *behind you*!"

She spun around, and in that same motion the specter vanished, bursting into shards and scraps of shadow that faded into the night.

Margery.

"Nothing's there," Alex said.

But I could still sense her: Margery Lemont's spirit had its talons dug deep in my heart, my blood turned to poison in my veins.

I shook my head. "It was . . . She was there, I swear. She was *right there.*"

How did the poem go?

And then the spirit, moving from her place,

Touched there a shoulder, whispered in each ear, . . .

But no one heeded her, or seemed to hear.

"This is bullshit," Alex declared.

"No! Alex, don't—"

Too late. She swept the planchette from the board and stabbed the incense out. "It's not real, Felicity. Calm down."

No. No, this was all spiraling out of control. We had to end the séance properly. Margery was still here, lurking, the veil between our world and the shade world gone thin and diaphanous at Samhain. It was only too easy for her to shift into our sphere.

I'd prepared for this possibility: a tiny bowl of ground anise and clove to be ignited over a charcoal briquette—enough to protect against the cruelest spirit, or so I'd been assured by the library's copy of *Profane Magick.*

Alex scattered the spices across the floor, rendering them useless.

That was the moment, I decided later, that set everything in motion, the moment the devil's wheel began to turn, my blood spilled on Margery's skull and Margery's hands tangling in the threads of our fates. We'd cursed ourselves. *I am going to kill you,* she'd made me say. And she was right.

It had an absurd sense of inevitability about it. I kept thinking about the séance the Dalloway Five had held, the one that was interrupted. About Flora, dead three days later. How each girl died in mysterious circumstances which couldn't be explained, until finally Margery herself was buried alive. It was almost like whatever spirit they'd raised had cursed them—and wouldn't rest until every one of those girls was dead.

But at the time, I let Alex convince me. Once the lights were on, it all seemed rather ridiculous: The candles had guttered because we'd left the window open, which also accounted for the chill. The figure I'd seen behind Alex was her shadow stretching and shifting in the candlelight. Everything had a reasonable explanation, and Alex was right. The spooky atmosphere, the old school legends, Samhain: we'd let it get to us; that was all.

I didn't tell her how I couldn't stop dreaming about Margery after that night, or how I slept with anise and clove under my pillow to keep her away.

A few months later Alex was dead, and now . . .

Now I can't hide from the truth.

9

The postcard never emerges. I search everywhere in the following days, even the hole in the back of my closet, but it's no use. The card is gone, vanished into the place where lost things go.

Or, perhaps, into someone else's possession.

I started reading *We Have Always Lived in the Castle* this morning for my thesis. I wonder if Merricat's brand of magic would work here—if I could tie a black ribbon in knots and bury it in the back garden with a murmured incantation, and tomorrow I'd wake to find the postcard back on my wall, where it belongs.

Not that I do that kind of thing anymore. If the postcard is lost, it will have to stay lost.

Later in the day, right before we're meant to head to Art History, Ellis knocks on the frame of my open door and says, "Let's skip."

I've just finished packing my notebooks into my satchel; when I look back Ellis is leaning against my wall, arms folded over her chest and one heel tipped against the baseboard. She's wearing trousers and a starched-collar dress shirt, the formality of her cuff links and suspenders somewhat undermined by the way her hair is pulled up in a messy knot, like she just woke up.

"Class, you mean," I say.

"I was thinking we could go into town instead," she says. "There's this little antiques shop on Dorchester I've been meaning to explore."

The whole thing smells suspiciously of pity. Bridget Crenshaw might have evaded the torment of being partnered with me for our project, but that hasn't stopped her from trying to turn half the school against me. Incredible how much damage one girl could do in just two days.

I'd heard about it from Hannah Stratford, of all people. "You know you can talk to me," she'd said, after accosting me in the cafeteria line. "If you want."

I hadn't understood what she meant, not until she went on:

"My sister was sick like that, too. She tried . . . you know. To"—Hannah had lowered her voice to a stage whisper—"*kill herself.* She's better now, but I just . . . I figured, if you needed to talk—"

"I didn't try to fucking *kill* myself."

"Oh!" Hannah's face had flushed the same mauve color as her fingernail polish. I doubted her embarrassment even had anything to do with the mistake; she'd just never heard me swear before. "I only . . . I heard . . ."

I'd stared at her, letting her fumble her way back to safer ground.

"It's just, Bridget said—"

"Bridget said," I'd repeated, and Hannah stammered an apology, finally flitting out of line to go join the queue for sandwiches instead.

Bridget said.

So now I wasn't just a murderer; I was suicidal, too.

I didn't understand how Bridget could have found out. Not the *killing myself* part—I'd never tried to kill myself—but . . .

The fact that I'd been gone last semester was no secret. I'd spent four months at a private residential facility tucked away near the Cascades, listening to people with rows of degree certificates on their walls explain to me that it *wasn't my fault,* that I'd had no choice, that just because I took my knife and sawed through that rope and killed my best friend, that didn't make me a psychopath. As if I didn't know that already.

News travels fast at Dalloway. The rumors must have reached Ellis by now.

But even if this is pity, it doesn't change the fact that I want nothing less than to go to that goddamn class and sit there and watch Bridget Crenshaw make tragic faces at me from across the room.

"All right," I say, and take the notebooks back out of my bag.

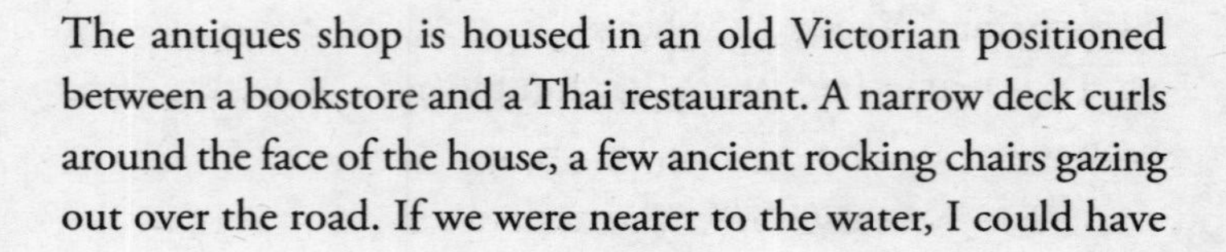

The antiques shop is housed in an old Victorian positioned between a bookstore and a Thai restaurant. A narrow deck curls around the face of the house, a few ancient rocking chairs gazing out over the road. If we were nearer to the water, I could have imagined an old widow perched in one of those chairs, dressed in black but still peering through her binoculars at the sea, waiting for her love to finally come home.

Ellis precedes me up the stairs. The deck looks like it was whitewashed once, but it's now more gray wood than white paint. A little bell tingles over the door as we go inside. Ellis smiles over her shoulder at me, and I can't help grinning back; it's so very *Ellis* to be charmed by something that old-fashioned and simple.

A shriveled woman sits behind the front desk. She gets to her feet when we enter, although that doesn't make her more than an inch taller at most.

"Can I help you girls with anything in particular?"

"We're browsing," Ellis says.

The woman's smile is as wobbly as her knees. Her hands grip the edge of the counter like she needs to hold on to keep her balance.

Alex will never be this old.

"Well, if you need me . . . ," the woman says, and I can't look at her anymore. I turn away, pretending fascination with a nearby lamp carved in the shape of a naked lady.

Ellis wanders farther back into the store, and I follow, watching her pale hands drift over the shapes of old furniture and cloudy vases.

"I love these," Ellis says. She holds up a handful of marbles, all different colors. She rolls a few into my outstretched palm. Each sphere has its own unique starburst at its center, dye exploding into glass and glinting in the lamplight.

"They remind me of my grandmother's house," I say.

Ellis gives me a quizzical look.

"She had vases filled with marbles and cut flowers. Seashells, too. It was a beach house." I'd taken one of those marbles and swallowed it once, hoping, I think, that the magic they held would grow inside me like a seed, would become a part of me.

"Which beach?"

"Beaufort. On the Outer Banks of North Carolina."

"I've never been," Ellis says. "Maybe that's embarrassing to admit since I'm from Georgia—I could have gone anytime."

"You're not missing much."

That was a lie, although I'm not sure why I told it. I'd loved my grandmother's house. I loved the way the sea crashed in against the rocky shore. I loved the dunes held together by repetitive wind patterns and tall grass. I loved the way the dock felt under my bare toes, the smell of salt, and the crabs we caught in little wire cages.

I'd also loved the sound the steam made as it escaped the crabs' shells when we boiled them alive.

Are they screaming? I'd asked my grandmother, simultaneously horrified and fascinated, and she'd covered the pot with a lid to stop me watching.

"Where in Georgia?" I ask. The conversation has fallen into a silence that doesn't feel entirely natural. Or maybe it's that I want Ellis to keep talking about herself, about mundane things—hometowns and summer holidays—normal topics normal people discuss.

"Savannah. Does your grandmother still live in that house?"

"She died a few years ago. The house belongs to my aunt now."

"Too bad." Ellis pours the marbles back into their bowl. "You must miss her."

I dip my hand into a basket of lace shawls that smells like dust. Ellis examines a sculpture of a soldier astride a rearing stallion, the horse's mane tangling in the wind.

My grandmother died three years ago now. Sometimes it's hard to remember the topography of her face or the sound of her voice. I wonder if we all fade from memory so quickly after we pass. I wonder if one day I'll forget what Alex sounded like, too.

"Isn't this much better than class?" Ellis asks when I don't answer. "Why sit in a stiff metal chair staring at dozens of laminates"—she trails her fingers along the line of the horse's flank—"when you can *touch*?"

I stare at the movement of her hand, a work of art in itself somehow: elegant knuckles and almond-shaped nails, a smudge of ink on her thumb.

She catches me looking. I draw one of the shawls out of the basket; I drape it over my shoulders, a mourner in white.

This time, I smile. "It's better."

Ellis laughs and steals a wide-brimmed hat from a nearby mannequin, perching it atop her head. It makes her look like a character from an Agatha Christie novel; she has become a hard-boiled detective in herringbone with a nose for blood.

"I think you're missing something," I say, and pass her an ebony walking stick, half bowing like a Victorian valet for her mistress.

"Perfect." She raps the foot of the cane against the floor, playing her own part with aplomb. "Carry on, madam."

I hook my arm through hers, and we meander through the maze of artifacts, maneuvering around scratched furniture and piles of old license plates. Ellis digs up a pair of pince-nez, and I find myself in ivory lambskin gloves.

I spot a cast-iron kettle that looks ancient, like it might date back to the eighteenth century, and I wonder if it really does—if one of the Dalloway Five might have used it, if something of their ousia, their essence, would cling to any object they'd touched.

"Don't you ever wish you could go back?" Ellis murmurs, gaze turned up toward the chandeliers; their light glitters off the lenses of her glasses. My gaze snaps away from the kettle, back to her. "To some other time," she says, "when things were a little wilder. When the rules were a little less clear."

It's the opposite of the usual line. *A simpler time. A time when a lady was a lady.*

"Maybe. I hadn't really thought about it." I rub the edge of a tablecloth between my thumb and forefinger but feel only the friction of my age-softened gloves. "I suppose it depends on *where* I was, too. I wouldn't want to get burned at the stake as a witch."

"Oh, but can you blame them? You *are* a witch. I don't doubt you would have poisoned the village crops, salted their fields, and led their daughters into temptation."

My breath freezes in my lungs. But Ellis isn't even looking at me—she has a painted figurine in hand and seems very interested in the whittle-work.

For a second all I can do is stand there, sucking in air and clenching my fists; the leather creaks as it stretches over my knuckles.

And then, at last, I manage to push the words past my throat: "Just their daughters?"

Ellis glances back. She's taken off the pince-nez; the frames dangle from one idle hand. "It takes one to know one."

It isn't an accusation. It isn't anything. It's . . . a *statement*. Of fact.

I take off the gloves.

Ellis is still watching. She watches me fold the gloves and place them on the table, watches me pretend to look at the tablecloth embroidery.

"It's nothing to be ashamed of," she says.

A dry laugh rasps out of me. "I know that."

"*Are* you ashamed?"

"Of course not." The words are sharper than intended. I grit my teeth and try again. "No. But that doesn't mean I'm ready to tell everyone."

Ellis holds up both hands, palms out: a surrender. "Fair enough. Forget I said anything."

Only now that the seal has broken, it's impossible to go back. And maybe I don't want to forget what she said.

Ellis heads into the next room, and I trail behind her like a second shadow. She hasn't told anyone, either. If she had, I'd have heard about it. It would be in the interviews, the profile pieces.

"My girlfriend wanted me to come out," I say, standing there in the middle of a Persian rug as Ellis drops into an emerald-cushioned armchair. "I wasn't ready. But she kept pushing."

"She sounds like a bitch."

I shrug. "She wasn't. At least . . . not most of the time. Not to me." I don't want to say *Alex wasn't a bitch.* That wasn't, strictly speaking, true. But *bitch* felt like a harsh word to apply to a girl who was fighting so hard to make space for herself in a world that didn't want her. Alex was many things. She contained multitudes. And to say she was a bitch *sometimes* was to erase everything else she was: brave, stubborn, passionate, affectionate, a girl who would destroy empires to save someone she loved. "She was of the opinion I didn't want to tell anyone because I was worried I wouldn't be popular anymore if people knew."

"I doubt that would have been the case."

"No. It wouldn't have. Alex was out, and no one cared. Everyone worshipped her."

I realize I've said her name only after it's already fallen from my lips. Ellis is unfazed, her knees crossed and the top leg swinging: a feudal marchioness presiding from her throne. Maybe she'd already figured out Alex and I were together, our relationship inevitable as any plot twist in Ellis's book.

I shake my head, an odd smile twisting at my mouth. "I don't know. I'd rather wait until after I've graduated. It seems like such a cliché, doesn't it? Lesbians at a girls' school."

"Hey now. I happen to like that cliché."

I laugh. "I bet you do." All at once I'm giddy, as if buoyed up on champagne fizz. The chandeliers seem brighter; the brass seems brassier. The dust flickers like diamond shards in the window light. On impulse I steal Ellis's hat, tipping down the brim to gaze at her from under its shadow with a cocked brow.

"I'd have smoldered at the stake right next to yours, no doubt." Her smile is more subdued than mine, but it's still there. It's *real,* crinkling the edges of her eyes. She seems younger suddenly, just a girl wearing a ridiculous pair of glasses, sitting in the middle of a shop filled with everyone else's castoffs, all the memories no one wanted to keep.

I offer her the hat back; she shakes her head and says, "It looks better on you."

We move into the next room, which is full of books—everything from leather-bound tomes with gold foil lettering on the spines to frayed mass-market paperbacks. I pull out a particularly thick one and let it fall open to the middle page, bury my nose against the paper, and inhale.

"Tell me about her," Ellis says. "Alex. What was she like?"

I open my eyes to look at Ellis over the edge of my book; she stands just a few feet away, ignoring the shelves entirely.

It's the moment I've been waiting for, of course. This is the moment when Ellis finally musters the nerve to ask me how it *felt,* to write for her the emotional arc of the Dalloway Five murders.

And so she wants to know about Alex's murder.

I didn't kill her.

I almost say it, but the words don't come. Instead I lower the book, slowly, although I don't put it down. It feels better to clutch the book to my chest, leather binding gripped in both hands.

Maybe I owe Alex this much, after what I did. Maybe if I put it to words . . .

They say knowing the name of a thing gives you power over it. And right now, I need power. As much of it as I can get.

Ellis can write whatever she wants.

"She was . . . very clever," I say. I'm surprised by how even my voice sounds, almost like it doesn't hurt. Almost like I don't care at all. "She was in Godwin House, too. She read satirists, mostly."

Ellis doesn't say anything. It's the oldest trick in the book, but it works; now that I've started talking, I can't stop.

"She was funny. Sometimes that was a bad thing—if you got on her bad side, she could be . . . not *cruel,* not necessarily, but . . ."

I don't want to disparage her. Not to Ellis Haley. Not to anyone, actually.

And because if Alex was cruel, then some might say that's motive for murder.

I press my thumbs in harder against the book's spine. "She liked dogs. You couldn't take her anywhere—she'd have to stop every time she saw a dog. Had to say hello. She'd run into traffic if it meant she could pet a Labrador on the other side of the street. She was terribly allergic, but that didn't seem to make a difference."

"That's sweet," Ellis says.

"It was. *She* was."

God. I hadn't ever talked about her this much. Not even to Dr. Ortega, in therapy: *Talking will help,* Dr. Ortega had said. *Remembering her how she was. . . .*

"She was outdoorsy," I say. "She liked climbing, hiking, that sort of thing. I mean, she was a professional—or gonna be. She qualified for the very first Olympic sport-climbing team. She summitted Everest. Twice."

All at once it's harder to breathe, as if the air in here has become heavier. I can see dust motes sparkling in the air, dead skin particles from a hundred patrons, possibly even from the former owners of all the trinkets for sale in this place. I imagine that dust draping over us like blankets, suffocating us.

"I know this must be hard to talk about," Ellis says softly. She has one hand on the surface of a nearby table. She doesn't move, just says: "Because of the way she died."

I swallow. The back of my throat feels like it's covered in grit. "Right."

For a moment we both stare at each other, Ellis's eyes unblinking over the frames of those rickety pince-nez.

I try not to think about the abortive scream as Alex fell, cut off too quickly as she hit ground. I used to hear it everywhere: in my nightmares, in movies. Right now it echoes in the hum of the old record spinning on the turntable by the front desk, the music gone silent, static prickling at our ears.

I didn't want her to die. I never wanted her to die. But I'm not innocent, either.

That's the thing the doctors kept missing at Silver Lake, with their trauma therapy and white pills and cloying pity: That I'm the *reason* she died. If I hadn't been there, if I hadn't walked into Alex Haywood's life, she'd still be alive.

Ellis is looking at me like the doctors did, now—examining me, dissecting me for her goddamn book the same way those doctors might have used me for case studies. Like I'm confused, or misguided, or broken. Like I'm incapable of killing an ant, never mind a girl.

"I swear to god," I say, "if you tell me it *wasn't my fault—*"

"I wasn't going to say any such thing."

"Good."

She lifts a brow. "It was an accident. Everyone knows that. Everyone who read the papers, anyway."

I break first. I look away, down at the book still held against my chest. The dust threatens to make my eyes water.

"Yes," I say. "Well." *The papers don't tell everything.*

Silence stretches out long and taut—easily broken.

I slide the book back into its place on the shelf. When I'm turned away from Ellis, it's easier to speak. "Everyone says I'm a murderer."

"You aren't a murderer. I research murderers, I should know."

I make a sound that's meant to sound derisive but comes out strangled, bitter—as if this whole scenario could get any more humiliating. I rub the heel of my palm against my brow, not that it does much good.

"Hey," Ellis says, and she has both hands on me now, grasping my shoulders to look me in the eye. "Hey. Listen to me. The death wasn't premeditated. You didn't have malevolent intent. You loved her."

That isn't what Alex said. Alex insisted—she'd *insisted*—that I couldn't possibly love her, that I didn't want her, I just wanted to own her. It had been so . . . unfair, so brutally and callously unfair, as if the past year of our relationship had meant nothing to her.

I grimace. "I know. I know I didn't murder her—not *really.* But . . . we'd been fighting. I was still so . . . *so* angry at her. And maybe if I hadn't been distracted, maybe if I'd . . . if I'd paid better attention . . ."

Maybe I could have saved her.

I can't know for sure. How can I prove, even to myself—?

I know I'm not a murderer, but the difference between *murderer* and *killer* seems insubstantial sometimes. I was responsible for her death.

Our argument feels ridiculous now. We'd been fighting about the same thing we always fought about: Alex had called me spoiled, said I didn't appreciate how lucky I was to have grown up the way I did. It was the kind of comment that never hit well with me. Especially not when we were staying in Colorado, with my mother, with my mother's empty wine bottles and empty words.

If Alex and I hadn't fought . . . maybe I would have made a different choice.

Or maybe I would have gone down with her.

"You couldn't have saved her," Ellis says. "It was an accident."

She must be able to tell I'm unconvinced, because she sighs. She takes the hat off my head and puts it aside, as if she needs to see me properly.

"It was a long time ago," she says. "It's done now."

It doesn't feel done to me.

Whether Ellis is using me for her story doesn't seem to matter anymore. All I can think about is the spaces between the words I just said, all the confessions I didn't speak aloud.

How could I explain the way Alex's accident was the period at the end of a very long sentence—the conclusion of a long-owed debt?

I'm afraid if I close my eyes I'll find myself back there, one year ago, with the candles and the incense and witches whispering in my ear. With that ritual Alex and I tried to enact, the one that Alex ruined, the ritual that cursed us.

"We were climbing Longs Peak," I say. "We'd gone home to stay with my mother. For . . . Christmas, you know. We'd begged and begged her to let us go off and do one peak alone. Alex was . . . very persuasive. It was December, so we'd expected storms, but . . ."

When I close my eyes, I still see white. Everything there was white, the snow blinding.

Only the storm had come later.

"They never recovered the body, so they couldn't do an autopsy to be sure, but we'd both been trained to recognize pulmonary edema. When you're up at that altitude, sometimes it . . . Your lungs can start to fill with fluid. That's what happened to Alex. She was in a lot of pain and starting to find it hard to breathe, so we . . . The most important thing at that point is to get down to a safer altitude as quickly as possible. . . ."

Stupid, so stupid. We should have turned around as soon as Alex had started showing symptoms. But we were reckless, and as far as we had been concerned, we were immortal.

Ellis was perfectly, thankfully silent.

"You have to summit Longs Peak before noon, or you risk getting caught in a storm—that's how people die up there. And we'd kept climbing too late. By the time we started to descend . . . that's when the storm began. There was so much snow everywhere it was impossible to see anything, and we . . . *I* made a wrong decision. We descended off a cliff. Or I mean . . . Alex. She was caught in midair. I was still on the mountain. I couldn't . . . I wasn't strong enough to pull her up. She was too heavy—she had my oxygen."

I bite down on my inner cheek. The sharp flare of pain is enough to keep me going.

"The storm was bad. The snow . . . it was shifting. We were both . . . We weighed too much, with both of us. The snow was going to break. And we'd both fall." I nod, just once. "So I cut the rope."

Ellis touches my elbow. I startle. I hadn't realized she'd approached, and now she was right there, close enough I could have counted her eyelashes. The pince-nez have vanished again.

"She was screaming," I whisper. "The whole time. She was screaming for me to pull her back up."

The confession drops into the space between us like a lit fuse. And there it is: the nasty truth.

"Alex begged me not to, and I cut the rope anyway."

Ellis takes in a shallow audible breath. Her hand is still on my arm, at least—she hasn't recoiled in disgust.

"I don't understand," she says. And neither do I. *Neither do I.* My breath shudders in my chest, and I turn away so she won't see my tears.

Ellis's hand tightens on my arm, and she moves back into my line of sight until I have no choice but to look at her.

"I don't understand," she says again. "Alex didn't die on a mountain. She died here, at school. She drowned."

10

Ellis's words land heavy in my mind, and I rock back on my heels, away from her touch.

She drowned.

I can still see Alex in my memory, her lips tinged blue and her hand shaking where she gripped her ice pick. I still feel the frigid wind tearing at my hair, the snow wet against my cheek. It feels as if that reality has pressed itself up against this one, like I could reach into the dusty air and tear it apart and find myself back on the mountaintop. We were *there.* We—

"I read it in the paper," Ellis is saying; I barely hear her, barely see her. "She fell off a ledge by the lake. That's what you told the police, anyway. You said she couldn't swim."

No.

That isn't what happened. I cut the rope. It was thick, almost impossible to saw through—my hand was numb by the end of it. She screamed the whole way down.

"That isn't what happened," I say. My voice sounds like it belongs to someone else. "I was there. I . . . No—"

"Felicity," Ellis says. She's being careful—careful like the hospital doctors were careful, careful like I'm insane. "What did you use to cut the rope? A knife? Where did you get it?"

I hesitate, mouth half-open, lungs full of dead air.

Ellis releases my arm; my skin is cold where she once touched me. Alex's skin was cold up on that cliff, slippery with tears, her flesh translucent like polished quartz.

No.

That's not right. I never touched her. She fell.

She *fell.*

"You were there," Ellis is still saying, slow and so perfectly concerned. "Remember? You said she lost her balance. You came back to campus, dripping wet, and said she'd fallen into the lake."

I remember. I remember standing in the foyer of Godwin House, the cold night at my back and muddy dress clinging to my legs. Ice water pooled on the floor. I remember MacDonald calling the police. I remember them picking Alex's red hair from where it had caught, tangled, around my fingers.

Oh god.

It was an accident. I had just kept saying that, over and over, a litany.

Where is Alex, Felicity?

What happened to Alex?

I can't stand anymore; my legs feel fragile as flower stems, and I sink to the ground. I'm shaking, and Ellis leans over me, touching hesitant fingers between my shoulder blades.

"They never found her," I whisper. I know that now. Ellis is right. I remember, I—

Ellis shakes her head. "Divers searched the whole lake and

half the Hudson shoreline. Eventually the police said her body had probably floated out to sea."

Why did I think she'd died climbing? That wasn't true. I'd never even gone climbing with Alex—I don't even know *how.*

Was that story easier than the truth?

Why was it easier?

Maybe I just wanted to believe Alex had died doing something she loved. I didn't want it to be up there on that ledge, the two of us fighting about, about—

And then she fell.

I tip forward, pressing my brow against my knees.

I can't escape the memories rising in me like a briny tide.

Alex, her cheeks pink with anger.

Alex, shouting.

"I tried to save her," I sob. I don't know when I started crying. It chokes me, the tears salty when they catch on my lips, soak my tongue. "I tried. I *tried.* I swam out after her, but she . . . she already . . ."

She must have hit her head too hard when she fell; she would have lost consciousness immediately. There was no dramatic struggle to stay afloat, no flailing limbs or splashing water. Just terrible silence. I dove under again and again, eyes straining against the black water, searching. I dragged my fingers through the silt at the lake bottom. I cut my hands on the rocky edge of that cliff, clinging there and gasping for breath as I realized it was too late.

Alex was gone. The lake had swallowed her up and carried her far, far away. She was never coming back.

"It wasn't your fault," Ellis says.

"You don't know that," I say, and I laugh. I know how I sound—wild and unhinged. The same crazy girl they all think I am.

This is just what Ellis wants to believe. It's what *I* want to believe, and that's precisely why Alex won't let me go. She haunts me because she knows, as I know, that if things had been different . . . if I'd climbed down after her faster, if we hadn't argued in the first place, if Alex hadn't been drinking . . .

Ellis's mouth puckers, but she doesn't pull away. Instead she reaches for my wrist, fingers curling light around my bones and holding there. "How did she fall?"

Ellis says it so gently, and I want to trust her. I want to trust her more than anything. I want there to be someone in this terrible and twisted world I *can* trust.

"She slipped," I whisper. "She'd had . . . We'd *both* had a lot to drink. We'd been at the Boleyn end-of-semester party, you know? And we . . ."

Alex in her black beaded dress, pearls in her hair. Her fingertips smelled like cigarette smoke. Her lipstick was smudged.

"We fought. I'd run out of the party. I just wanted to be away from her for a little while. To calm down. But she followed me up onto the cliffs. She kept yelling at me. And I—"

I don't want to think about it. I don't want to remember. *I don't.*

But I have to. Ellis is right; Dr. Ortega is right. I have to face this. I close my eyes and see Alex's lips parting in that O of surprise, her hair catching on the rings on my fingers. Too late. Regret always comes too late.

"She was, you know . . . gesturing a lot. She did that when

she talked. Especially when she was angry. And I guess she . . . lost balance. And she . . . stumbled. She . . ."

"None of that is your fault. You didn't force her to drink; that was her choice. You didn't make her fall."

I laugh, a strangled, bitter sound. "I don't know why you can't . . . why you don't *understand*—you're a writer, aren't you? You know nothing's ever that simple."

"What, because you argued first? People argue, Felicity. People get angry. It's tragic that she died while you were fighting, but she didn't die *because* of it. Alex's death was an accident." Ellis's hand slips into my hair; her thumb strokes my cheek.

God. I wish I were just a little bit less broken, a little less humiliatingly weak.

My mother would be so ashamed.

It's that thought, more than anything, that makes me suck in an unsteady breath and lift my head. I scrub the tears from my cheeks with the heels of both hands and stand, moving away from Ellis's touch and forcing a trembling smile onto my lips.

"I'm okay," I tell her. "Sorry. I don't know what . . . I'm not usually like this."

The words ring false; the version of me that was in the hospital, that lay curled up in a thin bed for weeks, drunk off grief and medication, knows the truth.

I've always been like this.

And Ellis knows it now, because she saw me break down in the middle of this antiques shop. She—god—she knows I made up a different story about how Alex died. And she knows that I believed it.

"I don't know why I said that thing about the mountain," I tell her, letting my gaze drift away from Ellis's face to fixate on the gloves on my hands instead. The leather has worn at the fingertips, a relic of someone else's hands, someone else's life.

Only that isn't true, either. Now that I'm here, now that I'm thinking about it, I remember. This was something Dr. Ortega had come up with. An exercise, trying to convince me that Alex's death hadn't been my fault.

Write me a story, the doctor had said. *Write Alex's death as it might have happened in another universe, without the fight.*

I'd written about mountains and snow and autumn storms, about a rope and a knife. Dr. Ortega had read it at her desk while I sat in the chair across from her, my hands folded primly in my lap, awaiting her verdict.

And how did writing this story make you feel?

"One of the articles I read about Alex said that she'd had a fight with another professional climber," Ellis says, pulling me back. "She'd gotten violent and broke the other girl's nose. She got kicked off the Youth Olympics team."

That's right. That's right, she did. Alex had called me in tears that summer night, crying so hard I could barely understand her over the phone. I'd shut myself away in my bedroom where my mother couldn't overhear and begged her to explain how this had happened. Only she couldn't.

There's no excuse, Alex told me. I messed up, I fucked up, I'm so . . . And between sobs I pieced together a story of relentless bullying, hazing, sabotage.

Alex's temper was something vicious and vibrant, flaring up bright as lit magnesium—although it never burned out nearly so quickly. It didn't matter if Alex's tormentor deserved it, if this assault was the period at the end of a very long sentence—if Alex, like anyone sick and tired of being treated as less-than because they can't afford the best equipment or the newest shoes, finally snapped.

Alex had attacked that girl, and she'd ruined her career over it.

"Yes," I say quietly. "Everyone wouldn't stop talking about it, even once we got back to school. Alex hated that. She . . . she hated the way people looked at her. So maybe that's why."

I'd wanted to give her a better ending. A happier one. One that was less violent, one where Alex hadn't been angry.

I sniffle and wipe my cheeks again, then finally look back at Ellis. "I'm sorry. I didn't mean to make a scene. I'm . . . fine."

"Are you sure?" Ellis says, and I nod. She presses her mouth into a thin line and turns away, pretending interest in the ancient, wilting books that line the shelves behind her.

A part of me doesn't ever want to leave this shop, doesn't want to step out that door and go back to campus, to the place where Alex died. I don't want to leave the reality I wrote for Dr. Ortega.

But I have no choice, of course. I don't want to lie to myself anymore.

I try to remember being on that mountain again, but this time the memory feels muddy and distant, like one of the framed sepia photographs atop the store's antique piano. I can't remember how the snow tasted on my tongue anymore. I can't remember the texture of the rope.

We spend another half hour or so in that shop without

speaking. Ellis buys the hat and I leave with a beautiful vintage copy of *Rebecca* that has a forget-me-not pressed between the pages.

We don't talk on the ride back to campus. But Ellis reaches over and touches my shoulder before we get out of the car. It's just for a moment, but I feel the heat of her hand there for hours before it fades.

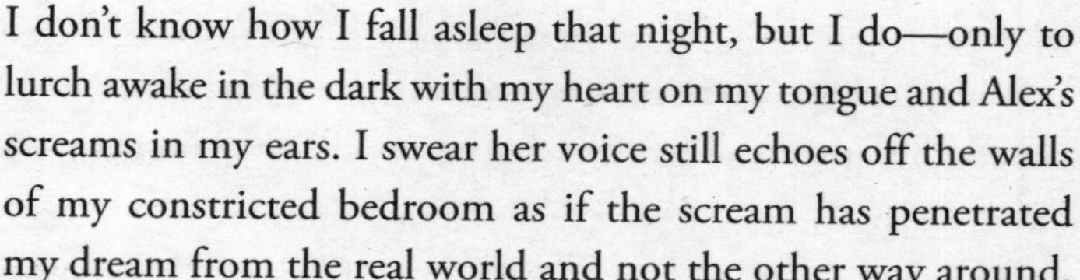

I don't know how I fall asleep that night, but I do—only to lurch awake in the dark with my heart on my tongue and Alex's screams in my ears. I swear her voice still echoes off the walls of my constricted bedroom as if the scream has penetrated my dream from the real world and not the other way around. I look at my alarm clock with one hand cupped around my brow, squinting against the glowing red numbers: it's three in the morning.

My stomach is uneasy, pitching like a sea at storm. I get up and turn on the lights, both arms hugged around my neck and my back to the door as I stare at my empty room. No one is here. No shrouded spirit emerges from hell to haunt me.

Then my gaze lands on the window. It's like getting shot in the throat, air cut off, ears ringing.

Fog had risen overnight, clouding the window behind my desk. And in that mist a perfect handprint presses against the glass from the outside, little rivulets of water dripping down the chilly palm.

In the light of day—on the other end of hours curled up

under my covers, sweating and sick to my gut, in and out of the bathroom until I've vomited so much it feels like I've expelled my spleen along with my stomach contents—I try to entertain mundane explanations for what I saw. But I couldn't recall ever pressing my own hand to my bedroom window, and it's too high up off the ground for a passerby to have touched it from the other side. I imagine some sinister creature slipping out from the forest, tall and faceless as the tree trunks, peering through the glass and watching me sleep. I imagine Tamsyn Penhaligon swinging from the oak tree.

I would have preferred the wildwood explanation, but I suspect the spirit who left this mark lives closer to home.

"Are you sick?"

I lift my head from my book. I've been reading in the main library since it opened at eight, escaping the dark shadows and slanted floors of Godwin for the comforting glow of fluorescent light. I couldn't stay there. Everything reminded me of how sick I'd been overnight, from the water glass to my toothbrush on the bathroom sink. And every corner felt like it shrouded secrets, Alex watching me from the shadows. Since coming to the library, I've finished *The Haunting of Hill House* and moved on to *Rebecca,* which, although a favorite of mine, is nevertheless consistent with the whole theme of eerie mansions haunted by the ghosts of dead women. My nausea throbs below my breastbone, insatiable.

It's been hours now, or it must have been; the campus, outside the library windows, has taken on the golden hue of late afternoon.

Ellis stands with her hip tilted against the wall of my carrel, long legs crossed at the ankles. She looks relaxed enough to have been there for a good while, myself too absorbed in du Maurier's words to notice.

"What?" I say, too belatedly.

"You look pale," she says, taps beneath one eye. "Dark circles. Are you sick?"

I don't know why she's asking, after yesterday. She knows why I'm upset. Maybe this is Ellis's way of showing concern without letting that concern bleed into pity.

But I don't need her concern. I slept last night, sort of. I got out of the house this morning. I'm far from Alex now; I just need time.

"I'm fine. Are you following me?"

She doesn't dignify that with an answer. "Get up. We're going."

"Where?" I ask, but I'm already shoving the book into my satchel and getting to my feet. Even the library gets tedious after nine hours. Ellis could be bringing me to Persephone's underworld and I'd be glad for the change in scenery.

I follow Ellis back to the Godwin House common room, where she pushes me down into the armchair by the window. "Stay here," she orders, and vanishes into the kitchen.

When I agreed to go with her, I hadn't thought she meant back *here.*

But I sink back against the cushions with a sigh, tilting my face toward the sunlight. It might be chilly outside, but the light is warm on my skin through the window; I imagine it sinking through flesh and taking up root in my marrow. There are no ghosts. No dead memories—of mountains or otherwise.

I won't let Alex get to me anymore.

Ellis emerges with a tray in hand, a teacup and pot balanced atop it. She slides the tray onto the ottoman and crouches down, pouring a steaming cup of jasmine I can smell from where I sit, the long petals unfurling against white porcelain. There's only one cup.

"Aren't you drinking any?" I ask.

"I can't stand anything decaffeinated," she answers. "Would you mind opening that window for me?"

I obey. The latch is old; it takes a second to get it unstuck and shove the glass up enough to let in a soft breeze. I don't think this window has been opened in fifty years. Perhaps longer—since the Dalloway Five lived in Godwin House and spilled blood on its ground.

Ellis perches in the other chair, drawing a cigarette case from her inside blazer pocket. "Want one?"

"No, thanks. I quit." Which is true. The taste of cigarettes reminds me of that last Boleyn House party with Alex.

I hope, whatever Ellis wants now, it doesn't have anything to do with that. With *her.* I was vulnerable yesterday, and allegedly that's a good and healthy thing to be, but I'm not terribly keen on a reprise.

She strikes a match and tips forward to light the cigarette, the cherry at the end flaring as she inhales. A familiar sweet smell curls through the air and my brows lift.

"Is that—?"

"Changed your mind?" Ellis says archly and passes the joint. Judging by her sly smile, she knows the answer already.

Her lips have left a crimson stain behind on the paper.

I take a deep drag, my mouth right over the imprint from Ellis's, and hold the smoke in my lungs until it goes stale. When I do exhale, all my tension goes out with my breath. Now this . . . this is something familiar, but something that isn't tied to Alex. I smoked for the first time at Silver Lake, a joint my roommate had smuggled in. The pair of us shared it out on the back steps, surreptitiously blowing smoke into the chilly winter air and counting down the weeks until our release.

Ellis draws one leg up onto the seat cushion, her posture long and graceful as a nineteenth-century dandy's.

"Drink your tea," Ellis says.

I obey without argument and watch Ellis over the rim of my cup as she brings the joint to her red-lipsticked mouth, lips pursing as if in a kiss.

"Didn't you sleep last night?" she asks.

That chill rolls through me again, like a cold bead of water cutting down my spine.

"Not much," I admit. "I woke up at three and couldn't fall back asleep. Nightmare."

I mentally cross my fingers that Ellis doesn't bring up yesterday and try to tie my bad dreams to those revelations. I want her to think I'm *normal,* not . . . fragile.

She grinds out the joint against the tea tray. "Well, it is the devil's hour," Ellis says, pointing to the grandmother clock. I suppose she was never able to fix the thing, after all.

Three o'clock. The same hour I woke up last night. The hour Alex first slipped into my nightmares here at Godwin House and the grandmother clock stopped working. I'd calculated it after that: three was also the time it had been when Alex and I left that party, when she chased me onto the cliffs.

"An unlucky number, three," Ellis muses. "You know it took three years after Flora Grayfriar's murder until all of the Dalloway Five were dead. Three years to the *day.*"

I do know.

"I see your research is going splendidly."

Ellis smiles. "Don't act so cantankerous about it, Felicity. I'm hardly going to start believing in magic and demons and so on just because I read about them."

Well, that makes one of us, I want to snap—but Ellis doesn't mean anything by it. She doesn't *know.*

Ellis Haley is a lot of things, but willfully cruel is not one of them.

Even so, I have to fight not to let my reaction show on my face. I don't want her to know how sharp those words cut. "An unlucky number," I agree instead.

"Are you done with your tea?"

"Oh. Yes. Thank you."

"Excellent." Ellis produces a book out of her satchel and sets it on the table, tapping her fingers against the spine. "Bring it here."

I don't question her. It occurs to me only after I've adjusted my position on the sofa to face her more properly and slid my cup and saucer across the table that it was a strange request. Still, now I'm here, sitting opposite Ellis in her brown pin-striped blazer, with the dregs of my tea going cold against the porcelain.

"Have you heard of tasseography?" Ellis asks. I can see now that the book she pulled out of her bag is titled *Reading the Future in Tea.* She must have gotten it out of the occult collection in the library.

"Tea leaves?"

A smile curls one corner of Ellis's mouth; her lipstick isn't even smudged. For some reason that frustrates me. "I thought you might. It seems very like you, with the whole interest in tarot and so on."

"You make me sound like—" I can't finish the sentence, but I'm sure my flushed cheeks communicate most of what I'd intended to say.

"No, I think it's endearing," Ellis says, which serves to make me feel even worse. "I've been reading about it for my book, of course. I think I'm going to write Tamsyn Penhaligon as a fortune-teller, so I'd better learn how to fortune-tell myself. Do you mind?"

I arch my brows questioningly.

"Can I read your tea leaves?" Ellis clarifies.

"Oh." I almost don't want her to. Every time I've read my own future in the cards, it's been dark and incomprehensible. I'm not sure I want Ellis to see me so keenly. But I find myself saying, "All right," and the grin that splits Ellis's face is almost worth it.

"Fantastic. Go on, pick up your cup. . . . No, other hand. Left hand. Swirl what's left of the tea three times from left to right."

"Now what?"

"Now put the cup upside down on your saucer and leave it there."

I do. The clink of china is too loud in the quiet room. "I can't believe you decided to learn how to read *tea leaves.*"

"Method writer, remember?"

Perhaps it's not that Ellis learned tasseography that surprises me. It's that she chose to learn about it from that book she's now perusing so closely, finger skimming down the text on the page as if to keep her place. It's easier to imagine her learning from experience instead of from a book: Ellis in some smoky London salon, lounging on a silk chaise and smoking opium while a veiled mystic reads her future from the grounds.

We sit there for about a minute before Ellis gives me permission to rotate my cup three times then lift it upright.

"Which direction is south?" she asks, and when I tell her she makes me point the cup handle that way, then reaches across the table to slide my saucer toward her.

Ellis curves over the cup, her gaze flicking from the little bundle of leaves clustered opposite the handle to the flecks smeared about its belly. Her face is set in a mask of concentration; I wish I had the ability to slip into her mind and page through her thoughts, to read them as easily as she seems to read me.

"Was I supposed to think of a question?" With tarot, usually you ask a question. I don't know if the same holds true for tea leaves.

"Oh, I have no idea. I suppose I can read your fortune more generally, if that's all right with you."

It's very all right. I'd rather her ask a broad question and be unable to interpret the answer than ask anything specific myself—like whether Alex's ghost will leave me alone. Like whether I'll ever be able to piece myself back together again.

"There's a cross," Ellis says. She flips through the tea leaf book to the index, trails her finger down the long list of keywords until she finds the right one. "That represents death—not surprising, perhaps, given your history. It's toward the bottom of the cup, which signifies events that occurred in the past."

I lean forward a little, trying to peer beyond the fall of Ellis's errant hair and into the cup. I can't make sense of any of it, of course.

"A mountain," she says. "That's usually powerful friends. Oh, and apparently you're going to be very successful in your career, that's nice. Maybe that's where you meet said powerful friends?" She trades me a quick grin. "We also have something that looks like a hand." She has to check the book again, flipping back and forth between chapters. "That means relationships, either you helping other people or them helping you. Or it means justice. But that seems like quite the departure from the other interpretation, doesn't it?"

"I think you're very bad at this," I inform her with a wry grin.

She smiles and tilts over the teacup again. "All right, last one. This looks kind of like a bird . . . that means dangerous situations. But it could also mean you're being watched by spirits—I'm not sure which. Perhaps the ghosts of the Dalloway Five come to haunt their witchy inheritor?"

Spirits. Or *spirit,* singular. I've tried to ignore the heaviness in this house, but after last night . . . that handprint on the window, right after I realized the truth . . . it's too much of a coincidence. My tongue tastes metallic.

Alex used to say I was too obsessed with the Dalloway Five, with magic in general. She told me I was being irrational. She told me I was crazy.

But I'm not irrational, and I'm not crazy.

Some things are too dark to be seen—or explained.

I must have shivered visibly, because Ellis shuts the book and pushes the cup away, her gaze meeting mine across the table.

"Don't worry," I tell her with a false smile, "I'm not frightened by some soggy—"

The crash of ceramic shattering is so loud it feels like a gunshot. I'm on my feet, dizzy, staring across the room, where a potted plant just fell off the fireplace mantel, scattering pottery shards and black soil across the hardwood floor.

It's her. I knew it. She won't leave me alone. Not now, not ever. *It's her, it's her—*

Those words are stuck on a loop in my head now, trembling in my mind. Ellis pushes the saucer aside and tilts in closer, her eyes as wide and gray as cold pond water.

"Felicity," she starts, reaching for me; I flinch away.

"It's her," I gasp. I want to press a hand to my face, but I don't dare close my eyes. Even here, even with Ellis, Alex won't leave me alone. "She won't ever . . . She . . ."

"Talk to me, Felicity."

I suck in a shallow, sharp breath and force myself to look away from the plant. It must have been freshly watered; dark liquid seeps along the floor, staining the fringe of the nearest rug.

"What's going on?" Ellis demands.

I sit, but I'm shaking badly enough that Ellis must feel it

when I brace an elbow against the table. "Nothing," I say, trying to calm myself.

But Ellis has scented blood, my soft underbelly exposed, and in this context—as in all contexts—she is nothing if not a shark. "Tell me."

I twist my hands together in my lap, hidden under the coffee table. An exhale heats the nape of my neck; I wonder if Ellis can see Alex behind me, her skeleton fingers closing around my throat.

"You're going to think I'm stupid."

The look Ellis fixes me with then is tight and disapproving. "I would *never* think you were stupid."

You've done it now, a voice scolds in the back of my head. Because it's too late. I've gone and made this an enigma for Ellis to unravel. I have to say something, or else she'll never stop picking at the knots—and if I unspool at Ellis's hands for a second time, I'm not sure I'll ever manage to stitch myself back together again.

I grimace. "It's . . ." *Spit it out.* No evasion, nowhere to hide. "Do you believe in ghosts?" I ask. "Real ones."

To her credit, Ellis doesn't laugh.

"I believe that ghosts are a culturally universal phenomenon," Ellis says. "Whether I *personally* believe in them is neither here nor there; plenty of people do, and perhaps they know something I don't."

I almost want to laugh. It's just that the response is so characteristic, so terribly *Ellis,* that I might have predicted it.

For all that I've been hiding from Ellis, she's hid nothing from me. She's an open book.

"How academic of you."

"That's me," she says. "An intellectual."

Ellis's gaze is wary still, but the fear has relaxed its grip on my shoulders, and they slump now, my hands going limp at last. "I don't know. Maybe I'm imagining things."

Ellis says nothing. She waits in silence, and I keep talking to fill it.

"But . . . ever since I came back here, to Godwin House . . . I feel like she . . . Alex . . . like she might be . . ." God. I need to stop prevaricating. I need to put words to this phenomenon. I need to call it what it is, name the thing and steal its power. "I think she's haunting me."

Ellis's gaze flicks down to the teacup, its muddled leaves with their messages of death and betrayal. *My* betrayal, of course, of Alex.

"And why shouldn't she?" I go on, voice dropped to a whisper now. "Ghosts are restless spirits. And she died because I . . . I'd want vengeance, too."

"You think she believes you murdered her," Ellis says.

I shrug. "I don't know what Alex thinks."

But I know what everyone else does. I see it written in the surreptitious glances, the whispers behind cupped hands. I remember Clara's fingers miming scissors at the Boleyn party. Before, in my muddled mind, I'd thought they'd blamed me for cutting the rope. Now I know they don't believe my story of what happened at all.

For several long moments Ellis just looks at me, eyes narrowed and her mouth set in a flat line. I almost expect her to renege on what she said yesterday, to tell me *You're right—you're a killer,* to launch into a typically Ellis inquisition about why I did it and how it felt. How convenient for her to have a real-life murderer right here, prepared to color in the white areas of her fictional psychopath.

But then—

"All right," Ellis says. "Enough of this. You're going to help me with my project."

"What project?"

"My research for my novel," she says. "I need to somehow reconstruct the experience of the Dalloway murders, so I was thinking I would plan them. If I take their deaths as inspiration, if I design a modern version of the murders as I think they *could* have happened—if I take all the steps but the last—then I can write it. And"—she arches one brow—"you can help me."

This time I really do laugh, the sound barking out of me like a dying person's cough. "Why?" I say. "Because you think I know something about murdering people?"

I did lie to her, after all. I lied, and the memory of it still hangs like smoke in the air between us, poisoning our lungs. There's too much I managed to forget about that night with Alex, and Ellis knows it now.

What else does she think she knows about me?

What else does she suspect?

"No." Ellis pushes the cup and saucer aside and leans over the table again, her elbows planted on the wood and her chin resting atop a shelf of both hands. "Because you know everything there is to know about the Dalloway Five. Because you've *researched* them—you've clearly done your homework. Not to sound too utilitarian, but I'd like to capitalize on that."

"There's a whole occult library at this school," I inform her. "You could just go there."

"It's not only that. You didn't kill anyone, Felicity, not maliciously, and you aren't being haunted. There are no ghosts, there's no magic, and you didn't kill Alex. I'll prove it to you. Besides," she adds, "if you help me with this, maybe you can go back to your old thesis. You know so much about the Dalloway witches; that knowledge shouldn't go to waste. It's all those horror novels making you believe in ghosts. Reality is reality. It's pretty clear you've strayed far from *that* in recent weeks. Don't you think it would be grounding, to look history in the eye and name it what it is?"

"I haven't lost my grip on reality," I argue, but it's a moot point. I have. I demonstrated that just yesterday. I want to argue that plenty of people manage to believe in ghosts and witches without others questioning their sanity, but I suspect Ellis would find some way to twist my words.

"Help me," Ellis says. "I want to reenact the Dalloway murders. Not for real, of course—but we could figure out how they were done. Because it wasn't magic, no matter how impossible they seem. Maybe someone wanted to frame them, to persecute the Dalloway girls for the crime of possessing their own agency. It would have been easy, back then, to convince people that five odd, educated girls were witches. We'll go through each death, one by one, and figure out how they were accomplished *without* the use of magic. And of course, it will be good for me to understand the mechanics of it all, for my book."

A ridiculous proposition. I know that. I *know* it. But Ellis watches me with eyes lit from some arcane internal light, one long strand of black hair fallen into her face. All I want is to compulsively tuck it back behind her ear—it's intensely distracting—but I find myself saying: "Fine."

"Fine?"

"*Fine.* I'll help you. We'll . . ." A giggle rises in me, helpless; I've never been a giggler. "We'll re-create the Dalloway murders, and you'll write your book, and then we all live happily ever after. Not the Ellis Haley ending I expected, but I can appreciate a plot twist as well as the next person."

Ellis rolls her eyes, and I spare a thought to wonder if I'm the first person who has ever managed to make Ellis Haley do something so pedestrian as *roll her eyes.*

"This will be good closure for you," she says, rising to retrieve the broom to clean up the broken pottery. "Trust me."

"I don't," I tell her, but we both know that makes little difference.

Whether I trust Ellis or not, I need to do this. I need to understand what happened the night Alex died. I need to know if some shadow of Margery Lemont has curled up in my heart, guiding the movements of my hands and the words in my mouth. The ghost raised by the Dalloway Five didn't rest until all of them were dead. I need to know if I'm cursed by that same fate. If raising Margery's spirit in our unfinished ritual cursed me and Alex. If it killed her.

I need to face whatever caused the broken ceramic shards on the floor, the misty handprint on my window.

I need to face the truth.

11

I don't tell Wyatt I'm researching the witches again.

Maybe it's because I know what she'd say. I can visualize the precise character of the disappointment that would settle over her features. I can even imagine her deciding to call my mother, who would call Dr. Ortega, who would ask if I've been taking my medication.

Better to wait, to prove I'm healthy—stable—before I tell Wyatt the truth.

And there's research to do, not just for myself now, but for Ellis as well if I'm going to help her write this book. I reread my old notes a dozen times, but they're full of references to primary source material, questions scribbled in the margins that I meant to answer later, when I could go back to the occult collection.

There's no other option. I need to access the original sources before I can get anything else done. Wyatt gave me a signed permission slip last year, which is what it takes to get into the occult library as a student. They say it's because the books are old and rare, but really it's because the administration is afraid more students will turn out like me. I have no idea if my old permission slip will still work, but I smile at the front desk librarian anyway as I pass it over with my student identification card.

"Good evening," I say, and I notice even as I'm speaking that my voice has taken on crisper enunciation—my mother's accent, laden with all its connotations of privilege and power. "I need to access the occult collection. Felicity Morrow."

The librarian examines the slip and then scans my card. She shakes her head.

"I'm afraid your permission to view this collection has been revoked," she says, passing my ID back across the desk.

Of course it has.

"Are you sure? Can you check again?" I ask.

The woman just spins her computer monitor to show me the screen, where it says my name and, in bright-red font, DISALLOWED.

I know for a fact that Ellis has been going into the occult section; that's where she got the book on tasseography, after all. Still, something in me balks at the prospect of asking her to go for me. I don't want to open up the possibility for questions I can't answer.

So I return to Godwin House and pack myself a sandwich and a water bottle, then go back to the library and claim a carrel on the fifth floor—the emptiest floor, housing the school's encyclopedia collection. I occupy myself by reading the rest of my latest Shirley Jackson book, then type out a few new paragraphs of material for my European History essay.

Eventually even those few students who had ventured up

to the fifth floor drift away, the last of them packing up when the lights flicker, a sign that the library's about to close for the night.

I've been one of those reluctant students before, lingering as long as possible to finish just one more chapter, one more page. The librarians will come through any minute, checking to make sure all the students have egressed and gone back to their houses; I know that much from experience. But I also know they won't check *everywhere.*

I take my sandwich and go sit in the stacks, eating my late dinner and listening to the echo of heels on hardwood as one of the librarians makes her rounds through the carrels.

Then the sound of a door shutting and the lights turn off, plunging me into darkness.

I pull out my flashlight and flick the switch. The amber beam of light casts a narrow channel through the gloom. The stacks feel taller like this, looming watchful in the darkness as I pass. Perhaps this wasn't such a good idea; my skin prickles at the nape of my neck as I take the elevator to the basement, which encloses the occult collection. I'm afraid to look behind me, knowing that if I do I'll find *her* there, dripping lake water on the tile floor, eyes like black pits above sharp teeth.

I dart out of the elevator as soon as it hits ground; the doors can't slide open fast enough. Only it's worse once I'm ducking under the velvet rope and shouldering through the door into the occult section. If Alex haunts me, haunts the school—if Godwin House is the epicenter of her power—

then this would be the epicenter of *theirs*. The Dalloway Five.

I find myself gazing through the iron grate at a leather-bound copy of *Malleus Maleficarum,* my breath coming in shallow gulps, afraid to look too deeply into the shadows.

This is my problem. Despite my fear, despite all the ways this obsession ruined everything for me, I *want* to be back here. I'm drawn to these books like a moth to a struck match. I can't stay away.

I used to spend hours in this room, poring over the papyrus boards of *Grimoirium Verum* and caressing its cobra-skin spine. I scrawled pages of notes from *The Book of Paramazda.*

I should be flipping through pulp horror novels and having nightmares over *The Yellow Wallpaper.* I should be spending my afternoons in the general stacks with cozy, comfortingly fictional books, then returning home to hot tea and a warm bed. I shouldn't be picking the lock on the Godwin case, washing my hands at the sink, settling in under the amber glow of a desk lamp to read.

But the Dalloway occult collection is the only place in the country where I might find the information I need: how to unravel the curse Alex and I brought down upon ourselves, how to close the ritual a year too late.

The spine makes a faint cracking sound when I open the second volume of the Dalloway records, its heavy leather binding settling reluctantly against the surface of the desk. The smell of it hasn't changed. It's like the inside of a grave. The title, in brown ink, is inscribed in eighteenth-century calligraphy atop the first page:

Report of the Trial of

Margery Lemont, Beatrix Walker,
Cordelia Darling, & Tamsyn Penhaligon,

On an Indictment for the
Murder of Flora Grayfriar

The trial took place in 1712, well before the advent of photography, but like most of us at Dalloway, the accused girls came from money. A portrait of Margery Lemont has been preserved here in the bowels of the Dalloway library; it hangs on the east wall next to the painting of her mother, the founder. When I look up from my book, Margery is watching me with a cool and impenetrable gaze. The artist painted her in luscious pale silks, her black hair tumbling loose over her shoulders, in defiance of the style of the time. Her nose is long and narrow, her lips faintly smiling, but it is her eyes that have always captured me most. Pale green along the lower curve of her irises, they deepen to black past the meridian of her pupils. A pinprick of light gleams against that shadow but fails to illuminate.

Some say she haunts the school along with the rest of the Dalloway Five—Godwin House, in particular. That legend isn't true, of course; or it wasn't until Alex and I made it so.

Flora Grayfriar was found exsanguinated in the woods, says this particular record, her sternum split and her white dress soaked red. She was the last body in a series of smaller corpses to be found: a slaughtered rabbit, a bloodless sheep. The trial makes no mention of a musket wound, although the account of the herbs and flowers strewn about her body is repeated here.

I reread the girls' testimonies. It's hard to imagine that they were alive once, pink-cheeked and vibrant, when the tales of their deaths loom so large.

In fact, tonight I reread the entire record of the murder trial, although I've scoured it enough times I nearly have it memorized. There are other accounts, of course, but I keep coming back to this one. Maybe a part of me heuristically assumes that if it was reported in a courtroom, it is likely a truer account of what happened—although I'm sure that isn't actually the case. Every time I read I think I'll find some new detail: another hint about what spells they cast, what arcane arts they practiced that required Flora's death—if any. It's useless. The girls claim they never touched Flora. They do admit to having held a séance, the details of which I had bastardized last year for my ritual with Alex. But the girls insisted it had all been in the name of good fun, a joke between friends, nothing more insidious. And nothing to do with Flora's death.

Never mind that some townspeople testified they'd seen the girls holding bacchanals in the woods, drunk on cherry wine and consorting with devils—this wasn't Salem. Nor was it Norfolk, Virginia, where Grace Sherwood survived the water test and was acquitted of witchcraft; or Annapolis the year following the Dalloway trial, where Virtue Violl was similarly found innocent. The town leaders were educated and wealthy, not Puritans; they did not believe young girls were capable of such satanic cruelty.

Or perhaps they were just afraid of Dalloway's then headmistress, the daughter of the Salem witch.

If being Deliverance Lemont's daughter had saved Margery

from the stake, it hadn't kept her alive for long. And if the town's leaders were too scholarly to believe in magic, well, that did not apply to the common folk who relied on healthy crops and cattle to survive. If the girls at the school were witches, and if they were to turn their evil eyes toward the fields and farms, the town could not endure. Normal hardworking people can't live off tuition and inheritance money, after all.

At least, that is what historians commonly believe happened to the girls. Fevered and idiotic mobs out for brutal justice.

And so one by one the Dalloway Five died—each in mysterious circumstances, each horribly. Flora Grayfriar's ritual murder was avenged with their blood.

These are the deaths Ellis wants to recapture. These are the deaths she insists weren't caused by magical means, although I still don't understand what she thinks is the alternative. I don't get the sense she buys the mob account, either.

I want to interrogate the concept of the psychopath, Ellis had said.

Maybe she believes Margery is responsible.

It's what I believe, too. She confessed, according to later records, once the trial was complete. She *confessed.* Angeline Wilshire, the baker, claimed that Margery Lemont boasted about murdering Flora as the devil's sacrifice while buying bread one Sunday. Allegedly, Margery had said that she was possessed by a spirit, or a demon. And if Margery was responsible for Flora, then why not the rest of them, too?

The demon part is what used to suspend my disbelief.

Yet Alex and I were there the night Margery Lemont's ghost stepped out of legend and into the real world. I invited her into our lives, and I kept her here against her will. I still feel her fingers tangled up in the threads of my fate.

If Margery really had been possessed . . . if the girls had failed to close the séance, if they'd trapped a spirit in our world who would not rest until all of the participants were dead . . .

Who is to say she hadn't done the same to us?

How long will you punish me? I ask the ink that inscribes Margery's name.

But that's not why I'm here. Or at least, it's not the only reason.

I pull out my notebook and turn to the list of references, cross-checking the values against the tome open on the desk before me. I take notes for Ellis—anything that could conceivably be relevant, anything that suggests Margery's guilt, paired with book and page numbers in case she wants to come herself.

When I'm finished I return the trial record to its glass case. I should leave. I've done what I came to do. There's no need to look at any of the other books.

But I can't stop looking at the spellcraft tome in the case nearest the door. It's bound in a blue so old it appears nearly gray, the cover stained dark where some ancient witch spilled her wine while reading.

My hands clench into fists. I really shouldn't. I *can't.* If I start with this again, I'll never be able to stop.

On the other hand . . . On the other hand, it was so difficult to get in here. I can't be sure I'll ever have a chance again. And what if Ellis could use some spells for her book? It might be helpful.

In for a penny, in for a pound—

I open the case and take out the spell book, carrying it quickly to the reading table. Irrationally, a part of me thinks magic won't infect me if I don't touch it for long.

My mouth has gone dry as I stare down at the book. And it *is* just a book. It holds no special power. It can't hurt me if I don't let it.

The leather bends easily as I open the cover, worn soft by a hundred years of hands. The thick parchment paper is scratchy against my gloved fingers when I turn the pages.

This book has more than one author. The handwriting is all different—sometimes steady and slanted, sometimes erratic. Sometimes the ink is thick and black; other times it's a pale red brown so faint I can barely read it at all.

I flip over my notebook and uncap my pen again. My own calligraphy is shaky—blotches welling at the tail of each letter, jagged cross-strokes—as I copy down a spell for banishing evil spirits. But Ellis might want it.

And me . . . I won't use this incantation. But I'll have it, just in case.

I turn the page again, and abruptly it's hard to breathe. The air has gone heavier, wetter, like I'm choking on tar.

A full illustration consumes the verso, a young woman kneeling, nude, at the feet of a tall figure with a bone-white face. The mask is gaunt and elongated, with curving horns and black pits where the eyes should be, its nostrils sharp and jagged: a goat's skull. The figure reaches out one spindly arm, dripping blood, to paint a sigil on the woman's brow.

Initiation.

Members of the Margery coven don't talk about it often,

not outside the rituals. Even Ellis probably doesn't know initiation exists. The secrets of Dalloway are given only to a select few: those of us thought worthy, those of us strong enough to survive our fear. But behind closed doors, in secret gatherings of two or three girls from each house, some of us lean into the dark.

Will I ever forget the way Alex looked that night? They'd positioned us facing one another, the two new initiates of Godwin House. Alex was in flannels and a tank top that exposed her slim collarbones and muscular shoulders. She'd looked so out of place surrounded by the elder girls in their black robes and skull masks.

They lit candles and burned herbs. They chanted in Latin and Greek and Aramaic—a bizarre and meaningless mix of languages, it strikes me now, but at the time it felt like the shadows grew taller and wilder, shifting with our occult power. The night was endless and magnificent; it could have lasted three hours or three days. When they smeared the goat's blood on my brow, it was still fresh, cutting down my face and catching in my eyelashes. With my hands bound, I couldn't wipe it away; I could only sit there as scarlet tears streamed down my cheeks.

That was the night I felt like I had finally become one of them—a girl of Dalloway, a girl of Godwin—heiress to the witches who planted the stones on which we stood.

That was the night I first wished magic were real.

I shut the spellcraft book and put it back where I found it. I feel as if the darkness breathes out a sigh behind me as I leave the library: as if the spirits there had been watching, waiting for me to go.

It's a silent and solitary trip back to Godwin House, especially once I've left the quad and must tread through the woods up the hill. The windows of Godwin are black and shuttered; I'm left with the strange impression that its soul has been sucked out through the cracks beneath uneven doors.

I don't go in. Instead I slip around back, shoulder open the rickety door to the gardening shed. The small stone structure is steeped in shadow, a gloom somehow more complete than pitch.

I find the masks where we always kept them—even if I spent a year away, even if the sisters who initiated me have graduated, some things never change. I crouch on the pounded-earth floor of the gardening shed and stroke a finger around a mask's hollow mouth; shears and trowels, which had concealed the memento mori of our craft, litter the floor around me.

I might have been expelled from the Margery coven, but Ellis hasn't.

Ellis is in the kitchen when I return to the house, her typewriter set up on the table overlooking the forest behind Godwin, face and page both lit only by a single flickering candle. She twists round to look at me when I come in, and the light shifts in shadows across her face like panes of stained glass.

"I have an idea," I tell her.

If Ellis wants to understand the Dalloway witches, if she wants to prove that magic isn't real, she has to become one of us first.

12

"This is perfect," Ellis says once I've explained the Margery coven. I told her of the sanitized version of a coven that exists between the other houses, of course—but also about the Dalloway Five dancing nude and worshipping old goddesses around towering bonfires, taking arcane herbs. Stories of their magic have survived at the school even throughout the most austere administrations.

And so help me, I don't care what Dr. Ortega says anymore. The legend is real.

At the very least, Ellis should know about the Margery coven. She should see if she can be initiated.

"It's magic," I tell her. "Or the Dalloway Five believed it was. Doesn't that run *contra* your entire thesis?"

But Ellis is still pacing the narrow kitchen, the soles of her Italian leather shoes clicking against the stone floor. "Not at all. It's no different than the spiritualist séances of the Victorian era—people went wild over the idea of mediums who could commune beyond the grave. It was occult as entertainment, nothing truly paranormal. Who says the Dalloway girls couldn't have enjoyed the same kind of fun?"

"This was 1711, not 1870," I say. "That kind of fun would get you killed."

She stops pacing and turns to smile at me, a scant foot away from where I stand. She lifts a hand and trails it along my temple, tucks a stray lock of hair behind my ear. I barely remember to breathe.

"No, this is perfect," Ellis says a second time. "I promise. But who cares about those posh modern girls and their party coven. Let's make our own."

My air comes back all at once; I choke on it. Ellis pats my back as I cough until my throat is raw.

"I beg your pardon?" I croak at last.

I wanted Ellis to join the Margery coven. I wanted her to wrap herself up in the shroud of their dark games—not drag me down with her. The Margery coven felt safe. They didn't practice real magic—their craft was all about aesthetics and pretension, the foolish games of wealthy girls who wanted to feel powerful, who wanted to touch the hem of night's cloak but nothing further, nothing *real.*

"Real magic is something different. Real magic has risks."

Ellis lifts one shoulder and drops it. "Let's make our own coven. Why not? If I'm to do this properly, like a real method writer, I should explore the same pastimes the Five explored. Even if they didn't die by magic, some still believed they practiced it."

My palms are clammy as I press them to my face and suck in several hot, recycled breaths. I'm well aware of my own hypocrisy: I try to get her to join a coven, and then I balk at the very idea. But Ellis doesn't understand—even if she can flirt with devils, I can't. I can't.

"Some things shouldn't be toyed with, Ellis. Magic is dangerous."

"Magic isn't *real,*" Ellis says.

"You don't know that."

She sighs. "I suppose, if you're the kind of person who also chooses to be agnostic as to the existence of deities or fairies in the garden. Yes, there's always a *chance* it's real. But is that what you really believe?"

My jaw hurts from gritting my teeth so hard. "You know I do."

"I told you that I'd prove there was no magic involved in the Dalloway Five's deaths. There's no magic, period. We can make our coven as *magical* as you like, but no demons will rise from the underworld to meet us. And besides . . . this could be precisely how the girls are killed in my book. The Margery character needs to lure her victims away from safety. This is how."

I think that once we're out there in the forest, under the moonlight, she'll see things differently. Who knows what lurks in the woods, which beings rule the cold space beneath the trees?

Still, perhaps this is harmless. Perhaps I'm overreacting: maybe Ellis's presence alone would serve as a shield, her rational mind stalwart against the insane. I spend the rest of the night thinking about it: planning what spells we could try, how we could adapt magic that might have worked three hundred years ago for the modern day.

It isn't until the next night that my fear surges back like a briny sea, my body frozen at the door of my bedroom with my shoes on but my coat still clutched in both hands.

Something about this feels wrong. I promised I wouldn't do magic anymore; all those fantasies from last night about bonfires and bacchanals reveal their sharp edges when dusk falls.

I'm afraid that if I take this leap, there will be no coming back. I'll free-fall forever.

But that's why you have *to do it,* a voice whispers in my head, one that sounds suspiciously like Ellis Haley.

I need to be able to touch the dark without being consumed by it.

We had sent the invitations as three notes, handwritten on paper Ellis tore out of the backs of books she doesn't like and slid through the uneven cracks beneath the Godwin House bedroom doors:

Meet me here at midnight. Tell no one you're coming. Then a set of coordinates, signed with Ellis's name.

The times Ellis gave were staggered, to ensure that no one runs into each other as they leave the house—every one of the Godwin residents thinks she is coming alone.

I exhale and make myself open the door. Ellis is waiting for me downstairs, already masked. She emerges from the poor light like a slim black bone, inhuman and hollow-mouthed. It's difficult to imagine a soul exists behind the void of those empty eye sockets. In the Margery coven they told us that when the initiated wear the mask, their spirit departs their body; we are possessed instead by the ghost of a Dalloway witch. One of the Five.

I press my hand against my chest, and my heart thumps against my palm. *My* heart?

Or someone else's?

This is a mistake.

What if this is what Margery wants? Her spirit could be watching me, waiting patiently for my willpower to snap. She could possess me while I'm vulnerable, one foot already stepping into the night. She would force me to dance on her strings. To kill until the dead are satisfied. To perish so that her ghost can rest.

Perhaps I was never haunted. Perhaps this whole time Margery knew, and Alex knew, they wouldn't have to chase me.

They knew I'd come looking.

The darkness lends a sense of intimacy, of import. We move through it like specters, silent—we become part of Godwin House, sprouted from the uneven floor and shadowed corners, descendants and daughters of witches who died centuries ago.

And then we're outside, we're in the forest, following the witches' footsteps deep enough that the house vanishes into the night's open mouth, until the dark space beneath the trees hangs heavy enough that even our breath sounds muffled. An owl hoots somewhere nearby, warning of our passing. The Greeks believed witches could transform themselves into owls to stalk their prey. I can't stop thinking of the figure Ellis saw in my teacup: the bird, *dangerous situations.*

"They aren't coming," I say after we reach the clearing. The forest seems to close in around us, sharp-toothed and hungry. I take off my mask; I can't stand feeling half-blinded, unaware of what lurks just out of sight, in the corners of my eyes.

"They're coming," Ellis replies.

I don't believe her, but I get ready anyway. My bag has everything we need, materials retrieved from the hole in my closet wall: candles and herbs, a vial of goat's blood I bought from the butcher in town.

When a twig snaps I lurch upright, half expecting to see *her,* Alex. But it's just Kajal emerging from between the trees, a smudge of dirt on her knee and a scowl on her face.

"Morrow," she says. "What are you doing here?"

I know the moment she spots Ellis, from the way her spine stiffens, the reflexive half step back and away. I turn to look just as Ellis is lifting the goat's-head mask away from her face.

"It's me," she says.

"What the fuck, Ellis!"

Ellis draws a cigarette case out of her pocket. She pauses long enough to light one and blow smoke toward the stars before she says: "I'll explain when the rest arrive."

I'm caught there between them, Ellis pale and serene, Kajal shifting her weight from foot to foot as she clearly debates running back to Godwin. But she doesn't. She stays, watching in wary silence as I finish building a circle out of candles and black tourmaline. Ellis might be right—we aren't in any danger from Margery or her kin—but the protection of the crystals make me feel better all the same.

Clara and Leonie arrive over the next fifteen minutes, Leonie appearing perfectly coiffed and all but presidential, as if she were somehow transported to the middle of the woods by hired car rather than by traipsing over twig and stone. Clara looks rather worse for wear, but she doesn't complain. Perhaps she's pleased to have been invited at all.

Ellis stands at my side, her fingers pressing against the back of my elbow: careful, steadying. I doubt she knows how much I need that anchor right now.

Leonie recognizes Ellis's mask. I can tell from the way she hesitates but doesn't flinch when she sees it—the goat's skull is less horrifying if you've seen it before. Perhaps she's one of the Margery coven's newest members, inducted while I was rotting away in a hospital bed.

Does she know, then, that I was once a sister too?

That I was excommunicated?

"Ellis," Leonie says slowly, carefully, "what is that?"

Ellis, who had resumed wearing the mask after she finished her cigarette, tips it away from her face again. "It's a mask, Schuyler. What does it look like?"

"Where did you get it?"

"From me," I interject. "She got it from me. I was part of . . . Well." I can't say it out loud; even though I've been excommunicated from the Margery coven, it feels like their rules still bind me. Leonie's dark gaze holds mine, steady and knowing. "I gave it to her," I say.

"I thought we could play a little game," Ellis says, finally discarding the mask altogether and smiling at us, her acolytes, gathered for her homily. "You've heard of the Dalloway Five, I presume."

Nods all around.

"Your book is about them," Clara ventures. "The witches."

"That's right. And you know my style—I'm a method writer. They say the Dalloway girls were witches, or at least that they had séances and cast spells. So I must as well."

Clara gazes adoringly at Ellis as if Ellis had just offered her true and everlasting friendship for the low price of her eternal soul. Leonie and Kajal exchange looks.

"I think it's a wonderful idea," I say at last, because it's clear these two aren't convinced but are too nervous to contradict Ellis to her face.

"Me too," Clara adds.

Kajal twists a lock of black hair around her finger. "I suppose it could be fun. . . ."

One left. Ellis turns her gaze toward Leonie, and Leonie sighs, then nods. Our pact is sealed.

"We need a name," Clara says. Her tone is too bright for the setting, at odds with the heavy tree cover and the treacherous vines snaking underfoot.

A name. It feels irreverent somehow to *name* what we're doing. Then again, to Clara this *is* a game. She doesn't understand how magic can pull you in, pull you under. Every spell is a pomegranate seed on your tongue, binding you to the underworld.

Maybe not for everyone. But it is for people like me.

the red berries of the mountain ash
and in the dark sky
the birds' night migrations

"What did you say?" Leonie is looking at me strangely; I must have spoken aloud.

I swallow. " 'The Night Migrations,' " I say. "You know, the Louise Glück poem."

Blank stares answer me. My discomfort aches inside me like a swallowed rock.

"From *Averno,*" Ellis says after a moment, and when I turn to her, she's smiling. "In which the poet writes of Persephone and her marriage to the underworld. The poems circle the same question: how one's soul could possibly endure when life's beauty vanishes from reach."

"Yes," I whisper.

Alex wrote an essay on those poems. Her copy of *Averno* probably still resides on the Godwin House shelves.

Ellis nods once, as if a decision has been made.

"Welcome," she says, "to the Night Migrations."

The silence that follows stretches out like a long ribbon, silky-smooth; we are all like changeling children hanging on to Ellis's every word.

"There are rules," Ellis continues. "First: no talking about the Night Migrations. Not unless we're here in the woods, or at any other meeting location."

"This isn't Fight Club," Kajal says.

"No, but it's more fun this way," Ellis answers. "Second: Felicity and I choose when and where. There will be no argument or discussion on this point. Third, you will know the week's meeting time and place from a note we slide under your door. Since you won't be discussing the Night Migrations with anyone else, you won't know what time the others are told to arrive. But I *will* tell you that the arrival times are staggered. The journey to our meeting location is part of the experience. As in life, every woman must make her journey alone."

Ellis's gaze flicks toward me then, and I think I catch a glint of something like amusement in her gray eyes—although that might just be the candlelight. If our game were real, the journey of the Night Migrations would play out as it does in the real world: born alone, die alone. *Now,* one of the *Averno* poems reads, *her whole life is beginning—unfortunately, it's going to be a short life.*

"And what is that?" Kajal says distastefully, pointing at the circle I've constructed, then at the assortment of mouse skulls lined up along the rock. All of them collected last year, all found in Godwin House. I hadn't thought them uncanny until later, after Alex died.

"You don't get to play the game if you don't follow our rules," I say.

Beside me, Ellis smiles.

The next morning my memories of the initiation are blurry, oil paint bleeding into water. I remember the way the others looked on the forest floor, dead leaves and bracken scattered in their laps. I remember painting the blood on Ellis's brow, Ellis gazing at me as if she could see through my mask and into the heart of me.

My fingers were still on her skin, wet and scarlet, as she murmured my name.

Whatever else the others felt, I knew what I saw in Ellis's eyes last night.

Euphoria.

The most vital part of any occult ritual is the closing. Witches, Druids, and Auguries might interface with creatures of the Dead, but we are also obligated to protect the mortal world from arcane influences. When we open a door, we must also shut it, or risk inviting Evil in.

—*Profane Magick*

Alexandra Haywood, the elite mountaineer and the second-youngest girl to summit Denali, has disappeared while attending her boarding school. She is 17. Haywood was recently in the news for her involvement in a physical altercation with fellow climber Esme Delacroix. An anonymous detective speaking to the Associated Press said the police are considering multiple theories. Divers are scouring the campus lake in case of an accidental drowning, but detectives have not ruled out the possibility that Haywood ran away to avoid public scrutiny over the assault.

—Excerpt from an article by Mariely Reyes,
journalist at *Sport Climbing Quarterly*

13

"I got something for you," Ellis says.

She has appeared in my doorway without invitation, which is becoming something of a habit. She's wearing a tweed waistcoat and a cravat, one hand tucked behind her back.

I look at her forehead for signs of the bloody sigil we painted there last night, but her skin is clear and clean.

I shut my laptop halfway, so that the technology doesn't offend her vintage sensibilities. "Not more tea leaves."

"Better," she assures me, and comes into the room without being asked. "Put out your hand."

I do. She places on my palm a package wrapped in brown paper and tied with a neat length of twine. I glance up and she nods, so I tug at one string, and the bow unravels, the paper falling away to reveal—

"Ellis." My voice comes out half a gasp; I'd be humiliated by that gasp if I weren't so busy staring at the tarot cards that fan out between my fingers. They're matte black, lined only with the faintest threads of metallic gold tracing out the shapes of skeleton figures, a glossy jet finish poured into the

cages of skulls and bones so they glint in the afternoon light. "These are . . ."

"I thought you'd like them," she says.

I drag my gaze away from the cards and back to Ellis's face. A small smile has caught about her lips, a smile that feels genuine not because it splits across her face or crinkles the corners of her eyes but because of the softness to it—and the way her gaze lingers on mine. I hold out the deck of cards, and she chooses one from the middle, then flips it over to show the Magician.

"Whatever it is you're trying to do," I interpret, "you will succeed. All the power you need is in your hands."

"I certainly hope so," she says.

I pack the cards away in a position of honor on my shelf, right next to the candles and my one photo of Alex and me, taken by the lake with evening sunlight blazing like fire in Alex's hair. The photo used to live in the closet with all the other paraphernalia of my old life; I only managed to look at it again last night. And then, gazing at the pair of us and the smiles on our faces, I felt guilty shoving her back into the dark.

"Is this her?" Ellis asks, coming up to stand at my shoulder.

"That's her." I stare at Alex's face: the soft uptilt of her nose, her cinnamon-dust freckles and red bow lips. The Alex in that photo had no idea she would be dead within the year.

"You look young," Ellis says, and I suppose I do. I'm laughing, one arm slung over Alex's broad shoulders, like I think I'll get to keep her forever.

"It was two years ago. I was sixteen."

We'd just moved into Godwin House. When this photo was taken, I still didn't believe in ghosts.

Ellis looks for a second longer before finally turning away, taking claim to my desk chair, and leaving me to sit on the edge of my bed. "There's something else," she says. "I'd like to finish my book by the end of this year, which means we don't have much time. I still need to figure out how the deaths happened."

"All right." I reach for my notebook, grabbing it off the desk where it sat by Ellis's elbow. She hands me a pen.

I hold the pen for a moment, the weight of it like a bad omen. Maybe last night was a mistake. It's not too late to take back my agreement and put an end to this.

But then Ellis starts talking, cutting the thread that twines through my doubts.

"First," she says, "the hypothetical victims. Four deaths, one for each of the Dalloway witches—not counting Margery Lemont, of course, my narrator."

"A bit morbid," I say. "We aren't going to be acting this out ourselves, are we?"

Ellis laughs. I realize now it's the first time I've heard her laugh, the sound bright and clear as winter bells. "You're delightful," she says. "Of course we will. We will each have the singular opportunity to inhabit the histories of Flora Grayfriar, Tamsyn Penhaligon, Beatrix Walker, and Cordelia Darling. It will be like a game."

"A game," I echo.

Ellis nods. "A game. Don't be a spoilsport, Felicity—this will be fun."

Fun.

I grip the seat of my chair with my free hand, palms gone damp. The prickle at the nape of my neck must be the breeze drifting in through the cracked window, chilled as it rolls off the lake.

Ellis and I have very different ideas of fun. But she needs this. And so, it seems, do I.

"Fine. I presume the magic isn't real in your book, considering your position on the subject. The witches aren't really communing with the devil, they're just laboring under the oppressive weight of societal expectation."

"Oh, yes," Ellis says, and kicks out one foot to knock the sharp toe of her oxford against my shin. "Witchcraft is just a metaphor for female grief and anger. I told you that."

"Right. Of course. How could I forget."

"That's why this will be good for you, Felicity," Ellis says. "So that you *don't* forget."

It feels the slightest bit juvenile, the two of us sitting around in my room like this, talking about hypothetical murder—a scene better suited to children at sleepover parties, huddled under the covers clutching flashlights. But Ellis has likely never worn pajamas in her life, never mind attended sleepovers. Perhaps our plans become sophisticated by the mere virtue of her presence.

"Let's talk about method," Ellis muses, propping her chin against one hand and gazing out my window as if she can glean ideas from the pattern of the shadows in the woods. "Each of the Dalloway Five died a different way: Flora was stabbed, Tamsyn strangled, Cordelia drowned—"

"I'm not stabbing anyone," I say.

The look Ellis gives me is a shade shy of derision. "Felicity, this isn't—"

"I'm not fake-stabbing anyone, either."

She sighs. "All right, we can each take on a different murder. If I have to consider stabbing someone, then it's only fair that you strangle Tamsyn."

"Good, the easy one. All I have to do is string her up on a noose. *Forty feet above the ground.*"

That's why people thought these deaths were magic—they all happened in incredible, impossible ways. There's no explanation for how Tamsyn Penhaligon's corpse was found swinging so high up that tree, too high for anyone to have climbed without the branches breaking under their weight.

"Yes," Ellis says, "but the murders don't need to be *exact* replications. We both know historical representation of fact is more or less political propaganda. We need to find ways for the Five to have died that *approximate* their recorded causes of death. A story told again and again is never the same story as the original. So Leonie should be strangled, as in the Dalloway myth, but not by a noose. What about—*oh.*"

"What?"

Ellis sits a little straighter in her chair now, eyes glimmering with an unseen light. "A garrote."

"You mean like . . ." I gesture as if tightening an invisible wire around my neck.

"Precisely. Minimal blood, silent; it's ideal. They used to use it during war, to kill sentries without alerting other enemy soldiers."

I really don't know where she acquires such information. I've read Ellis's first book. It has nothing to do with war, which means this wasn't part of her research.

But I have to admit, I like the idea. It seems . . . Romantic, with the capital *R,* conjuring visions of dashing heroines and vicious assassins, of hazy London streets and the click of horse hooves on stone, gas lamps burning, the flick of a cloak in the dark.

It seems like precisely the kind of fate that could have met a person in 1712.

"A garrote," I echo, and find myself tracing a circle on my notebook, over and over: a circle of piano wire perhaps.

"Do you like it?"

Pleased is not an expression I'm accustomed to seeing on Ellis Haley's face, but it's infectious; I find myself smiling back at her as I write down the method: *garrote.*

"All right," I say when I look up again. "You know, one of the interesting things about the Dalloway case was that there were no suspects—everyone just claimed the girls' deaths were the inevitable price of witchcraft."

Margery's directly so, if you consider being buried alive by vengeful townspeople to be a fitting end for her magical crimes.

"Yes, that's my point," Ellis says, perhaps a bit impatiently. "It's terribly convenient, isn't it? The witches all die in witchy ways, no murder about it. Do you really believe that?"

I don't want to dignify that with an answer. Especially when we both know what the answer really is.

"Fine," I say. "But is that what you want to do in the book as well? I thought you were going to have Margery be the killer?"

"Are you two planning to come down for supper?"

I snap around toward the door at the sound of the voice. I was too quick to avoid looking suspicious; for her part, Ellis is perfectly unfazed by the appearance of Leonie Schuyler in my room. Today, Leonie wears a tartan skirt and a neat blazer furnished with an elaborately knotted silk scarf: the very picture of an old-fashioned schoolgirl. She no longer has the loose coils of before; now her hair is a cascade of braids entwined with delicate gold thread. She didn't even mention she was going into the city, but she must have: everything about her looks professionally styled. For some reason I'm struck by the reality that the other Godwin girls have lives that don't involve us—don't involve *Ellis.*

"That depends," Ellis says. "It's Kajal's turn tonight, right? What did she make?"

I wonder if Leonie can hear my heart beating from all the way across the room. It certainly feels like it's about to pound its way right out of my chest.

"Coq au vin," Leonie says. "With a side of hasselback potatoes and salad. She made some kind of vegetarian version of the chicken for you, Ellis."

Vegetarian coq au vin sounds repulsive to me, but Kajal's a fantastic cook, so I put aside my notebook and we follow Leonie downstairs. Ellis glances back at me as we descend, her hand trailing along the railing and her scarlet lips quirking, the only acknowledgment of our shared secret.

Once she's turned away I let my fingertips graze mahogany. I touch the same place she had touched, and it's like a cord drawn taut between us—as intimate as skin.

14

Things change in the days following that first Night Migration.

Whether the magic was real or not, something bound us together in those woods. Leonie puts music on the record player, Kajal dances in a red dress. Even Clara seems to be more at ease, her smiles coming quicker when we laugh over dinner. It feels like *Godwin* again, the way it did before. Like we're sisters.

That first week is painted in vivid color. I read tarot for the other girls in the common room: Kajal half-drunk making me draw cards for her again and again until she gets the results she wants, Leonie draping a veil over her head like the High Priestess, Ellis curled up on the sofa studying the Magician. Clara plants herbs in window boxes that wilt two days later; she cries about it, even though they're just plants, and for some reason I feel sorry enough to comfort her.

It takes that whole week for me to define what's happening, to say *I'm happy,* in those words. But I say it, a declaration made while standing on the coffee table with my arms outspread, a declaration that earns whoops and applause from the rest of them, Ellis helping me down with one black-gloved hand.

I'm happy. Ellis was right: I'm getting *better.*

I bury what's left of my pills in the backyard under Tamsyn Penhaligon's oak tree, pressing quartz into the soil above them. I don't need them anymore. I'm not that *person* anymore. I'm not the girl who saw ghosts in every corner, who feared her mind was host to a darker and more parasitic presence.

I'm going to be all right now.

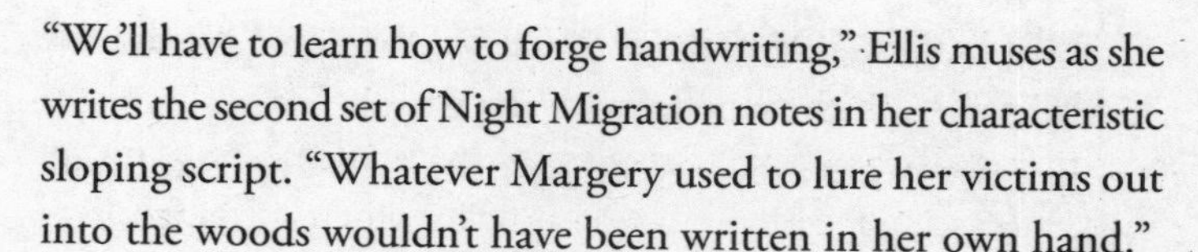

"We'll have to learn how to forge handwriting," Ellis muses as she writes the second set of Night Migration notes in her characteristic sloping script. "Whatever Margery used to lure her victims out into the woods wouldn't have been written in her own hand."

It is starting to seem to me as if Ellis has an answer for everything. She wants us to break into a locked building just to find out if we can, to mark the locations of every security camera around Godwin House, to research the best way to remove bloodstains from clothing. I have no idea how much of this, if any, will make it into Ellis's book.

"I doubt Margery wrote notes at all," I say, but Ellis shrugs and adds a flourish to Clara's name on the final envelope.

"Perhaps not. But this way's more fun, don't you think?"

Tonight, Ellis chooses the location, one much closer than the clearing I sent us to last time. It's a brief walk through the forest, dead leaves crunching underfoot and the beams of our flashlights bobbing amid the branches.

Ellis and I get to the meeting place at 11:40, five minutes before Leonie is supposed to arrive, just early enough to try and get a fire started. Ellis is dressed in hues of charcoal gray and black; she all but blends in with the landscape, a shadow among shadows. Next to her, in ivory, I feel like a lantern. This time, we forgo the masks.

"A new moon," Ellis says, turning her face toward the starless sky. "I don't know why the myths always pair a full moon with the uncanny. Total darkness is so much more paralyzing."

"I suppose under a new moon, you're less likely to die by meeting a ghost than you are tripping over your own feet."

Ellis laughs. "Or perhaps you'll be murdered by the two Godwin girls, in the woods, with the garrote."

Just two weeks ago, I would have flinched. Tonight, I smile with her instead.

I crouch down on the forest floor and pick up a long stick, prod at the weak shambles of our fire. It's still smoldering coals and flickering twigs—hardly the rapturous bonfire we'd envisioned. I blow on the coals, and sparks spray into the air like fireflies. We'd built a circle of stones to keep from accidentally burning the woods down, but that risk is starting to feel very distant indeed.

"We should meet in a graveyard next time," Ellis muses. She leans past me to light her cigarette on the flames, which have finally started to ignite the gathered timber.

Leonie arrives soon thereafter, then the other two; they plop themselves down on the ground as if they've forgotten to care what happens to their tailored skirts.

Ellis positions herself by the fire, posed such that the flames appear to be licking up the straight legs of her trousers, consuming her. She holds her book in both hands: a reverend presiding over her flock.

"Ex scientia ultio," she says.

Only the crack and snap of smoldering wood answers her, like gunshots in the empty night. In the half-light we look like ghosts.

I've never felt like this before. The Margery coven was different—constructed for alumnae connections and nepotism, not sisterhood. *This* . . . this is real.

"What happened to the goat's blood?" Kajal says.

"It's a poetry reading." Leonie has clearly spotted the book in Ellis's hand. I half expected it to come out sounding derisive, but it doesn't. There's an upward tilt to the words, delight making music of Leonie's voice.

Ellis lifts *Averno* and smiles.

"It seemed appropriate," she says, "given our name."

We stand in a circle around the fire and read—Ellis first, then she passes the book to Clara, who takes over. Around the circle two times, thrice. Ellis unearths a flask of bourbon from my bag, and we drink that, too, choking down the bitter liquor and telling ourselves it doesn't taste like gasoline. By the time we have read the last poem, my mind feels pleasantly liquid, my thoughts floating on the surface of a golden sea. Clara clasps both my hands in hers and smiles like a child, Kajal dances in the bracken and Leonie lies on her back, dirt forgotten.

"Look how easily they give over to emotion," Ellis murmurs, her fingers slipping into my hair, her lips whisper-cool against my ear. "No drugs or magic necessary. Couldn't the Dalloway Five have done the same?"

But if this is magic, it isn't the kind the Five practiced. I'm sure of it. For once, the forest is empty of ghosts, the sky clear and glittering. Nothing evil can touch us like this. We're dryads cavorting in autumn, wood spirits breathing out starlight.

Eventually, though, even dryads must sleep. We stagger home in single file, bramble-cut and smelling of campfire smoke. The next day Ellis tears a poem out of *Averno* and pins it to her bedroom wall and tells me this is it, the beginning of everything, the first page of our story. A story that has no dark corners, just us, just happiness and freedom.

Strangely, I believe her.

Sunday, Ellis and I go down to the lake. Ellis has brought a picnic basket with cheeses, cranberry juice, fennel crackers, and a map of the surrounding terrain.

The lake glitters gold in the early-morning sunlight, its surface calm and even. I know Alex's body isn't in there—the silted floor was searched by divers, every cave scoured along the shore—but I can't help shivering.

"What's this?" I ask, pointing to the map.

She unfolds it across the grass and gestures to the lake with her cheese knife. "The lake," she says. "And here"—she points a half mile east, on Godwin grounds—"is where Cordelia Darling's body was found."

So that's what this is, then. Another murder, dissected and resolved.

"With water in her lungs," I murmur. Cordelia Darling had drowned on dry land, reason enough for some to suspect witchery.

I just wish Ellis had brought me here to discuss a different Dalloway Five death. Anyone's except Cordelia's.

Ellis has assembled a little sandwich of cheese between crackers; she offers it to me, and I take it just to have the distraction. The taste is sharp and peppery all at once.

"You can see where Cordelia was found from here," Ellis says, and she touches my chin, gently directs my face toward the sunrise. "Look."

Yes, I can see it. The patch of grass is as indistinguishable as any around it, especially from this distance. Godwin rises above Cordelia's temporary grave on its wooded hill, shuttered windows and uneven gables: a shadowy tombstone.

"I know what you're going to say," I tell her. "Someone drowned Cordelia, or she drowned on her own, and then she was carried a half mile that way. Mystery solved."

"Mmm, yes, the answer is rather obvious, isn't it?" Ellis says with an arched brow; I can't tell if she's making fun of me.

But this time, it's my turn to have the upper hand. "The lake didn't exist in the early eighteenth century," I say. I tap the map. "This was just a valley. The lake itself was man-made as a flood prevention measure in 1904. There was just the Hudson, and it runs narrow through here."

Ellis's brow furrows, and she hunches over the map again, presumably to examine the little topographic lines that show the steepness of the cliffs and depth of the valleys around Dalloway School. "Really?"

I take another bite of cracker. "Really."

"Curious," Ellis murmurs, and I can't help but feel somewhat gratified that I've finally said something to throw her off balance. It feels like winning.

"Besides, even eighteenth-century bigots knew that it's not impossible to carry a skinny teenage girl half a mile across land," I say, "soaking wet or otherwise."

Ellis looks up. "Yes. But we also know that it doesn't take that much water to drown a person, considering. You could drown in your bathtub. You could drown in a shallow puddle of rainwater."

"You could," I agree, "but then why not leave the body in the bathtub to be found later? Why take her outside? That only makes you more likely to get caught."

It's enough to make Ellis fall into pensive silence for the next several minutes. I occupy myself with the cheese and crackers, and drink a long swig of sour juice straight from the bottle. Ellis squints out across the lawn toward where Cordelia's body was found. The way her face scrunches up cuts a wrinkle right below the single freckle on her cheekbone.

"Are we really doing all of these?" I ask her eventually, after she's finally reached over to steal the cranberry juice from me.

"All of them," Ellis says, with a faint lilt of surprise to her tone. She looks at me. "What else, Felicity? There's no better way for me to write about their deaths."

I sigh. "Lovely. When will we be finished? I do have my own thesis to work on, you know."

"It won't take too long," Ellis promises. "I have to be done by the end of winter if I want to get the book written and revised by deadline. I'll need all of spring to work on revisions."

"Fine. But you still haven't explained to me how Cordelia Darling's body ended up drowned on dry land."

Ellis's gaze cuts back toward the lake, her eyes narrowed against the bright sunlight. "Isn't it obvious?" she says. "Whoever drowned her brought her out here to make it *look* like magic. They wanted the Dalloway girls to be blamed for it. And they got what they wanted."

I track a path along the ground, from the lake across the field, back up the hill toward Godwin House perched like a bird of prey upon the rocks, silently observing. If they'd been looking, someone in the house would have been able to see what happened. But they hadn't looked, and so the mystery persists.

"You said you're writing Margery as the villain," I mention eventually.

"I am."

"Then why would she want to frame her own friends for the deaths? Why not frame the townspeople?"

Ellis shrugs. "Who knows? The mind of a psychopath is an uninterpretable thing. Perhaps she thought it was more entertaining that way, to sow fear and hysteria among the coven—who can you trust, who can't you, and so on."

I find myself unpersuaded, but I nod anyway.

"There's just one thing," Ellis says. She dusts the cracker crumbs from her hands and pushes to her feet, offering to help me up after her.

"And what is that?"

"Pick me up."

"I *beg* your pardon?"

Ellis's brow arches. "If it *was* Margery who killed all the others, she would have needed to drag Cordelia Darling's body out here, wouldn't she? But we've seen the painting of her. She wasn't a large girl."

Ellis is the furthest thing from a corpse. She's bright-eyed and impatient, watching me with arms crossed over her chest and the wind blowing stray black hairs across her face. And yet when I crouch down to lift her she feels like dead weight in my arms. I take two steps and stumble, my breath lurching in my throat.

"Steady now," Ellis murmurs, her breath hot against my neck.

I grit my teeth and take another step. "What did you eat for breakfast, rocks?"

"Well, I am prodigiously tall for my age. I weigh quite a bit more than you do."

I make it another three feet then give up, unceremoniously dumping Ellis onto the grass and collapsing next to her, sweaty and breathless. She falls onto her back, arms splayed across the dirt, and for a moment I worry I've hurt her somehow, broken something when I let her go—but then she says:

"Margery could have dragged her."

"What?"

Ellis stays right where she is, loose-limbed and still. "Margery dragged her. She wouldn't have needed to *carry* Cordelia across the field. There are other ways to transport a body. This isn't proof she wasn't involved."

My hands twist up in my dress. "I'm not going to drag you anywhere."

At last Ellis pushes herself up onto her elbows, fixing me in her gaze. "No," she says after a moment. "You don't have to. You could, though. If you tried."

She crawls back over to the picnic blanket, leaving me standing there, aching and damp-faced, behind her until she's poured fresh glasses of juice and called for me, and I, obediently, follow.

"Go without me," Ellis says the night of the Lemont House Halloween party the following week; she's sitting in the common room on one of the high stools by the windows, gazing out down the hill, with her dark hair tumbling about her shoulders and ink stains on her sleeve. "I need to write."

We might have grown closer, but the four of us still make an awkward crew without Ellis's grounding presence. Even so, we go without her. Leonie's brought a flask; she passes it around as we traipse down the drive and across the quad, sharing Ellis's bourbon (of course; no escaping Ellis's influence, even in Ellis's absence) and each other's spit. I'm the only one who bothered dressing up—the others are all costumed in their usual plaid skirts and cable-knit sweaters, Leonie with a beret perched atop her head, and Kajal's skinny legs all wrapped up in wool stockings. My Persephone costume seems absurd in juxtaposition.

"I wish it was only Godwin House," Clara sighs as we pass

a knot of giggling first-years with their flimsy disguises: sexy nurse, sexy vampire, sexy priestess. "I wish we were here and no one else."

A murmur of agreement rolls from one of us to the next, and it's only after I've said my part that I wonder if it's even true. Do I wish we were alone? Do I think we're so different from all the rest of them? Better, even?

"A school just for Godwin girls," I muse aloud, saying what I know they want to hear. "We'd establish our own new theoretical perspective on the classic literary canon. They'd cite us in books."

"Invite us to speak at conferences."

"Interview us in the *Times.*"

"Debate whether we're idiots or geniuses."

"We're both," Leonie says, and even Kajal laughs.

But I can't share their levity. A year ago Alex and I left this same party, went back to Godwin with the stolen Margery Skull concealed under my coat. We lit candles and spilled blood and called up the darkness.

This year, Samhain itself doesn't fall until later in the week. But I can feel it approaching, the veil between this world and the next stretching ever thinner.

What might cross over when that veil splits?

I wish Ellis was here now, her arm looped through my elbow and her lips grazing my ear as she murmurs secrets. It's easier to forget my ghosts when I have her.

The event is well under way by the time we arrive. We're greeted by a girl wearing a top hat and a sour expression; clearly she drew the short straw for door duty tonight. The girl takes our coats and our bags and ushers us into the house proper, watching impatiently as we shuck off our shoes.

I regret that part soon enough. The floor is already sticky with spilled beer, red plastic cups are stacked on nearly every flat surface, and a few students dance with themselves in the living room where someone's pushed all the furniture up to the walls.

"It's a good thing Ellis didn't come," Kajal says, and Leonie neatly sidesteps an intoxicated girl who almost stumbles into her on her way to the drinks table.

She says it because she thinks Ellis wouldn't like this kind of party, but I'm not sure I agree. I could see Ellis perfectly at home here; even with her dress shirts and suspenders, even in shiny bespoke shoes, she would inhabit this space the same way she does every other: like she belongs.

"I'm going to get a drink," I say, and shoulder my way past a knot of rowdy Claremont House students to peruse the libations on offer. Almost every bottle left contains tequila.

This party is nothing like the Boleyn House fête at the start of the year, but I'm reminded of that night all the same. Clara is talking to Leonie about something inane, using gesture as punctuation, like she thinks everyone in this room ought to stop and listen to what she has to say, like she thinks she's more important and more interesting than anyone else here. The murders Ellis and I are plotting might be hypothetical, but I can't help thinking that one day, someone will get sick of Clara and push her down the stairs.

The tequila sloshes over my fingers when I pour it into a cup. Cheap clear liquor, the kind that burns on the way down and on the way back up, but erases the memory of everything that happens in between. I start drinking, and once I start, I find it hard to stop.

Just like your mother, a voice murmurs in the back of my mind. It should be enough to inspire sobriety, but thinking of my mother only makes me drink more.

The party slides into a blur of faces and bodies. I'm with the Godwin girls for most of the beginning; I remember that much. But then somehow I end up in the Lemont backyard under glittering market lights, slow jazz playing on vinyl, swaying with my hands reaching toward the sky. I find a beautiful girl who has eyes like night and skin cool as water. I tell the girl that, as I slide my touch along her cheek. A serial killer sort of thing to say—*I love your skin*—but she smiles at me.

"So forgiving," I murmur. Her hand has caught my dress, thumb pushing a button free at its collar.

She looks nothing like Alex. Her hair is brown, not red. Her complexion is dark, not pale. But when I kiss her, I see Alex all the same.

Possession, I think, just for a moment. But is it really such a strange possibility as to be *im*possible? This girl's hands are Alex's hands, her tongue Alex's tongue. I want to lace our souls together and make her forgive me.

The kiss breaks, and the girl touches my lips, our breath shallow and hot between us. "Do you want to go upstairs?" she says.

The answer rises to my mouth, but before I can say yes, I spot her: Ellis Haley, a slim figure in a tweed suit, watching us from across the backyard with her cigarette burning down to ashes in one hand.

"What is it?" asks the girl who isn't Alex. When I look at her, she has her brows knit together and uncertainty written all over her face.

I take it back. This girl isn't possessed. Alex has never been uncertain about anything in her life.

My gaze flicks back over her shoulder. Ellis is already gone.

"I have to go." I extract myself from her arms and chase after the spot where Ellis had stood. The air still smells like her cigarette smoke, but the crowd has swallowed her up; I spin around, but all I see are strangers.

It's freezing out here. How had I not noticed how cold it is?

Everyone out in the backyard exists in their own little world; I have to shove my way through with sharp elbows to get back inside. But inside is worse. Bass thumps through the floor, the windows sweating with the humidity of so many bodies; I trip over someone's discarded shoes and hit the ground hard enough that it sends shock waves ricocheting up from my knees.

"Are you okay?"

It's Hannah Stratford, of all people. She crouches down next to me, her mouth in a little pink O of affected concern.

"Fine," I say.

She has her hands on my arm anyway, helping me up. I wonder if she saw me kissing the ghost in the backyard. I wonder who else saw, how many whispers are passing from lip to ear: *I saw Felicity Morrow . . .*

Ellis watching me, her cigarette an ember in the dark.

I kept being lesbian a secret for years. Now I've thrown it away to join the rest of the trash littering this house.

"Are you drunk?" Hannah asks, a question stupid enough to rival her first.

"No," I say. "I just hate everyone."

It's not what she expects to hear. She frowns, her mind working overtime to square that with the Felicity Morrow that exists in her imagination.

"You're drunk," she decides at last, and settles my arm around her shoulders even though I'm mostly steady on my feet. "Maybe we should get you home. . . ."

"I can walk, thank you." I shift out of her grasp and reach up to grab my hair, pulling it into a ponytail. For some reason that makes me feel more sober. "I'll see you around, Hannah," I say.

I can't find my coat at the door, so I stagger home without one, teeth chattering by the time I'm climbing the hill to Godwin House.

The door all but slams shut behind me.

"Ellis?" I call her name from the foyer.

No one answers. It's late; even the light beneath Housemistress MacDonald's door is dark.

I drag a plaid throw blanket off the sofa and wrap it around myself. Godwin House is old and badly insulated; it's not much warmer than outside.

There are other reasons it might be cold, Alex's voice murmurs in the back of my mind. I shunt her aside.

I climb the stairs to the second floor. Unlike MacDonald's room, Ellis's light is still on.

I knock.

There is no response.

"Ellis? It's me." A beat. "Felicity."

Still no reply. But I can hear the creak of a floorboard as she—what? Shifts in her chair? Moves across the room?

Ellis is in there. She's just ignoring me.

I hover in the hall a moment longer, staring at the strip of yellow light under her door, hoping to see a shadow cross the floor and betray Ellis's position. But nothing else moves. I imagine her sitting at her desk, watching the door the same way I watch the door. Waiting me out.

So I do it. I leave.

I let her win.

The girl became a crow, the crow became bones,
bones became dust. I wonder now if such curses
are bestowed only upon the wicked.

—Ellis Haley, *Night Bird*

Patient is emotionally labile, with increasingly erratic mood swings and heightened environmental reactivity. Positive symptoms observed: fixed delusions and auditory-visual hallucinations that are refractory to therapeutic intervention. Will recommend and discuss antipsychotic treatment regimen with pt's parent.

—Medical record note, Silver Lake Recovery Center

The Devil has my consent, & goes & hurts them.

—Abigail Hobbs, confessed witch,
The Examination of Abigail Hobbs at Salem Village,
April 19, 1692

15

When I wake up next morning—late, with a pounding headache and the taste of old socks in my mouth—Ellis has already left Godwin House.

I drink her leftover cold coffee in the kitchen and swallow as many acetaminophen as I can handle on an empty stomach. Then I make myself take a shower and get dressed and apply my makeup with a tight jaw and a steady hand. I'm not going to be that girl. I'm not the kind of girl you ignore.

"Where's Ellis?" I ask Housemistress MacDonald, standing in the doorway of her office.

"You look very pretty today, Felicity."

"Thank you. Have you seen Ellis?"

MacDonald gives me a look that suggests she's surprised I don't already know the answer to that question.

"It's Saturday, dear. She's at fencing practice."

Of course she is.

I find out where practice is held by looking up the fencing team's website on my phone, then set off across the quad with a coffee thermos clutched in one hand and the sofa throw wrapped around my shoulders; that coat I lost was the only one I had.

I haven't been in the athletic complex yet this year. *Before,* I used to go all the time: tennis, treadmill, the climbing wall with Alex. Now I'm an interloper in foreign territory.

The building where the gym is located used to be a hospital—Saint Agatha's Sanitarium—or so I'd read once, from an old property record buried deep in the Dalloway library archives. The interior still bears relics of that history. The training room used to be a morgue; the drain on the floor would have carried away blood and fluids during autopsies. The erstwhile surgery is now the locker room, but the observation balcony still circles overhead, empty seats gathering dust, ghosts watching us undress from above.

Patients at Saint Agatha's used to have to pay a fee when they were admitted. The money was intended to cover burial costs.

The fencing practice suites are on the fourth floor. I let myself in and stand against the wall, watching identical women in masks jab and slash at each other. There's something elegant about it—something that reminds me of dance. The swords are slim steel cutting through space, long limbs that move to a rhythm only the dancers hear.

Even though all the fencers are in the same white uniform, wearing the same mesh masks, I spot Ellis almost immediately. No one else is so tall, so slim-shouldered and narrow-hipped; no one else would move so decisively.

If the rest of them dance, Ellis preys.

She spots me a few seconds in, falling into a backstep as

her faceless mask turns toward me; her opponent lunges, and the blade snaps against Ellis's chest.

I smile.

Ellis tugs off her helmet and stalks across the floor toward me. Her hair has frayed free from her bun, wisps plastered to her sweaty forehead, and her cheeks have gone red. "You distracted me."

"You ignored me last night."

She braces the tip of her épée against the tile, a conquistadora. "Is this supposed to make us even?"

It's the same game we'd played before the start of the semester. This time, I won't lose.

"Why didn't you answer your door when I knocked?"

"I was writing, Felicity. I didn't want to be disturbed."

"Really. Because I'd assumed you were done writing for the night, considering you came to the party after all."

She stares at me for a long moment, one bead of sweat cutting a path down past the bridge of her nose. Her mouth is a flat line. "Perhaps I found myself reinspired."

My lips quirk up. And, at last, Ellis is the first to look away.

"Come on," she says, grabbing my elbow and steering me toward the door. "I'm done practicing anyway."

I wait outside the locker room while she showers and changes out of her lamé. It's a cold walk back to Godwin House, Ellis's wet hair frosting over as we tramp across the quad, then melting all over the floor as soon as we're inside. I go straight to the fireplace in the common room, my hand shaking as I strike a match three, four times before it lights.

"Shit," Ellis murmurs, breathing into her cupped palms.

She's still trembling as she comes to sit down on the floor with me, both of us huddled together and waiting for the flames to catch. Her hair drips onto my shoulder; I feel the ice all the way down in my bones.

"It's only October twenty-ninth," I say. "It's going to get worse."

"I don't want to think about it."

We sit there for a while without speaking, the silence punctuated only by the crackle of wood as it alights. Ellis's fingertips are whiter than the rest of her hands, as if that part of her body has died.

I wonder how long it took Alex's body to turn that color. I imagine the cold winter preserving her flesh, her corpse broken but beautiful as a winter doll.

"Are you going home for Thanksgiving?" Ellis asks eventually.

I shake my head. "My mother's in Paris until the new year. I think she forgot there's a holiday."

"I'm not, either," Ellis says. "I already have to go back for winter break. That's quite long enough for me."

I'm dying to ask Ellis about her family. She never mentions them, and I have no idea if her parents are still together, if she had a happy childhood, whether her family supported her dream of being a writer. Maybe a normal person would ask. But only people with loving families like talking about them; when people ask about my mother, I always lie.

"There's nothing back in Savannah for me, anyway," Ellis says, and I glance over, not entirely able to hide my surprise.

"What do you mean?"

She sighs and shifts back onto her elbows, reclining against the rugs and stretching her feet toward the hearth. "We lived out in the middle of nowhere—not really the city proper. My moms have an estate on hundreds of acres; the nearest neighbor is miles away."

"Don't you have school friends?"

"I didn't go to school," she says. "My parents were the kind of rich people who felt that spending hundreds of thousands of dollars on a small army of private tutors was a better investment than Emma Willard. Of course, that meant Quinn was my only friend—and they started at Yale when I was eight. That left the tutors. And the dogs, naturally."

I assume Quinn is Ellis's sibling; clearly the Haley parents have a fondness for surnames as first names.

After a moment I lie back as well, settling in close enough that I can feel Ellis's chest rising and falling with every breath, my head nestled in the crook of her shoulder. "Is that why you started writing? Because you were bored?"

"Maybe. Probably." She drapes a hand over her eyes. "Yes."

I turn my face toward her and inhale; her hair's still wet, but it smells like lemon.

"My mother's crazy," I confess. It's easier to say when Ellis can't see me. "Better now, perhaps; or perhaps she's traveling so often I don't notice anymore. But when I was younger . . . you never knew which version of her you would get. Maybe today she thinks you're the best person in the world, or maybe not. Maybe her life is falling apart and it's all your fault."

Or maybe she's drowned herself in another bottle of vintage Clicquot and needs you to rescue her again.

Ellis doesn't say anything. I'm grateful for that—I don't

know that there's anything she *could* say that would be better than silence. Her hand falls from her face to drape across my knee instead, the two of us like twin corpses side by side. Her eyes are still shut.

"She never saw herself as the problem, though," I go on. "First it was my anxiety that was the culprit. Then, after Alex, it was that. She was so humiliated by the idea that she'd produced me. Like it was the worst sin in society, to parent a child who . . . who had to be institutionalized. All I want is to be better than her."

The confession falls out of me like a stone. And once the words are spoken, I can't take them back.

I half expect Ellis to laugh and tell me how I've failed, that my mother was right to be ashamed.

But instead Ellis lets out a heavy breath. "Well. My parents were never around, but I have to admit . . . maybe I lucked out on that front." She looks at me now, turning her head so that our noses all but brush. Her breath is warm against my lips, her face so close I can see every delicate pore.

All of a sudden my heart beats a little faster. I can't stop thinking about the way Ellis moved with that sword in her hand, sweat-slick and intentional.

I sit up too abruptly, digging my nails into the rug beneath us. "I have to go," I say. "I just remembered I owe Wyatt revisions by Monday."

Ellis pushes herself up more slowly, but she doesn't get off the floor when I stand. "All right. Will we be seeing you for dinner?"

"Oh. I don't . . . maybe. We'll see."

"Felicity, wait." Ellis stops me when I'm already halfway out of the room. I pause and look back over my shoulder; she's still sitting on the floor, firelight flickering off the wet gleam of her hair. "I was thinking . . ."

For a moment she almost looks her age, the set of her features softer somehow, lips parted. But then the effect passes and she's Ellis again.

"The next Night Migration . . . perhaps you should take the lead again. Half the point of this project is my proving magic doesn't exist. So why don't you teach us some magic?"

My breath has stopped moving in my chest; my blood has gone still in my veins. I blink. And in that split second I see her again—Margery Lemont—her pale face rising behind Alex's frame.

"I don't know if that's a good idea."

Ellis tilts her head. "Why not?"

"I shouldn't be doing magic. Not anymore."

"You've done magic already. You initiated me into the Godwin coven, didn't you?"

"That wasn't magic. That was just a ritual."

"What's the difference? It doesn't need to be anything dark and terrifying. One of us can cut her finger and you can attempt a healing spell, if you like. But I want to give you a fair chance to prove magic *is* real before I disprove it for good."

I don't have a good argument in response to that. I should, but I don't. Ellis seems to know that, to taste my surrender like blood in the water, so I nod once and escape before she can think of any other harebrained ideas.

It's true that I have essay revisions due Monday morning,

but after I make it upstairs and sit myself down at my desk to work, I realize I can't concentrate. The words blur together on my laptop screen and a painful beat pounds in my temple, despite all the pills I gulped down this morning.

I can't do this. I can't do magic again. It's not even about Ellis—I can't do this to *Alex.* Even if this ghost is all in my head, it's . . . callous, it's sick to just . . .

It's been less than a year since I watched my girlfriend plummet to a watery death. I should be more concerned with Alex's blood on my hands than the smell of Ellis's hair.

Magic is what got me in trouble in the first place. Only now, because Ellis has asked it of me, I'm only too willing to give in.

But maybe I am a monster, because now she's all I can think about.

16

I drew a card from my deck when I woke up. The Nine of Swords. I replaced it, shuffled, and drew again, and got the Nine of Swords for a second time.

Fear and nightmares.

So even before I see her, I know Alex is coming tonight.

I've already written to Wyatt to ask for an extension, and since then I've been metaphorically chained to my desk. I keep my hands on the keyboard as if that will force me to use it, but my attention keeps drifting away from my laptop and out my window toward the quick-approaching night. Dusk falls faster now than it did, a curtain dropping over the horizon and trapping us on a darkened stage. The snow brings its own silence.

It's Sunday. It's Samhain.

My gaze has drifted from my computer again, past my own face reflected in the window and toward the woods. At first I think it's a trick of the light, a reflection from my own bedside lamp in the glass—but then it *moves.*

I slam my laptop shut and lurch across my desk, pressing my

nose to the windowpane. Even with the double glazing installed since I left last year, the glass is frigid against my skin.

There. There, in the woods, a figure shifts between the trees.

Even from this distance, I can see Alex's red hair.

The moonlight reflects off her skin and lends it a strangely iridescent quality, like a white opal dropped underwater. Her movements are inhuman, her incorporeal form like a wisp blown from place to place, flitting between trees and vanishing, only to reappear a moment later farther away.

She's not real, she's not real, she's not real—

She's real.

I shove back my chair and grab the tartan throw from where I'd tossed it on the foot of my bed, wrapping the wool knit tight around my shoulders as I clatter down the stairs and out the Godwin House back door.

The temperature has plummeted since Ellis and I cut across the quad after fencing practice the other day. My breath clouds in front of my face as I dash across the short field behind Godwin. Already my teeth are chattering; I'm too aware of my bones caught beneath my skin, of my own mortality in the face of Alex's . . . of Alex's . . .

I don't know what she is now.

By the time I'm ensconced under the tree cover, I start to wish I'd brought a flashlight, or at least my phone—something I could use to light the way. As it is, branches cut my cheeks, and I trip over unseen roots, stumbling from trunk to trunk and blinded by my own adrenaline.

"Alex?"

My voice doesn't echo; it's swallowed by the forest, the silence somehow more complete in the wake of my words than it was before.

The air out here is granite-dry, sucking the moisture from my skin and making my lips feel raw. I twist my hands tighter in the knit throw and slow my pace, too conscious of the way the tree cover consumes the light of the moon, the way the snow muffles every step. If something were to come up behind me, I wouldn't hear it until it was too late.

The nape of my neck prickles. I whip around, but there's nothing there, just the blank faces of dying trees and the penetrating dark.

My breath is too loud now. I tug the edge of the tartan blanket up over my mouth, like that could muffle the sound. It only succeeds in making me feel half suffocated by the damp heat of my own air.

"Alex?" This time her name comes out softer, quavering like a baby bird.

I have no reason to think Alex's ghost is benevolent. She might have drawn me out into the night with any number of motives. She might intend to kill me.

I never should have trusted her absence. I never should have doubted her ghost was real. I knew she was here, knew it in my blood. Why would Alex's spirit leave me alone if Margery's curse won't? Margery claimed Alex the same night she claimed me: the night of my séance.

My fault. All of it—my fault.

I stop in a clearing, turning in slow circles. I can't watch every angle at once; I can't guarantee that the moment I turn my back on that tree, this one, her specter won't slip from between the vines to close cold fingers around my throat.

"I'm sorry," I whisper. If she hears me, she gives no sign of it.

Then I turn on my heel and sprint out of the woods as fast as my feet will carry me. I stumble and trip over rocks and roots, stagger up the steps to Godwin House, and all but collapse in the back hall, dripping melted snow onto the floorboards and shivering in the sudden heat.

I place black tourmaline along my windowsill, a defense against whatever—whoever—I saw. But when I climb into my bed, I can't sleep.

I'm afraid to close my eyes.

I've planned the third Night Migration, notes written with Ellis's leaky fountain pen and slid under doors, folded and tied with twine. Kajal finds me the morning after I deliver the notes while I'm making tea in the kitchen, her eyes red-rimmed.

"I can't come tonight," she says. "I know we're not supposed to talk about it, but I didn't want you to end up waiting for me."

"Are you sick?" I ask.

Kajal grimaces, an expression that comes across as pained. "Yes. I suppose it's that time of year, isn't it? I don't doubt I'll infect all the rest of you by the end of the week."

"Oh no. I'm sorry. Here, let me make you some tea. And don't worry about tonight, really; you should rest—"

"What's going on?"

We turn to find Ellis in the doorway, one hand braced against the frame, already dressed in a blazer and twill trousers despite the fact it's not even eight in the morning.

Kajal sneezes into her elbow then scrubs the heels of her hands against her cheeks. "I'm ill. I'm not going to make it tonight, obviously, so I just thought—"

"Don't be ridiculous," Ellis interjects. "Of course you'll make it tonight. It's just a little bug. We couldn't have a meeting without you."

"I really can't." Kajal's hair is usually perfectly coiffed, silky and coaxed into loose waves; today it's pulled into a messy bun and tied off with a scrunchie. She looks like she needs to be in bed, not tramping through the frigid woods.

But Ellis's frown deepens, and she pushes off the doorframe, stepping farther into the kitchen. "You have to come. This isn't optional, Kajal—you made vows during initiation. You're bound to us now."

"It's fine, Ellis," I say, and I find myself having shifted to put my body between Ellis and Kajal—although I don't really remember moving, although I know Ellis wouldn't hurt her. "Magic isn't real, remember? So there won't be any evil spirits rising from the grave to punish Kajal for taking one night off."

Of course, the vows we all made during initiation weren't that kind of vow anyway—I'd been so careful to keep magic far away from our earlier rituals, to be *good*—but it's an argument that will work on Ellis. That's all that matters. And if she still wants me to practice magic tonight, to *perform* for her like a prize horse, she'll agree.

Ellis's expression has gone still and smooth as marble, a

sculpted neutrality that I don't know how to interpret. But I stay where I am, my feet rooted into the stone floor, into the uneven foundation of Godwin itself.

At last a slim smile cracks her mouth, and she nods, once. "Fine," she says, and she says it calmly enough that I almost believe she doesn't care anymore. "As you like. I hope you recover well, Kajal."

She turns and goes without another word, and the vacuum of air left by her absence makes it hard to breathe. When I look at Kajal, she's leaning back against the kitchen counter like she's been exsanguinated.

"Ellis will get over it," I tell her, and I offer an arm that I don't expect her to take. Only she does, leaning her weight in against my side and letting me help her out into the common room to curl up on the sofa. I drape one of our ugly knit blankets over her reed-thin legs and tuck it in around her hips. "Can I get you something? A book? Tea?"

"Tea would be nice," she admits, and I spend the rest of the morning checking on her, making sure she eats something between bouts of editing my English paper that's now due at the end of the week.

When night falls I leave without Ellis. I've chosen a field farther up in the mountains for tonight's meeting—far enough away that I have to steal an unlocked bike from Yancey House and pedal my way through the hills. By the time I make it to the right coordinates, I'm sweaty and out of breath. The bike chain catches at my skirt as I dismount, ripping the hem.

"Fantastic," I mutter, hopping on one foot to examine the damage. The chain has left a smear of grease along the ankle of my tights, too. This isn't even the final location—I plan to move us somewhere new once the others have arrived—and I'm starting to regret that choice, the same way I'm starting to regret the sacred materials I've packed in my satchel. The bag hangs heavy against my thigh, an unignorable reminder of my own foolishness.

As usual, I shouldn't have let Ellis pressure me into this.

Leonie is already here, crouched down by the start of a little fire and blowing on the embers like she can coax it into existence despite the damp.

"I don't know why Ellis can't schedule these indoors," Leonie says, stabbing at the coals with a stick. She blames *Ellis,* of course, even though I'm the one who planned tonight's meeting. "It's November. It's absolutely freezing."

"If we aren't uncomfortable, we aren't having the true experience," I say in my best Ellis impression, which earns me a snort and half a grin from Leonie.

"Well, maybe next time you can be the first one out here," she says. "Tell Ellis to schedule me last."

It must have rained up here earlier, then froze after dusk fell. The stones we're meant to sit on are slick with ice; the grass is crunchy underfoot. I put my satchel on the ground and sit on top of it, feet stretched toward Leonie's meager fire.

"I'm ready for Thanksgiving break," Leonie says. "Kajal's coming back with me, you know."

"You're from . . . ?" I know Leonie said, the night I first met her, but I don't remember. I'd been too busy thinking about myself—and Ellis.

"Newport. So it won't be any warmer than this, I'm afraid."

"Are you planning to do anything fun?"

She shrugs; the gesture looks oddly stilted, but that might be because of the cold. "I mean . . . My grandmother's sick. Dying, probably. So . . . not really."

I flinch and wish I could take the question back. "Oh. I'm sorry."

"It's okay." She tosses the stick into the flames, abandoning her attempt. "She's getting old. It was going to happen sooner or later."

"Even so."

Leonie sighs and sits on one of the frigid rocks, gloved hands planted in the grass. "She was the first Black student at Dalloway, you know. Desegregation of schools had just passed in the Supreme Court, and Dalloway wanted to look progressive—so they had to find an appropriately bright, appropriately wealthy young Black girl to play the role. My great-grandmother was rich, an inventor, and my grandmother really was a genius. The Schuylers have attended Dalloway ever since."

My brows rise despite myself. "I didn't know that." I suppose there always has to be a first, but it never occurred to me how utilitarian it all was, how Leonie's grandmother might have felt less like a welcomed admission and far more like a weapon.

Leonie nods, twisting her signet ring around her pinkie. "She's why I'm here. Thomasin and Penelope, too, I suppose."

It takes a moment for me to place the names: Thomasin is a sophomore, Penelope a junior. They're both Black.

"There's just three of you," I say, surprised, and then immediately flush. "Sorry. That was a silly thing to say."

"Not really." Leonie stops fidgeting with her ring and places her hands flat on the rocks beneath us, leaning her weight back so she can tilt her face toward the starry sky. "You're right. Three of us. My grandmother was so proud to be an alumna."

"I'm sorry she's ill. I can't imagine." Which is true; I never knew my grandparents. My mother didn't speak about them, and they didn't bother to get in touch.

Leonie glances toward me. The light reflects off her dark eyes like a million fractured diamonds. "I found out that my grandmother knew all the great Harlem Renaissance writers, back in the day. Zora Neale Hurston, Anne Spencer . . . She never mentioned them. Not until she was dying. And now it might be too late."

She chews on her lower lip. I wish I knew her well enough to reach over and take her hand, but most of our interactions have been under Ellis's watch. I only know the parts of Leonie that Ellis wants to see.

I need to figure out a way to change that.

"Anyway," Leonie says eventually, "I'm going to record her stories while I'm home. Kajal's helping. I feel like there ought to be some kind of archive, you know?"

"I think that's a wonderful idea." I smile when I say it, and I genuinely do admire Leonie for that. And I envy her. No one in my family cares about literature at all. My mother views my love of reading with the same vague bafflement with which she viewed my former interest in running—a hobby one might reference in polite conversation, but ultimately unnecessary.

If she knew I want to study English in college, that I hope to be a literature professor one day, my mother would die from sheer disgrace. A society woman doesn't need to work, and in fact, ought not.

"I'm glad we decided to start doing these," I say after a few long moments. "The Night Migrations. Ellis thinks it will help with her book, so . . ."

Leonie laughs. "Oh. Right, yes. It's so silly, isn't it? The rituals, the theatrics of it all. Even worse with the Margery coven—it took me ages to get the smell of dead goat out of those robes. But it's fun. It shouldn't be, but it is."

Yes. It is.

Maybe it's all right to love this. Maybe it's okay to find comfort in the darkness, as long as I don't let myself take it too far.

And I can't help myself. I have to know; I have to know if *Leonie* knows. I wet my lips and start: "Listen, Leonie, about the Margery coven—"

But Leonie shushes me, grabbing my wrist and pointing across the clearing. "Look."

A light has appeared in the woods, bobbing between the trees; eventually the forest releases Clara onto the horizon. She's bundled up in what looks to be two cloaks, her flashlight beam shaking with how bad she's shivering.

"Did you *walk*?" I say, horrified.

"How else was I supposed to get here?"

"Bike," Leonie and I say in unison, then exchange glances.

Clara makes a face and comes to stand at the other side of the fire, rubbing her hands together and apparently refusing to sit in the wet grass.

Eventually a pair of headlights curve around from the far

end of the field—there must be a road over there that I missed on the map. The vehicle lumbers over the hill and comes to a stop twenty feet away, the engine running for another solid ten, fifteen seconds before it shuts off. I'd be worried about who might have driven up here in the middle of the night if I wasn't equally confident that the likelihood of some stranger finding us here, at the random coordinates I chose in the middle of the woods, is next to zero.

I don't recognize Ellis's truck until she emerges from the driver's side wearing riding boots and a shearling coat. She tramps across the dead ground without a flashlight; when she's close enough, I realize she's not even wearing gloves.

Ellis doesn't say a word about Kajal, or about anything else for that matter. When she comes to a stop between me and Clara, she's at such an angle to the fire that the light casts her features half into shadow.

"Who are we reading this time?" Clara asks. "Sylvia Plath?"

Ellis shakes her head. "Felicity's in charge for this one. I think she had her own idea. Didn't you, Felicity?"

I nod and rise to my feet at last, dusting off the bark and bracken that cling to my skirt. "It's a bit of a hike," I tell them, kicking damp leaves over the fire. "Come on."

I lead them through the forest, down the slope of the hill, occasionally pulling out my phone to check the coordinates. It occurs to me only now that I have no idea how the others have been locating the Night Migration spots—none of them have mobile phones.

Surely they don't use compasses?

After ten minutes' walk we emerge into a clearing, and from

the soft murmur behind me, I can tell that the others recognize this place—from photographs of the town's history, if not from real life.

The church has been abandoned for over forty years now; the windows are boarded up, the front door padlocked, although I suspect the police were more concerned about squatters than witches. The white clapboard exterior is stained near black in places, as if with soot, though according to the property records there was never a fire. Even the steeple lists slightly east, the ancient cross that used to crown it toppled over and hanging nearly upside down.

The Margery coven has held initiation here for twenty-six years. I wonder sometimes if that's the real force that's eaten away at the building's integrity, the irreverent power of reckless rich girls and their pretense at faith corroding the relics of life.

"I'm not going in there," Clara announces, stopping short near the creaking fence that circles the churchyard.

The rest of us exchange looks. Sometimes I think Leonie and Kajal, at least, regret including Clara in our games. She's younger, impressionable in a way that doesn't lend itself to creativity. And as much as I know none of them believe in magic like I do, at least the rest of us take the Night Migrations seriously.

"It's all right," Leonie says, with surprising gentleness. "It's just an old building."

And of course she would have been here before; she knows from experience.

"Nineteenth-century, I think." Ellis wanders closer, peering up at the shuttered windows and trailing a hand along the clapboards. Even in the moonlight, I can see her fingertips come away dirty. "I wonder why no one bothered to maintain the place; it could have been a historical landmark."

Clara still looks dubious, but she wanders closer to Ellis all the same.

"It was built in 1853," Leonie says, and when I turn to look at her she's gazing at the crooked steeple, her hands in her pockets. "Commissioned by the people who owned Dalloway at the time. It was even briefly used as a sanitarium in 1918 during the Spanish flu pandemic."

I stare at her. "How do you even know all that?"

"I'm a historian," she explains as she moves closer, drawing one hand free to touch the door frame. "I've read a lot about Dalloway's history."

I've never read anything like that in the Dalloway library. Only now do I wonder if Leonie has been going off-campus for her research—if, during all her trips to the city, she found records about Dalloway that I've never seen before. Records that, perhaps, Dalloway wishes would stay buried.

I draw the key out of my skirt pocket and open the padlock; we Margery coven girls had cut off and replaced the police's original lock with one of our own. I suppose whenever the coven decided to excommunicate me, it didn't occur to them to take my key.

The church door swings open with a whine, and I instantly sneeze. If the Margery coven held another initiation here at the start of the semester, the dust has already returned.

"Come on," I say, and flick on my flashlight.

The others trail behind me, which is a little ironic considering none of them even believe in ghosts. I cast the glow of my light toward all four corners of the church, counting the usual landmarks: the baptismal font, the pulpit, the pews draped in ancient white blankets. Nothing is out of place. No one else has been here in weeks. No one alive, anyway.

There's still a splatter of goat's blood on the floor, presumably where the others drew the chalk pentacle for this year's initiation—the one I wasn't invited to. Clara spots it and yelps, lurching back against Ellis's chest. I can't help but laugh.

"It's probably just paint," I say, even though I know better, and I kneel down over that stain to shrug my satchel off one shoulder and start unloading my materials. I pass around a jar of cloves and instruct the other girls to place the cloves under their tongues and murmur a consecration.

Clara giggles and grimaces as she swallows her clove, like she thinks it's a silly formality and not sacred liturgy. Leonie discreetly spits hers out.

I suck my clove slowly, luxuriating in the warm, earthy spice of it, the way it makes my tongue feel slightly numb, the perfume that dies when I crunch down. The bitter taste lingers long after I've swallowed.

I light two candles—one white, one blue—and set three snow-quartz crystals in a small bowl. Another bowl I fill with rainwater, poured out of a steel thermos I appropriated from Godwin's kitchen.

The spell isn't anything I got out of a book. I invented it. It just feels *right,* each element of my altar connecting to something real out there in the world, like threads. Sympathetic magic: like tugging on like.

I dip holly berries in the rainwater and then roll them in sugar until their garnet skin is frosted and glittering in the candlelight. At last, with a rain-wet finger, I trace a fractal on the floor—lines and angles splintering off one another in perfect symmetry.

The others watch me work in cautious silence. I'm not sure if Ellis somehow warned them not to speak or if some part of them inherently knows. But when I lift my head, they're all seated in their semicircle around me: waiting, like students, for an instructor's command.

I invited them, but for this, their presence is irrelevant. They're only here because Ellis needs five of us, five to match the five dead Dalloway witches. She doesn't have five tonight, and that almost ruined everything. But it doesn't matter.

This spell is about *more.* It's about me and Ellis. About magic—and whether forces exist too powerful and arcane for us to understand.

"We're going to summon snow," I tell them. "Close your eyes and clear your mind. Try to imagine the way snow feels, tastes, sounds as it blankets the ground. Then repeat after me . . . We call upon the north wind: greet us with your breath and bless us with your gift."

It sounds a little silly when I say it out loud, but Ellis closes her eyes and repeats my words, and so the rest of them follow.

A chill sinks into my skin as I turn my gaze down to the holly in my lap, the yellow candlelight dancing on the surface of the rainwater and casting shadows across the backs of my hands. I smile and close my eyes as well, let myself sink into the space that always opens up for me in rituals like this—a quiet space in my chest, a secret space. The only place I ever feel truly calm.

I was wrong to think magic was dangerous. Alex might be. The witches might be. But not this.

Never this.

"Listen," Ellis murmurs.

For a moment her voice is the only thing echoing in my mind, soft and heavy as the dusk all around us.

And then I hear it: the soft patter of snow falling on the church roof.

Leonie lets out a startled yelp—and when I open my eyes, she's laughing, face turned up. Beside her Clara has gone still and wide-eyed, arms wrapped around her middle and hugging herself close. If her curves became edges, if her curls were wild and tangled instead of neatly restrained, she might be Alex come back to life.

"It worked," Leonie exclaims, already on her feet and spinning in place, like a child who just learned that school has been canceled. "Felicity! It's *snowing*!"

My gaze flicks over to Ellis, who has a tiny smile settled about her lips as well, although her smile is harder to read. I can't tell if she believes me, or if she's mocking me.

Leonie darts across the church to throw open the doors. A flurry of snow scatters in across the floor, and I'm on my feet, too—we all are—abandoning the candles and crystals and holly berries to stand there on the edge of the night with winter stinging at our skin.

For some reason, it doesn't feel cold anymore. Or maybe that heat is from the flask Leonie presses into my hand, the rhythm of Ellis's voice steady like a heartbeat when she pulls out a book of poetry and reads to us, our bodies flung on the church floor like discarded dolls.

Leonie's flask empties, then Ellis's, and it's twenty minutes until the feeling hits. But then the euphoria pours over me like cool water, and I'm alive, I'm alight, sliding my fingers through sugar and tasting it on my tongue, snow falling on our faces through a hole in the desecrated roof.

This is better than any Boleyn party, I think, and let my fingers twine together with Ellis's, my other hand linked with Leonie's, Ellis's thumb rubbing heat against my knuckles and the air gone thick like syrup. I'm drunk enough now that the world has gone to watercolor—all shapes and motion without texture.

We end up back in the woods somehow, Clara with a torch held high overhead. I don't remember where she found such a big stick, or how she managed to ignite it with the wood so damp, but we follow that flame through the darkness, wandering in circles and curving lines with blood searing our veins.

I touch a tree trunk and am amazed by how rough the bark feels, how much I want to press my face against it. Leonie trails her fingers through my hair, and I could kiss her, almost do. Only then we're moving again, reciting poems in shouts to the shadows and daring the ghosts to come out and play.

I don't know how long the high lasts. It could have been all night; it could have been an hour.

But I wake up the next morning lying on a bed of bracken and melted snow. There's frost on my lips and crystallized on my lashes. I'm cold enough that I've forgotten how to tremble.

It's several seconds, several gulping breaths, before I convince myself I'm not dead.

What happened?

I've been drunk before, but it was never like this. Did I really have that much? I can't remember how many times the flask was passed into my hand, how many times its mouth met my lips.

The forest is quiet as the interior of a mausoleum. Whatever protection last night's spell had given me is gone now, melted like ice.

Last night didn't summon snow.

Last night summoned *death.*

I stare into the trees, waiting for her to reappear: The spirit with white eyes and poisoned fingertips. Alex with her tangled hair and lake-drenched dress. I know she's there, because I can feel her watching me; every shift of wind through the pines is her voice whispering.

I need to leave. I can't be here. *I need to leave.*

I stagger to my feet and almost trip over the body.

"Shit!"

It's Leonie, her dark skin silvery beneath the light dust of snow that covers it. She's still, so still—a corpse in bespoke—and we never should have come here, never should have let ourselves fall asleep.

Only then she moves, curling her fingers into a fist, mouth twisting with discomfort. I glance away, and that's when I realize we're all here: Ellis huddled under a tree with her coat tugged in tight, Clara asleep in a pile of leaves with her cheeks gone pale and damp.

Her red hair in the snow is bright as spilled blood.

I gag and whip away. *Don't think about Alex. Don't. Don't think about—*

There's movement in the trees. Oh god—I see it. I see *her.* Barely more than a shadow, but I'd recognize her anywhere. I press my hand over my eyes so I don't have to see. Only then memory is painted across the black velvet space behind my eyelids: Alex on that cliff, hair knotting in the bitter wind, her cheeks flushed in anger—and she was shouting at me, she wouldn't stop shouting, and so I reached out and I *pushed—*

"Felicity?"

That's Ellis's voice. And so it must be Ellis's touch that finds my shoulder, turning me away from Clara, from the bodies scattered on the forest floor like discarded trash.

"Felicity," she says again, and cold fingers slide up the nape of my neck to grasp my skull. "It's okay. It's all right. We fell asleep. But everyone's fine."

I can't breathe. The air is too thick out here, oxygen-poor and stinging like broken glass. It floods my lungs like cold water. How long can one survive without air? How long until my body collapses in on itself like Alex's did? Twenty minutes? Thirty? The lake closes overhead. I sink into the dark. The earth swallows me whole.

"Shh. Just breathe."

I can't.

"Breathe."

I'm crying now, the tears sliding down my cheeks. It's not cold enough for them to turn to ice, not yet.

I didn't kill her. I don't have the capacity for something like that. I'm just . . . I'm losing my mind. I'm—

Margery. It's Margery coiled like a viper in my heart, making me think these things.

"Felicity. Can you look at me?" Someone brushes the tears away, their touch skimming my face as if to map its topography. "Look at me."

I look.

Ellis is close enough that for a moment all I can see are her eyes, cloud gray and steady. Her hands are on my cheeks. Her lips are flushed.

"You're all right," Ellis says again, and strokes my hair like a mother with her infant, and that's when I realize the others are awake now: Clara and Leonie both standing there staring at me, Leonie's hand over her mouth, Clara's gaze wide and hungry.

I can still hear Leonie's voice echoing in my skull: *It's so silly, isn't it?*

Ellis exhales softly; I feel the heat of it on my skin. Finally, her touch drops from my face down to my shoulders; she rubs my arms hard.

"You're soaked," she murmurs. "Come on. We should get you home."

I don't remember the walk back to the truck. When I try to envision it, I see four bedraggled girls with numb noses staggering over fallen logs and lurching past pools of snowmelt. Ellis's arm around my waist keeps me upright, Clara trailing behind like a watchful shadow.

Ellis bundles me into the front seat and drapes a blanket over my lap. I twist my hands up in the wool and stare out the window as we trundle over uneven ground and back out to the one-lane gravel road.

It's only five minutes back to Dalloway. I don't know why it felt like we'd gone miles that night, thousands of miles, like we'd traversed the globe a dozen times over.

Kajal's asleep when we return, and Clara is too timid for confrontation, which means there's no one to fight me for the third-floor shower. I turn the water as hot as it will go and sit on the floor underneath the spray. My mind is a blank sheet of ice, a still lake that stretches far toward the horizon. I contain nothing. Everything inside me is cold and dead.

I remember this feeling; I felt this way in the hospital—like my very soul was constructed of laminate floors and fluorescent light. Sterile. The first several nights I cried for my mother. A mistake, because she never came. And even if she had, I probably would have regretted it.

But that place didn't ruin me. I was cursed already. The Dalloway witches had carved out my heart and consumed it for heat. I had nothing left to give.

I get out of the shower only when the water has gone lukewarm, then stand there in front of the mirror, dragging a brush through my hair over and over until my hand shakes. I get dressed in dry clothes and lie down on my bedroom floor.

Ellis finds me like that sometime later. I don't get up even when I hear her knock, or when my bedroom door opens.

She settles in next to me and rests her hand on my brow. After a few seconds I shift and let her tug my head into her lap, her fingers combing through my hair.

"It's the comedown," she tells me with surprising gentleness. "Nights like that can leave you feeling terrible. This happens sometimes."

It doesn't feel like a comedown. It feels like the world is fracturing and falling apart.

I'll never drink again, I tell myself. I want to believe it this time, but I'm no better than my mother.

I open my eyes and gaze up at Ellis. She looks less familiar when seen from upside down, her features gone alien and surreal. "I forgot the bike," I say.

"We can go back and get it later."

"It wasn't even my bike. I stole it."

A soft breath bursts from her lips, and I recognize it a beat too late: a laugh. "In that case, we might as well not bother. I don't know if a bike would fit in my truck anyway."

"I could ride it home."

"You could," she agrees.

Ellis is close enough that I can feel her breathing; her stomach shifts against the back of my head every time she inhales. Some part of me feels, bizarrely, like we all died out there in the snow. I cling to this small evidence that she's alive. That we both are.

"It snowed," I murmur. "I knew it would. Believe me now?"

Ellis twists a lock of my hair around her finger. "It's November, Felicity. It would have snowed regardless."

I sigh and don't bother arguing. Ellis was the one who wanted me to prove magic to her, after all; if she doesn't want to believe me, that's her prerogative.

I think about her breathing, and the rug beneath me, the wax still burned into the silk fibers from when I knocked over the candles the week Ellis and I met.

"I'm going to help you through this," Ellis promises, her hand still stroking my skull. "There's no ghost, and there's no magic. I'm going to prove it to you."

17

I invent reasons to stay in my room the next day: too much homework, food poisoning, I overslept. The truth is, I can't bear to face Leonie and Clara now that they've seen me in that state.

"It was the whiskey, Felicity. Everyone understands that," Ellis says with a note of impatience to her tone. It doesn't matter. I saw the way they looked at me. I know what they're thinking.

But Kajal wasn't there, so I find myself spending time with her instead. She's also a Wyatt student, and it's easy to commiserate over Wyatt's ridiculous standards and share French pressed coffee as we read through our assignments. "First she wanted me to talk more about the rhetoric of silence in late Victorian literature, and now she wants me to delete everything," Kajal bemoans.

The next night I find Kajal in her bedroom with a bottle of pills, neatly swallowing one tablet with a glass of water. Our eyes meet and she immediately frowns.

"Can I help you, Morrow?"

"No," I say quickly. Only, then: "Well—no. But . . . I take those too." They're antidepressants. I would recognize this particular med's shape and color anywhere. I attempt a smile. "I hate how they make me feel. Like I'm underwater."

But if I expected some kind of commiseration, all Kajal gives me is a thin grimace. "Yes, well, not all of us can afford to quit taking our medication on a whim, Felicity."

My hands clench in fists. "I didn't," I say. "I don't— It wasn't a whim."

"Regardless, we aren't going to talk about it." Kajal neatly screws the top back onto her medication bottle and drops it into her desk drawer. The sound of the drawer sliding shut feels like punctuation at the end of a sentence: a dismissal.

Two nights after that terrible Night Migration, I lurch awake with sweat plastering my shirt to my spine, my nightmare still sour in my mouth. When I shut my eyes, I see bodies in the water with white fingers and cold lips. It's Tamsyn Penhaligon, it's Cordelia Darling, it's Flora Grayfriar with blood on her throat.

And as if to make things worse, my laptop crashed the night of the last Night Migration. I'm forced to borrow a Godwin House typewriter while my computer is sent off for repairs, but now, after two days without it, I discover I prefer the analog method. I like how it's difficult to depress the keys of a Remington, that I can't lounge with my hands sprawled over a keyboard with the words flowing unedited from my fingertips; I have to be *deliberate* in my choices. I must pick each key in sequence. I must think about what I want to say before I say it, or risk having to retype whole pages' worth of argument.

There's something so freeing about cutting myself loose from technology in some small way. No more stressing over profile pictures or whether my social media feeds reflect the kind of golden, idealized life I want everyone to think I have. No more virus scans or junk mail or counting likes. If I want to look something up, I go to the library. If I want to talk to someone, I talk to them. And everyone I'd talk to is in this house.

I decide that once I do get my laptop back, I won't use it. I'll hide it under my bed to collect dust. I need the physical anchor that my typewriter provides; I need that stability.

"We should practice," Ellis says, three days after the ill-fated Night Migration, after I've finally recovered from some of my chagrin—or, rather, was forced to recover when Ellis refused to leave me alone. I watch her from my place, curled up on her bed with a Christie mystery, as she tips her desk chair back farther and farther, as if testing how far she can go before she loses balance and cracks her head open.

"Practice what?"

Ellis's chair clatters back into place. "A murder. What else?" A grin cuts across her mouth, and she opens her desk drawer, pulling out a length of twine. "The garrote."

"*I* don't need to practice that," I inform her. "I'm not the one writing about psycho witches."

And there's a difference between talking about how something might have been done and physically re-creating it. Especially something this brutal.

"But you *are* the one who's convinced she's being haunted by the ghost of her dead ex-girlfriend. If anything, you should go first."

Ellis holds out the twine, shaking it in midair until I sigh and snatch it out of her grasp.

"What am I supposed to do with this?"

"Do what comes naturally. Put it around my neck and act like you're trying to strangle me." Ellis pushes back her chair and rises to her feet, drawing her hair up into a messy bun to expose her throat. "You should come at me from behind."

Of course. Naturally. How else would one attack a murder victim?

I wrap the twine around the palms of both hands and position myself to Ellis's back. She's taller than I am; I'll have to drag her back to reach. If anything, that should help my cause: Her own height will put pressure on her larynx—the garrote will be harder to escape.

I step closer, holding the cord taut. The nape of Ellis's neck is long and slender, fair-skinned with a tiny freckle positioned off-center from her vertebrae. I can see her pulse beating in her carotid artery, just below her ear.

"What are you waiting for?"

Nothing. I'm waiting for nothing.

I rise up on the balls of my feet and wrap the cord around Ellis's throat, tugging her back a sharp half step—she makes a soft, surprised sound and grasps at the twine. She arches and ducks free, kicking her heel against my ankle so that I stumble and swear.

There's a thin impression on Ellis's neck when she turns to face me again, the flesh gone slightly reddish but otherwise unmarked. "What was that?" she says, laughing. "You couldn't have killed a child with that effort."

"I wasn't trying to kill you at *all.*"

"You won't kill me," Ellis says, and from the way she says it I get the distinct impression she finds this exchange distastefully remedial. "Really. But you have to make sure your victim can't escape. Or do you really think you're capable of chasing someone down and killing them by brute force when they're already fighting back?"

"I'm not planning to kill anyone, period," I argue, and one of Ellis's brows pops up.

She doesn't say it, but I can still hear those words hovering unspoken in the space between us: *Even Alex?*

My chest aches, badly enough I press my closed fist against my sternum and press down hard. Ellis would never say I'd killed Alex. And even if I insisted on my own responsibility, I know what Ellis would argue back: *People fight, Felicity,* she'd say. *People drink, and they fight, and accidents happen.*

I haven't told her about the séance, or Margery Lemont. How sometimes I wonder if Margery's spirit has burrowed itself into my body, curling up tight and cold around my heart.

And yet here I am, pretending to murder Ellis. Putting the garrote around her throat, where, if I truly was possessed by Margery, it would be only too easy for her to take over my body and draw the twine tight.

Possession doesn't exist, I hear Ellis say. *Magic doesn't exist.*

Only it does. Just because Ellis can't see it doesn't make it not real.

"My turn," Ellis says. "Give me the garrote." My palms are damp as I shove the twine back into her hands; she twists it around her knuckles hard enough the skin blanches. "Turn around."

I do, slowly. Knowing Ellis has no intention of letting me die doesn't do much to quell the way my heart has started to race. What if she makes a mistake? She might not *mean* to hurt me, but if she draws the cord too tight, if she holds me too long, it would be an accident, and I'd still be just as dead.

I'm about to tell Ellis I've changed my mind when she snaps the cord around my neck.

I stumble back against her chest, both hands grasping at the twine. But Ellis drags it tighter, crossing the cord behind my neck and eking out a wet, convulsive noise from my windpipe. Her body is firm and unshifting, even when I jab an elbow back at her stomach, her breath hot in my ear. The twine digs in, a white-hot streak across my throat. I try to tell her to stop, but my voice doesn't work. I can't breathe. I can't—

Ellis jerks me sideways, and for one reeling second I think she's about to break my neck. But it's only to turn me toward the mirror.

We're both reflected there: me with my face gone scarlet, my throat straining against her makeshift garrote and Ellis's fists clenched around the twine.

"See?" Ellis says. In the mirror her eyes are bright and alive with their own internal light, shoulders rising and falling with a shallow tremor. "You can't escape. You can't resist—not effectively, anyway. I've compressed your carotid artery, so there's very little blood flow to your brain."

I can barely even understand what she's saying. My thoughts have gone to static, blurring out at the edges. Ellis tips her head in against mine.

"Like this, see? Even with you fighting back . . . you'll be unconscious in thirty seconds. Within another minute, you'd be dead. Just like Tamsyn Penhaligon."

She's going to kill me.

The thought flares in my mind, red and lethal. Tears leak from my eyes, hot on my cheeks. I taste copper.

Only then Ellis lets go. Color blooms back into the world, and I stagger. I would fall to my knees if not for the way Ellis catches me with an arm around my waist.

"There," she murmurs. "There . . . You're okay. Did you think I was going to hurt you? I would never hurt you. You're safe."

I'm still crying. The sobs come out hoarse and inhuman, like my vocal cords have been dragged over asphalt. My throat burns.

Ellis's hand is in my hair, stroking it like I'm a frightened animal. My mind circles around and around the white noise of encroaching death. Of suffocation.

Is this how Alex felt after she hit the surface of the lake, the first shocked gasp as water came flooding in? Did she see the same haze seeping into her vision—her intoxication fading as terror clawed up her spine?

She might have survived the fall. But even then, Alex didn't know how to swim.

I twist in Ellis's arms to press my face against her shoulder, and she lets me cry, patting my head and murmuring soft, meaningless phrases as my tears and snot dampen her starched shirt collar.

"Why did you do that?" I ask when I've finally gotten my breathing back under control. I withdraw enough to look at her, wiping my wet nose with the back of one hand. "You didn't have to . . . to *do* that."

"We were practicing," Ellis says, with a faintly confused tilt to her tone.

"Right, we were *practicing,* not . . . not . . . You could have killed me!"

Something complicated passes over Ellis's face, and she lurches forward, grasping my shoulders with both hands. Her fingertips dig in hard enough it nearly hurts. "I would *never* kill you," she vows, her eyes gone wide. "Felicity, I swear to you, I'll never let anything happen to you. I'd rather die."

I blink against a fresh wave of tears. Ellis's thumb skirts up to brush one of them away; her touch lingers on my cheek afterward, her skin cool where mine now feels feverishly hot.

I suck in a shaky inhale. "You need to be more careful," I tell her at last, my voice steadier than it was. "I'm not one of your characters, Ellis. If something happens to me, you can't throw out that page and rewrite it."

Ellis looks stricken, her pupils black enough they almost consume all the gray in her eyes. Her hand on my face quivers very slightly. "I know," she says.

She strokes her fingers back through my hair, tucking a stray lock behind my ear. We're too close, her hand too near my throat. She has a tiny scar on one of her eyebrows, one I've never noticed before; it's mostly grown in but still visible, a hint of asymmetry in an otherwise ordered face. For some reason that's all I can think about.

But then she moves away, out of reach. Her larynx bobs when she swallows and, belatedly, she leans over to pick the twine garrote up off the floor. "Well. That's what it's like, I suppose."

Somehow I'd managed to forget this was an experiment.

Ellis retrieves a dove smoking jacket from the back of the chair and slings it over her shoulders, grabbing her satchel and a notebook. "I'm going to the library to write this down. I'll see you at dinner later?"

She leaves me in her room, the door left ajar but all her personal effects still here lined up on their shelves and in their drawers as if awaiting my perusal. I almost wonder if she intends me to snoop. This feels not unlike an invitation, something very, very *Ellis.*

I catch my own gaze in the mirror. My nose is cherry-colored still, my face slick with sweat or tears or both. My hair looks the way it does after I've run six miles, a tangled blond halo. I don't look a thing like Felicity Morrow.

I don't snoop, but I do look at the things she has left out in the open: the row of poetry books lined up in alphabetical order on the shelf by her bed, the Montblanc on her desk, a teacup bearing not tea but a single white dahlia in full bloom.

There are no photographs of family or friends. No secret phone charger or even so much as an uncharacteristic paper clip, although there is a row of half-burned votives along her windowsill. For some reason it seems stranger to me that Ellis wouldn't have finished each candle in sequence than that she'd own, say, a pair of headphones.

The impulse to start looking through her drawers is almost too much to bear. I escape while I still have the will to leave.

18

The next morning, I wake to find a note slid under my door. It's written in Ellis's handwriting: the coordinates and time for the next Night Migration.

But when I follow them that evening, they don't lead to a copse in the woods or the peak of a black hill; they take me to a dingy rental car agency a mile down the road. Ellis stands out front under the flickering yellow lights, smoking a clove cigarette like a character from a noir film.

"Good, you're here," she says, and stabs the cigarette out on the plaster wall. "Let's go in."

I glance over my shoulder, half expecting to find the rest of the girls standing there, wearing impatient expressions. The lot is too empty, nothing but cars and puddles of oil where cars used to be. "Where's everyone else?"

"Just us tonight," Ellis says. "I thought we could have our own private Night Migration."

The thought makes me uneasy; I can still feel the garrote cutting into my skin. Ellis saying she wouldn't actually kill me doesn't help matters as much as it should. I tug Kajal's coat closer around my shoulders and stay in place. "Why?"

She fixes me with a tight look. "Why not? If you don't want to come, you can always go back to Godwin House."

I dig the heel of one shoe into the cracked sidewalk. The snow has melted, but the cold still reaches to the bone.

"Don't be ridiculous. Of course I want to go." It doesn't sound nearly as persuasive as I'd like, but Ellis just smiles and leads the way through the swinging glass doors and into the fluorescent glare of the agency.

She orders us a plain, inconspicuous sedan. I catch sight of the ID she passes over the counter—it's her photo but not her name.

"Your car's in A-4," the rental agent says as he gives Ellis the keys. "Enjoy your trip, Miss Breithaupt."

Outside, in the parking lot, Ellis spends far too long adjusting the side-view mirrors and switching radio channels, the car idly puffing exhaust into the night air and the heat blasting.

"Where are we going?" I ask when I can't stand it any longer. " 'Miss *Breithaupt*'?"

At last Ellis appears satisfied with the angle of her seat, and she glances over at me, says, "I'm seventeen, silly girl. I can't rent a car without a fake ID."

She digs out a pair of driving gloves from her inner jacket pocket and pulls them on with expert efficiency. I try not to stare at the way the leather creaks as Ellis curls her fingers around the steering wheel, grip firm and dominant. I recognize them belatedly as the same white gloves we'd found at the antiques store—Ellis must have gone back and bought them.

We drive east, cutting along winding Catskill roads. A fog picks up as we move deeper into the forest; our headlights reflect off white gloom, eliminating the sight of anything past ten or fifteen feet.

"Maybe we should pull over," I finally suggest, squinting into the mist. "I don't understand how you can drive in this."

"Don't be a coward, Felicity; we're perfectly safe."

I shut my mouth over my response. What I *want* to say is that even Ellis Haley can't control the weather—but I have the feeling it's going to be a long drive, and I don't want to irritate her this early.

The radio station Ellis has chosen plays the blues, mournful notes that make me think of smoke. I wonder if the music is another thing Ellis is trying to make herself like, the same way she's forcing herself to enjoy whiskey. Or perhaps this is one of those rare glimpses into who Ellis Haley really is, something organic that grew from her heart.

I realize where we're headed after we've turned off toward Kingston and follow a slim road skirting outside the city and into the wooded hills. But I almost don't want to believe it. I stay silent in my seat, gripping the handle above the window, until Ellis rounds a corner and the cemetery gates come into view.

"No," I say. "No. I'm not . . . Why would you *bring* me here?"

Ellis shifts the car into park and twists around to grasp my wrist and say, "It's okay. You can do this."

But I can't. I can barely even breathe; it feels like something is crushing my chest, my bones, my lungs.

"It's just a grave," Ellis says. "You can visit a grave."

"I can't."

"Didn't you go to her funeral?"

I went to Alex's funeral. Of course I did. That was right after the accident; I was still floating in the numb, medicated haze of trauma. But I remember enough. I remember how empty Alex's house felt without her; how Alex's mother flinched away from me at the wake. Even the reverend looked at me like I was original sin herself walking among them.

It takes me a long time to nod. "Yes. I . . . Yes. But that was a long time ago."

"Then it's time to pay your respects."

Ellis reaches into her satchel and passes me a book. *The Secret Garden.* An older edition, the spine cracked and the pages gone the color of saffron.

"You told me this was one of her favorites," Ellis says softly.

I take the book and hug it close to my chest. All at once my face feels tight, a pressure building behind my eyes.

Maybe Ellis is right. Maybe I do need closure.

"Come on," Ellis says, and opens her car door. I sit there a moment longer, breathing the overhot, dry air, then make myself follow.

The cemetery is small and out of the way; I doubt most of the people who live in Kingston even know it exists. This is what Alex's family could afford. The wrought-iron gate creaks when Ellis opens it. When I curl a hand around one of the prongs, the metal flakes against my palm and stains my skin rust.

Alex's grave rests under the shadow of an oak. Although the snow has melted everywhere else, it's still chilly enough here that ice clings to the tree's roots and laces the curve of Alex's headstone. Ellis has brought a lantern; she sets it down by the stone; it casts a dull gold light for five feet in every direction before the darkness swallows all sight.

We stand at the foot of her grave. ALEXANDRA IRENE HAYWOOD, BELOVED DAUGHTER. She died six days before her eighteenth birthday.

"The coffin's empty," I say. "They never found her body. Well, not empty. We all left something for her. A favorite necklace, a square of lace sprayed with her perfume . . ."

"What did you leave?"

I swallow hard. "I wrote her a letter. Ridiculous, I know. She'll never read it. But . . ."

"It's not ridiculous," Ellis says. She reaches over and grasps my shoulder, squeezing once. "I'll give you a minute. All right?"

She heads for the car and I crouch low, toward the frozen earth. A spray of black hellebore grows by Alex's headstone. I offer a thin smile. Hellebore, in witchcraft, is used for banishment and exorcism. If Alex's body were in fact here, maybe the presence of that flower would have been enough to keep her spirit confined.

"I'm sorry," I tell the grave. It feels so inadequate. It feels like a lie. "I . . . I didn't know what else to do. I was scared. I tried to save you—I tried. I tried to *help,* but you . . . you weren't . . . You have to understand."

I can practically hear her voice: *I don't* have *to understand anything.*

"It was the séance. Margery Lemont cursed us, because we trapped her in our world."

Saying it aloud here, to Alex, it sounds insane.

I get down on my knees, tilting forward to press one hand

against the cold dirt. I try to summon her spirit. I wish I had wormwood or dandelions, herbs good for evocation. Not these god-awful hellebore, taunting me in an ironic twist of fate. I'd tear them up if it weren't for the fact that touching hellebore is bad luck—and irritating to the skin, besides. Some part of me feels guilty, too, at the prospect of ripping up the only flowers that adorn Alex's grave.

Please, I think in the direction of that darkness that hovers, omnipresent, on the fringes of my awareness—the darkness I've come to associate with Alex's ghost. *Please listen to me.*

Silence answers.

At last I sigh and settle back onto my hips, opening Ellis's book in my lap. The pages are hard to turn; age has stuck them together and stiffened the binding.

"Chapter One," I read aloud. *"There Is No One Left."*

I glance toward the headstone again, as if to see if Alex is paying attention. The stone is as gray and faceless as before.

I keep reading anyway, all through chapter one and well into chapter two, until my throat starts to feel dry and hoarse. I close the book and, after a beat, lean forward to rest it against the headstone. Another gift to a girl who has no need for gifts. Not anymore.

Something painful catches in my chest, and I press my brow against the chilly soil, eyes clenched shut. A tear leaks past my lashes and drips onto my fingers. *Useless, this is all so . . . I'm so useless.*

I shouldn't be here. Alex was always the smart one. Alex was going to *be* somebody. You could tell by the way the instructors fawned over her work, how effortlessly everything came to her. She would write an essay overnight, drunk with a joint in one hand, and next thing you know she's won the English department's Best Paper Award. Alex was applying to the Ivy League. We all knew she'd be accepted anywhere she wanted to go.

Not like me. I'm the spoiled rich girl who lurked at the fringes of Alex's halo, stealing her light.

The crunch of frozen ground breaking makes me look up. Ellis stands by the stone with her weight braced against the handle of a shovel.

"I think we should dig her up."

I gape at her, my heartbeat suddenly beating hard and high enough that it feels like I'm gagging on blood.

"What?"

Ellis is as placid as ever. "You said the grave was empty, right? So there's nothing to be afraid of. There's no body to desecrate. Maybe seeing that for yourself will give you closure."

I stumble to my feet, dirty hands tangling in my skirt. "No. Absolutely not."

"You can put the book in her coffin," Ellis suggests in a very rational tone. "You can perform a spell to put her spirit to rest."

"Ellis, *digging up Alex's grave* isn't going to fix anything."

"And ignoring the problem will?"

I can't. I can't do this. I turn away from her, staring out into the forest instead, the blackness of night somehow more complete now than it was when we first came.

"Where did you even get the shovel?" I say. I'm aware of how my voice sounds: wild, hysterical, cracking on the word *shovel* like I'm a breath away from total delirium.

I make myself twist back toward Ellis, who's still standing there like this is a perfectly normal conversation to have in a graveyard past midnight.

She gestures vaguely over one shoulder. "The caretaker's shed. The lock was easy to pick."

I'm not hearing this. This is absurd.

"You're insane."

Ellis shakes her head very slightly. "I'm not the one who's seeing things, Felicity. I'm not having breakdowns in the woods and warding off ghosts."

I press both hands over my face, careless of the way it smears grave dirt on my cheeks. God. *God.*

"I'm not digging up that grave," I say.

"Fine, then we won't. It was only a suggestion."

Ellis takes the shovel back where she found it, and I stay there, my feet planting roots in the earth. This time in Ellis's absence, the air is colder. I feel Alex's ghost like breath on the back of my neck.

Maybe Ellis is right. I am crazy. Just like my mother.

We drive back to the car agency in relative silence, Ellis's gloved thumb tapping against the wheel and my hands gripping my knees.

It's past two by the time we're home, but as late as it is, I don't think I'll be able to sleep.

"Are you okay?" Ellis asks once we're back inside Godwin House, lingering on the second-floor landing. The light from the overhead lamp casts odd shadows on her face. "I didn't mean to push you. I wasn't trying to—"

"I'm fine," I interrupt. "Sorry. I just . . ."

Why am I apologizing? Of course I didn't want to exhume my ex-girlfriend's grave. Ellis is the one who should be asking forgiveness.

Even so, I can't find the nerve to say as much. I chew at my lip and brace my back against the wall, both arms wrapped around my stomach. Ellis's thumb scrapes at the finish on the stair banister.

"Look," Ellis says at last. "I only want to help. You know that, right?"

I stare at her in silence.

"You already knew that grave's empty. I thought this would give you closure. I want you to understand. . . . I can't keep seeing you torture yourself like this."

"Well, I'm sorry it's so *painful* for you," I snap. It feels like I'm biting the words off a sheet of ice. "Seeing me. *Like this.*"

"Felicity—"

"I'm going to bed."

I take the stairs up to the third floor two at a time and kick my door shut so hard it slams. I brace, anticipating the rap of Alex's broom handle against the floor.

But it never comes. Alex's ghost, if it exists, doesn't care about noise.

The only thing down there, I tell myself, is Ellis Haley.

And Ellis Haley can go fuck herself.

My intent beinge only to construct a School for Young Ladies, a Place of refuge and education in Etiquette, soe these imperiled Young Ladies might prove usefull to Society and to God.

—Deliverance Lemont, accused Witch
and founder of Dalloway School

Bury my bones deep, that I might feel the flames of Hell.

—Last words of Margery Lemont,
buried alive in the year 1714; recorded
by those present at her burial

19

I'm on my bed, paging through my well-worn copy of *I Capture the Castle,* when my phone rings.

It takes me a moment to realize what the sound is. It's been over a week since I've used my phone; for the most part I've left it plugged into the outlet behind my desk and forgotten about it. But now I dig it out from where it's fallen, between my trash bin and the wall, and thumb open the screen.

"Mom?"

"—humidity levels really must be checked every day . . . Oh, Felicity? Is that you?"

I sit in my desk chair. "Of course it's Felicity. You're the one who called me, remember?"

My mother's still in France. It sounds windy on the other end of the line; I imagine her on a yacht off the coast of Nice, wearing a beige sundress and ordering the staff to bring her more drinks. It's still November, even in Nice, but I can almost imagine my mother's money going so far as to buy good weather, God herself susceptible to Morrow bribes.

"Oh, right. . . . Well. Dr. Ortega thought it might be a good idea if I checked in on you, now that the semester's getting on. . . ." *Almost over* is what she means. Dr. Ortega probably told her to call me weeks ago.

I stay silent. Another gust of wind, loud through the speaker.

"So how have you been, honey?"

My mother has never in her life used pet names.

"Fine. Everything's fine."

"You're sure? I just mean, Dr. Ortega said you haven't been checking in with her like you were supposed to."

So my mother is still in contact with Dr. Ortega. I can't decide if I'm more surprised—my mother has never taken such a close interest in my well-being before—or irritated.

"I've been busy," I say. "I have a lot of work to do, actually, I should—"

"Are you coming home for Thanksgiving? I should be back stateside by then."

I make the decision on impulse, even though I have nowhere else to stay, even though campus will be closed over the holiday. "No. I'm going home with a friend."

"Oh? Which friend?"

"You don't know her." I hook my ankles around the legs of my desk chair. "But you're always welcome to come and visit next semester. If you want."

She doesn't want.

A long pause drags out behind my words. My mother would love to prove me wrong, but even Cecelia Morrow can't deny her nature. "Maybe. . . . I'll be quite busy in the spring. I'll have to check my calendar."

"You do that."

"Are you sure you're all right? You sound a little . . ." She doesn't seem able to find the word. My mother has never been much of a poet. "Have you been taking your medication?"

"I told you, I'm fine. I have to go, actually. I'm meeting my friend to work on our final project."

"Is this the same friend you're visiting for break?"

"Yes. Same friend. She's right here; I have to go. I'll talk to you later. Tell Dr. Ortega to stop worrying about me."

I hang up before my mother can say anything else or demand to speak to the imaginary and impatient friend.

I drop my phone behind my bed and sink lower in my desk chair, turning my face toward the ceiling. I'm still like that, eyes half-shut, when someone knocks at my door.

It's Kajal. "There's a visitor downstairs for you," she says. I recognize the dubious edge to her tone and frown.

"Who?"

"Some little third-year girl. She kept asking if Ellis was here, too."

Hannah Stratford.

"Did you tell her I was gone?"

Kajal's mouth twists into something that is almost but not quite a smile. "I told her you'd be right down."

I sigh and follow Kajal down the stairs to the entryway, where Hannah Stratford stands in the foyer, bowed under the weight of a massive brown box.

"Hey!" she says, breathless and staggering with the effort of keeping herself from tipping over. "I was just in the mail room. This came for you!"

A dark, mean part of me wants to keep watching her struggle, but I shove it away. I'm not that person. I've tried so hard not to *be* that person. So I move forward to take one end of the box, and when it slumps lower in Hannah's arms, it exposes her flushed, damp face grinning over the edge of the cardboard.

"You didn't have to bring it here," I tell her. "They would have called."

And now I'm wondering why Hannah was looking at the names on packages in the first place.

"I know, but it's been forever since I've seen you, so . . ."

Hannah nudges the box against my chest, and I step back, letting her guide us up the stairs. We have to pause on the landing for Hannah to catch her breath; I position myself in front of the corridor, in case Ellis makes the mistake of emerging from her room while Hannah is still present.

Eventually we manage to lug the box to the third floor and shove it onto my bed. Hannah's shoulders heave. I'm perspiring a little myself.

"What's in it?" Hannah asks.

I eye the box, which is plastered with FRAGILE stickers and has my own home address scrawled in one corner. "It's everything I didn't bring with me when I came back to school." My mother had said she'd send it at the start of the semester. I'd almost forgotten.

"Oh! Cool! You should open it."

I look at her, long enough that anyone else would have gotten the message. But Hannah Stratford stays precisely where she is, beaming at me patiently with her hands clasped in front of her.

I wonder if I ever looked like that. I wonder if I ever smiled so easily.

I dig out a knife from my desk drawer and slice open the tape, unfolding the cardboard flaps to expose the box's contents. Hannah watches on, fascinated, as I sift through all the artifacts of a life lived so long ago it feels like it happened to someone else. There's a handheld video-game system—that can go in the trash, obviously—some art prints I bought two years ago in Granada, hiking books filled with glossy photos of trails in Albania and Greece and Turkey from trips me and Alex will never take. It's a box of useless things.

Hannah dives in the moment I withdraw, pulling out my tennis racquet. "I didn't know you played," she says, delighted. "We should go down to the courts sometime."

I used to do intramurals at Dalloway. I didn't even bother signing up this year.

"This is a really nice racquet," Hannah says, rubbing her thumb over the brand name engraved into the handle.

"You can keep it."

"What? No, I couldn't. . . ." Of course, she's already smiling.

I dump the hiking books back into the box and close the flaps. "I'm not going to play, so it might as well get put to good use. Take it."

Hannah's grip tightens around the racquet, and even though she opens her mouth to protest more, I can tell she's already made her decision.

"What are you two troublemakers up to?"

Hannah spins around so quickly she drops the racquet, then swears and snatches it back off the floor. Ellis leans against my open doorway, arms crossed over her chest and a crooked smile curving its way up her mouth. She'd climbed the stairs so quietly I never heard her coming.

"Ellis! Hi!" Hannah lurches forward, saving me from having to respond.

Ellis draws her gaze away from where it's fixed on my face, but belatedly, just in time to let Hannah grasp her hand. "Hello. Have we met?"

"Sort of. I mean, I'm friends with Felicity."

Ellis makes eye contact with me over Hannah's head, and I shake mine, very slightly.

Hannah barrels on: "And we were both at the Lemont House party last month! Do you remember? You left so quickly . . ."

"What do you want, Ellis?" I say.

Hannah's mouth snaps shut, and Ellis takes the opportunity to extract her hand from Hannah's grip, pushing off the doorframe and taking a step into my room. "It's personal."

At last, Hannah seems to catch the hint. She clutches the tennis racquet to her chest and backs out into the hall, her gaze flitting back to Ellis even as she says, "Okay. I'll see you later, Felicity. Thanks for the racquet."

Ellis kicks the door shut with her heel.

I linger by the bed, my own arms folded now and my chest a cage for my heart as it throws itself against my ribs. "'It's personal'?"

"It is," Ellis says. She moves in, sitting down in my desk chair and crossing her long legs at the knees. She sits as if she owns the place.

"I don't want to talk about what happened in the graveyard."

"We're going to have to talk about it," Ellis says. "You were very upset."

"Sometimes people are upset, Ellis. Let it go."

She shakes her head. "I can't. You know that." She digs a thumbnail into the wood groove of my desk, tracing it toward one corner. "I don't like this tension between us. I want you to trust me."

"I trust you. There—are you happy?"

Ellis fixes me with a narrowed gaze. "I mean it. You're right, I shouldn't have pressured you the other night. It was a strange request. I know that now."

A strange request. It's as if Ellis thinks we all live in books. At least then it would be easy enough to delete what happened in the cemetery, make me forget, and start over.

I sigh and drop down onto the side of my bed, the box of nonsense bouncing with my weight.

"I'm not angry," I tell her. "Not really, anyway. Not for long. I know you were only trying to do the right thing."

"I *was,*" she insists, and releases the desk to lean forward and grasp my knee instead. Her fingers curve all the way around my kneecap, swallowing the entire joint. "I . . . God help me, Felicity, but I care about you. I want you to be happy again."

Again? She's never seen me happy. She doesn't even know what that looks like.

"All right," I say. And when she turns her hand palm-up on my knee, I take it, lacing our fingers together. "All right."

It's a lie, of course. I have no intention of being happy, for Ellis or otherwise.

But what else am I going to say? Ellis sees me.

I need to be seen.

Things ease between me and Ellis the week following that conversation. I'm grateful for it; with the end of the semester approaching in a flurry of final papers and projects, I don't think I could have sustained my resentment without unraveling in some other way.

Although it might already be too late for that. I dream about Alex almost every night now, even when I'm not having nightmares. She's the girl at the café in my dream about Paris; she's the woman with soft fingers touching my lips; she's falling and falling and falling into an endless dark.

I'm not the only one worried about final exams looming at us from the other side of break. Godwin House is consumed in a constant fog of low-grade panic. Kajal has realized she's on the cusp of an A and a B in AP European History, and her score on the final essay will determine whether she makes dean's list this semester. Meanwhile, Clara, whose record is in somewhat more dire straits than Kajal's, refuses to emerge from her room. Leonie spends half her time in the library—and I have started to regret my decision to eschew laptops. It's much more difficult to write a fifty-page essay on a typewriter than one would think. I don't want to find myself rushing to get it finished in the few weeks after Thanksgiving.

Wyatt calls me into her office midweek to check up on thesis progress. She wants to see pages—pages that, of course,

I don't have, because I'm not writing about the topic we agreed upon. I escape by telling her the truth, or part of it at least: I'm writing on a typewriter, so I only have one copy. I'll show her after break.

That buys me a few weeks to invent an excuse for why I'm writing about witches again.

Ellis is the only one of us who seems relatively at peace. "My main concern right now is finishing the book," she tells me, both of us sitting on the common room floor with the materials for our Art History project arranged on the rug in front of us. "Everything else is secondary."

"That's easy for you to say. Even if you fail out of Dalloway, you still have a writing career."

She shakes her head. "I only have a writing *career* if I publish another book. And to publish this book, I need to finish it first."

I sip my coffee. The taste is strong and bitter, the way Ellis likes it.

Ellis highlights a line on another page then finally sits upright, fixing me in her gaze. "Are you all right?" she asks in that characteristically blunt way of hers.

"What? Yes, of course. Why? Don't I look all right?"

"You look exhausted," she says. "Have you been sleeping?"

"No," I admit. The truth is, I've been doing my best to stay awake; my nightmares have only gotten worse since our ritual at the church. "I can't sleep."

Ellis's mouth tightens, but at least she doesn't say anything more on the subject. Perhaps she knows how little I want her pity. Instead she shoves one of our new library books into my lap and says, "You're in charge of chapters fourteen through eighteen."

The reading is a slog, but we get through it. Then Ellis wants to dissect the Dalloway murders again; she's stuck on the scene with Beatrix Walker's death. She was found with all the bones in her body broken, as if she'd fallen from a great height, but she was *discovered* indoors, far from anywhere above ground level.

"Someone obviously moved the body, like with Cordelia," Ellis says, sounding almost exasperated. "The simplest explanation is always the best. Why assume witchcraft?"

"But how did she fall? There's nowhere on campus high enough—not in the eighteenth century, anyway." Except for the cliffs where Alex died.

I grit my hands into fists.

"Maybe she didn't fall at all. Someone could have broken her bones individually." Ellis lies down on the common room rug, her limbs splayed out. She lifts one wrist in demonstration. "A hammer here." She touches her ribs. "A kick to the chest."

I shift over her, straddling her middle, and brace one hand against her sternum. My hair has fallen forward, long pale strands tickling the skin at Ellis's throat. "But she'd be struggling," I point out. I add pressure to my hand, holding Ellis in place. "And screaming."

Ellis gazes up at me, eyes steady and unafraid. "Not if she was dead first."

We finally call it a night around one, Ellis stretching her long arms toward the ceiling as I collect all our notes and other detritus.

"Again tomorrow?"

"Six sharp." Her grin is quick; I want to memorize it.

My room feels dark and barren when I go upstairs. I've been spending more and more time in the library with Ellis, enough so that coming back here even to sleep feels foreign.

I should have brought more books when I came back to school, perhaps. More photos, maybe a few potted plants—something to bring life in wintertime. Something aside from the incense and crystals and candles I dug out of my closet hiding space, meager wards against the dark.

I trail my fingers along the spines on my bookshelf, tracing past *Little Women* and *The Bluest Eye* and *Wide Sargasso Sea.* I've read all these a dozen times, have loved them more at each iteration. But then my hand brushes an unfamiliar leather binding, and I stop, the air suddenly frozen.

The Secret Garden. It's the same copy Ellis gave me in the graveyard, the same copy I left leaning against Alex's headstone, with its old pages and embossed gold foil.

I'm sick to the blood, sick in a way that makes me certain I shouldn't touch that book. I should leave, should burn this place to the ground.

But I can't help myself. I slide the book out of its space between two Austens with shaking hands. When I open the ancient pages I smell something familiar, something that isn't glue or rotting paper. It's jasmine and vetiver. It's . . . Alex. It's Alex's perfume.

Pressed between chapters three and four is a sprig of hellebore.

20

I drop the book, and it thumps to the floor, releasing a cloud of dust as I stagger back. The walls are closing in on me, the room airless. It's a feeling like standing on a precipice, the world dropping out from under you, and nothing but sky between you and certain death.

I spin around, expecting to find Alex there, with skeleton fingers reaching for my throat. Her face bloodless and pale, withered with decay. Her mouth sucking in air like a broken vacuum, and frothy blood leaking from her lips—I'd watched videos of drowning victims online after I remembered the truth; I know what it would look like. The way her chest would heave as she tried to breathe. The gut punch, her back curling, as she couldn't exhale.

The room is empty, but it's not empty. I feel her. She's here. She's in every corner, every shadow. She's above me, inside me. She's black ice in my veins.

She's the shadowy figure flitting between the trees, watching us sleep in the snow.

I stumble out of the room and down the creaky Godwin

stairs, dragging against the wall and gripping the banister, as if that could keep me from falling if Alex's spirit made me throw myself down. The light is off in Ellis's room when I manage to get my disobedient legs to carry me along the corridor. Tripping over the fringe of the rug, I press my sweaty hands against her lintel.

For a moment I'm sure I'm about to vomit all over her door, but I swallow bile down and knock instead. She doesn't answer, so I knock again and again, until I'm just pounding and shaking and sobbing. The time it takes for Ellis to open the door feels like a thousand years. But she does open it, and I tip forward and into her arms.

Her hands find my back hesitantly, as if she's never held anyone so close before. She's in a silk dressing gown; it occurs to me on some distant level that I've never seen her so undressed.

"What is it?" she asks, slowly smoothing her touch up and down my spine. "What happened?"

I can barely get the words out. They're like broken glass in my mouth, deadly.

"Alex," I manage at last, and a fresh shudder rolls through my body.

"What about Alex?"

I'm still trembling, but Ellis pushes me back enough to look at me properly, her gaze traversing my face as if she can interpret something new from my tears and snot.

"The . . . the book," I say, after taking a few unsteady breaths. "The one we left at her grave."

"The Secret Garden," Ellis provides.

I nod. "It's . . . It's in . . . It showed up in my room. The same . . . the same copy."

Ellis's gaze sharpens. "The same? You're sure?"

"Of course I'm sure!" My voice pitches loudly enough that Leonie opens her door down the hall and peers out at us, blearily asking what's going on.

"We're okay," Ellis says, and she tugs me into her room and kicks the door shut behind us.

"It's the same book," I tell her again. My voice is a little calmer now at least. I don't feel quite so much like I'm suffocating. "It's . . . Alex. I *told* you. I told you going to that graveyard was a bad idea! Now she's angry. She's . . . she's never going to leave me in peace!"

Any other day, perhaps I'd have taken a moment to be pleased with myself; I've clearly presented a mystery to which Ellis Haley has no ready answer. She stares at me with a look on her face I've never seen before, like she doesn't believe what she's hearing.

It occurs to me in that moment—away from the proximity of the book itself—that there's another explanation for its reappearance.

"You," I choke out. "*You* put it there. Didn't you?" I shove her with both hands, and she falls back on her heels, which for some reason strikes me as not good enough. I push her again, harder. *"Didn't you?"*

"No," she snaps, and when I move to hit her, she grabs both my wrists, squeezing tight. "Felicity, are you even hearing yourself?"

"I should think you'd prefer an explanation that doesn't

involve *ghosts,*" I snarl. "You were at the graveyard. You saw the book. You *brought* the book. It would have been so easy for you to go back and get it again."

Ellis's grip strengthens, and she shakes me slightly. "Why? Why would I do something like that? I've been trying so goddamn hard to get you to realize you're delusional—"

"Delusional?"

"Well, you are! What else do you call all this nonsense about ghosts and witches and magic books and . . . I wouldn't mess with you like that."

I don't know how to believe her. The Ellis I know—the Ellis I thought I knew—wouldn't do that, it's true. But . . .

"Then explain the book," I demand. "If the ghost isn't real, explain that to me!"

She shakes her head very slowly. "I can't. I . . . I'm going to have to think about it. I'm sure there's a normal reason behind all this."

"Right. The only normal reason I can come up with is that you put the book in my room."

"Yes, you've mentioned that option." Ellis makes a harsh noise, exhaling through clenched teeth. "But I don't know when I'm meant to have chased down this book of yours. We've been practically inseparable since that graveyard trip—you're always with me. And if you aren't with me, one of the other girls is."

Only that isn't true. Yes, we're together a lot; Ellis and I are constantly studying, or working on our project. Other times we're with the rest of the girls: on a Night Migration; in the common room, reading poetry; on an outing to a nearby farm to pick up fresh meat and dairy, fascinated as the farmer shows us the beehives on her property, a thousand buzzing insects settling over our arms and the nets over our heads.

But we still have to sleep. Ellis could have crept out at night and returned to the graveyard for the book, carried it back home, and bided her time until she could slip it onto my bookshelf.

Ellis wouldn't do something like that, I tell myself. She might be a lot of things, but she isn't malicious. The whole point of this project outside of researching for her book is to prove to me that ghosts *don't* exist—so why would she do something to convince me that they do?

Alex, a voice in the back of my mind insists. *It was Alex. That was your first instinct, and it's true.*

"I'll show you," I say. "Come up to my room, and I'll *show* you the book."

Ellis takes a shallow breath and says, "Tomorrow. Yes, I want to see it, but . . . Felicity, it's really late. I was half-asleep when you knocked."

Of course. I can only imagine what a madwoman I looked throwing myself against her shut door at one in the morning, crying about books and ghosts. Accusing her of torturing me. I scrub both hands over my face, rubbing away what's left of my tears. "I'm sorry."

"It's all right," Ellis says.

"No. No, it's . . . Sorry. I'll let you sleep."

She gives me a thin smile and trails her fingers along my cheek, her hand dipping back toward my ear before falling to her side. "Tomorrow," she says again.

I have no choice then but to take myself back up the stairs to the room and that horrible book still lying discarded on the floor, the pages all bent now and the smell of Alex's perfume still pungent in the air. I refuse to touch that cursed thing. I leave it where it lies and grab a handful of dried dandelion from my stash of herbs, sprinkle it in a circle around the book, as if that could keep her ghost at bay.

I can't sleep in here.

I grab my pillow and duvet off the bed and head back downstairs, this time into the common room, where I make up a temporary bed on the sofa and curl up there, facing the hearth. Even here, I'm afraid to have my back to the room.

Eventually I rock to an uneasy sleep. In my dreams I'm chased by monsters with long, reaching hands, flickering lights, and blood on ice.

I lurch awake hours later with my heart in my mouth and cold sweat damp on my lower back. But it's already daylight, the sun streaming in through the east-facing windows. Leonie and Kajal are in the kitchen. I can hear their voices chattering as they clang about with pots and pans; that must be what woke me.

I drag a hand through my sweat-salty hair and press my brow forward against bent knees.

Maybe I dreamed what happened last night. Maybe it was all some horrible nightmare. Maybe—

"There you are," Ellis says, standing over me. "I was looking for you. You wanted to show me that book, right?"

She's already dressed, in a jacket with elbow patches, like some absentminded professor. Still in the couch, in my wrinkled yesterday's clothes, I feel like a child caught out-of-bounds.

"Right." All the terror of last night seeps up like groundwater—diluted now but still nauseating, still potent. I shove the duvet aside and bundle it and the pillow under my arm, carrying them up with me to the third floor.

Ellis trails behind like a tall shadow. I find myself glancing back, as if to make sure my Eurydice still follows.

"I still can't explain it," I tell her as we turn onto the landing. "I don't know how it got back here. And we both . . . we've been *here.* We did leave it there, right? I'm not imagining things?"

"We'll figure it out," Ellis says, firm and confident, as usual. More confident, I note, than she'd sounded last night.

I push open my bedroom door and step inside, and the duvet falls from my arms.

The book is gone.

The circle of dandelion petals is still there, a ward against evil spirits, but the book itself has vanished. The only thing left is the hellebore, fallen in the middle of my ward like an ill omen.

"It was *right here.* It was right—"

I'm breathless, light-headed. It's a feeling like being eviscerated.

Ellis moves into the room behind me, cutting past the bundled-up blanket to gaze down at the herbs littering my floor. She doesn't say anything, but she doesn't have to. The thin line of her mouth says enough.

I round on her, heat rising in my cheeks. "I swear it was here. Last night, it was on my shelf. And here—I dropped it *right* here. You believe me, don't you?"

Ellis's eyes flick sidelong to catch mine.

"It was here!"

"I believe you," Ellis says, too slowly.

I shake my head, catch a lock of my hair, and start twisting it around my knuckles, tugging until it hurts. "Someone must have taken it," I say. "Someone came up here, someone . . ."

"Who?" Ellis asks. She's infuriatingly calm. "Who would have come into your room and stolen this book? What would anyone want with it?"

"I don't know. I don't—"

I shove past her, banging the door open and darting down the hall toward the stairs. Ellis is on my heels almost immediately, calling my name; I ignore her and clatter down the steps, spinning around the bottom landing fast enough the banister rattles under my grip.

I burst into the kitchen. Leonie is by the stove, an omelet sizzling in a skillet, Kajal cutting up a fresh bell pepper at the island. "Did you take it?" I demand.

Kajal puts down her knife. "Take what?"

"The book. There was a book in my room. Someone took it."

I sense Ellis slipping into the kitchen behind me.

Kajal and Leonie glance at each other.

"I don't think any of us would have gone into your room without your permission," Leonie says, with a gentleness that is both surprising and irritating. It's the same tone the nurses took with me at the facility: cautious, soft, like anything else would fracture me. Like I might get violent if they spoke too loudly.

All at once I'm aware of how this scene would look to an observer: Myself, wild-haired and hysterical at eight in the morning, demanding that someone confess to theft. Ellis, behind me, grim.

They think I'm insane. They all do.

"I'm sorry," I gasp out, too late. "I'm sorry. I don't . . . I barely slept. I . . ."

"It's okay," Leonie says, in that same too-calm tone.

I clench my teeth so hard my jaw hurts.

"Maybe a nice cup of coffee," Ellis suggests at last, and she touches my elbow as she moves past me to the cabinet.

I stand there and stare at her back as she takes down the pour-over cups and filters, opens the ceramic box of fresh beans, and pours a tablespoonful into the grinder.

Leonie offers a hesitant smile across the island. "Do you want an omelet? We have plenty of eggs."

I can't speak. I'm afraid if I do, I'll start crying and I won't stop. So I shake my head, feeling my face crumple a beat before I escape the kitchen—back upstairs, back to my damn room with the dandelion on the floor and the scent of Alex's perfume long since dissipated. I pace from the window to the dresser and back once, two times. It's cold, it's so cold.

The book was here. I know that much for certain. It was here, and then it was gone—the book we left at the cemetery, the book that smelled of Alex's perfume.

She's here.

I push the thought away, but a sick ribbon of nausea is tied to it. I can't stop thinking about her.

She's here.

I grab a candle from my collection and kneel down on the floor in the middle of that dandelion ring. I strike a match and light the flame, whisper, "Please go. Please. I'm sorry. Please leave me alone."

I don't know if I'm talking to a ghost anymore . . . or to something else.

A rap sounds against my doorframe. I jerk my head up; Ellis stands there with a mug of coffee cupped between both hands.

"I thought you might still like that coffee," she says quietly.

I fall back onto my heels and exhale. At least when she's here, the room feels warmer. "Thanks."

I hold out a hand, and Ellis moves deeper into my bedroom, crouching down next to me and passing the mug. It's still steaming hot; the liquid burns my tongue when I take a sip. I'm glad for the pain. It's steadying.

I wish it were bourbon.

Only as soon as I think that, I think of my mother, with her empty wine bottles, glass shattered on the marble floor, and gag.

"I'm worried about you," Ellis says.

I snort. "I know. So's my mother. She called the other week to *check in.* For the first time all semester, but at least she's performing her maternal duties."

"What did you tell her?"

The coffee's just as hot when I swallow it a second time. I clench my eyes shut and drink it anyway, my tongue numb and dry-feeling after. "I told her I was fine. I . . ." I laugh, "I told her I was going home with someone over break so I wouldn't have to see her instead. I suppose I'll have to get a hotel room in town."

"Or you could stay here with me."

My heart seizes in my chest. "What?"

"Stay here with me," Ellis says again. Her hand finds my knee and squeezes once. "My parents will be traveling most of break, so I got special permission to stay at the school. My sibling, Quinn, is coming up to visit; I'm sure they'd love to meet you."

A quavering smile rises to my lips despite myself. I shake my head. "I wasn't trying to invite myself, for the record."

"Duly noted. Please say you'll do it."

I've never wanted anything more in my life. "Yes. I'll stay."

Ellis grins and swats my leg before her hand retreats back to her own lap. I find myself bereft in the wake of her touch. I want more. I want her touching me everywhere.

I want more, I suspect, than Ellis has the capacity to give.

21

With the campus empty and Godwin all to ourselves, being at Dalloway feels like summer again.

Ellis and I play records in the common room with the volume turned up loud, hang out of bedroom windows with lit joints and our heads full of stars.

I know that I'm unwell. I know I shouldn't keep denying it. I'd hoped distance from Alex's death would erase the fear scrawled on the walls of my mind, but it hasn't. Dr. Ortega once described psychotic depression as being like a gun: my genetics loaded the chamber with bullets, my mother passed the weapon into my hand, but Alex's death pulled the trigger.

So maybe I imagined the book. Maybe Ellis is right and it was never there—maybe I *wanted* it to be there. Maybe I wanted Alex to punish me.

And maybe it's all right to admit that.

Ellis's sibling arrives on the third day of Thanksgiving break, their vintage Mustang barely visible through the trees around Godwin. From the third-floor hall window, I watch them ascend the path on foot, a narrow figure silhouetted against the setting sun.

"Ellis," I call out, just loud enough to be heard from the floor below, where Ellis is hard at work on her novel. "Quinn's here."

Even from upstairs I can hear her chair scrape against the floor, then the clatter of her feet on the hardwood as she races down the stairs. I follow, trailing belatedly after Ellis out into the cool dusk, where she has thrown both arms around the newcomer, who squeezes her tight enough that Ellis's feet lift off the ground.

They're dark-haired, like Ellis, and tall—also like Ellis. But when they set Ellis down and I catch sight of their face, I realize they're nothing like their sister at all. Their face is too open, too heart-on-their-sleeve. I don't know how I can tell such things from a glance, but it feels true. Our gazes meet over Ellis's head; Quinn's is steady and black-hued.

"Felicity, this is Quinn. Quinn, Felicity," Ellis says at last, a saving grace. "My friend from school that I told you about."

"All lies, I'm sure," I say, and when Quinn offers their hand, I shake it.

"I imagine Ellis didn't talk about me very much at all," Quinn says.

There's no good response to that; it's true, after all. Ellis only mentioned them twice. I know they're much older than Ellis, by about ten years. I know from Ellis's use of gender-neutral pronouns that Quinn is nonbinary. And I can tell by looking that, aside from their basic appearance, they have a lot of other things in common with their sister—at least if the blazer and flamboyant gold cravat are anything to go by.

"I know a little," I end up saying, and Ellis folds her hands behind her back, smiling like a proud gallery curator who has just introduced a patron to a brand-new work of art.

Quinn gestures to the house. "Shall we go in and get to know each other, then?"

We head inside and to the common room, Ellis pushing me down into my favorite plush burgundy armchair. Quinn takes the seat opposite, lounging on the chaise and lighting a cigarette. I find myself unsurprised they're smoking indoors; Ellis does it often enough that the shock has worn off. Perhaps she got the idea from Quinn.

For her part, Ellis heads directly to her hidden stash of bourbon—the bourbon, I recall, that Quinn had gifted her. My gaze lingers too long, watching her elegant hands move to drip bitters into three crystal glasses. I manage to look away only when I realize Quinn's watching me, assessing.

I clasp my hands together in my lap and attempt a smile. I feel like I'm trying to impress someone's parents on a first date. Not that I've ever had one of those. Not really.

"Tell me about yourself, Felicity," Quinn says.

What is this, a job interview? I dig the side of my thumbnail into my hand to keep from saying something I'll regret. "I don't know how much there is to say. I'm not a very interesting person, I'm afraid."

"Felicity's being modest," Ellis says. "She's the best academic in Godwin House, and I include Housemistress MacDonald in that assessment."

I don't blush easily, but I blush now. I hope the light here's dim enough that Quinn doesn't notice. "That's not true."

"What is your favorite class?" Quinn asks.

"English literature, broadly," I say. "But I'm doing my thesis on the portrayal of witchcraft and mental illness in genre novels."

Ellis frowns over her shoulder at us. "I thought you said you were writing about horror novels or something."

"I *am,* but . . . I did so much work before, when my thesis was still about the Dalloway witches. It seemed a shame to let that all go to waste."

"Are you sure that's a good idea?" Ellis says, stirring one of the drinks. "After . . ."

Fortunately for me, Quinn takes that moment to step in. "Mental illness in genre," they say. "Are you more interested in accuracy of portrayal? Or the significance thereof?"

"Mostly how depictions of mental illness are used to build suspense by introducing uncertainty and a sense of mistrust, especially with regard to the narrator's perception of events, and the conflation of magic and madness in female characters."

"See?" Ellis says, returning with two of the cocktails in hand. "I told you she was brilliant."

Heat rises in my cheeks, and when she hands me one of the drinks, our fingers brush. Does her touch linger a beat longer than necessary? Or am I imagining things?

Quinn glances down at their drink and lets out half a laugh. "Old fashioneds? Really, Ellis? You're seventeen, last time I checked."

"Are you going to turn me in?" Ellis says.

Quinn shakes their head. "No, but I *am* going to mock you mercilessly. When I let you try one of my whiskey sours over the summer, you hated it so much you puked in the hydrangeas."

Ellis turns a delicate shade of rose; I'm fascinated. I don't think I've ever seen her embarrassed.

I relate far more to the old Ellis than the new one, but I take a sip of my old fashioned anyway. I can tell intellectually that the sweetness is balanced perfectly by the bitters, that neither overwhelms the heat of the bourbon—that it's an objectively good drink—but I still hate it. I set the glass aside on the end table and hope Ellis won't notice if I don't finish.

"What else?" Quinn presses me. "Where are you from? Where did you go before Dalloway?"

"Jesus, Quinn," Ellis says, her tone sharp—still ruffled by Quinn's taking her down a peg, I imagine. "What is this, the Spanish Inquisition?"

"It's okay. I don't mind," I say.

Quinn allows me a slight smile from across the room. Maybe I've won myself some credit with them after all.

"I'm from Colorado originally," I tell them, "but I went to the Fay School before Dalloway. That was a long time ago now; I'm a senior."

Senior plus, really, but Quinn doesn't need to know this is my second attempt at finishing my prep school career. Assuming Ellis hasn't already informed them of my flaws.

I decide not to give Quinn the chance to guide the conversation, by asking the next question. "My mother's Cecelia Morrow. Of the Boston Morrows."

Not that it needs to be clarified; my mother's flight from the East Coast, unmarried and pregnant by a stranger, had been what passed for a scandal back in the aughts. Everyone knew all the nasty little details, no matter how fiercely my grandmother had tried to obscure them.

Quinn performs a dramatic shudder. "New Englanders."

"You're such a snob," Ellis says affectionately. She has curled up on the sofa, long legs flung out along the floor and crossed at the ankles. Her trousers hitch up high enough that I can tell she's wearing sock garters.

"What about you?" I shoot back before Quinn can resume the interrogation. "I already know where you went to university. But I don't know what you studied."

"Statistics."

"Quinn's a poker player," Ellis elaborates.

"If my trans-ness didn't murder our parents, the gambling certainly would have." Quinn's slow smirk suggests they don't mind that at all. "Ellis has always been the darling child, although I can't imagine why. She's just like me."

Ellis rolls her eyes, but it seems good-natured. She leans over, and Quinn hands her their cigarette.

"I think it's almost time for bed," Ellis says, blowing her smoke toward the ceiling. "It's getting late, and you had a long drive."

"Kicking me out already?" Quinn's grin is slow and mischievous; I don't have the impression they mind being bossed around by their little sister.

But I *am* surprised Ellis is attempting it in the first place. I get the sense she's trying to reassert some kind of dominance after Quinn called her out for the fake whiskey habit.

"Oh, we'll see quite enough of each other over the next few

days, I'm sure," Ellis says. She stabs out the cigarette and gets to her feet, finishing off her cocktail in a few long swallows.

It means I have to gulp down the rest of my old fashioned as well, and I waver a little when I stand. I tell myself that's fatigue; I'm not such a lightweight as to be thrown off balance by one drink. "It was nice meeting you, Quinn. I'm sure I'll see you tomorrow."

"Bright and early," they say, clapping Ellis on the shoulder one last time before heading for the door. "I'm staying at a hotel in town. Not far at all; feel free to call if you need anything."

And then they're gone, as quickly as they arrived. If I were alone, I might wonder if the whole thing had been some bizarre drunken fever dream.

Ellis stands in the hall with her arms crossed, staring at the space where Quinn had stood.

"What?" I say, a teasing edge creeping into my tone. "Sick of them already?"

Ellis shakes her head. "Of course not. Although I do wonder why they bothered to come all this way if they're only going to make fun of me."

A sharp sound bursts out of my chest, almost a laugh. "Ellis, they weren't making *fun* of you. They were perfectly nice."

"Oh, yes, that's Quinn. *Perfectly nice.*"

She stalks back into the common room, and I follow, sitting next to her on the sofa and—after a moment—patting her knee.

"Well they aren't staying in Godwin, at any rate, so you'll have plenty of breaks," I say.

She sighs and tips her head back against the upholstery. Her cheeks are still pink. Maybe it isn't embarrassment; maybe she doesn't have nearly the alcohol tolerance she leads us to believe. "Yes," she says. "Even so, perhaps we should have gone down to Savannah instead. My parents' house is massive—you could get lost in those halls. We'd have had all the privacy we desired."

"We could have, yes."

I don't ask her what we'd need privacy for. I'm afraid the answer would be something horrifically mundane.

"I used to call the house Manderley," she says. "We weren't near enough to the sea for the comparison to be perfect, but it was close enough."

"Is *Rebecca* one of your favorites, too?"

"Of all time." Ellis tilts her face toward me again. "Although I always related more to the eponymous mistress than our dear narrator."

"I can believe that," I say, and she reaches out and slips a hand into my hair, her thumb skirting the curve of my ear. I do my best not to shiver.

Maybe the privacy she wanted in Savannah wasn't so mundane, after all.

In the firelight, Ellis's eyes glitter like polished pewter. "I'm glad you stayed with me," she murmurs, her voice as low and soft as the velvet sofa beneath us. "I would have been lonely if you hadn't."

Her words stay with me even after I've gone upstairs to bed, repeating in my mind as I light my candles and tuck tourmaline under my pillow.

I'm glad you stayed with me.
I'm glad you stayed.

The next morning, Quinn arrives early and makes breakfast, which we eat together in the dining room; the formal mahogany table is incongruous with the casual breakfast, but Ellis insists. We eat toast dipped in soft-boiled eggs and a side of bacon. "All Quinn knows how to cook," Ellis informs me in a conspiratorial whisper, which earns a flick on the temple from her sibling.

After breakfast Quinn has to drive into the city for some poker thing, leaving Ellis and me to spend the morning reading. We splay ourselves across her bed, Ellis's hair pooling by my elbow and my toes curled under her thigh; my horror novels aren't so scary when we're like this.

But after lunch Ellis makes me leave her alone to write, and I'm left to wander through Godwin's empty halls: Past Kajal's room, the door left open so I can see her neatly made bed, her shoes lined up along the wall beside her desk. Past MacDonald's locked office. Through the common room, the kitchen, then upstairs again, to lie on my back in the hallway and feel gravity trying to pull me sidelong, the tilted floor daring me to roll left and press my nose to the baseboard.

I close my eyes and press my palms to the hardwood, feeling the texture of the grain against my thumbs.

Is this what it feels like to be a ghost? To haunt the same halls over and over, waiting for someone to see you, to speak to you, to call for you or send you away again?

Quinn returns in the evening. I find them in the common room, drinking a martini garnished with lemon peel, flicking through the pages of one of Godwin's books too quickly to actually read the words. I have no idea where they conjured up gin.

"Did Ellis abandon you?" Quinn says without looking up.

"Predictably." I brace my hands against the back of the sofa. "What are you up to?"

"Nothing. I'm bored. Do you want a martini?"

Good lord, does anyone in this family do anything besides drink all the time?

But I can't afford to be impolite. And besides, growing up with my mother, I can't exactly pass judgment. "If you're offering."

Quinn lets the book fall shut and gives me that grin again—the sincere one, all teeth. It feels like a victory, winning that smile. "Follow me."

We retreat to the kitchen, where Quinn produces liquor bottles from a plastic grocery bag on the counter; they must have run by the store on their way back from New York. Quinn mixes a fresh drink and drops the lemon peel in with a flourish. When I take a sip, it's dryer than I'm used to, the taste of vermouth strong in the back of my throat.

"It's good," I say anyway, and Quinn snorts.

"If you don't like it, we can do shots instead."

It's a joke, of course—and a good thing, too, because the martini Quinn made is *strong,* and the second one they mix is stronger. We both end up sprawled on the common room rug, the room spinning overhead and little waves of heat coursing through my stomach.

"This was a mistake," I mumble.

"No such thing," Quinn says, although the slurred way they say it suggests the contrary.

I don't understand why my mother enjoys this so much. I'm afraid to move, for fear I might detach from the earth and spill unanchored into the sky, my tongue thick and heavy in my mouth.

Or maybe I'm afraid of losing control like she did—drunk in our gallery with a knife in hand, ripping all those priceless works of art to expensive shreds.

I drape my wrist over my eyes, but that only makes the spinning worse. "How often did you get to see Ellis?" I find myself asking. "After you went to Yale. I guess you didn't come home much."

A long silence passes in the wake of those words, long enough that I squint over at Quinn and start to wonder if I've said something wrong. But at last Quinn exhales and tilts their face toward me, says, "Not much, no. And god knows Karen and Jill weren't home enough, either."

It takes me a second to realize Karen and Jill must be Ellis's mothers. Quinn's, too, although perhaps not very good ones.

"That must have been hard," I say.

"Depends who you ask, I suppose. I survived just fine. Ellis, though . . ."

I'm still trapped in the thick gauzy space of intoxication, but something about the way Quinn says it injects a shot of adrenaline into my blood. And suddenly I'm a little more awake, a little more alert.

"What do you mean?"

Quinn's eyes are slivers of obsidian glittering beneath their half-lowered lashes. "I mean it fucked Ellis up. She was always a little insecure, but . . ."

Insecure? "Are we talking about the same Ellis here?"

"Same Ellis. I don't know what kind of persona she puts on at school, but yeah. Because . . . well."

Quinn blows out a heavy burst of air and pushes themselves upright, turning toward me properly, with one knee drawn up. Something about the way they're sitting reminds me so keenly of Ellis: the body language, perhaps, or even just the clothes. And yesterday wasn't a fluke; they dress exactly alike. I wonder if Ellis did that on purpose, modeling herself after her older sibling—if she hero-worships Quinn and can't tell the difference between admiration and appropriation.

Maybe, in some small ways, Ellis is human after all.

"Fuck it. Look. Ellis was always a little weird growing up, you know? She was one of those gifted kids. I'm smart, but Ellis . . . she was on a whole 'nother level. The tutors almost couldn't keep up with her. She'd get so *bored,* so damn pathologically bored. She needed constant stimulation or she'd throw these tantrums and give the whole house migraines."

It's not hard to imagine a young Ellis—in my mind, wearing a miniature version of the adult Ellis's knife-crease slacks and glen check blazers—hungry for knowledge, for *more,* and bursting with fury when that need was denied.

"Anyway, when Ellis was ten our parents went abroad for

the winter. They were supposed to be gone a couple months, so they left Ellis with our grandmother in Vermont. Only then there was this terrible storm . . . They got snowed in, and the power went out, and Nana died."

"Oh god." I don't even want to think about what that was like: Ellis, solitary in that house with her grandmother dead, her parents gone. "What did she do? How—?"

Quinn arches a brow. "Ellis was alone for four weeks. It took three weeks for the snow to melt, but the power company was stretched so thin with all the outages that they didn't get around to fixing our grandmother's house that whole time."

It would have been freezing cold, the snow pressing in against the windows and the grandmother's body slowly rotting upstairs. And as it got warmer, the stench permeating the house inch by deadly inch. I imagine Ellis shutting doors to keep out the smell, barricading herself in smaller and smaller spaces until there was nowhere else to run.

"It was six miles to get to the nearest neighbor," Quinn went on. "And with the snow . . . I mean, Ellis was ten. She decided it made sense to hole up and wait it out."

As indifferent as my own mother might be, I can't imagine her allowing something like this to happen. I have to keep reminding myself that Ellis's parents had left her with her grandmother, that they had every reason to think she'd be safe.

Only she wasn't safe. *Clearly* she wasn't safe.

"But then your parents came back. So she . . . she was all right." I stare at Quinn, half begging them to end it. Knowing Ellis is here, that she survived, isn't enough. I need the story to be finished.

"They came back all right," Quinn says grimly. "They came back early, in fact. But Ellis had already run out of food. Our moms weren't supposed to return for another three weeks. Ellis didn't have anything to eat. . . . She ended up strangling her pet rabbit and eating him. Raw. You have to understand—she was desperate. . . . She didn't have a choice."

Nausea lurches up my throat, the taste of bile and old gin flooding my mouth, convulsive and sickly; I swallow it down. Ellis . . . She—

"I did have a choice, actually," a voice says from behind us. Quinn and I both lurch around so quickly it sends the room spinning all over again.

Ellis stands in the doorway, one hand braced against the frame, resplendent in a tailored suit. Her expression is so neutral that I can't tell if it's an affectation or if she genuinely doesn't care what we've said—what *Quinn* has said.

Her hand drops back to her side, and she arches a brow. "It was eat my rabbit or eat the dog. And I wasn't going to shoot Muffin."

"Of course not," I whisper, so softly I barely even hear myself say it.

"I'm sorry," Quinn is saying, already on their feet, swaying slightly, their face gone green. "I shouldn't have said anything. Ellis . . ."

Ellis's lips press into a sharp smile. "It's all right, Quinn. Felicity understands. Everyone has a backstory."

Our eyes meet across the room. I feel like I'm seeing Ellis Haley for the first time, turning over memories like fresh stones: When I told Ellis about Alex, she never said it wasn't my fault. She'd said, *You didn't have malevolent intent.* There was a difference, which Ellis—Ellis the writer, Ellis alone in the dead of winter—understood better than anyone.

"I was coming down to tell Felicity I'm going to bed," Ellis says. She toys with the corner of the nearest accent table, as if caressing the grain of the wood. Or as if she has more to say, something she's holding back.

I discover what that something is an hour later, when I go up to bed myself and find a folded square of paper on my floor, tied shut with a length of black ribbon: coordinates and time, signed with Ellis's name.

Another Night Migration.

22

The coordinates take me back to the church an hour before nightfall the following day. The setting sun casts a yellowish hue over the clapboards, the shadow of that upside-down cross stretching long and black across the dirt—nearly to the forest's edge.

Ellis leans against the wall by the door. Beside her is a gun.

I stop at the tree line, staring at her from twenty feet away. Although of course that distance would mean nothing to someone with a finger on the trigger. "What is that for? Where did it come from? You—"

"Don't worry," Ellis says, pushing herself to standing. "It's nothing sinister. Quinn keeps this rifle in their car for self-protection—it's a southern thing."

A southern thing. My throat is still so dry I have to swallow against it several times before I'm even able to speak again. "I'm not asking why Quinn has it. I'm asking why *you* have it."

"For the Night Migration," Ellis says slowly, as if I'm perhaps a little bit stupid. "Flora Grayfriar's death. It's one of the last loose ends we need to tie up: we need to reframe how she died. How Margery killed her, rather."

I shake my head. "There are too many versions of that story. Which one are you claiming is real?"

Ellis picks up the gun and props it against her shoulder. I feel like my head is full of marbles, all of them rolling over each other, bumping against the walls of my skull, too many to count. I can't think straight with that *thing* in Ellis's hands.

"I still don't understand why you need a gun."

"The hunting explanation," Ellis says. "Remember? One version of the story says that Flora was found shot in the stomach. It could have been a hunting accident, or one of the townspeople, but my money's on Margery. Someone heard her confess, after all. Why confess to something that isn't true?"

"I don't—"

"Just a coyote, Felicity," Ellis says with a little laugh. "There are dozens of them out in these woods. Obviously we aren't going to shoot each *other.*"

I move closer to her now, although what I really want to do is drop onto the ground and sit there in the dirt. I don't know how to argue with Ellis about this. It's like trying to convince someone the grass is green when they insist that anyone could clearly see the grass is *blue.*

"Okay." I press my hands to my face and exhale heavily. "So you want to go hunting. Is that it?"

"I want to see if an unskilled girl would be able to shoot something in near darkness and actually hit her target. And I want *you* to see that, too: No altar, no ritual. Just a girl who shot another girl in the woods. No spirits or sorcery necessary."

"The body was found on an altar. None of the accounts dispute that fact."

Ellis shrugs. "Sure. But that doesn't mean the magic was real. Just that Margery wanted to make it *look* like it was real."

The explanation feels half-baked to me. I can't put my finger on why at first, but then: "We've gotten to the part of your method writing where you need to kill something?"

But Ellis just smiles and shakes her head. "Not remotely. You already heard I killed that rabbit, after all. This is for *you,* Felicity. This is the central part of the Dalloway story, as close to the heart of the so-called witches as you can get. But you don't have to perform a ritual to pull a trigger."

"I know that," I snap.

"Knowing isn't the same thing as *knowing.* You know up here." Ellis taps her temple with one finger. "But you don't know in here." She presses that same hand over her chest. "You've tied those girls to magic so closely in your head that the knots will never unravel on their own. That's why we're doing this, Felicity—that's the whole *point* of the Night Migrations. You need to walk in their shoes without magic. You need to see them as humans: as fallible and impulsive and mundane as anybody else."

Maybe she's right. She's been right about enough so far. So much of this has been in my head, the product of fear and some kind of chemical imbalance in my brain. I'm not sure I *want* to see the Dalloway witches as human, though. I want them to be like me.

But when Ellis starts off toward the woods, I follow.

According to her, coyotes are best hunted in the last hours

of daylight. The sun is already dipping low toward the horizon by the time we step under tree cover, the gold light glinting off the lake and burnishing auburn in Ellis's hair. I let her walk in front of me. It's not that I don't trust her; I just feel better when I can keep my eyes on the gun.

"I saw a few traps out here last time. Watch your step," Ellis says as we step into the shadow of the woods, her rifle cradled in the crook of one elbow.

My gaze tracks the ground, but all I see is dead leaves.

Ellis had told me, as we set out from the church, that our first goal was to cover as much ground as possible. Apparently coyotes move quickly and don't often linger in one place for long—and in the woods, our call won't travel far. We won't spend more than ten or fifteen minutes in any one position before moving on.

We don't speak much once the trees have closed behind us. Silence reigns, broken only by the chattering of birds as we move beneath their nests. I feel the cold more completely now that we're in shadow. I clench my hands in their leather gloves and pull my scarf tighter around my neck. Ellis's cheeks are flushed, the only sign she feels the same.

We've been out for twenty minutes or so when Ellis stops all of a sudden, reaching one hand back to catch my arm. She gestures, and I look.

Tracks in the dirt: fat paw prints with widely spaced toes, perfect enough to publish in a textbook. We've found the coyote's hunting territory. Ellis shoots me a quick grin, her face half shadowed under the brim of her flat cap, and starts off along the trail.

The forest falls quieter the deeper we go. The birds no longer signal our arrival; perhaps they sense the presence of a greater predator than us. The shadows thicken, stretching out like slim fingers, then lacing together until their shade rises like tidewater underfoot. I keep my gaze on Ellis's back; her shoulder blades shift visibly beneath her jacket, and for some reason I can't stop staring at them, the slow steady movement of her body through the brush.

Or maybe it's not that I can't stop watching Ellis. I find myself wary of looking *away,* certain that if I turn my eyes out toward the forest I'd find something else gazing back at me.

"Wait," Ellis says, throwing out one arm. I almost run into her but stop myself just in time.

"What is it?" I ask, but she doesn't need to answer—I see it a split second later.

Past where Ellis stands, about ten feet away and half concealed by the shadow of a fallen log, lies the mess of a kill.

A deer, I think, although it somehow seems too massive to be a deer, white bones gleaming where they thrust spearlike from the gore of tattered flesh and organ. Here and there the remnants of tawny fur ripple in the slow breeze.

It's grotesque. I take a half step closer, the scent of blood like copper in the air. Ellis doesn't hold me back, but she does lift her gun up to her shoulder, ready if anything should dart out from between the trees.

Near the carcass, the rotting leaves are slick and almost mushy underfoot. The corpse *is* a deer's, as it turns out—the antlers fractured and useless, one black eye staring sightlessly toward the dusk sky.

"Can coyotes do that?" I breathe.

"Maybe," Ellis says. "But this is probably a wolf kill." Her fingers press against the back of my neck. They're gloved, but it's still enough to send a soft shiver rolling down my spine. "How long ago do you think it died?"

I crouch down in the bracken and take off my gloves to trail bare fingers along the deer's flank. The fur is cool, but my hand comes away sticky.

I turn and show her. "The blood's still warm."

"Less than ten hours, then," she says. "Be careful. Wolves might still be in the area."

The air feels thinner as we move on. I don't glance behind me. I know I should be afraid of the wolf, or *wolves,* that killed that deer, but instead my mind keeps circling the memory of Alex's ghost in the woods, a slim white figure darting between shadows. As certain as I'd felt earlier tonight that she wasn't here, it's harder to believe that as the forest darkens. Even the branches seem to take on new form, like bony fingers reaching for flesh.

I straighten my shoulders and keep my gaze ahead. I want to seem ready. I can't afford to show fear where Ellis can see.

"We should try now," Ellis says after we've walked another five minutes past the kill site. "I'll set up the call."

We kneel down in a cradle of oak roots, close enough that our shoulders brush; I feel it every time Ellis breathes. We've placed the call fifteen feet away, a tiny electronic speaker that plays the sound of a rabbit in distress—squealing, screaming for mercy.

The way Ellis's rabbit might have squealed when Ellis wrung its neck.

I glance sidelong at her, quick and surreptitious, but if she is thinking about that winter it doesn't show on her face.

We stay there, frozen still, until my legs start to ache and my body goes cold. The dark pitches deeper now—my eyes adjust slowly—and the frozen ground is hard against my knees.

The recorded rabbit screeches, a terrible sound that tightens something in my gut like a twisting wire. The sound goes on and on and on, until that's all I can hear. Not even my own breath, not even my heartbeat.

Then I see it.

The coyote creeps in slow, padding across the fallen leaves in unnatural silence. Every couple of feet it pauses and glances around. At least twice I swear it sees us, those yellow eyes glinting through the shallow light and fixing right at the hollow of our tree.

Next to me Ellis doesn't move, barely seems to breathe. Her finger is steady on the trigger.

I'm not the one who has to shoot the creature, but my hands are sweaty all the same. I stare through the shadow at the coyote as it sniffs at something on the ground: innocent, oblivious.

All at once I don't want her to do it. I can't let her.

"Ellis—"

She glances sidelong at me, one brow lifted. I extend my hand, and she hesitates, then gives me the gun.

It's heavy against my shoulder, heavier than I expect. The grip of it is polished wood, chilly on my cheek as I brace the rifle and put the coyote in my crosshairs.

The creature still hasn't noticed we're here; it nudges its

nose at a pile of leaves near the call, searching for its prey. I wet my lips and curl my finger around the trigger.

Ellis's hand touches my shoulder, so lightly, a barely-there presence that nevertheless sends a shudder down my spine.

I shoot.

The crack of my gunshot ricochets off the watching woods, a flock of birds exploding from a nearby bush and scattering toward the sky. I startle and fall back against the tree trunk, the gun dropping into my lap as the coyote drops to the ground. Ellis loses her grip on me when I fall, but a grin sharpens her mouth—and in a moment she's gone, moving forward across the decaying leaves. I'm frozen in place for several long seconds, the rifle's kick still quaking through me—or so it feels like, at least. But then I force myself to my feet and clamber along behind her.

I won't be weak. I can't be afraid anymore.

The coyote's still alive when we get to it. Its torso shudders with every breath, a black spot blooming quick on its fur. The eyes roll in their sockets, as if the beast thinks it can find escape from some quarter, might still have a chance at living.

Ellis braces her gun over one shoulder and inspects it critically. "That's a kill shot," she states at last. "It won't live much longer."

Up close, the coyote isn't nearly as threatening as my imagination had made it out to be. It's smaller than I expected, about the same size as Alex's shepherd-husky mix and similar in features. Its black nose is almost delicate somehow, whiskers quivering as its breath starts to slow.

Ellis quivers too—a very slight tremor to her hands, detectable only because I notice everything about her. It's so easy for Ellis to pretend disaffection, as if our childhood traumas don't trickle like rainwater through the bricks of our lives. As if she doesn't care.

But I know Ellis better than that now.

She crouches down next to the body and swipes her gloved fingers through the bloody mess at its chest. "Come here."

I obey. What else is there to do but obey? And Ellis rises, one hand tipping my face toward the light as the other paints the coyote's blood in a quick line across my cheek.

"It's an old English tradition," she says as I take in shallow breaths and fight the abrupt urge to touch my face. "For those new to the hunt."

I grimace and wipe the blood off my cheek as soon as Ellis's hand falls away. She laughs.

"What?" Ellis says. "Isn't this the Dalloway way—all weird and bloody?"

"I'm *sure* I don't know what you mean."

She gives me a conspiratorial grin and tugs off one glove to lick her thumb. "You missed a spot."

Her damp finger scrubs away the last of the blood, lingers perhaps a beat too long. I still feel her touch even after she moves away to examine the coyote again. Its eyes track her approach, half-lidded and half-alert. But already its pupils are clouding, its fangs matte and dull instead of slick with spit.

Nausea roils up in the back of my throat, and I turn away, retreating a safe distance to huddle down at the root of a sugar maple. I don't know what Ellis is doing with the coyote's body, and I don't care. The gun lies discarded in the leaves, two feet to my left; overhead, the sky beyond the cover of trees is starry and vast. My world is a globe forty feet in diameter, spinning and spinning and spinning.

One would have thought Alex would have died on impact, after she fell from that cliff. But she didn't. I stood there frozen for a long moment, watching her struggle, black lake water sluicing over her face and filling her mouth. And by the time I made it to the shore, she was already gone, her body sinking into the low current, her lungs heavy with fluid and dragging her down.

I know she died. But . . .

What if she hadn't? What if she'd survived—half-drowned in the cold air, her bones shattered. Could she have dragged herself out of the water and away from the rocks, into the woods, still drunk? Would she have wandered through the dark, living off mushrooms and tree bark? Would she have stayed there, watching me, waiting for the chance at revenge?

Maybe what I think is her ghost isn't that at all, but is instead some arcane shade of what Alex might have been, a zombie crawling through its half-life and seeking its creator.

"The coyote is dead," Ellis says.

I look up. I hadn't heard her coming back, but she's here now, crouched on the ground in front of me. My whole body feels stiff and weak, as if I haven't moved in years.

Ellis's lips curve into a frown. "Are you all right?" she says, a softer edge rounding her tone. Her gloved hand tilts my chin up so that I have to meet her gaze. "Felicity. Tell me you're okay."

The darkness around us is now absolute. I can barely make out Ellis's features, can't even tell the color of her eyes. They're pale like glass but *alive,* flickering with light. Or maybe I'm just dizzy, exhausted, half-frozen. She cups my cheek.

I exhale. My breath shudders out of me to cloud in the wintry air. "I'm okay."

"Are you sure?"

I nod. Ellis's teeth catch her lower lip for a moment, but then she stands, offering a hand to pull me up. She tugs me away from the coyote's carcass and into a streak of moonlight that filters through the forest canopy.

I must be mad, truly mad—as if killing that coyote knocked my brain off-kilter—because I find myself deliriously thinking how beautiful Ellis is. Her skin is pewter in this light, all her color reduced to myriad shades of gray, like a black-and-white photo given life.

"I can't believe I killed it," I say.

"I can't believe you killed it, either," Ellis admits. Her hand is on my waist, steadying me as I stagger over fallen branches. "You didn't have to."

"I had to." I don't know how to explain it to her, not fully. I don't even know how to explain it to myself. But I couldn't . . . After everything, after the story Quinn told me about Ellis and her rabbit . . . I couldn't let her pull the trigger. I couldn't make her do that again.

Or maybe I just needed to know if I was capable of it. If I had that dark streak inside me, running black and cold enough to take a life.

It turns out I do.

"Come on," Ellis says. She laces her fingers together with mine. "Let's go back."

23

I don't remember much of the trip out of the woods and up to the house.

What I do remember is Ellis's hand gripping mine the entire time, the taste of sweat on my lips. The common room light is on when we ascend from the garden up to the house proper, but we evade Quinn entirely. Instead Ellis takes the steps two at a time; I go behind like a pale shadow, my bared hand cold as it trails along the banister.

She goes to her room, and I follow.

I kick the door closed behind me and Ellis pulls off her gloves finger by finger, watching me with this wary look, like she still expects me to bolt.

"I told you I'm fine," I say. It comes out more persuasively now, my voice steadier away from the dark.

"I know what you said."

"And you know I'd tell you if I wasn't fine." I offer her a small and wavering smile. "Shame has never stopped me from falling apart on you before."

She laughs and the taut thread tied between us eases a little. Eases, but doesn't unravel.

Ellis presses her bared hand to my sternum, right above my heart. I wonder if she can feel it beating against her palm—too fast now.

"You're brave, Felicity," she says. "You're the bravest person I know."

And then she kisses me.

The dizzy feeling doesn't abate. Instead of swaying on my feet, I cling to her with both hands, my head spinning and her tongue in my mouth. Ellis's body is hard and firm, and I can't stop touching it; she presses me back against the shut door as her open mouth skims my cheek. I arch closer as she peppers kisses along my jaw, my throat.

"I've wanted you," she murmurs, and those three words are sudden heat; when she pulls back, my lipstick is smeared across her mouth, a scarlet streak cutting past her jaw. Her lips are parted and still damp.

I need to kiss her again, but when I try she tilts away, then smiles. "I want to hear you say it."

My breath cuts out of me in shallow half gasps. Both my hands twine in fists around the fabric of her shirt.

"I want you, too," I say.

Ellis's smirk widens. This time when she kisses me, it's harder, more desperate. I'm desperate, too, shucking off her jacket and waistcoat, Ellis's fingers fumbling over the buttons on my shirt in turn.

My hands find her waist, smoothing down toward her

narrow hips. God. I can tell just from this, even with her body clothed in thick tweed and wool, that she's strong. Powerful.

I need more.

Ellis's forearms bump against mine as she unknots her tie and yanks it free. The drag of that fabric against her collar sends an unexpected shiver down my spine.

Maybe any other day, or with any other woman, I would have been embarrassed. But there's something about this night—or about Ellis herself—that makes me feel confident. Sexy.

Invincible.

The rest of our clothes come off, and then we're moving, the backs of my legs hitting the edge of the mattress. Then we're on the bed, and Ellis is there, touching me.

I wonder if my skin feels hot against hers. I'm burning up inside.

"Fuck," I gasp, and Ellis laughs against my collarbones.

"Oh dear," she murmurs. "Language, Felicity."

I love the way my name sounds on her voice: husky and low, gravelly in a way that makes me shiver. Being here with Ellis, like this, feels inevitable: as if I could trace our friendship back to the day we met and discover roots there, the original seed of something that would become *this*.

And what is *this*? I'm not sure I know the answer. Maybe it doesn't matter.

Ellis performs her work with the slow, determined care with which I imagine she writes her books, leaving me breathless and blinking up at her as she leans down to kiss me again.

"Not fair," I say—accuse, really—and Ellis smirks into the

kiss, reaching for my wrist to slip my hand down the waistband of her underwear instead.

She's flush-cheeked and breathless once she's finished, lifting her head to meet my gaze. This time when she kisses me, it's languorous and warm. Then she shifts to kiss my throat, my sternum . . . and lower.

"You're—"

You're incredible. You're inexorable. You're merciless.

I don't even have the ability to speak.

When you read about sex in books, it's always described like a magical event, something sacred enacted through the profane: two souls joining on the metaphysical plane while two bodies entwine below. I had never understood that before now. But with Ellis it's different than it was with the girls I've been with before—even Alex. Ellis is something new, and it feels like she creates and unravels me in the same moment, a sentence she writes and erases and rewrites, a product of her wants and imagination. I feel like she *invented* me.

I wonder if she feels the same.

After, I'm left limp and feverish, staring at the ceiling as Ellis shifts back up the length of the bed to settle her body next to mine. She trails a finger along my cheek, toward the corner of my mouth.

"There," Ellis says, as if she's accomplished a task. She kisses the place her finger just touched.

I coil in closer, and she smiles a small and careful kind of smile, a smile that conceals secrets.

We fall asleep together, Ellis's arm thrown over my stomach

and my face tilted in against her shoulder. And for once it is so easy to forget I've ever known anyone else.

Quinn leaves for Georgia two days before classes are meant to resume. It's snowing when Quinn drives off, fat white flakes dusting the green roof of their Mustang, and within minutes the snow has covered the tracks the tires made on the drive, as if they were never there.

Ellis and I are never far apart now. She touches me frequently, as if still amazed that she can: her fingers laced with mine while we read, her hand slipping into my hair as she passes behind me in the kitchen. I've stopped finding her touch as unsettling as I did, although it hasn't gotten less thrilling. I want to memorize the warmth of her skin, the way her eyes sparkle like smoke quartz when she laughs.

"No one has ever understood me like you do," she told me after that first night we had together, tangled up in the sheets and awakening before dawn. I keep turning those words over in my mind, engraving them into the firmament of memory. I don't want to forget this. *No one understands Ellis Haley like I do. No one ever will.*

I'll have to go back to my own room tomorrow, when the other students return. But for tonight, again, I share Ellis's. I lie beside her in the narrow bed and focus on the heat of her body, the weight of her arm around my waist.

But without her easy smiles and calm words, the walls close in.

I keep thinking about the graveyard where Alex's empty coffin was buried. I wonder if the book is back there now, covered under several feet of snow, with its pages gone soft and illegible. I wonder if Alex searches for me even now—if she'll find me hiding here in Ellis's room, hiding where I think I'm safe, and drag me back down into her hell.

The gentle respite of our week's vacation has gone. The clock has started ticking once more, a second for every heartbeat.

I twist under Ellis's arm, the dorm room bed small enough it knocks our knees together, and she mumbles in her sleep, rolling onto her other side. I curl up against her back, gazing at the nape of her neck and trying not to think about the sound the storm makes right outside her window—trying so hard not to wonder if that's a figment of my imagination or if a girl's voice carries on the wind, calling my name across the snowy hills.

Ellis comments on my insomnia the next morning, the pair of us sitting in the kitchen with tea and coffee, the sunlight outside reflecting white off the snow.

"Didn't you sleep last night?"

I press both hands into my lap and stare down at my tea. I don't want to see the look on her face right now: concerned, knowing. What we have together feels fragile, not even two days old. I want to seem *better* now. Sane.

"A little," I say. "I had a hard time getting comfortable. Perhaps I shouldn't have drunk some of your coffee last night."

She grins. "Yes, well, that was your own mistake. You're the one who stole my mug."

A drop of relief trickles down my spine. Ellis is letting it go. She believes me. She doesn't assume the truth: that I was up all night obsessing once again over witches and ghosts.

"What's your plan for the day?" I ask.

"Write," she says, perhaps predictably. "Maybe try to get a little reading in before the others get back. What about you?"

I keep gazing out the window. The trees are so thick, so icy, I can't see farther than a few trunks deep. Past that the world blurs into gray fog. "I was thinking I might start running again . . . but it's too cold today. So maybe I'll be reading, too."

But once breakfast is finished and Ellis has absconded back to her room and her typewriter, I don't read. Instead I search the titles on my bedroom bookshelf for *The Secret Garden* (absent) and position a row of candles and dried dandelion along my windowsill. The lit wicks flutter against the glass, a feeble barricade against whatever moves out there in the woods, drawing ever closer.

Margery's curse still waits for me. I might have killed Ellis's coyote, and she might have proven their deaths could happen without magic, but that doesn't make me free.

I don't want to bother Ellis—I don't even know if we're *together.* Even if we are, I don't want to be the kind of girlfriend who hangs around constantly, present to the point of frustration. So I stay upstairs until I hear the front door open and shut again, Leonie and Kajal's voices carrying up the stairs as they stomp in from the snow sometime near dusk.

I meet them in the kitchen. Leonie, for one, seems especially pleased to see me; she grins and throws her arms around me, squeezing tight enough that I can't help but laugh.

"You came back!" she exclaims when she finally lets go.

"Of course I came back," I say. "Why wouldn't I come back?"

Some of the delight dims on Leonie's face now and she falls onto her heels, Kajal quickly busying herself with the teapot. "No reason," Leonie says unconvincingly. "How was Colorado?"

"I didn't go," I say. "I stayed here with Ellis, at Dalloway."

Leonie and Kajal exchange looks. I wonder if they've been talking about me on the ride back from the airport, if they were taking bets on whether I'd be readmitted to the mental hospital before the end of term.

The silence hangs heavy between us. We all try not to look at one another, Leonie grinding the edge of her nail into the groove of the wood counter, Kajal waiting for the water to boil.

"I like your new hair," I end up saying eventually, gesturing toward Leonie, whose braids have been replaced with loose waves that reach her waist.

"Thanks. I just called in for the appointment yesterday. Your sweater looks nice, too."

"Oh," I say. "Thank you. It's vintage."

"What's for dinner?"

Ellis has appeared in the doorway, one hand on either side of the frame: a saving grace wearing houndstooth. Her gaze lingers on me a half second longer than it does anyone else.

"Clara said she'd go by the grocery store on her way back," Kajal says. "I don't remember what she said she was going to get, but it seemed like she had a plan."

The plan, it turns out, involves tacos. Somehow that's

the absolute last thing I ever expected to see the Godwin girls consume. But consume them we did, sitting around the dining room table dripping hot sauce and sour cream. Kajal picks at hers, but Ellis sucks the salsa from her fingertip, a sight that makes heat bloom low in my stomach.

I help Clara clean up after dinner, once Leonie and Kajal have retreated to the common room and Ellis is upstairs—no doubt pounding away at her typewriter, creating the world's next literary masterpiece. If Clara had expected me to disappear over break like the others had, she doesn't show it.

"How was your Thanksgiving?" I ask, feeling suddenly congenial. Clara is too focused on herself to notice anybody else.

"It was good," she says, glancing over her shoulder at me as she scrubs down the stove top. "I went back to Connecticut and spent some time with my family. My little sister just turned four. She was running all over the house, getting into things—she tried to start herself a bath and ended up flooding the whole third floor. I mean, I'm pretty sure I wasn't that stupid when I was four, right?"

I didn't know her when she was four, obviously. "I'm sure you weren't."

"Well, at least she didn't drown herself," Clara says charitably. "Although not for lack of trying. Good thing it was too cold for beach trips."

"It snowed almost the whole time we were here," I say. I'm at the sink washing dishes, done with the cast iron and moving on to the cutlery.

"Oh, I *know.* Ellis told me. That sucks. Actually, I think I might skip classes for a few days and go somewhere. Like, apparently there's this spa closer to the city, and it's like . . . rustic? Only not really. You stay in a tent, but it has heating, and a bed, and a phone line. And it isn't dirty."

So, glamping. If Alex were here, she'd have quite a few choice things to say about that. Clara might look like Alex—at least from behind—but the two of them have nothing in common.

All of a sudden, I miss Alex more than anything. I miss the way she laughed. I miss how she always wanted to be outside, constantly wandering under the sun and trees. Leaves stuck in her hair, always with a book in her bag.

And somehow thinking about Alex now . . . it doesn't hurt. Or at least not the way it did. Maybe there's still a chance to repair things with her spirit, to make amends.

Maybe, at last, Alex can rest.

"I hope you have a great time," I tell Clara, surprising myself with my own sincerity. "It sounds wonderful."

When I do go back to my room, the shadows don't seem as dark as they once did. The air is easier to breathe, despite the pitch dark outside. I gaze out my window for a while, waiting, but no figure emerges from between the trees. No chill creeps up my spine.

I can still hear my mother's voice echoing in my head, condescending, faux concerned: *Have you been taking your medication?* But it helps. I'm getting better. So I call the pharmacy and head out to pick up my order. As soon as I get back to Godwin, I swallow a pill with a glass of tap water and close my eyes.

It's surrender, in a way, but it's not something to be ashamed of.

That night, I take down the letters Alex sent me. I tie them in a neat stack with a length of ivory ribbon and slide them into my desk drawer. I leave the photo of us, pinned next to a postcard Alex sent me one summer.

I fall asleep easily, and I sleep well.

Perhaps too well.

24

I oversleep.

By the time I make it downstairs the next morning, everyone's already had breakfast. The others have left for early-morning extracurriculars, and Ellis is curled up fully dressed on the common room sofa, dead to the world.

I stand there for a little while, watching. I've seen Ellis sleep before, of course, but this feels different somehow. Maybe there's a vulnerability in sleeping out in the open, without a blanket. Or maybe it's that Ellis has never seemed the type to drowse in libraries.

She's wearing a point-collared dress shirt, still tucked into her trousers. One of the shirt buttons is undone; I glimpse the slightest swell of bare skin past white fabric, rising and falling in slow rhythm with her breath.

I grip the back of the sofa so I won't give in to the urge to reach down and brush back the hair that has fallen across her eyes. I don't want to wake her—not if she was up writing all night.

Robbed of my usual spot, I take my book back upstairs to

the little reading nook nestled under the window at the far end of the third-floor hallway. Classes are barely back in session—a good excuse not to read horror and mystery. But I find myself choosing *Strong Poison* anyway. It's not fascination with the macabre. It's not that perverse need to terrify myself, a twisted penance for my crimes. I *want* to read Sayers. I want her elegant Oxonian prose, the fierce wittiness of Harriet Vane, the thrill of a chase.

Wyatt told me the mark of a true scholar was passion for the subject above all else—passion that resumed despite obstacles, the academic circling back to her true love again and again.

I think of the college applications I submitted before break, little missives darting off to Princeton, to Duke, to Brown. None of them were sent with much hope. The future had felt like a distant and abstract construct, a life that belonged to another Felicity—a mirror image of myself existing in some parallel world, a girl who stood a chance at living past the end of the year.

When I was a child, I found it so hard to imagine ever turning sixteen. *Sixteen.* The age was laden with implication: sweet sixteen celebrations, cars, makeup, drinking at parties, and kissing lips I'd never remember. Only then I turned sixteen, and the impossible age became eighteen.

And once I was eighteen, I hadn't been able to see ahead past May. Alex's ghost was a rising fog that obscured possibility, swallowing up every line that led into June, to July, to nineteen. None of the Dalloway Five had lived past eighteen; why should I?

I sent those applications because it was what I was expected to do.

Today, for the first time, it finally feels real.

Maybe Ellis will come with me. We'll share a one-bedroom apartment in Manhattan. I'll attend classes at Columbia during the day; at night I'll return home to find Ellis still tilted toward her typewriter, notes and half-read books scattered over her desk like fallen leaves.

When I wander down to the common room for lunch and a break from my thesis, Ellis has vanished from the sofa. Leonie is back, though, perched at the kitchen island with a cup of coffee, scribbling away in a notebook.

"What are you working on?" I ask, and she immediately slaps the notebook shut, like she doesn't want me to see.

I lift my brows, and after a long beat she wipes a hand over her eyes and shakes her head. "Sorry. I . . . well, I've been writing my grandmother's story. A novelization of it, anyway. Don't tell Ellis?"

"Why would Ellis care?"

Leonie shrugs. "I don't know. Maybe she wouldn't. But . . . well, writing is kind of *her* thing."

"Ellis doesn't own writing. If you want to write about your grandmother, you should."

Leonie twists one of her waves around her forefinger and looks like she doesn't believe me. I know Ellis better than anyone now, and I'd like to think Ellis would be pleased to hear that someone else has discovered a passion for writing and creation.

I also know what it is to have a secret you've held close to your chest for so long it starts to poison you—to fear that if you show it to anyone else, it might poison them, too. But when I finally told Ellis about my mother, she hadn't been poisoned.

She'd understood.

"I wanted to ask you about something," I say once I've mustered the courage.

Leonie nods slowly. "Okay," she says. "Go for it."

"You were in the Margery coven. Weren't you?"

Leonie releases her hair. I can't define the expression that settles on her face, her typically serene features twisting for a moment—almost as if in disgust. But the look is gone so quickly I might have imagined it. "Yes. I suppose I still am."

Well, I'm not, I almost say, but I swallow the words. Instead, I take a breath, one that shakes in my chest.

"What do you think of them?" I ask.

Leonie pats the seat next to her at the island, and after a beat, I take it. She crosses her arms over her shut notebook and meets my gaze straight-on.

"You really want to know?" she says.

"I really want to know."

A smile cuts across Leonie's red-lipsticked mouth. "I think they're full of shit."

I almost choke on my own laugh, startled, amazed—Leonie has to be the first person I've ever met to just come out and say it. But she's right.

"They're all bluster. They make it seem like the coven is the only path to success after Dalloway, but that's just propaganda."

"It's not entirely propaganda. Margery girls always succeed."

"Because they're rich, not because they're Margery. They're rich and they're white."

My teeth catch my lower lip. There's a bladed quality to Leonie's voice; I've never seen her like this.

"Why did you join then?" I ask.

Leonie shrugs. "Why does anyone join? And I liked it, at first. They liked me, too. Only then last year I mentioned that one of their little bits of historical legend was technically inaccurate, and all of a sudden they started treating me differently. It was . . . let's say illuminating."

"That's horrible."

"Right? But that's my point. They're horrible."

I sit with her words for a moment, turning them over in my mind like stones. She's right, of course. She's right, but I didn't want to admit it before. The Margery coven was all about appearances—from their feeble gestures at "magic" to their rejection of Leonie. Their rejection of me when I got sick.

I wonder what part of the legend was inaccurate—if this is another piece of knowledge Leonie acquired during her research off-campus. I wonder how limited my own understanding of the Dalloway Five is, if by studying only what I found in the library, I've trapped myself in a certain view.

I only ever wanted the Five to have been witches. I only ever saw what I wanted to see.

Not like Leonie. For Leonie, it was never about what she wanted—it was about discovering the truth.

"I'm really sorry, Leonie," I say at last. "I . . . That's repulsive."

Leonie rolls her eyes, but her smile is good-natured as she says, "See? Now you're getting it."

I head to the fridge and take out the cheese plate Clara and

Kajal assembled last night after dinner, peeling off the plastic wrap and bringing it back to the island.

"Do you want to know something?" I say, impulsive, but suddenly I *want* her to know this about me. Leonie has confided in me about her dream of being a writer. I want to trade one secret for another.

She opens her notebook again, setting her pen down at the binding. "All right."

I'd told Ellis, of course, if indirectly. I told Alex. Maybe putting words to this part of myself has already drained the secret of some of its power, because it's easier now to meet Leonie's gaze across the table and say, "I'm lesbian. It's a little bit of a secret. . . . Or . . . it was. Maybe not anymore."

To Leonie's credit, she doesn't even look surprised. "Oh. That's cool."

"It is cool," I agree, and I grin before I can stop myself. Leonie smiles back. And for a moment it feels like there's a cord drawn between us, a link.

"For what it's worth," Leonie adds, "I don't think anyone in the house would think any differently of you, if you ever decide to tell them."

I'm sure that's true. It's never really been about fear of exclusion—not lately, anyway. Maybe it just felt like such a personal part of my identity. Maybe I didn't want to let anyone so close.

Ellis has changed all that.

When evening falls, three of us Godwin girls play rummy in the common room till fatigue takes over. Clara is already off on her glamping trip, although I have no idea how she managed to get permission to skip class for something like that. And Ellis returned to the house after dinner, but she'd darted straight upstairs without speaking to anyone. Judging by the glassy look in her eyes we'd all gathered she was writing, too absorbed in the world of her characters to remember the rest of us existed.

"I don't know what you did to her over break," Kajal says as we're all heading upstairs to our respective rooms. "But whatever it is, it worked. I was starting to think she'd never finish that damn book."

The heat that rises in my cheeks has nothing to do with Ellis's book and everything to do with *what I did to her over break.* I wonder if it's written all over my face—if they both can tell exactly what I'm thinking, despite my efforts to appear cool and unruffled as I bid them good night on the second-floor landing.

The candles on my windowsill have burned out; they're stubs of melted wax now, the wicks charcoal smudges impossible to relight. I scrape the wax off with the edge of a ruler. It's slow work, but I don't stop until every sign of the candles has been rubbed away. In their place I put a row of colored flat marbles I bought at the antiques shop I went to with Ellis that one time. I'd gone back before break to purchase the pince-nez Ellis had worn. I'd meant to give them to her as a gift for surviving midterms, but I forgot; they presently rest in a velvet-lined case hidden in the back of my desk drawer. Maybe they'll make a better gift for when Ellis finishes her book. She can revise with the glasses perched on the end of her nose, red pen in hand.

The clock on my desk ticks past eleven, closer and closer

to midnight. I ought to sleep. It's Tuesday, but if I get in the habit of sleeping in too late it's going to be hell getting myself out of bed for Art History. Eight on Tuesday morning is an ungodly time for a class, but at least I only have to do this for a few more months.

Then summer. Then, I hope, college. The city. A new life.

I've sworn off sleeping pills, but after half an hour of lying in bed and feeling equally as awake as I'd been at dinner, I flip my lamp back on and wander over to my bookshelf. I love Virginia Woolf, but to be completely frank, *Mrs. Dalloway* always puts me right to sleep.

I trail my fingers along the spines, past *Oryx and Crake* and *The Secret Garden*—

No.

Time goes still—this moment, this *room* existing outside the rest of the universe—as I jerk my hand back to my chest and clutch it there, not breathing. The old book is nestled there on my shelf, the cloth binding slowly peeling back from the spine and the lettering of the title faded to gray.

It's not possible. It's . . . I'd finished this, the nightmare was *over*. I blink, almost expecting the book to vanish when I open my eyes again, like a trick of the light. But no. Nothing has changed.

I tug the book free with shaking hands.

A black dust tumbles from between the pages, scattering to the floor at my feet. I press my fingertips to the cover, and they come away dark.

Grave dirt.

My mind is full of static, a roaring sound that drowns out

all else. I open the book, half expecting to find another wilted hellebore bloom.

And there on the title page, in Alex's handwriting, an inscription:

I never told you that I love you, but it's true. It was always true.

Those words. . . . they're *my* words, from the letter I wrote Alex a week after she died.

The letter that was buried in her empty casket.

I slam the book shut and grip it between both hands, as if that will erase what I saw. My gaze flits back out the window, past the colored marbles—I should never have blown out those candles, should *never* have let down my guard—and out into the thick night.

The first time I found this book in my room, I'd thought it must be Ellis playing a prank. But she wouldn't have any way of knowing what I wrote to Alex.

Then I'd thought I might have hallucinated the book.

I'm not hallucinating now.

I open the book again and reread the inscription. Alex's handwriting is . . . There's no mistaking it. Even so, I dig out the old letters she sent me and crouch down on the floor, comparing the swoop of Alex's *s* in the book to her calligraphy from when she was still alive—the spiky peaks of her *n*'s, the way she always forgot to add punctuation and just began the next sentence with a capital letter.

Alex wrote this inscription. Resuming my medication hasn't chased her away, and she didn't vanish in the face of what Ellis and I built together. She's here. She's always been here, her ghost called back by the legacy of magic sunk deep into the bones of this school, the dark curse that infected me the night I spilled my blood on the Margery Skull.

Enough.

I can't live like this.

It's time to face Alex.

It's time to pay for my crimes.

Sympathetic magic, must mirror a curse to undo it.

—A note, in Felicity Morrow's handwriting,
appended to her thesis materials

Margery was a silhouette against the trees, but the way the mob's firelight caught on the whites of her eyes made her look crazed. Demonic.

"I did it," she whispered. "And I would do it again."

—From a manuscript by Ellis Haley

25

The graveyard is in Kingston; it's too far away to walk.

I steal Kajal's bike and ride it into town and rent a car at the same place as last time with the false ID my mother gave me as a misguided sixteenth birthday present; the last thing I want right now is to sit in the back of a stranger's cab for an hour, fielding questions about what I'm studying at school, why I'm out so late, why I look like I've seen a ghost.

Blanketed under snow, the cemetery looks nothing at all like it did when Ellis and I last visited. The tombstones rise out of the gloom like onlooking specters, black and silent. It's four in the morning by the time I arrive, the night as dark as it will ever get and the cold reaching down into my bones as I step out of the car and let myself in through the iron gate.

The snow has fallen ankle-deep; it's a slow trudge past the mausoleum and toward the silent oak tree that stands watch over Alex's grave. The hellebore has been buried under that weight, and as I approach, the grave looks unmarked. Undisturbed.

It's only once I kneel down by Alex's headstone that I realize the snow there has been shifted. It's not the pure faultless blanket that covers the other graves; the snow here has been freshly shoveled back into place, someone's meager attempt to hide what they've done.

I twist around, expecting to find a shadowy figure standing behind me, but the cemetery is empty of all but the dead.

Alex never died in that lake. We didn't find a body because there was no body to *find.*

While I ran down from the cliff to find her body, Alex pulled herself out of that black water and staggered into the woods, vanishing without a trace.

Of course she did. She could have. Her career was over, her reputation ruined. Everyone thought she was violent now, too emotional, too unprofessional. She'd told me there was no escape, that she could run and run as far as she wanted, but she'd never stop being Alex Haywood.

She dug up her own grave and read the letter I wrote. That's why the snow is disturbed. That's why the inscription appeared in the book. Because Alex *did* write it.

Then what's in her grave that she wants me to find so badly?

All at once, I no longer feel the cold. It's a strange heat that blooms under my skin, smoldering in my chest like fury. I push to my feet and make my way along the winding path that leads to the caretaker's shed. The padlock hangs unlocked around the door, not even frosted over. I kick the door open and stumble into the dull warmth of the interior.

The dust knocked down off the rafters makes me cough. I pull my phone out of my back pocket and flick on the flashlight app, the beam illuminating the dark corners of the space. *There.* A shovel rests against the far wall, tip down. I drag it out of the shed. I should have brought gloves; my fingers are already white-tipped and numb where they curl around the handle.

When the blade cuts into the snow, it makes a crunching sound, like ice snapping. I dig up that first shovelful and pitch it to the side, my heart already pounding as I thrust down for another load.

I feel oddly dizzy—light-headed—with a sense of double vision, as if I can see a second pair of hands alongside my own, a second shovel, black soil breaking beneath the blade. My palms ache with phantom blisters; I taste old salt on my tongue.

It's at least ten minutes before the tip of my blade hits dirt. I've cleared a rectangular space the approximate length and width of a coffin. My chest aches, sweat sticky under my coat. But this isn't over. Not yet.

I dig the shovel down once more, cutting through frost and soil and heaving, again, again, *again.* The sun starts to rise over the distant horizon, a dull gray glimmer that only casts the shadows into sharper relief. I stare at the name on Alex's headstone, the letters blurry through the sweat that beads on my lashes.

I'll find you, I tell her. *I'll fix this.*

I don't know what I'm fixing.

I start to lose track of time. The world condenses down to this: the snow soaking into my socks, the dirt under my nails. My breath clouding at my lips, and the calluses that swell on my palms—swell, then burst, then bleed.

I never thought how long it would take to dig up a grave.

I never considered how the shovel handle would get slippery under my grip, that I'd end up stomping on the shovel blade to force it deeper into the ground, that I'd be on my knees in the dirt as the hole got deeper and deeper, until I'm standing in the pit and digging beneath my own feet.

The spade thumps against something solid, and I stop. The sky overhead is slate gray as I tip my face toward it, gasping for air and shutting my eyes. I've forgotten how to be afraid. Even the mist that rolls in off the mountains and wells up around the tombstones doesn't frighten me anymore. I am closer to shade than girl. I am no more substantial than bone dust.

I scrape the dirt off the lid of the coffin, exposing wood gone dark with too much soil ground into its veins.

All I have to do is open the casket.

Yet I find myself kneeling down in the chasm of Alex's grave, both hands pressed against the lid of her coffin and my eyes squeezed shut, taking in a shuddering breath and trying to chase away the sense, even now, that I am being watched.

I wish her body were in here. I wish I could press my cheek against the cold wood and feel some shadow of her on the other side. I could practice the same necromancy as Alex and I did that night we spoke to Margery Lemont—inscribe letters on the coffin lid, let Alex's spirit move a planchette from word to word.

But a ghost didn't dig up this grave. That work was done by living hands.

The seal on the casket is broken; it's easy to hook my fingers under the lid and yank it up, the hinges creaking as the coffin opens.

And even in this dim light, dawn still pewter over the hills and the cover of snow draping everything in silence, I recognize her.

Alex.

26

Alex was on her fifth cigarette—the fifth cigarette to go with her fifth drink—her dress disheveled and her cheeks sunset red as she spun little Hannah Stratford around in a circle. The lit cigarette left a stream of smoke in its wake; I flinched every time it careened past the drapes.

"Let me take that," I said, edging closer. "You're going to burn the house down."

But Alex just laughed and twirled Hannah again, who was tipsy and giggling and clearly delighted just to have caught Alex's attention at all. "Don't be a spoilsport, Felicity. Dance with us."

"I don't dance. You know that." My glass was slippery against my palm; I downed what was left.

Hannah reached for me with her free hand. "Come on, Felicity. It's fun!"

People were starting to stare. Whispers exchanged behind hands, glances darting between Alex and me.

I shifted closer and lowered my voice to little more than a hiss. "You're making a fool out of yourself, Alex. Let's go home."

Alex stopped dancing. The centrifugal force sent Hannah spiraling, staggering until she was caught by the helpful arms of a senior girl I distantly recognized from Greek class.

Alex's hair had frayed out of her chignon, tangling wild like a red halo about her face. She looked, in that moment, every bit the role she'd been cast in the papers: mad, aggressive. *Violent.*

She drew closer, and closer again, until my heart pounded not from the alcohol but because I was briefly certain she was going to kiss me and force me out of the closet right then and there—

But Alex's mouth just twisted meanly, and she said: "Yes, well, you'd know all about making a fool of yourself. Wouldn't you, Felicity?"

It felt like all the air had been sucked out of the room. The party went silent; the feeling of all eyes on me made my skin itch.

"We're going home. Now." I started toward the door, but I didn't get far.

Alex's voice cut through the thick air between us like hot steel. "Everyone knows you're crazy," she shouted. She was drunk, the words coming out slurred and uneven. She was drunk; she didn't mean it. But she said it anyway. "All this bullshit about witches and magic and dead girls. We all know the truth."

I spun on my heel and stalked back to where Alex stood, weaving on her feet. I could smell the liquor on her breath from a foot away. "And what's that, Alex?" I said. "What's the *truth*?"

Alex took in a sharp breath. *Don't say it,* I urged her mentally. *Don't say it.*

She was going to say it.

I could see it in her eyes, because I knew her—I *knew* her—and Alex was the kind of person who was never cruel on purpose but who was inevitably cruel regardless. She just couldn't help herself.

"You're obsessed with magic because you can't stand to live with yourself otherwise. Because if you don't have witches to blame all your *shit* on, if you can't pretend that you've been chosen by Margery Lemont or *whatever,* then that means nothing you do is magic's fault. It's just *you.*"

I laughed. It came out cold and callous, like the laugh of a villain in a children's movie. "You want to talk about taking responsibility for your own actions, Alex? Really? Or do you just want me to reassure you one more time that you're perfect and Tes started it, and if you broke her nose, then it's her own damn fault?"

I went too far.

I knew that before I even finished saying it, but I said it anyway, and it hit Alex like a bullet hitting its target. She reared back, the color drained from her face. All at once she didn't look angry anymore, or *cruel-aggressive-violent-mad.*

She just looked scared.

"Alex . . . ," I started, but it was too late.

She flung her glass onto the floor, where it shattered into a thousand pieces against the marble. I yelped and flinched back, and that was all the head start she needed. Alex shoved her way past the gathered crowd toward the front door, and I was behind her—too far behind her—so even when I had broken out of Boleyn and onto the quad, she was already a distant pale speck running toward the lake.

"Alex!"

I sprinted after her. It couldn't end like this; I couldn't just leave her alone after . . . after saying something so terrible. She was unstable. I knew that. She'd been off ever since what happened over the summer with that other climber, and if I left her to her own devices, she might—

I didn't know what she might do.

Alex was a world-class athlete; she was too fast. By the time I made it up to the cliffs, I was heaving for air, one hand pressed to the stitch in my side.

She stood on the ridge, silhouetted against the white moonlight and still. I approached slowly, half-certain that any sudden movements would fracture her.

"Alex," I said again, once I had the breath to speak. "I'm sorry. I didn't mean that."

"Yes, you did," she said. She had her back to me, both hands clenched in fists at her sides. "You meant every word of it, just like I did."

I gritted my teeth and shook my head. "Please. Let's just talk about it. Okay? Let's go back to Godwin House. We can . . . I'll make tea, and we can talk."

Alex turned at last to face me, her hair tangling in the wind in front of her face. She looked wild and feral, like a creature out of legend.

"You were right," she said. "I haven't taken responsibility for what I did. But I was right, too, you know. This whole witch business has gotten to you. Like, sometimes I don't think you even hear yourself properly. Fucking . . . séances, Felicity? Dead girls and curses and demonic possession?"

I recoiled. It wasn't *demonic*—I'd never said anything about demonic possession. But I had confessed to Alex one night, both of us curled up in her bed together, that I thought Margery Lemont's spirit was trapped in our world after that Halloween night. That because we didn't do the closing ritual properly, Margery had no way to leave our world. I had said that I knew Margery's intentions were evil. That she might use us to do evil things.

At the time, Alex had been so careful with me. But tonight her eyes were slate and cold, her mouth thin as wire.

"You need help. And you need to get a fucking grip."

"Go to hell," I managed to get out, but my voice was shaking. It was weakness, and to Alex, weakness was like blood in the water.

She moved closer, but I refused to be weak. I refused to let her pin me against the trees like a coward. I could feel Margery there, watching. Her eyes burned into the nape of my neck.

I stepped toward Alex and shook my head. "No. I'm not letting you do this. You're . . . You're being *mean,* Alex. Stop it."

"Mean," she echoed, and let out a breathy laugh. "Fuck you, Felicity. I'm so sick of this. I'm so . . . I'm so *sick* of you acting like the martyr all the time. Like you're so goddamn patient, and *understanding,* and if I'm not, well, that's just Alex being Alex, isn't it? Just evil, mean Alex, who talks back and curses and defends herself. But I guess standing up for yourself isn't very Dalloway, is it? I guess I'm just showing how *uncouth* I am, since I didn't go to goddamn finishing school and learn how to act like a perfect little princess all the time—"

"You—"

"But they'll figure you out soon enough, Miss Morrow. You can't hide it anymore, can you? You're fucking broken. You're batshit, just like your mother."

And I pushed her.

I didn't mean for her to fall. She wasn't even that close to the edge. But she was drunk, and when she lost her balance, she stumbled. For a split second I thought she was going to recover and lunge for me—

Instead she pitched, and dropped, and vanished, screaming the whole way down.

Alex died. Alex was dead. I killed her myself.

27

The shock of seeing that body in the grave sends me reeling back toward the crumbling wall of the pit I dug. Only there's nowhere to go, the space too cramped to allow for anything but this:

Me, half tumbling into the open casket, staring down at Alex's beautiful red hair tangled against the satin pillow, her pale cheeks and limp hands, the scarlet bloom of blood staining her white shirt.

No. No, *no*—

That isn't Alex's mouth, nor Alex's nose. Her cheeks have too many freckles, her body isn't decayed.

Not Alex's body.

Clara's.

I scramble back along the narrow space I've dug, flattening myself against the grave wall and staring down at the dead body of my friend.

And maybe I'm a terrible person, as dark-hearted as I've always feared, because my first reaction isn't to grieve. It's the cold and clinical assessment:

She hasn't been dead long.

I twist around and press my brow against the dirt, eyes clenched shut. I can't fake innocence. I knew it. *I knew it.*

The body in Alex's grave has a bullet in her stomach. Her throat is slit. Wormwood leaves wreathe her hair, and hellebore flowers bloom where her eyes should be.

She's the perfect picture of Flora Grayfriar's corpse.

This whole time . . . some part of me suspected, deep down. Some part of me knew how this would end, and I kept going anyway. Even with my eyes shut, the truth stares back at me.

For Ellis, this was never a game.

I feel as if I'm falling—a hundred miles through an endless pit, into water, cold and black and closing overhead, filling my lungs and flooding my veins.

Ellis killed her.

She really killed her.

My heartbeat is the only sound I hear as I force myself to face the coffin—the girl in the coffin—the *corpse.* I'm sick; it's the kind of nausea that devours. I shove the lid back onto the coffin with my heel, my mind suddenly tumbling through a litany of realizations—the kinds of realizations that become reflexive after studying murder for months on end.

My fingerprints are on the coffin. I shift forward, crawling across the lid with my hands balled in fists and my weight pressed against my knuckles to scrub the cuff of my sleeve against the places I touched. I hope those are the *only* places I touched. Can I be sure? Do I *know*? I should wipe down this whole coffin, should—

Only it's already dawn, the sun beginning to rise beyond the trees. Cold light filters down even into this hellhole. Someone could find me here. A mourner, or the cemetery caretaker back to shovel the snow and throw away wilted flowers.

I pull my phone out of my coat pocket, swiping away my notifications. It's seven. I'm already out of time.

I claw my way to the surface, elbows digging into dirt. Panic is a living thing, I discover: It twists and quivers in my chest. It strangles every breath. I don't bother with the shovel; I shove dirt into the open grave with both hands, tears freezing on my cheeks. I can't even feel my hands anymore, my fingers like rubber.

I don't know how long it takes to fill the grave. How long it takes to heave the snow back in place, or carry the shovel to the caretaker's shed, or scrub away my fingerprints. I can't fix the broken padlock. They'll know someone was here. How many minutes until they pair the broken lock with the disturbed snow atop Alex's grave? How much longer to exhume a body? How long, then, until they come hunting for a killer?

For *Ellis.*

I don't want to think about it—about what Ellis did. But now . . . here, with Clara's pale face rising like an unseen island to the surface of my mind . . . I can't evade it. Ellis did this. Ellis killed Clara. Buried her in Alex's grave, then . . . then . . .

All of it makes sense now. I don't want to believe it; Ellis had seen how upset I was. She had comforted me, had—

She'd manipulated me this whole time.

There's no better explanation for the book in my room, or for the grave dirt that fell from its pages. Even the inscription in *The Secret Garden* was a forgery; all those hours we'd spent copying each other's handwriting. Ellis had brought the book there. She'd brought it there to mess with me, to make me *think* I was crazy. She—

Ellis killed Clara. I tell myself those words, try them out on my tongue. "Ellis killed Clara." Ellis tried to convince me that I was haunted, or crazy, or both. She used magic to get to me. She told me magic was destroying me and then manipulated me into using it anyway. Then she killed Clara and lured me here to make sure I knew.

I don't want to believe it. But not wanting to believe the truth doesn't make it not the truth.

My hands are still numb when I shut myself in the rental car, but I can't afford to linger. I press my wrists against the steering wheel and manage to guide the car like that, down the steep hill and out onto the open road. I pull over a mile out, crank up the heat, and sit there with my fingers held up to the vents until they finally start to thaw. The lights from passing cars cut through the silver dawn light; I flinch every time one drives by.

The radio is on. The newscaster lectures us about some store closing in town: *A pillar of the community.* And why would they close that store? It's been there for fifty years. It's a family-owned business. *Sign of the times,* the newscaster says, and I agree. I've never in my life cared as much about village politics as I do right now, sitting in this car with dirt under my nails and sweat frozen at the nape of my neck, cheeks tear-streaked and hands shaking.

What will that family do next? Will they open another store? How can they show their faces in public once everyone knows their failure?

Maybe they'll move. Far away. Somewhere no one who knew them will ever be able to find them again. They could change their names and cut their hair. Get a little cottage in the woods and become recluse. Eventually everyone will forget.

At last, once feeling and color has returned to my fingertips, I reach onto the passenger seat and grab my cell phone. I swipe up the screen and stare at the keypad.

I should . . . call someone. The police, perhaps. That's what a normal girl would do. Call the police, the ambulance, the fire department, the goddamn National Guard—anyone and everyone.

Clara's death is a heavy stone. I want to pass it to someone else.

My phone is still in my hand when it rings.

I startle, badly enough that I drop the phone into the footwell and have to retrieve it, my cold fingers scrabbling down between my legs. The number is one I don't recognize, but my phone tells me it's from a Georgia area code.

All at once I'm transported back to the Dalloway main library: Me and Ellis sitting on the floor in the stacks, leaning against opposite shelves with our knees bumping together. We were in the true crime section. We'd read about a murder case, solved because the culprit made a phone call at the scene of the crime. The cell signal pinged off the nearest tower, and that easily, the murderer's alibi became worthless.

I turn off my phone. It feels like it takes years for the screen to go dark, that infernal unknown number mocking me the whole time.

Is that enough? I didn't pick up; maybe I'm safe.

Only I already know that's not true.

If the police find out about Clara's body—if I become a suspect—they'll know I was here.

They'll think I killed her.

28

The return to school passes in a watercolor haze. I pull over at a gas station to vacuum out the rental car, suddenly terrified that a grain of grave dirt will be all it takes to identify me. I wash myself off in the grimy bathroom with paper towels and industrial soap as best I can, black water swirling down the drain. I vomit in the smelly public toilet. I drop off the rental car and ride Kajal's bike to campus. I can barely keep balance. I almost run myself into a ditch at least twice.

But I make it.

It's barely past nine when I trudge into the house, exhausted and sick. My heart feels like a bird fluttering in my chest, weak and breakable. I don't think about the mud I'm tracking across the rug until I'm already in my bedroom, and by then I can't care anymore. The prospect of getting down on my hands and knees and scrubbing dirt out of the carpet feels like an insurmountable challenge.

I didn't even glance down the second-floor hall as I passed the landing. Maybe Ellis is in the room below me right now. Maybe she's waiting for me to find her.

I don't want to find her. I can't even look at her.

Instead I turn on the shower and crouch down on the tile floor as hot water pounds against my scalp. It sluices off the evidence of crime—grave dirt disappearing down the drain. It rinses me clean, the same way it did a year ago.

That shower is just what I need to crack open the shell I've built around myself; finally, the world sinks back in.

Clara is dead. (*Murdered. Ellis killed her.*) It's Tuesday; she's supposed to return tonight from her camping trip. That means a few short hours before people start to wonder what happened to her. If I'm lucky—if I'm *very* lucky—the cemetery caretaker doesn't come in on Tuesdays. Maybe it will snow again overnight, a layer of ice all I need to conceal any sign that Alex's grave was desecrated.

And what is the evidence that ties me to the graveyard?

Alex's connection to me, of course. That's one.

The grave dirt in the rental car. I vacuumed it out, but I hadn't exactly been in the best state of mind; it's possible I missed some. But how easy is it, really, for a forensic team to link dirt to a specific location? Surely all the dirt in the Catskills is essentially the same.

The phone call. That's what will get me. That's my weakness.

But even that is circumstantial—I can come up with a good reason to have been all the way out in Kingston early Tuesday morning. They'll need more evidence than my proximity to Alex's grave to prove I *killed* Clara.

This is just another one of Ellis's mind games, isn't it? She wants me to *feel* responsible, the way I was responsible for Alex.

I need to talk to her.

The thought makes me want to start running and never stop. Ellis killed Clara. What reason do I have to think she wouldn't kill me as well?

Only if she wanted me dead, she could have killed me a dozen times already.

This is about something else. Ellis must have had a *reason.* She made me go all the way out there to that grave, tricked me into digging Clara up . . . And why? Was this another part of her game? Margery Lemont was buried alive, after all.

But Clara wasn't.

And *I* wasn't.

I shudder, wrapping my arms around my middle and hugging tight. God, I hadn't even considered the possibility that Ellis would have sent me out there to die. After all, she had me dig Clara up. She could have been lurking in the shadows, waiting until I had the lid off the casket. And then she could have shoved me forward and nailed me in.

She could have killed me just like Margery was killed, and I would have walked right into her trap.

But she didn't, and that in itself opens a new question: Why would she expose herself like this to me? I could turn her in. I could tell the police *precisely* why I was in Kingston.

Maybe I should. I don't know why I haven't, in fact. This isn't a matter of petty theft or trespassing. Ellis killed someone. She killed our *friend.*

Somehow, though, betraying Ellis to the police never feels like a real option. I should feel more than I do. I should grieve Clara. I should cry and scream and beat my hands against the walls.

Instead I pace from one end of my room to the other, wet

hair dripping cold down my bare back. I try to remember Clara in the sunlight, Clara's skirt catching the wind as she crosses the quad toward the library, Clara with a stack of books and her pen stuck in her mouth, Clara during the Night Migrations, a dryad amid the trees.

Is that how Ellis caught her? A note slid under the door the night before Clara's camping trip, a set of coordinates signed with Ellis's name?

I imagine myself explaining the story in a cold police station room, confessing that I drove all the way to Kingston, I stole a shovel, I dug up Alex's grave and found Clara's body. I could insist that Ellis killed her.

But—*no*—but . . . what if she didn't? What if I did?

What if I killed Clara, then forgot about it, the same way I forgot I'd pushed Alex until Ellis made me remember?

What if this is the curse playing itself out again and again, an endless string of deaths to satisfy an insatiable bloodthirst? If this *is* the curse, the evidence will only point to me.

Checkmate, Margery Lemont murmurs from the darkness.

I tug an extra-long sweater over my head and don't bother with the rest of my clothes. I dart down the hall in my underwear, faltering when a floorboard creaks, terrified Kajal will emerge from her room and ask where I've been.

I avoid looking at Clara's door altogether.

On the second floor Leonie's room is open and empty. Ellis's door, though, is shut. I can't tell if her light's on or not.

I knock anyway. No one answers, of course. I don't know what else I was expecting. If she's in there, she won't answer for me.

My pulse is beating fast—so fast. I read once that a

hummingbird's heart beats over a thousand times per minute. I feel like that now, like my heart is just a quivering lump of meat inside my chest. Am I afraid? Or just . . . *angry.*

I shouldn't even be here. It's foolish, reckless—a good way to get myself killed.

Even so, I call Ellis's name, pounding louder. No response. I grab the knob, but the door is locked from the inside.

"I know you're in there," I accuse. "Open the door."

Silence, still. Just like that time after the party: Ellis's insistence that she'd been *writing,* too busy to see me. It's not even ten in the morning, and with all the times I've found Ellis up fully dressed and working well past four a.m., I refuse to believe she's out of bed with her nose to the grindstone.

I press my brow against the wood and strain to hear something, *anything:* the click of typewriter keys, or the soft strains of classical music played on vinyl, even the soft susurration of Ellis's breath. But there is nothing behind that door. It might as well open up into the void of space, an inevitable tumble into the crushing heart of a black hole.

I stalk back up the stairs and into my room, kick the door shut behind me. I lie down on my bed, press my face into my pillow, and scream.

By the next evening, Clara has been missing for a whole day. Too long to be extracurricular. Too long to be innocent. I skip class and stay in bed as the sun tracks its course across the sky, but after dusk falls, there's a knock at my door.

I consider staying in bed and pretending I'm not home. But sooner or later someone's going to come looking for Clara. And when they do, I can't afford to seem suspicious.

I crawl out from beneath the sheets and shuffle across the rug and open the door.

Ellis blows past me with her arms full of typewritten pages and a feverish glow in her cheeks.

"I did it," she says, clutching the book to her chest and staring at me like she doesn't really see me at all. "I finished the book, Felicity. I finally finished it."

I stand there in the doorway, wishing I had something to hold in my hands. A weapon, maybe.

"Clara's dead."

Ellis shoots me a sharp glance, something almost disapproving to the set of her mouth as she shuts my bedroom door. "I know. You don't have to say it so loudly."

She watches me like she's expecting a specific kind of response to that. I have a feeling it isn't the response that creeps up the back of my throat, bilious and sick:

"You killed her. You . . . You . . ."

Ellis sighs, and at last she moves to set the stack of pages down on the corner of my desk. "Okay. I suppose if we *must* have this conversation . . . yes. I killed her. And it *worked,* Felicity. It worked! I'd spent months trying to push through this scene. You don't even know how many sleepless nights I wasted trying to eke out just one more word, to find the perfect phrase or image."

The knot in my chest loosens slightly. It was her. It was Ellis. Not the curse, not the witches, *not my fault.*

It wasn't my fault.

She draws closer, and I cannot move, not even to pull out of reach. Her hands curl around my wrists, drawing my arms up to press my fists against her chest. She's near enough that I can smell the cigarette smoke that clings to her hair. I can see new shades layered in her eyes: pale-gray water over black stones, lurking below the surface.

Ellis smiles.

"It's done now. I did it. Thanks to you. I can't even tell you how much I . . . This book. It's the best thing I've ever written. You understand, don't you?"

I don't know how to reply to that. What is there to say? I can still see Clara's cold body in the back of my mind. The blood on her stomach. Her blank gaze.

"You killed her," I say again.

Ellis drops my wrists. Her arms fold over her chest, and she shifts onto her back foot, her attention suddenly gone clinical. "Yes. I shot her, in fact. Twice, in the gut. And then I slit her throat."

If that admission is intended to make me feel sick, it works. I shake my head as if I can shake that knowledge out of my mind.

"I used Quinn's hunting rifle," Ellis goes on. "The same gun you used to shoot that coyote. It has your prints all over it."

The air in the room goes still.

I don't know how I'd imagined it happened. But now all I can see is Ellis with that gun, Ellis's hands wrapped in gloves, Ellis pulling the trigger.

"Why?" I croak. "You . . . Why?"

"Because I had to be sure," Ellis says evenly. "It's the same reason I had you go to Kingston and dig up her grave: to place you at the scene of the crime. I can't have you running off to the police and telling them what I did, can I? I'm sorry, Felicity. I'd hoped it wouldn't come to this. I don't *want* to betray you. Please don't make me."

I pace toward the window and look out. Ellis says something behind me, but I don't hear her. Static roars in my ears, my lungs gone breathless. I press a hand against the frigid glass. Not that it helps.

Never mind the dirt in the rental car. Never mind the dug-up grave, or my cell signal pinging off the tower in Kingston, or Clara's body in Alex's coffin. Ellis doesn't play by half measures. Whatever she's done, she will have left no weakness in her plan.

I sense her coming up behind me; it's all I can do not to whip around to keep her in my line of sight. Ellis grasps my shoulder, squeezing very slightly.

"Don't touch me."

Her hand falls away. I hear the soft shifting sound of her breath. The hair on the back of my neck prickles.

"I want to make sure you have the full picture," Ellis says, "so listen carefully."

I don't need the full picture. I don't want to know how thoroughly Ellis has shackled me. But I can't stop her from talking, either, so she goes on:

"Think how it comes across. Clara and Alex . . . they could be twins. Or sisters, perhaps. It's not just the red hair—they have remarkably similar features. After that hospitalization, your mental instability is established. Everyone in this house has seen it—your obsession with those old dead girls, thinking you're cursed. Of course, the police won't need to make such inferential leaps. I wrote a letter to Clara in your handwriting. It's a very . . . well. Let's just say it wouldn't look good for you if that letter were found in Clara's room, among her things. It would be easy to slip the letter into a notebook or under her pillow."

I turn around. Ellis has taken a step back, thumbs tucked into the pockets of her pin-striped trousers. Her words reverberate through my head, playing and replaying until they lose all meaning.

"A letter," I echo.

"Yes. And the fingerprints on the gun, naturally—mine are on file from my arrest a few years ago, you know, so I'm accounted for. Clara's body will be found in *Alex's* grave—the grave of your own ex-girlfriend, the girl everyone thinks you killed. Not to mention your cell phone places you at the scene of the crime. My phone, on the other hand, was in my room the whole time."

"You don't have a cell phone," I croak.

"Don't I?"

She slips a hand into her pocket and draws out a slim device. Not the newest model, but it doesn't need to be new. It just needs to work.

Ellis's mouth quirks in half a smile. "I did warn you about the dangers of technology."

And now that I think back, I realize Ellis never told me explicitly that she didn't own a phone. I'd just assumed from the way all the Godwin girls eschewed computers and social media and texting; I'd figured they were taking a leaf from Ellis's book. I had thought she started that trend.

Perhaps she did. Perhaps she'd planned this far earlier than I realize.

"But you don't need to worry about any of this, as long as you do the right thing," Ellis says. "Don't go to the police, and I won't plant that note. I won't tell the cops where to find the gun. Or Clara's body."

Clara's body. *God. I'm going to be sick.*

Only I can't show Ellis that kind of vulnerability. She'll tear open my underbelly the moment it's exposed.

I must look as awful as I feel, because Ellis offers me a rueful smile and catches my wrist, her fingertips pressing in over my pulse point. "Why do you think I chose you for this?" she says. "It wasn't to ruin your life. I wanted to *help* you. Don't you feel better now? You're standing here arguing with me because you *know* you didn't kill Clara Kennedy. And you didn't kill Alex, either. Not with magic, at least."

"It doesn't matter if you turn me in," I say. My voice sounds as if it's coming from somewhere distant, echoing across the expanse of time and space to reach my ears. "You said it yourself: they'll think it was me anyway. They'll have me on the cameras at the rental spot. My cell phone . . . in Kingston. The moment they realize the grave has been disturbed . . ."

Ellis shakes her head. "Why would anyone even think to check a graveyard miles away? Clara could be anywhere."

Only she isn't *anywhere*. She's in that coffin. If they do find her body, it will look like I murdered her in cold blood. Or in a psychotic rage.

Sickness lurches up the back of my throat, and I pull out of Ellis's grasp, hunching over one of my potted plants with a hand clasped to my mouth. But nothing comes up. I'm gasping by the time Ellis helps me straighten upright, my tongue coated in a metallic taste.

"God," I say. "If they suspect me, if they find even a *shred* of evidence . . ."

"You could have been in Kingston for any number of reasons. Besides, cell phone records require a subpoena—they'd have to have other reasons to suspect you in order to even look into that. As long as you play along, they won't *have* those reasons."

"Get out."

"Felicity, I promise you won't—"

"Get *out*!" I shove at her with both hands, knocking her a stumbled half step back.

Ellis moves out of reach, dragging her fingers through her already-tousled hair. "All right. All right, I'll go. . . . Be careful, Felicity. Remember what I said."

I'm not likely to forget.

She leaves, taking her manuscript, and I'm alone again. I don't want her to come back. I wish I had never met Ellis Haley.

But in her absence the walls close in on me. I'm left alone with nothing but the watch ticking on my wrist and the inescapable knowledge that sooner or later, my time will run out.

I have a huge and savage conscience that won't let me get away with things.

—Octavia Butler

Beware, for I am fearless, and therefore powerful.

—Mary Shelley, *Frankenstein*

29

Two and a half weeks ago—one week before Thanksgiving break, two weeks and approximately two days before Clara's death—Ellis and I were in the library, ostensibly finishing our Art History project but really just procrastinating. The rare books section was too quiet at night: the kind of quiet that didn't suggest the absence of voices so much as their silence, watchful eyes and wordless mouths. I'd had Ellis commandeer several books from the occult collection, the pair of us shut away in the mustiest part of the stacks, breathing the smell of dust and old paper.

"Give me your hand," I'd demanded.

Ellis glanced up from the text she'd been reading. "Did you know some people claim they can read the future in animals' entrails? It's called extispicy."

"Yes. Give me your *hand*."

She obeyed. I turned her wrist so her arm rested palm-up across my lap.

"What are you doing?" Ellis said, leaning in and peering over my shoulder at the book I had laid open by my knee.

"I want to read your palm."

Ellis's lips quirked up. "All right, but . . . why?"

"Because I'm curious. Because I want to know more about you. Do I need a reason?"

She was still looking at me like I was a particularly interesting science project, which I took as tacit permission.

"You're left-handed, right?" I'd watched her practice forgery often enough to know, and we lefties have a bit of a radar for one another.

Ellis was still giving me that odd look, but she nodded.

I turned her hand to glance at it from all angles, cross-checking with my book whenever I wasn't sure about an interpretation. "This is your dominant hand," I told her. "All the readings here represent what you come into later in life. The other hand would be your innate characteristics. So this hand is more important, as you might imagine."

I trailed a finger along the length of her heart line, and Ellis didn't move, didn't even flinch. I wanted to believe she was *too* still, like she was trying very hard not to appear unsettled.

"What does my palm say?" Ellis asked at last.

"You'll have a long life. Healthy. And—you might have guessed this—you're a creative person. These branches here suggest ambition and achieving impossible goals."

Ellis grinned. "That's me."

I flipped to the next page and examined Ellis's hand again. Her palm was smooth, rosy, her fingertips callused by the keys of her typewriter. A fleck of ink stained the inside of her index finger. If I were one of those charlatans who owns a shop in the seedier part of town, thick with incense smoke and draped in gauzy veils, I might have told her, *You're a writer, aren't you?*—and that would have been how I seized her trust and suspended her disbelief.

"But . . . you should be careful about the friends you let into your life," I continued. "You shouldn't trust anyone. A mysterious older figure will spell destruction and a fall from grace."

A quick and sharp grin cut across Ellis's face. "I knew Wyatt had it in for me."

"Better run," I advised very seriously. "Change your name, change your identity, flee the country—"

"—burn this place in my wake—"

"—salt the earth so nothing grows again."

We both laughed, Ellis harder than me, hard enough that her cheeks went pink and she tipped forward to press her brow against my knee. Her long fingers curled around my ankle and stayed there. As if I would ever move when she touched me like this.

Of course, when Ellis read my palm in turn, she didn't even reference the book. She just told me that I would live forever, become very famous and very wealthy, and share all my money with her.

Nothing in Ellis's fortune gave any sign of what she really was. I should have paid better attention. I should have marked the smaller crosses and stars on her skin, should have found the truth written in her flesh.

I should have known she was a killer.

The police arrive on campus first thing Thursday morning, twenty-four hours after Clara fails to return to classes after her trip. I locked myself in my room after Ellis left and haven't emerged since, so I don't know what took them so long. I don't know if the Godwin girls didn't want to snitch on Clara if she was on a bender somewhere, or if Ellis had convinced them to wait.

Maybe it doesn't matter.

From the reading nook at the hall window, I watch the police cruisers roll up to the bottom of the hill, watch them tramp up the drive in their blue uniforms and murmur inaudible things into their radios.

The last thing I need is for someone to tell them I've been hiding in my room since Clara's disappearance. So I change out of my pajamas and into real clothes, brush my hair and pull it into a low chignon, apply a hint of pink lipstick—enough to look like Felicity Morrow, a good girl, of the Boston Morrows—and I go downstairs.

Ellis is already in the kitchen, sitting perched at the window, gazing out toward the woods. Her charcoal sweater is too big for her, swallowing up her torso. She has a coffee in hand. She doesn't look at me, and I don't speak to her.

What else is there to say?

The police interview us all separately.

"When did you notice Clara was missing?" Officer Ashby asks, once I'm settled alone with her and her partner, Officer Liu, in Housemistress MacDonald's office.

"She didn't come back from her camping trip on Tuesday."

"How long did it take for you to realize something was off?"

I have both hands in my lap. I refuse to twist my fingers

together, knot them up in my skirt. I don't want to seem nervous. "I don't know. Last night, I suppose. We all assumed she was at one of her clubs. . . ."

"Didn't you call her?"

"Clara doesn't have a cell phone," I say.

Ashby's brows flick up. "You're telling me a high school girl doesn't have a mobile phone?"

Officer Liu snorts. But when I look at Liu, she doesn't say anything, just shakes her head and holds up both hands, a derisive smile settling on her lips.

"We prefer to focus on our *work,*" I say.

"I'm sure," Ashby says, leaning forward like she wants to come across as reassuring. "Felicity, is Clara Kennedy the type of person who would run off like this? Did she give you any reason to believe she didn't want to come back to school?"

I shake my head.

"Has she been acting strangely lately?"

Another no.

Liu taps short nails against her ceramic coffee mug. "I have to ask the question: Did Clara have any enemies? Anyone who might want to hurt her?"

The back of my throat has gone bone-dry. I lick my lips and swallow, but it doesn't help.

"No. Of course not. Everyone loved Clara."

Loves. I should have used the present tense. The way Liu and Ashby exchange glances suggests I'm not so lucky that they haven't noticed.

"You were here last year, weren't you?" Liu says. "When that girl died?"

"Alex Haywood." I can't help myself. Alex wasn't *that girl.*

"Alex Haywood," Liu repeats. "A strange case. I looked it up. A girl falls from a cliff . . . drowns in the Dalloway lake . . . then disappears. Never found."

I feel as if my brain has been clipped free from my body, floating far overhead. I barely feel human at all.

"Yes."

"You were there. You saw her fall."

My throat has gone tight; I want to clear it, but I don't dare make any noise that could seem like discomfort. Or like remorse.

"I was there," I say. "Alex was my best friend. She fell. It was an accident."

"An accident."

"She was drunk."

"Yes. So you told the police."

Ashby's lapel has a tiny mustard stain on it, small enough that I hadn't noticed at first. Now I want nothing more than to rub at it with a wet dishcloth and wipe it away. I stare until the mark goes blurry.

"Here," Ashby says, relenting and passing me her handkerchief; I squeeze my eyes shut and dab away the tears. I retain enough presence of mind to be faintly disgusted with myself: these tears are what will buy my safety. No matter what I say, neither Ashby nor Liu will suspect I killed anyone. When they look at me they see my mother's money and white skin. They don't see a murderer.

But that's exactly what I am.

"I don't know what happened to her," I whisper. "Maybe

she . . . She could have tried to crawl away for help. . . . Into the woods. And then . . ."

And then the wooden handle of the shovel was against my palms, splinters catching under skin. I'd stolen the shovel from the janitor's shed. I couldn't dig six feet deep—only three, but it was enough.

Her body had looked pale and broken on the dirt when I dragged her out of the lake, less than human, waterlogged and cold. I had been relieved to cover it up—first with soil and then with stones.

I remember thinking it was a sign, that she had died as Cordelia Darling died. That I'd buried her as Margery Lemont had been buried—in the crawl space under Godwin House, built into its stone foundations, where she belonged. I had thought maybe this would be enough to sate Margery's appetite.

Only Margery Lemont had never existed. Not as a spirit haunting me, anyway. She had just been a too-clever girl living in a time when being clever made you dangerous. And she'd paid for that with her life.

The two officers let me retreat back to my room, clearly considering themselves married to a schedule. I leave my door open and sit on the floor, curled up close enough to overhear the echo of voices up the stairs while remaining hidden from passersby by the angle of the door itself. Ashby invites Ellis into MacDonald's office next. I can make out the click of the door shutting, but no matter how hard I strain my ears, their voices are silent to me.

I give up on this plan and creep down the stairs on sock feet to the second floor. Ellis's room is locked, but I can pick the lock;

at least there was one skill I'd taught myself during our murder plots that Ellis didn't know about. And the Godwin House latches are ancient, unfussy; they pop open without a fight.

Ellis said she had a document, a file, collating all the evidence against me. A letter to Clara written in my handwriting. I can't be sure when I'll have another chance to search her room.

Ellis has made her bed, folding in the sheets and draping a chunky knitted throw blanket along the foot. A book lies open atop the pillow: Shirley Jackson, *We Have Always Lived in the Castle.* Her typewriter sits on her desk, closed under a case now that she's finished her book. I open it, but there's no letter hidden against the keys.

Ellis's bookshelves are crammed full of an eclectic mix of titles, everything from mystery to classics to texts in the original Latin. There's even an odd copy of a Nancy Drew book, dog-eared and with a broken spine. There are no photographs. Not of herself, not of her moms or Quinn or childhood friends—just a framed portrait of Margaret Atwood tilted against the full set of Atwood's books.

Ellis's épée hangs from a hook on the wall. Her fencing gear is folded in the dresser. I dig through her sock drawer, shoving aside underwear and a collection of broken fountain pens to find . . . nothing.

Wherever Ellis has hidden that letter, the one allegedly written in my own hand, it isn't here.

Downstairs, the office door creaks open. I've run out of time.

I flee back to the third floor and shut my door, turn the latch. My heart pounds as I crouch there on the floor, ear pressed to the wall—I'd left Ellis's bedroom unlocked. But no footsteps ascend. She doesn't come knocking.

She doesn't *care.*

I won't let Ellis Haley set the terms of my downfall. One way or another, I need to get ahead of her.

At my desk, I take out a sheet of writing paper and uncap a pen I stole from Ellis's room. I write a letter, painstakingly slow, copying Ellis's handwriting from the Night Migrations notes as best I can.

Dear Clara . . .

The calligraphy is a poor imitation. The content of the note itself doesn't read like it's in Ellis's voice. I rip it up and start over—two times, three, before I decide it's good enough. Not a perfect match, but then again, no one knows Ellis like I do. No one else would be able to look at these words and tell they'd never fall from Ellis's mouth.

There's a chance I'll never need to use this letter anyway, I tell myself. Missing isn't dead. No one has any good reason to suspect me.

Not yet.

30

Most missing persons are found within the first seventy-two hours, or so I've heard.

I'm not sure why that is—if it's because the evidence trail is easier to follow closer to the actual moment a crime was committed or because most missing persons cases don't involve any kind of violence at all. Maybe most missing people come home eventually, a little smudged perhaps, a little blurry-minded or tattered around the edges, but safe.

The police discover Clara's car abandoned on the side of the road; her prints were the only ones on the wheel. "Maybe she left it there herself," Leonie says, picking the polish off her bitten-down nails. But the suggestion only brings the other possibility into sharper relief: *Or maybe the killer wore gloves.*

Ivory gloves, purchased from a local antiques shop and still smelling like lavender.

Clara's parents arrive, elegant people who speak very little and blow through Godwin House as if they find its existence unsavory. Perhaps they should. The sinking, uneven floors and faded rugs look shabby and dangerous juxtaposed with anyone from the outside. Our visitors seem out of place and out of time. I find myself wondering briefly if we at Dalloway have clipped ourselves out of the usual dimension and found a new one. If we exist on a separate metaphysical plane from all the rest, and these interlopers are mere trespassers. If Dalloway will reject them like a host rejecting its parasite.

I should tell someone. *Kajal, perhaps,* I think as we sit alone together at the breakfast table, Kajal pushing her eggs around the plate and eating none of them. Only Kajal is pieced together as fragilely as I am these days. If I apply the slightest pressure, she might crack.

I could tell Hannah Stratford, who has latched onto me in the wake of Clara's disappearance. Hannah appears at my side every time I venture out to class or the library, or make an appearance in the main dining hall, always with her face stitched in a perfect expression of concern.

"What does Ellis think?" Hannah asks me one day as she's accompanying me across the quad—because I so clearly need a chaperone. "Does Ellis think Clara was"—her voice drops to a stage whisper—"*murdered*?"

No. I'm not telling Hannah Stratford.

MacDonald, then. I could sit in her office, like I'm doing now, and open my mouth and confess it: *Ellis Haley killed Clara Kennedy. Her body is buried in Alex Haywood's grave. I saw it myself.* It sounds unbelievable even to my own ears. No matter what pulp novels would have one think, high school students are not known for their malevolent cunning. Ellis has no reason to kill Clara. She certainly has no reason to frame me.

The story sounds just like that: a story.

"Are you all right, Felicity?" MacDonald asks, her eyes huge and owl-like behind her wire-rimmed glasses. "I know how close all you girls are. Have you been hanging in there okay?"

"We all miss Clara," I say. In the past week I have gotten very good at choosing my words. I use the present tense. I blend myself in with the larger group—no individualism, part of a faceless whole.

MacDonald nods, and for a moment I think she's going to let me leave. Only then she shifts forward, reaching across her desk to clutch my hand, squeezing hard enough that I flinch.

"I'm so sorry," MacDonald tells me. "I know she's your friend. What a year for you. . . . No one should have to lose two . . . two . . ." She breaks off, tears welling in her eyes.

"I'm sure Clara's fine, Housemistress."

But we can both tell neither of us believes that's true.

MacDonald sniffs and, producing a handkerchief from her jacket pocket, dabs at her nose. "Well," she says. "You'll let me know if you need any support. Won't you? Perhaps . . . perhaps you should call your mother and have her come. . . ."

"I'm quite all right," I say as firmly as possible. "Thank you. I'll let you know if I need anything."

I go upstairs to my room, and I find the letter I wrote in Ellis's handwriting. I bring it downstairs and slide it under Clara's pillow.

Wednesday the police show up with a subpoena to search Clara's room.

Godwin House is a mess: crime scene technicians and officers, yellow tape bracketing off Clara's door, strangers tramping through our sacred halls.

I don't have to wonder what they make of us. I hear Liu and Ashby talking outside the front door as I lurk in the common room, doing my best to overhear.

"A thousand bucks says that girl's dead by now," Liu is telling Ashby. "We'll find her body floating in the Hudson in a few days, bloated up and half-rotten."

I think about where Clara's body really is: buried six feet underground, pale and bloodless. Still preserved, perhaps, by the cold and snow.

"Think one of the housemates killed her?" Ashby says, and my breath freezes in my chest.

I can practically see Liu shaking her head. "What a weird lot. The outfits. The vocabulary. Did you see the way that one girl reacted when I asked what Clara did for fun? I might as well've asked if Clara liked torturing small puppies in her spare time."

"Well, it *is* Dalloway," Ashby says dryly. "You heard about this place? Apparently they've got some real secret-society-flavored shit going on. I'm talking like séance parties, Satan worship . . ."

No one worships Satan at Dalloway. No one even believes in any of the magic—no one except me.

I can't listen to more of this. I slip away from the door, back up the stairs toward my room.

I only make it to the second floor.

Ellis stands on the landing, a slice of shadow in all black. She lifts an envelope in one hand and arches a brow. "We need to talk."

Ellis leads me back into her bedroom, shutting the door behind us with a jab of her elbow. The air in the room feels alight with electricity, sparking and shivering between us like a lightning bolt that started a forest fire.

"What is this?"

She holds the letter aloft. My eyes glance off my own handwriting, which looks even less like Ellis's from this angle.

She has positioned herself between me and the door—there's no escape, short of hurling myself out the window, that doesn't involve passing close enough for her to grasp my arm.

Ellis had promised she wouldn't hurt me, not unless I forced her hand.

Only I just tried to frame her for Clara's murder. Does this count as forcing her hand?

You can't believe Ellis's promises anymore, I tell myself.

"It's a letter," I answer, keeping my voice low in an effort to sound firm and controlled. "You started this game, Ellis. Don't act like two can't play."

Even from here I can see the way Ellis's shoulders rise and fall with swift, shallow motions. Her usual calm has been whittled away, revealing something brighter—something dangerous.

"I never put that letter in Clara's room," Ellis says, although I can't think of any other reason why she would have found this one. "I told you I wouldn't. I promised I wouldn't try to frame you unless you made me. Why would you do this, Felicity? *Why?*" Her voice arcs upward in pitch, louder.

I glance toward the window, but the police cruisers are already pulling away from the house, descending the narrow lane toward campus proper. Everyone else is in class. There's no one to overhear.

"You're the reason I came to this school," Ellis says all of a sudden, and my attention snaps back to her. I take a quick step away, toward the bed. "Did you know that? I read about you in an article on Alex's death. I didn't care about the Dalloway Five. I wanted to write about *you*."

She says it like that's an excuse—like I should soften into her arms and forgive her.

But all I can think now is . . . what Ellis must have thought of me. How pitiful I must have seemed to her: the girl who may or may not have killed her friend, the girl who believed in ghosts, the girl who went mad. And I've proved her right, haven't I? I've proved Alex right, too.

I meet Ellis's gaze and feel something cold close around my heart, a feeling like a door slamming shut.

"No," I snap, starting toward her abruptly enough that Ellis rears back, even though I never reach for her, never close my fist. "No. I won't let you destroy my life for entertainment. I'm not Melpomene, to inspire your next great and tragic art. You don't have the right."

Ellis's cheeks have gone pallid. She stands out against the backdrop of her quick-darkening room like a ghost in the night. "Is that so?"

For the first time, I think she might actually kill me. I can see her the way Clara must have seen her in that moment—a vengeful spirit ascended from hell, charging ceaselessly toward annihilation. My gaze flicks over to the épée hanging from its hook on the wall, equidistant from both me and Ellis.

And Ellis, it seems, has the same idea.

We both lunge for the sword at the same time, but Ellis—who has spent years training for this, has poured hours into practice at the gym, soaking her lamé with sweat in pursuit of mastering this sport—gets there first.

"Stay where you are," she demands, poised in perfect posture with the sword outstretched, its blunted tip inches from my face.

"Or what?" I laugh. "These swords aren't sharp. What are you going to do, poke me with it?"

But Ellis doesn't move, her gaze fixed, unblinking, around the vicinity of my shoulders.

She holds the blade with her right hand. All those times I watched her practicing forgery . . . She isn't left-handed. I could never have faked her handwriting, and she made sure of it.

My chest hurts with every breath I manage to take. And there's no way to know what Ellis is thinking: If she is even now calculating the worth of leaving me alive. Or if she will invite me on a final Night Migration, if my body will curl up with Clara's corpse and Alex's ghost in the ruined grave.

I can't stay here.

I dart forward, but Ellis is faster. It's a simple motion, a flick of her wrist, and pain erupts on my cheek. I stagger back, one hand rising to touch the blood that drips down my skin.

"Don't move," Ellis snaps.

This time, I obey.

The tip of Ellis's sword trembles. The edge of it is stained red.

"I can't trust you," she murmurs, but she isn't speaking to

me. Her voice is low, tight. It's not a statement; it's a realization. "Sooner or later, you'll betray me. Next time—"

The slam of the front door cracks the tension like thin ice. I startle, and for a moment Ellis is frozen in place, épée grazing my throat.

Then Kajal's voice calls up the stairs: "Is anyone home?"

Ellis's sword falls away, dangling from one limp hand. We stare at each other, Ellis's eyes pale and wide, her throat shifting as she swallows.

I tilt my chin up. "I suppose you'll have to kill me some other day."

I edge past her, shoulders brushing the wall in my effort to keep distance between us. Ellis's gaze follows me until I've left and shut the door behind me, another barrier between me and her.

For however long that lasts.

31

Ellis and I circle each other in that house like twin vultures over dying prey.

If I am in a room, she is sure to follow. She stalks at my heels, silent and watching, as Leonie ropes me into a game of checkers, as Kajal asks me to help pin her too-large skirt. Such casual activities, and yet they're frayed, fraught. Leonie's hand shakes when she moves the checker pieces. Kajal flinches when my fingers graze her spine.

We are all ghosts in this house, waiting to hear the death knell.

I don't sleep that night, or the next. Even with my desk chair lodged under the doorknob, I flinch at every creak of the floorboards outside, every scrape of branches against my window. I light candles for protection. But if those couldn't frighten off my own phantoms, they won't do anything against Ellis.

My world reduces to sensation. The lights are too bright, sounds overloud. People speak to me, and although I hear them and respond, two minutes later I can't remember what they said or what it meant. Ellis and I exist on opposing planes.

We scratch at that veil between us. Eventually, one of us will sweep it aside and move in. Eventually, one of us will lose.

Alex hasn't left. Even knowing that so much of her presence was Ellis's machination does very little to erase her from my mind. I still see her in the shadows. I still watch her flit between the forest trees. Her voice wakes me in the night. Her memory stains my soul.

Maybe I'm being unfair to Ellis. Maybe some nightmares are real.

My mother appears at Dalloway on Friday night, an apparition trailing expensive perfume. For a moment I almost don't recognize her, standing in my doorway with her hair spun in careful curls and her pink Isabel Marant dress. She got thin in Nice.

"What are you doing here?" I demand.

"Miss MacDonald called. She said your friend had gone missing." My mother looks as if she doesn't know what to do with herself in this place, her gaze darting from the books on my shelves to the candles on my desk to, at last, the tarot cards scattered across my floor. "Felicity, what's all this?"

"Nothing. You shouldn't have come."

Surely Cecelia Morrow had better things to concern herself with—better *vintages*—than her mad daughter and the dead bodies that seem to fall in her wake like cut flowers.

My mother drifts forward and kneels to stare at my spread. It was a bad spread, full of dark omens; I'd drawn the Hanged One and thought of Tamsyn Penhaligon swinging from that tree, strangled to death. I'd burned anise and clove over the cards to ward off her curse.

Now my mother trails a finger through the ground spices and then rubs it against her thumb, a faint grimace passing over her lipsticked mouth. “I thought you were past this,” she says.

“It’s for my thesis.”

“Felicity . . .”

I know what she’s going to say. She’s been talking to Dr. Ortega, who has filled her ears with stories about my paranoia, my obsession with the Dalloway Five. It was no use explaining how all academic passions veer toward obsession. She wouldn’t understand that magic can be a metaphor, like Ellis said. That magic doesn’t have to be *magic* for it to mean something. That sometimes magic is a salve over a burn, and it’s the only way you can heal.

“I’m fine,” I tell her. “You can go home. Go back to Aspen, or Paris, or wherever. Don’t worry about me.” I laugh. “You never do.”

“I *do* worry about you. Felicity . . . darling . . . are you still taking your medication?”

“Yes.”

“Can you show me the bottle?”

My next breath is too sharp, hissing through my teeth on the inhale. “Why is it any of your business? Why are you here, pretending I’m the one who’s crazy—I’m not the one who’s crazy! I’m not the one who spends every hour of every goddamn day with her head in a wine bottle. I’m not devouring Xanax and ripping up priceless artwork and then telling everyone I’m *perfectly happy.*”

I can’t tell if I’ve hit my mark. My mother’s face is as expressionless as the surface of an icy lake. Perhaps even now her emotions are drowned in six glasses of Côtes du Rhône red.

"I think," she says eventually, rising to her feet and dusting the spices from her hand, "you should take another leave of absence. Dr. Ortega said they can have a bed ready for you as early as next Friday."

"Fuck you."

This, at last, garners a reaction, my mother's mouth forming a tiny moue of shock and her hand immediately rising to cover it. "Felicity Elisabeth, that language is *not* appropriate—"

"Fuck," I say again. "Fuck, fuck, shit, goddamn, fuck, shit!"

The flush that darkens her cheeks is lovelier than anything she could buy at Chanel. "You aren't well," she says. "It's clear that Housemistress MacDonald was right about that. It's perfectly understandable that losing your friend would have this effect on you, after what happened last year."

Perfectly understandable. My mother has never understood a thing about me, not since the day I was born and she handed me off to the first in a string of nannies. "I'm not leaving," I say.

"You *are.* I had to talk to the police for you. Did you know that? The dean told me that you were being interviewed. I had to call the police and tell them you were nothing but a sick girl, grieving her friend. I had to tell them you were *fragile,* that you—"

What she means is that she had to call one of her powerful East Coast friends and make *them* talk to the police.

Or that she had to pay.

"I'm eighteen," I inform her. I grin, wild and sharp. "I'm eighteen. I'm an adult. You can't make me do anything."

My mother looks so small to me now, a stick-limbed figure closed in a shell of designer clothing and an old-money name. A single tap and she might break.

"I might not be able to force you to get help, but I can speak to the dean and have you withdrawn from school."

I shake my head. "No. You never cared about being my mother before. Don't you dare start now."

Her shoulders quiver. For a moment I think she might cry. But then Cecelia Morrow lifts her chin and nods, just once. "I see."

"I bet you do."

I escort my mother to the door of Godwin House, stand in the foyer, and watch her figure retreat down the winding drive until she is nothing but a pink speck quickly obscured by the trees. She never belonged here. She never should have set foot on this unhallowed ground.

I close the door, and she is gone.

When I return to the kitchen, Ellis and Leonie are making dinner. Ellis catches my eye and stabs her knife into a hunk of meat. I imagine her cutting into my flesh the same way, carving it off bone. Blood on the floor.

At last I understand.

In this, as in all things, I am alone.

It snowed Friday night. Saturday, at an assembly, the school tells us that the police are no longer looking for a girl. They're looking for a body.

Everyone stares at the Godwin House students as we drift home, draped in black. A lace veil flutters like a crown atop Kajal's dark hair. Ellis, for once, has nothing to say. She catches my gaze past the other two, and for a moment it's like we understand each other. We alone know what happened to Clara Kennedy. We alone understand the odd relief that seeps in now, our heartbeats in rhythm: *If they haven't found her by now, they won't find her. Not with the new snow.*

We got away with it.

That night I sit on my bedroom floor and pick at the place in the rug where I spilled wax, back when Ellis burst into my room and I knocked over the candles. Downstairs they've put Etta James on vinyl, the sultry notes of her voice broken occasionally by the unsteady, racking wave of someone's sobs. Four floors below me I feel Margery Lemont's bones reverberate in the earth, calling out to me. And some distance away—not far; it could never be far—Alex's. Two mad girls buried under Godwin House.

There are two weeks left in the semester. Two weeks until winter break and I escape this place, escape Ellis's eyes on me, the omnipresent threat of what she will do to me the moment we're alone. Two weeks with her fingers round my throat. Can I survive for two weeks—fourteen days—in this place?

Eventually I fall into an uncomfortable sleep there on the floor, my cheek pressed atop an open book and my knees drawn in close to my chest. In my dream it's me and Alex on top of a mountain, the wind catching Alex's red hair and tangling it about her neck. I shout and reach for her, but she's choking, she's choking . . . And she isn't Alex at all—she's Margery Lemont, black blood staining her veins and turning her skin gray, her eyes the color of the night sky.

I lurch awake. For a second I'm disoriented, the ceiling curving wildly overhead and my vision blurry. *That sound . . .*

Then it happens again: a slow creak at my door, someone turning the knob.

My heart seizes, and I pitch upright, watching as the brass handle twists toward the latch and catches. Gently, someone releases it back into place.

I stare at the door, stare hard enough that I can practically see Ellis on the other side of it with her head tilted in close to the frame, her pale fingers curving over the knob.

Go away. Go away.

Silence, for a moment. Then a soft scraping noise like nails against glass.

She's picking the lock.

I shove myself back on both hands, crawling until my spine hits my bookshelf. I need a weapon. I need . . . something, *anything.*

One of my running shoes has fallen under the bed. I lunge for it and untie the knotted laces, yank them loose. My hands are shaking as I rise slowly to my feet, twisting the slim lace around my knuckles as I edge closer to the door.

I press myself against the wall. The latch clicks open.

My pulse pounds in my temples, fierce and bloody. I brace the makeshift garrote between my hands and hold my breath.

Ellis pushes the door open a half inch, and it catches on my desk chair. The chair legs squeak against the hardwood floor and then go still.

Can Ellis see my empty bed from where she stands? Does she know I'm waiting for her on the other side of this door, fingers blanched white as the shoelace cuts off circulation?

After a long and terrible silence, the door shifts again, rattling against the desk chair. I catch the sharp intake of breath from out in the hall. I squeeze my eyes shut and clench both fists. But then, at last, the door closes.

She's gone.

32

I plot my own Night Migration.

The note is written in Clara's hand, copied from the passive-aggressive note she left me earlier in the year about leaving my dishes in the sink. I pick Ellis's bedroom lock while she's in class and leave it on her pillow, then escape to the library stacks.

The hours filter by in silent agony, punctuated by the pilgrimage of Dalloway students from carrel to shelf. I have hidden myself in the mathematics section, the last place Ellis would look. My hand grips the angelica root in my pocket, a charm against evil.

I wait until the sun dips low in the horizon and stains the sky in shades of gold and poppy. Then I take the stairs to the roof.

I haven't been this high up since Alex died. I creep toward the edge, my blood hot in my veins. It would be so easy to fall. No, not to fall—to jump.

I hear the air whistling in my ears, watch the ground surge up to meet me. I blink as the world plunges into darkness.

And then I'm here again. Poised on the edge, the wind catching my skirt and whipping it taut against my thighs.

The sun sinks lower, the fringe of the forest consuming the last of its light. I sit down on unsteady legs and turn my face toward the pewter clouds. I told her to meet me at 6:04—astronomical twilight, when the last light has gone.

She appears two minutes early, the stairwell door opening and falling shut loud enough that I can hear it all the way across the roof.

I don't turn around, even when Ellis's footsteps are right behind me. My spine is straight and still; my eyes are shut. My feet dangle so far above the earth.

But death doesn't come.

"Felicity?"

I look.

Ellis stands at my shoulder, clothed in mourner's black. She extends a gloved hand, and I take it, let her pull me up. I'm not wearing heels; she's several inches taller like this, free hand curling into a loose fist at her side.

"I thought you were afraid of heights," she says.

"I am."

Even now I can't look down. The world exists too far below us.

Then again, that's always been true.

"I never would have turned you in," Ellis says. Her gaze focuses past me, out over the darkening sky. I wonder if she is even speaking to me, really, or if she means these words just for herself. A private justification—a confession. "I only said that because I was afraid. I never collected evidence against you. I never wanted to hurt you."

I don't speak. My words are brittle ash in my mouth. Live coals that burn.

"I wish it didn't have to be this way," Ellis says. She still has my hand, her fingers laced together with mine. She squeezes lightly now, and I swallow.

The darkness is almost complete. The safety lamps have turned on down below, a field of little lights glimmering across campus and vanishing toward the woods. But their glow doesn't reach as far as we stand.

I'm too aware of all the little things keeping me alive: my quickening heartbeat, air cold at the back of my throat, the aching tension in my muscles holding me upright.

Ellis looks like one of the works we analyzed in Art History, a painting in chiaroscuro. Perfect at first glance, but lean closer and you'll see the brushstrokes.

"Me too," I say. "You made me who I am. You made me who I was always supposed to be."

Night hangs over us like a guillotine blade. Ellis lets go of my hand, and I count the seconds as they pass. *One . . . two.* We're alone at the top of the world.

She takes a shallow breath—I watch her shoulders shift as the air comes in—and I move forward.

This isn't like pushing Alex. That was an accident. This time I push hard enough to make it mean something, hard enough to hear Ellis gasp, hard enough that even when she reaches for me it's too late.

If I had all the words in the English language, I could not string them together adequately to describe the expression on Ellis's face when she falls.

Surprise, perhaps. But also a grim, inevitable recognition.

Ellis doesn't scream on the way down. I hear the crunch of her body hitting pavement, but I don't see the impact. I've already turned away.

The night is too silent now.

I return through the same door, descend the library stairs, and exit through the back. I don't want to see her.

I never want to see her again.

33

I leave the letter on Ellis's pillow, a confession in Ellis's own hand. They find her body, and an hour later they find the note.

Three days, I wait for the blade to fall. It never does. The police sweep in and out of the house, and I lurk in corners, waiting for someone's gaze to cut past the shell of Felicity Morrow and see what I really am. But they can't: No one sees past skin. No one senses the bones under this house like I do.

Ellis knew. Ellis saw me in a way no one else could; she saw the black and twisted heart of me. She took my hand and guided me into that darkness. She opened the door, and truth entered, and nothing can undo that now.

I'm surprised by the sympathy. Instructors I've never met stop me in the hall with well wishes. The dean herself invites me over for tea and hugs me before I leave, tells me to call her anytime. Even Kajal and Leonie orbit around me like they're afraid I'll break, appearing at my room with trays of coffee and cookies and books to borrow. They don't expect me to go to class. No one expects me to leave my room at all.

They think I'm mourning.

When Alex died, people could barely look at me. Everyone believed I'd killed her. Or at the very least, they believed there was something I could have done differently. Some way I could have saved her, or died in her place.

I murdered Ellis Haley in cold blood, and at last they lend me their pity.

The morning before I leave for Georgia, for Ellis's funeral, I venture out onto the grounds and go to sit by the lake, the Margery Skull in my lap and my feet stretched out toward the water. The sunlight is warm on my face, the birds chirping in trees and the lake water glittering at dawn. All last evening I had this feeling in my chest, a shivering sort of sensation; it started off as a low hum and has since crescendoed to glorious heights.

I still feel ghosts around me: the ghosts of the five Dalloway girls who defied the boxes and coffins the world tried to put them in. The ghosts of other women who attended or worked at this school, but whose legacies were forgotten instead of deified. The ghosts of every girl who came here and felt history beneath her feet. But I'm not haunted anymore. Maybe I never was.

I glance down at the skull, smoothing my palm over its cold and bony brow. I've kept the skull hidden in my bedroom, in that secret compartment in my closet, ever since I stole it from Boleyn for my séance last year with Alex. A bit of my blood is still dried there, brownish and crumbling easily when I rub it with my thumb.

The skull's eye sockets gaze blankly back at me, empty, lifeless. If Margery's spirit still clings to her bones, this will break the tie between us.

"I'm closing the ritual," I tell the skull. "I'm putting you to rest."

The clove and anise, when I burn it atop a flat stone, smells like Christmas.

Margery Lemont might have been buried alive, but I won't return her skull to the earth. Or to Godwin, for that matter. Instead I wade into the frigid lake, deep enough that the water ripples around my hips. I lower the skull in cupped hands beneath the surface. A few air bubbles escape, and for a moment I can imagine it's a last breath—a last goodbye.

Then I let go.

The skull sinks quickly, a weight falling out of sight, obscured by the shifting silt.

"Thank you," I tell her—Margery. Alex. Both of them. "For everything."

I emerge from the water shivering, mourning-black skirt sodden and clinging to my legs. I gaze back over the lake one last time, half expecting to see Alex's ghost rising from the waves, but the water is smooth as mirror glass.

It's a beautiful morning.

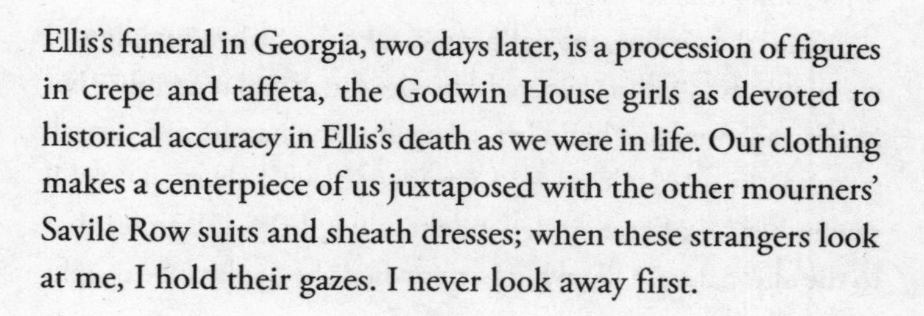

Ellis's funeral in Georgia, two days later, is a procession of figures in crepe and taffeta, the Godwin House girls as devoted to historical accuracy in Ellis's death as we were in life. Our clothing makes a centerpiece of us juxtaposed with the other mourners' Savile Row suits and sheath dresses; when these strangers look at me, I hold their gazes. I never look away first.

The whole thing is a subdued affair, Ellis's casket plain and unadorned, not a spot of whiskey to be found (except in Leonie's hip flask, which she passes down our pew while the preacher lectures on about innocence and forgiveness through faith). Ellis would have loathed it. I can imagine her sitting next to me even now, a birdcage veil tugged over her eyes and her fingers tapping together in her lap. A murmur in my ear: *Meet me in the bathroom. I want to fuck you.*

"Excuse me," I whisper to Kajal, and I edge my way out of the row, escaping down the aisle.

Alone in the church restroom, I lock the door behind me and pull out Ellis's silver cigarette tin from my pocket. *She would have wanted you to have it,* Quinn had said when they gave it to me this morning. I pick out one of Ellis's joints and light it with a struck match, inhale, exhale slow.

I never really liked to smoke all that much, but this feels right. It's appropriate, a final *fuck you.*

I catch sight of my reflection after, as I'm straightening myself up. My hair is still perfectly neat, lightly curled and drawn away from my face with a ribbon. My lipstick isn't smudged. I spritz fresh perfume on my neck, then I adjust my collar and practice a smile.

I look good in black.

After the service, the pallbearers take the casket outside and we all watch as Ellis is lowered into the dirt. I still remember her in herringbone, one hand braced against the handle of a shovel, standing atop Alex's grave. I wonder if that's always how I'll remember her: fierce, independent, alive. I think I prefer that to the alternative. I liked her better when she couldn't be caught off guard. I prefer to remember an Ellis who never would have let herself fall.

She isn't the girl in that casket, the same way Alex isn't the girl I buried under Godwin House a year ago. They both exist outside of time, fragments of memory and imagination—like Ellis's characters, in a way. They exist only insofar as I allow them to exist.

Beside me, Leonie shivers.

"What?" I whisper.

She shakes her head. Her lower lip blanches where she catches it between her teeth. "I don't know. I just . . . What if it's all true? The story about the Dalloway girls. What if this is history repeating itself? First Alex, then Clara, and now . . ."

I reach for Leonie's hand and squeeze it tight, and tell her: "Magic isn't real."

Quinn catches my eye from across the graveyard. In Ellis's absence they are a shadow of themselves, all their colors subdued without Ellis's light to brighten them.

Or perhaps that's how everyone looks to me now—everyone who knew her.

"Felicity," someone says, once the ceremony is over and I'm heading back to the car, flanked by Kajal and Leonie.

I turn. Two women have approached, each with a white lily pinned to her lapel. Ellis's mothers. I recognize them from the service.

"Oh," I say. "Hi."

Leonie's hand presses against the back of my elbow, but I wave her and Kajal away, offering Ellis's parents my best bathroom-mirror-approved smile. I try not to actively think about the fact these are the women who left Ellis alone that winter with her grandmother. Who didn't come back until their small daughter had been forced to do abhorrent things to survive.

One of them, the older one, steps forward and digs around in her satchel until she finds a stack of papers. She presses the pages into my hands, and I take them on reflex.

"This is for you," Ellis's mother says. "She would have wanted you to have it."

I glance down. The first page, typewritten in a familiar font, reads:

AVOCET

A novel

by Ellis Haley

"No." I try to shove the manuscript back at the woman who gave it to me, but she steps out of reach, both arms folding across her middle. "No. I don't want it."

"You have to take it," the other woman insists. "Please. It's the last thing Ellis ever wrote. She—"

I know what it is. I know, and I don't ever want to read it, don't ever want to crack open those pages and see what kind of mockery Ellis made of us.

"I don't care. I don't want to read it. I can't. Take it."

The two women exchange glances, but I don't wait for them to speak again. I bend over, set the stack of pages down in the damp grass, and dart away, chasing the distant figures of Kajal and Leonie, the mourners milling like ravens in the church parking lot.

When I glance back, Ellis's mothers are flitting around, chasing pages that have caught the wind, snapping desperately after paper and ink—the last that remains of their daughter.

Three years later

London is not where I thought I'd live, at the end of it all. I always thought I'd want mountains towering overhead, a wide-open sky and seasons as fickle as the sea. And yet here I am, with a flat in Mayfair, and a little dog, and a favorite bakery where they know me by name.

I've decided I like the city. I like the anonymity of the crowd, the way it feels as if possibility explodes around me in all directions. I like knowing I'll never go everywhere in this city, eat at every restaurant, meet every person who calls London home. There is always something and someone new. There is always a mystery I haven't solved yet.

I step out of the English building at Imperial College and head away from the Thames, into the bustle of the city proper. My phone buzzes in my pocket—my girlfriend texting me, probably, checking in again about dinner plans. Now that I'm almost done with my degree, I'm thinking about breaking up with her. I want to move on, opening up a new doorway in my life. Maybe I'll go to Paris. I'll meet a French girl with blond hair and a quick smile, one who will stay up all night naked in my bed. Perhaps she'll have a fixation with classic films—just to add character.

I don't want to go home yet and be confronted with Talia's demands in person, so I dip into a nearby bookshop and wander between the shelves, picking up books, only to set them down again. I'm so busy with assignments that it feels like I barely read for pleasure anymore.

I'm on my way out when I spot the display in the window: a full fifteen-book spread, complete with a photo of the author blown up to massive size. The poster announces the release of the posthumous masterpiece by Ellis Haley: *Avocet.*

My feet have grown roots that stretch deep into the floor. I stare at Ellis's photo and Ellis stares back, her gray eyes steady and alive, somehow, despite being printed by pixel. It's not the same portrait that was printed in her first novel. I know, because I spent hours staring at that original photograph back when we were still at Dalloway, fantasizing about what Ellis's mouth could do to me.

This photo was taken more recently. Ellis has the same hairstyle she wore when we were at school together, a few stray strands tumbling over her brow and her lips set in a flat line.

"Have you read it?"

I whip around. The bookseller stands over my shoulder, with both hands clasped in front of her lap, a hopeful expression painted over her face, an expression that says *I make commission.*

"No."

"Oh, well, you should." She chooses one of the books off the display and presses it into my hands. I glance down at the front cover: spare, minimalist, emblazoned with the gold medal of the National Book Award.

"I don't know if this is quite my genre."

"Literary fiction? That should be everyone's genre, I hope," the woman says with a little laugh. I want to hit her in the face. "But if it's any consolation, this particular book crosses over into the territory of mystery and thriller. It's about a female psychopath who falls in love with a beautiful woman who appears innocent at first glance but who"—she glances down at the marketing copy printed on the poster—"harbors deadly secrets of her own."

"Thank you. I'll think about it."

The woman at last seems to get the hint; her cheeks flush pale pink, and she retreats back behind the counter, peeking up at me occasionally from over her wire-rimmed glasses as she riffles through paperwork.

I turn my attention to the book in my hand.

So this is it. Ellis's magnum opus. The book she cared for enough to sacrifice anything: Clara's life. Her own. And all the rest of us bit players in her masterpiece.

I open the cover, flipping past the title page.

For Felicity. I did it all for you.

I snap the book shut. Abruptly the air seems to have been sucked out of the shop—the cashier and the shelves and the London street outside all falling away and plunging me into the darkness of oblivion.

Once again it's just me and Ellis, two figures emerging on opposite sides of a stage. Once more I feel her take my hand, drawing me into the night. It's been three years, but all at once it feels like I never left that place, Godwin House with its dark history and wicked shadows, magic drenching the stones and murder like a legacy passed from generation to generation.

I did it all for you.

I drop the book onto the table and leave, tumbling out of the bookstore and into the street. A bus blares past, and I'm blinded, I'm deafened, I'm falling and falling and falling through the cold.

I don't remember how I make it home.

Talia is in the kitchen when I do, a wooden spoon held in hand like a conductor's baton, surveying the bolognese that simmers on the stove with a moue of disapproval that suggests that if the sauce is a metaphorical orchestra, it's playing several measures behind cue.

"Felicity," she says, putting the spoon down as soon as she catches sight of me. "You look terrible. Did something happen?"

"Nothing. I'm just tired." The excuse falls from my lips like honey wine as I pull my pill bottle out of my purse and swallow one tablet; I've learned from experience never to be late on doses. "Is dinner almost ready?"

Talia seems happy to see me. She's a chef—or she wants to be, anyway. She has a job as a line cook at a small restaurant in the West End, hopes to work her way up. I'll miss her food when she's gone.

"All ready," she says. "Your mother called, by the way. She wanted me to tell you."

I make a face, and Talia rises up on the balls of her feet to kiss my temple. "I don't know why she bothers," I say. "I was clear the first time: I don't want her to be part of my life anymore."

Talia smells like nutmeg. When she steps away, I brush a bit of flour from her cheek and she smiles. She always smiles. "Maybe one day you'll feel differently." I won't. "Will you carry the wine up, darling? I don't think I'll have enough hands."

I kiss her again and obey.

We take the food up to the roof, which is strung with market lights and has a view toward Hyde Park, the city sprawling out below us, glittering as if with thousands of fireflies. Talia pours the wine and we toast to another year together, to wherever we go next, to the future Talia has constructed in her mind: the both of us, desperately in love.

After we finish the food, I watch her standing by the edge of the roof, gazing out over the streets so far below. Her hair tangles about her ears; she's kept it short lately, sensible. I step behind her and kiss the nape of her neck. My hands find her hips. Her bones feel fragile in my grasp, so easily fractured.

Alex felt the same way, her body docile, surrendering to the force of my weight when I pushed her off that ridge.

Talia leans back against me, warm and trusting, and says something about how cold the air is this high above the ground. A lock of her hair, black like Ellis's, catches on my lips.

What would Ellis say if she could see me now? A perfect character for one of her stories. Perfectly predictable.

I think about drowning, about euphoria, the red orchids I planted on Ellis's grave. I think how falling would be worse.

And here, my heart beating fast and the taste of ink on my tongue, the city opening wide below us like a waiting mouth—

—

It begins to snow.

Acknowledgments

Once upon a time, this book was a collection of disconnected ideas scribbled in a notebook: *lesbian dark academia,* or *plan the perfect murder but one of them takes it too seriously.* These ideas might never have expanded into this book if not for a phone conversation I had with my friend Tes Medovich, who loves *The Secret History* and elbow patches and Gothic architecture just as much as I do. I remember lying on my bed on my stomach, phone pinched between my ear and shoulder, and it was uncomfortable but I didn't care because it felt like my brain couldn't stop: each idea fed into the next, a cascade of plot points and scenes and little snapshots that perfectly encapsulated that tea-drenched, blurry-eyed, book-drunk aesthetic that is dark academia. So thank you, first of all, to Tes, for encouraging me to take these ideas and make them real.

Thank you, also, to my agents, Holly Root and Taylor Haggerty, who—when I described this book to them over the phone—stopped me one sentence into the pitch and told me to drop everything and write it. Right now. I'm so lucky to have these two as my agents, not least because I know they'll always tell me to write the thing I'm most passionate about, and that will always, always be the right choice.

To my editor at Delacorte, Krista Marino, thank you for seeing these girls so clearly and for loving Dalloway and its horrors. This book is so much stronger thanks to your input, and I can't wait to see what other twisty tales we cook up together. Thank you also to the whole team at Delacorte, particularly Lydia Gregovic, Regina Flath, Beverly Horowitz, Barbara Marcus, Elizabeth Ward, Jenn Inzetta, Kelly McGauley, Lili Feinberg, and Kristen Schultz. Thank you for helping me bring this story to life.

A million thanks as well to my authenticity readers, whose feedback helped make this book so much better—your expertise helped me explore a deeper level of meaning in this story, and I appreciate it more than I can say.

I wrote this book so quickly, and then of course it was an exercise in revision, layering muscle and flesh onto the bones and creating something whole. For that metaphor (and other feedback) I have to thank Victoria Schwab. Thanks as well to Emily Martin, who was there to hold my hand (figuratively, and occasionally literally) for every page, every triumph, and every stumbling block along the way. And of course, thank you to these friends and family, who were particularly supportive during the creation and revision of this book: Ben Scallon, Zoraida Córdova, Ryan LaSala, Nita Tyndall, Tracy Deonn, Rory Power, Claribel Ortega, Casey McQuiston, Christine Herman, and Ava Reid. Finally, to my parents, who didn't say a word about the sex scene. My endless gratitude for that.

About the Author

Victoria Lee is the author of *The Fever King* and its forthcoming sequel, *The Electric Heir* (Skyscape). In addition to being an author, she is a doctoral student, and a great follow on Instagram (@sosaidvictoria). She lives in New York City with her partner, cat, and malevolent dog and tweets @sosaidvictoria.